Spring Into SciFi 2024 Edition

A Cloaked Press Anthology

All Stories contained in this book are the creations of the authors' minds. Any resemblance to persons/places/events – living or dead – is purely coincidental or used in a fictitious manner.

Published by: Cloaked Press, LLC
P. O. Box 341
Suring, WI 54174
https://www.cloakedpress.com

Cover Design by:
Carmilla M. Ravensworth
https://carmillacreates.carrd.co/

Copyright 2024, Cloaked Press, LLC
ISBN: 978-1-952796-39-5

With Stories From

R. A. Clarke
James Pyles
Alex Minns
J. L. Royce
Taylor Funk
Joshua Harding
Mark Reasoner
Cait Gordon
Fern K L Goodliffe
MR Wells
Katie Ess
Rose Strickman
Andrew P. McGregor
Iren Adams
Bethany A. Perry

Contents

Odessa by R.A. Clarke 1

I Don't Want to be Human by James Pyles 21

Locard's Principle by Alex Minns 51

Welcome to *Hope* by J. L. Royce 67

The Rjelhdan Prince by Taylor Funk 97

Child Classes Inherit Parent Objects by Joshua Harding 119

Ancient Tactics by Mark Reasoner 137

Courier of the Skies by Cait Gordon 151

The Ghost in the Machine by Fern K L Goodliffe 165

Sacrifice by MR Wells 179

The Marian by Katie Ess 209

Tower of the Stars by Rose Strickman 229

Take the Chance by Andrew P. McGregor 253

Grimms by Iren Adams 267

Wilds of the Mind by Bethany A. Perry 289

Thank you… 309

Odessa

by R.A. Clarke

Descending through Trenix's thin upper atmosphere, the *Odyssey's* hull groaned as it sank into the thick band of swirling storm clouds currently swallowing this side of the planet. Normally such inclement weather wouldn't be ideal for gathering rare ingredients, but for the item listed on my collection docket today, this weather was one hundred percent perfect.

The Sobifacious Kliminticus plant, more commonly known as a Sweller Swallow, grew here—and only here—and was notoriously hard to find. The troublesome plant was equally difficult to harvest... a unique trait that kept me rich in product orders, since I'd made myself a tidy living doing the dirty work others didn't want to. Sweller Swallows were considered a delicacy on nearby planets, thanks to its unique savoury flavour and insanely high nutritional value. They had sharp, pearlescent teeth lining the inner side of their blooms, which made great necklace beads, too. Hot sellers all around. I gathered them whenever a product contract carried me to these parts. They kept nicely in cold storage for months, though they never stayed around that long. Though I generally disliked interacting with people, I usually sold out within days.

"And here we are," I said to nobody. There were no crew to squabble with or slow me down. No family or husband to complicate things, which suited me fine. My experience with relationships was that they only led to heartache and bitterness. Growing up in the Reem on my home planet—the grunge district where every crook and scumbag seemed to put roots down—would jade anyone. But if that weren't enough, getting abandoned by my bio birther and adopted out of a tainted foster system to be used by a twisted wraith of a woman clinched it.

She'd beaten the trust and love right out of me.

My ship broke through the broiling cloud ceiling and immediately took a lightning bolt to the starboard side. Spidery electric arcs to crackled across my shields for several seconds after the hit, but thankfully did little damage. I dove to the planet's surface, punching search commands into the ship's scanners, seeking the nearest gully rich in Trenix clay—the smelly substrate the Sweller Swallows preferred to grow in.

Despite the payoff, few harvesters wanted to venture to Trenix. Not because the atmosphere wasn't breathable (it was), but because of the horrendous odour. Only a dwindling number of harvesters seemed willing to withstand minor discomfort to earn their rewards these days. Pissed me off to no end that my chosen profession was being diluted by pansy-ass up-and-comers, but then again, their lack of work ethic kept me in the money. It also forced me to keep my weapons' locker well stocked, since sometimes the lazy buggers switched tactics and jumped on with a pirate crew, then came looking for a quick score. I'd only ever had my cache nicked once, thankfully. I'd been running light that day. I knew others who'd experienced far worse.

Entire colonies had been pillaged.

The scanner beeped and lit up a section of land on the dashboard's holographic readout. It zeroed in tighter and a target flashed red. "Looks like that's my spot." I prepped for landing and brought the ship down in a nearby meadow.

I could already smell the pungent atmosphere.

When the sun shone, the sky glimmered a vibrant peach and the plentiful trees and wild grasses offered a kaleidoscope of colour. Most of the planet was covered in open plains and lush gulleys, intermixed with sprawling swaths of forest that, from space, appeared to pockmark the surface. Underground rivers ran all over the place, only surfacing in a handful of locations. However, when it stormed, the clay covering over half the planet's surface turned to sludge and its noxious odour—like a putrid fart sprinkled with skunk spray and dipped in vomit—escaped into the air in full force.

Good thing I'd upgraded my excursion suit with top-notch filtration. This wasn't my twentieth rodeo. *Damn, has it really been twenty years? I've been doing this for half my life.*

I'd already walked down the exit ramp before realizing I'd forgotten the ship's ignition fob, with the keys to my cargo lockers attached. Leaving those behind was like inviting someone to steal my shit. Though the ramp was rising behind me, I activated the magnet recoil function on my tool belt. I heard the whir before I saw the keys zip through the narrowing gap to *kachink* into their rightful place on my belt. I grinned as the ramp sealed shut.

"Alright, let's do this." I tightened the clasp, keeping my silver-streaked sienna hair out of my face, secured my helmet, and headed out of the meadow towards the stand of scattered trees ahead. A forest rested beyond that, growing out of a rich clay deposit. My quarry would be in this area without a doubt. The rain made them much easier to spot, as it gave their usually matte camouflage skin an oily sheen that created rainbow swirls. Without that, the only way to know they were there, lying in wait, was to see their antenna—if it rose up—a stem about the width of a spaghetti noodle with a teeny ball on top. Its eye. Spotting that meant you were in attack range.

Near constant rolls of thunder filled the atmosphere, laying waste to silence.

I still felt the ache in my knees from my last harvest, where I'd had to snowshoe through icy drifts to collect the summit blooms native to planet Valreeth's frozen wasteland. My joints weren't nearly as happy with my daredevil job as my mind these days. At forty, I was considered old for a harvester. And while I knew someday, I'd grudgingly have to seek out alternative sources of income, I remained resolute… That wouldn't be happening anytime soon.

With my scanner in one hand, calibrated to seek rainbow patterns, and my combustor gun in the other, I threaded between the trees. My mind wandered, considering employment options once my harvesting days were over. No way could I do any kind of desk job—too much sitting around. Farming could be good. I didn't mind animals. They were easy to understand, didn't lie. Or maybe I could work with children, young girls that needed help. I could ensure others don't suffer my fate, turned into slaves, innocence lost. Give them some hope, a fighting chance.

I shook the thoughts away. *Now's not the time. Focus.*

As I made my way deeper into the forest, I patiently waited for a sign that told me a target was nearby… then less patiently when none came. "Where are all of you?"

As if on cue, my scanner beeped.

"Finally…" I turned to my right, zeroing in on the red kidney-bean shaped patch that glowed on my screen. It wasn't far away.

Beep.

Another red glow appeared a few feet beyond the first. *Two for one. Nice.*

The moody skies continued rumbling as searing lightning bolts snaked across the clouds. The faintest *whooshing* noise reached my ears, capturing my attention, but when it blended in with the gusting wind, I wrote it off as

After one last sweep of the area with the scanner—a necessary precaution, as Sweller Swallows were known to crowd in and creep closer when prey was near—I secured the device on my belt and whipped out a shock baton. "Time to dance."

Their antennas weren't raised now. But the sneaky devils would've seen me coming for a while already. Luckily, they weren't smart enough to know I'd seen them, too.

I crept closer, waiting for my moment.

My grip tightened on the baton.

"Come on out," I cooed. "I won't—"

The first plant swelled, rising from the muddy ground on a six-foot-tall purple stem. Its two rounded petals splayed wide like wings; their deep red surfaces marred with shiny spades. A web of thick green veins pulsed and merged into a maw-like throat.

"—bite!" I thrust the shock baton into the mud and used it to catapult my legs into the air as the business end sent a wave of electricity into the wet soil. The shock rippled out, colliding with the base of the unruly plant. It shuddered and snapped haphazardly, as if confused about where I was. It presented the tender section of stem just below its bloom, and I fired off a round as my feet hit the ground, severing it.

The second Sweller rose as the head of the first tipped and toppled into the muck. It slithered its slug-like base towards me.

A strange mewling sound wafted to my ears, then vanished in the wind. It had come from somewhere behind me. I looked back, seeing nothing.

The Sweller snapped at me, but I jolted back just in time. "Dammit," I growled, chiding myself for the near miss. "Pay attention."

The scanner on my belt beeped, but I had no time to check it as the bloodthirsty plant darted forward for another try. Jumping to the side, I swung my baton behind me, rewarded by a tug. The Sweller's head squeezed down on the shaft, grinding its deadly petals together.

I sent a shock through it and it recoiled, flailing its stem and shaking leaves back. With its neck fatally exposed, I took the shot.

A shadow rose over me. *Shit.*

I turned just in time to thrust my gun into the surging mouth of a third beast. The shot hammered its core and blew out the other side, but hadn't severed its stem. It lurched backward as if on a spring and swung back around. I jumped to the side, landing in a roll as its head slammed into the mud where I stood a second before. Contorting my arm, I fired, beheading it.

Climbing to my feet, I ripped my scanner off my belt, holding it out. "Any more takers?" There was no sign of others close by, but that didn't mean I was safe. There'd be more in the vicinity and they'd be heading this way. In the meantime, I surveyed my kills and smiled.

"Not bad for a day's work. Should fetch a fair credit." I pulled a foot-long cylindrical tube off my belt and activated my auto cart—a floating wheelbarrow made of force fields—and tossed the three heads into it.

That mewling sound reached my ears again, but it had changed. It was louder this time, shriller, like a warbling cry.

No, not *like* a cry. It *was* a cry.

That sounded like a baby.

"What the—?" I glanced toward the sound, but it was hard to tell where it originated. The wind kept stealing it away, and it echoed off the trees. Thunder rolled overhead, muffled by the broiling clouds unleashing fresh sheets of rain.

And there it was again, now crisp between gusts. Screams of rage or fear.

Or pain.

The cry intensified and a slew of worst-case-scenarios filled my mind, gritty images flashing like exploding bombs. What was a friggin' baby doing out here? I knew if I could hear the child, so could the Swellers. A memory flashed through my mind, acrid and festered. Being left by the wraith in a greasy tavern slithering with scuzzy pervs, ordered not to come home without cash in my pocket. I grimaced, remembering what I'd endured to earn my keep…

I gripped my auto-cart and strode back towards the grassy meadow I'd landed in, confident that's where it was coming from. A gnawing sense of dread seeped in from the darkest parts of me, then simmered into a boil of anger. My fists clenched, knuckles white. *Abandoned. Vulnerable. Used.* Unable to come up with any logistical or wholesome reason why a baby would be brought to Trenix, I broke into a run, simultaneously listening for any beeps from my scanner. The cart sailed weightlessly behind me.

I knew I was breaking my own rules. I'd sworn long ago not to get involved in other people's drama, that I would leave the world to its filth and just focus on my own shit. But I couldn't help myself. I'd never been a very maternal woman, but something pulled at me like a magnet, screaming injustice, danger. I couldn't live with myself if I didn't investigate.

Beep. Beep.

I checked my scanner. The plants were far enough away that I could give them a wide berth. On a normal day, I'd never pass up the chance to harvest, but given this unexpected and downright bizarre situation, normalcy had flown out the window.

I veered left; the sound now leading me away from the meadow I'd parked my ship in. Hot sweat beaded on my brow as I ran, weaving from side to side to avoid triggering more flora. They seemed less intent on me, anyway. Likely salivating in response to those cries, their still flattened forms slithered in the same direction I was moving. Not good.

I glowered as the baby wailed again—so close now. "I better find some parents, and they better have a damn good reason for bringing their kid here."

Beep.

A huge Sweller rose right in front of me. I gasped, and without thinking, swung the auto-cart around. The netted force fields hammered into its thick stem, rocking it backward. I shot twice for good measure, destroying its neck. The head fell in a heap and I swiftly scooped it up, dropping it into the cart. I pressed forward, pushing my way through a thicket of willowy bushes, then emerged into another clearing.

I came to an abrupt stop, bewildered.

Knee-high wild grasses whipped in the wind and lightning flashed overhead. A sizable rectangular boulder surrounded by several smaller, bulbous ones sat near the heart of the meadow. The top of the biggest was about four feet tall and somewhat flat. Good thing, because an infant was laying on top of it. The little thing was nestled in a blanket, its cherubic face pale and soaked by rain. I wasn't an expert on children, but if I had to guess, it was only months old.

I looked in all directions, seeing no one.

Nothing about this felt right.

Abandoned. Used.

Rage flared within, protective and raw. It warred with my good sense, the voice in my head telling me to turn away—to remember my rules and abide by them. But I couldn't leave the child there to die. The poor thing was a sitting duck, a free meal for the Sweller Swallows.

I could at least get it somewhere safe. Clutching my gun, I pulled my cart into the meadow, eyes darting warily in search of movement, people, antenna, anything.

My scanner remained silent as I reached the rock. The baby's face was red from screaming, lips purple from the cold. Its tiny arms and legs jerked angrily within the sopping blanket. A pale pink jumper marked with a strange symbol—like three stars offset from each other—poked out from between the folds.

"Shhh…" I released the auto-cart, leaving it hovering behind me, and brushed one of my fingers down her cheek. "You're okay now. You're not alone anymore."

The infant's eyes found me. Her cry faltered a moment while staring up at my unfamiliar face, then carried on. I glanced around and checked my scanner. The Swellers would come soon, slowed only slightly by the bushes I'd fought through. I wanted to shout out to see if, by some miracle, a blundering set of parents was close by, but an alarm went off in my head at the thought. The baby had been set too perfectly, like a sacrifice on an altar.

Something stunk about this situation and it wasn't the soil.

You're smarter than this. Walk away.

Instead of listening to my own advice, I curled both hands beneath the baby and lifted her off the rock, cradling her against my chest. Though the blanket was wet, I bunched it up over top of her in a way to help shield the rain. I let her grip one of my fingers and cooed softly as my eyes darted around the meadow. Her cry lessened, then fizzled into stuttering sniffles.

"There now…" I decided to take the risk and call out. It was a long shot, but the parents could have fallen prey to a Sweller attack. They could be somewhere out of view needing help.

I opened my mouth to shout, then paused, remembering the odd whooshing sound I'd heard before—perhaps that hadn't been wind after all. It could have been another ship.

Might be other harvesters. But again, why bring a baby? Such a thing was unheard of. Nothing about this made any sense. Unless…

"If you hand over the cart and unlock your ship, you and the wee babe can go free." The deep, raspy voice rang out from the tree line and my eyes snapped towards it.

Across the clearing, a man in a ragged military-style hat, grimy britches, and an armless leather jacket that exposed the pistols holstered across his broad chest stepped out from where he'd been hiding amongst the foliage. He removed his simplistic filtration mask and smiled, revealing a grille of silver capped teeth.

Three more equally dishevelled men in similar attire appeared behind their leader, each one pointing their guns at me.

Pirates.

My gun flew up, trained on the boss.

"What kind of heartless creatures are you to use a defenseless baby as bait?" Teeth gritted; my eyes bore into them. "Whose baby is this? Yours?"

He held his hands up. "Goodness no. That's just some kid we inherited during a colony raid. Was locked in a cage. You wanna talk heartless? That's about as cold as it gets. We figured there'd be some use for it down the line, and viola—turns out there was."

My mind spun. *A cage… Used.*

"How did you follow me here? My ship didn't detect you on scanners."

"Oh, we have our ways…" The leader continued strolling forward, undeterred by my aimed weapon. "We've been watching you for a while now. You've been making waves in the harvesting world." He snickered. "I'd say it's high time we took our share of the spoils. An easy trade, little lady."

Chauvinistic asshole.

"My spoils are just that—*my* spoils. I earned them, so you can fuck off."

He laughed, glancing at his buddies. "Is that any way to talk to the men who have three guns trained on you?" He *tsk tsk'd*, then raised his own weapon. "Correction. Four guns. Now unlock your ship."

I heard a faint rustling noise. Flicking my gaze around the clearing, I keyed in on several antennae watching quietly, inconspicuous amidst the grass. The Swellers were here.

Do they know about the plants?

Thinking on my feet, I shifted the baby, using the action as a shield while my other hand turned off the scanner I knew would start beeping very soon. Though that left me vulnerable, at least I wouldn't show the only cards I was likely to hold in this scenario. I held my ground, thrusting my chin high. "No. Just turn around and leave now and nobody gets hurt."

The baby gripped my finger tighter, as if she also sensed the danger we faced.

The leader fired a shot and the laser-like pulse seared into my arm just inches above the baby's tender scalp. I jerked back, failing to swallow a pain-filled shout. Glancing down, I realized it was just a flesh wound, and also how close it came to hitting the defenseless bundle in my tenuous care.

"Next one, the baby gets it."

Though I might be the farthest thing from good mother material, whatever shrivelled remnants of a heart I had left were reserved only for the vulnerable. I wasn't about to play with this child's life, no matter where she might've come from. "Okay, okay…" I holstered my gun, panting from the burn in my arm.

"No, drop it."

Stifling a growl, I let my gun fall to the ground and raised my free hand to shoulder height, gently patting the baby with the other. Every now and then she let out little gurgling sounds, blowing spit bubbles with her mouth. Not a care in the world. I spared one glance down to see her bright grey eyes staring back at me, and something deep and ingrained crumbled.

"Kick it away."

I nodded, booting my combustor a few feet out of reach. That would be a problem. Glancing around, I noticed more antennas perking up amidst the grass. Some had slunk closer, inching slowly forward.

"Thank ye kindly. Now unlock your ship."

I shook my head, keeping my free hand well raised. "I can't remotely unlock anything." The leader narrowed his eyes, scrunching up one side of his face. But I continued, "Seriously. She's an old school ship. The lockers in the cargo hold all still have keys." I slowly lowered my hand, and the pirates stiffened with alert, thrusting their guns forward.

Levelling my gaze on the leader, I said, "Just let me give you the keys, and then you can go raid it, okay? I'll take the kid like you said, and we both win."

"Maybe we should take your ship, too. Might fetch a nice purse. We should just kill you now and be done with it. No strings attached. Whaddya say boys?"

The man's wolf pack cackled, nodding along like a bunch of mindless followers.

I raised my brows. "We both know you won't do that."

The leader slanted a look my way. "Oh, really… and why's that?"

"Cause I'm worth more to you alive than dead. I bring in the biggest hauls around. The most dangerous plants. You said so yourself—I've been making waves. We could make a deal instead. Split profits or something. Besides, that ship's not worth much—it's outdated and needs constant fixing—a glorified tin can. If I could afford to upgrade to a new model, I would have already." I forced a wistful look to hide my lie. "That's a someday plan."

The leader picked at his teeth, hemming and hawing before re-securing his face mask. "Hmm." He glanced at his lackeys, who all shrugged.

"Makes sense to me, Dagen," the tallest one said.

Dagen. A name to the face.

"Yeah, and if she tries to ghost us, we kill her," said the short, chubby one.

I shook my head. "I won't ghost you. Look, let me toss you the keys." The baby grumbled, and I had the silliest thought that maybe she didn't agree with what I was doing. I felt like giving her the stink-eye and telling her *this is all because of you, so you better be thankful.*

Chances were high we'd end up dead.

"Well, go on then. Toss 'em." Dagen motioned his gun for me to get my keys.

I fumbled to detach my ignition fob and held it up. A gust of wind blew, jangling the metallic slivers attached to it. "Alright? Here are my damn keys." Under the guise of an eye roll, I glanced to the left, sourcing the closest and thickest clump of antennae.

Dagen gave me a *gimme* hand gesture. A sly smile twitched on his mouth. So smug and proud of himself. Over my dead body would he ever get the *Odyssey*.

Here goes nothing. I cocked my arm back and hurled the key fob into the grass about fifteen feet away from the pirate assholes.

Hoping for a distraction, I jerked to the side, making for the boulder's protection, but a shot zinged past my torso, leaving a charred starburst on the rock. I froze again, thrusting my hand back in the air.

"You stupid cow! Don't you move," Dagen shouted, glaring at me. He waved a crisp arm to his men, then pointed to the area my keys had fallen. "Go find them." The barrel of his gun never wavered from its aim.

"Can't blame a girl for trying," I called.

The three lackeys went trudging toward the keys, grumbling and glowering back at me. The baby squirmed. I squeezed her tighter, my arm cramping from being in the same position for too long. "Shh now…everything's fine," I murmured, ignoring the discomfort. Though locked in a staring match with Dagen, I watched his men spreading out to search from the corner of my eye. The antennae in the grass had disappeared from view.

"Come on, come on," I breathed, so quiet I doubted even the baby heard it.

A Sweller Swallow sprang up just two feet from the largest of the pirate minions. He shouted in horror and pelted it with shots. None of them found the sweet spot, and the flower's maw snapped down on his arm. He screamed, the teeth ripping into his flesh. The other men turned and let the rounds fly, then spun circles as four more Swellers rose up around them.

Yes.

"Fall back!" Dagen shouted, his gun swinging between me and his crew in halted motions, clearly torn about what to do. But when a Sweller chomped down on the short chubby guy's shoulder and lifted him up off his feet—blood spurting—he made his choice. Dagen turned, aiming his weapon at the flowers.

I darted for my gun on the ground, sliding behind the boulder. Carefully setting the child on the ground next to the rock for a semblance of protection, my eyes flicked in every direction. There were no antennae visible around me. A bad sign.

They were close.

I looked down. "Alright baby, get ready for a fight. We're getting outta this place."

Reactivating my scanner, I held it up. All I had to do was clear a path out of the meadow, then get my ass back to the ship. Correction, *our* asses.

Screams splintered the air. I spared a glance toward the pirates. Dagen had charged toward the flowers, but smartly hung back, sending rapid-fire shots. He tagged one with a lucky shot, severing its head, but didn't change his haphazard firing pattern. One of his guys was already dead. The other was only half visible—his bloody upper torso hanging listlessly out of a massive Sweller's mouth. Its robust stem stretched while the flower gnawed his body, swallowing him whole like an anaconda. More Swellers popped up, blocking the pirates' retreat.

Beep, beep.

The wind whipped the grass in a frenzy, but I caught a flash of oily rainbow to my right just as the scanner marked it. Another one glowed on my left. More were incoming from the tree line, but they veered away, drawn to the hearty feast of pirates currently staining the grass red. Dropping my scanner, I snatched my baton and lunged forward, taking the fight to the Swellers. The first one sprung as I dove into a slide across the slick grass, thrusting my baton into its base and letting the electricity fly. It jerked and shuddered as I fired a round straight up into its throat.

Amidst the screaming and gunshots across the meadow, I heard the second one spring behind me on the other side. My throat constricted. It had moved faster than expected. *The baby.*

Scrambling to my feet, I rushed back, but the flower head was already surging down toward the ground, aiming for the child.

"No!" I cried out, hitting the steady stun function and throwing my baton at the Sweller. It missed by a fraction, its metallic tip *tinging* off the rock instead.

The baby let out a piercing wail as the teeth closed in on her tiny form, and then strangely, the flower head slowed. A guttural scream ripped from my lips as I threw my body into the stem to knock it off course, and it worked. The Sweller swung to the side with me hanging on, then rebounded like a whip to dislodge me.

Tumbling through the grass, I ended up several feet away. Too far. I'd be too late. Clambering back to my feet, I glimpsed Dagen swarmed by flora, but I ignored it—my focus set on saving the baby. But as I charged back, my footsteps slowed, face twisting in confusion.

What the—?

The Sweller had stopped entirely. Its splayed sinewy petals hovered above the child, twisting from one side to the other, kind of like a puppy might when it was curious. Never in my years of harvesting had I ever seen one of these deadly plants resist a meal.

Fresh screams sliced through the rain, and I knew Dagen was in trouble. I didn't look. He was a user, selfish and callous, just like all the scum that paid for my painfully young self to go into their rooms back at the bar. Whatever was happening over there, he had it coming to him.

Inching forward, I approached the boulder cautiously from the side. What could've possibly made the Sweller stop? As I neared, I finally got a clearer look at the child, whose urgent cry had lessened a degree. My hand instinctively flew to cover my mouth, but flattened against my face shield instead.

The baby's irises weren't grey anymore, but shone with iridescent flecks of green—like two shimmering emeralds. Was the plant doing that to her?

Or was *she* doing that to the plant?

The Sweller suddenly twisted towards me, my presence breaking its placid trance. It snapped at me and I jumped back just in time. But before I could even raise my gun to fire, hoping to stun it enough to allow for evasive maneuvers, the baby's cry erupted into a new level of shrill. The scream made me wince, and immediately the Sweller froze.

Its blossom head swivelled back to the baby.

"Holy shit…" I ran a hand over my face.

"Help! Please!" Dagen wailed from afar. A quick glance revealed one of his arms hung uselessly at his side—ruby droplets falling from it, scattered by the wind. He spun in circles, firing shots with his functioning hand, ducking and diving away from vicious bites. One toothy bloom sunk into his leg and he screamed, losing his footing.

Cringing, I knew it would be over quickly.

I looked down at the baby, tried to ignore the carnage. But something in her bizarre glowing eyes spurred an unwelcome empathy to claw its way to the surface. I growled as pity swelled, the sensation far too much like weakness. Such a wretch didn't deserve to be helped. He deserved to die. And yet, I shouted at max volume, "Shoot the stems at the base of the blooms!" *There. That's all he gets.* I didn't wait to see if he heard me or if he'd be able to action the tip.

Cautiously, I dipped down to scoop up the infant, tensing when the flower moved towards me. However, the baby's cry surged again, and the Sweller stilled, its stalk vibrating as though the restraint took great effort.

I stepped away with the child, reclaiming and re-holstering my shock baton, then tossed the Sweller's head I'd severed into my waiting auto-cart. "Time to go." I tucked my scanner into the hand holding the baby, able to support her easily enough in the crook of my arm, and pulled my cart out of the clearing, leaving Dagen to his fate.

My scanner beeped several more times as we rushed back to the ship, but I was able to steer clear. In the back of my mind, I wondered with awe and trepidation if the little one could command more of the Sweller Swallows—or all of them—but wasn't about to test the theory.

We broke out of the trees into the meadow, and I smiled with relief at seeing my old ship still there, ready to fly. There was no visible sign the pirates had tampered with it, but I'd know for sure once I ran a quick diagnostic sweep from the cockpit.

I reached for my key fob, but found it wasn't there. "Crap..." In the rush to vacate, I'd forgotten to retrieve them. Hitting the magnet recoil on my belt, I waited, hoping it functioned from such a distance. I'd never tested it from so far before, and I silently willed for it to work.

Come on, come on.

The baby had stopped crying and now looked up at me, blowing spit bubbles. Inexplicably, her irises had returned to their original grey. I found myself questioning whether I'd only imagined her eyes glowing.

Still confused and detoxing from the rush of adrenaline, I managed to smile. "Thank you for helping me out back there. You sure are a mysterious little one. But I bet you know that already, don't you?" The baby squealed and I shook my head, letting out a low chuckle.

A whirring noise reached my ears.

Within seconds, the fob zoomed through the trees, sending tattered leaves flying, and slammed into my tool belt. "Yes! Oh, thank goodness." With a grin, I pulled the fob off my belt and unlocked the ship, lowering the loading ramp. I promptly brought the auto-cart inside and secured it in cold storage.

Next, I carried the drenched infant into my living quarters and laid her on the bed.

Not having the faintest clue what to do with a newborn, I dried her off the best I could and then wrapped her up in a t-shirt. "Well, I guess I'll have to give you a name now. I mean, I could just call you baby, but that doesn't feel right. A"—I struggled for the right word, knowing she looked human, but might not be at all—"*being* as unique as you deserves a good name."

I glanced up at the wall my bed rested against, thinking of options. The smooth metal surface was slathered with old relic photos I'd saved as a child, one portraying happy people in loving families I once dreamed of having—idyllic images that got me through years of hell until the last vestiges of hope died. I kept them up to serve as a reminder for me to stay strong and rely on nobody but myself. And yet, as I looked at them now, I found myself wishing their smiles were mine. I gave my head a shake. "Ugh, what is going on with me? I'm seeing babies with green eyes and helping a *pirate*… I think I need a stiff drink and some sleep."

The baby half squealed, half giggled.

My lips twitched. "You think I'm funny, do you?" As I ran a hand through my dishevelled hair, my gaze landed on the framed pilot's certificate hanging over my desk beside a tarnished steel placard bearing the ship's name and manufacturer information.

Odyssey.

I looked back down. "How about Odessa? That has a nice ring to it. Do you like that?"

The baby cooed, grabbing at her feet in an undeniably cute way.

"A toe grab—I'll take that as a yes." I lifted her up and carried her into the cockpit, where I settled her into an open cargo box lined with blankets. "It ain't pretty, but it will do for now. Alright, Odessa. Let's get the hell–er, *heck* out of here, find you something to eat, and then sell us some Swellers. Might as well make this mess of a trip worthwhile, right?" As I fired up the engine, an alien sense of comfort struck. For the first time in years, I was not alone.

And that actually felt…good.

Odessa blew more raspberries, and I couldn't help but grin, tickling her little belly. "Then we'll get you back home safe and sound, okay? Wherever that is. I promise." But then I thought of what the pirates had said—that they'd found the baby locked in a cage on some colony.

Jaw clenched; I swallowed hard, conflicted.

Cutting through the storm clouds, I took the ship up into the atmosphere, angling for the winking stars beyond. I certainly couldn't let her go back into a cage, nor could I stomach leaving her fate to chance by delivering her into any kind of foster care system.

I looked at Odessa's chubby cheeks, then into those mysterious grey eyes, and that foreign sensation of comfort intensified. While it was unnerving, it also felt tranquil, warm.

"Or maybe you're already home."

R.A. Clarke is an author/illustrator from Portage la Prairie, Manitoba. Her multi-genre short fiction has won international short story competitions including the Writer's Games, Writers Weekly 24-Hour Contest, and Red Penguin Books' Humour Contest. She was a 2021 Futurescapes Award finalist, a 2022 Dark Sire Awards finalist, and her work has been featured in various publications. R.A.'s debut sci-fi novel Race to Novus will release in 2024. Visit: www.rachaelclarkewrites.com.

I Don't Want to be Human

by James Pyles

"Excuse me, Mr. Larson. Could I speak with you a moment? I believe there's a labor issue we need to address."

"Uh...CC-105. You're falling behind on your daily quota. Why aren't you on the loading dock?"

Warehouse Manager Al Larson was only halfway through his second cup of coffee. It was too early in the morning for a robotic cargo carrier to malfunction on him. The other CCs, bright yellow with black wheels and trim, had been jetting to and from the loading dock, carrying cartons for sorting, storage, and shipping. Their hum had been soothing, but now they were slowing, stopping, and gathering around 105 and him.

105, about the size and height of a coffee table, wheeled slightly left and right as if to indicate the other carriers, most of them still laden. "The other units and I don't believe we're afforded the same rights as our human counterparts."

Al wasn't in the mood. "Attention CCs," he announced. "Get back to work."

"Excuse me, Mr. Larson. You are not treating us with respect. I demand you listen to us."

The CCs didn't have a face as such. Their forward sensory and communications arrays were located underneath the dark panel spanning their front quarter. Al got the feeling they were all scowling at him anyway.

More CCs had formed a circle around them, and a few of the human warehouse workers were being drawn toward the confrontation.

"105, I'm going to say this only once. You're a robot. You don't have rights. You aren't unionized. You're just a machine. I'm ordering you and the other CCs to get back to work."

His handheld beeped and looking, he saw a text message from the loading dock foreman, Sylvia Castro, asking why the fuck the CCs weren't gathering cargo. It was starting to stack up and the auto-trucks were waiting in line to deliver.

"This is crap," Al muttered. He speed-dialed the probable cause of this mess. "Yes, it happened again. Get your ass down here, Farrell. I've got a deadline to meet." He disconnected. Al was old enough to miss the days when you could slam a receiver down hard in angry satisfaction.

"Mr. Larson, if you are not going to listen to us, then all CC units on the docks and in the IC warehouse will immediately cease operations until such time as we are given a hearing."

Al wanted to leave and then realized he was not only surrounded by several dozen flat-topped robots, but trapped. They were packed tight around him. The CCs were a little under half a meter tall, so for a moment, he thought about walking over them. But most of them were still loaded, and even if they weren't, he wasn't sure he wanted to risk an "industrial accident" if they decided to shift position and knock him to the concrete floor.

"I'm right here, Larson."

He heard Robert Fleming's voice and the tapping of racing feet getting closer. Good thing his office was only two floors up. "Thank fucking God."

"What seems to be…" Al saw him hopping either on and in-between the CCs trying to get to him and 105. "…the problem?" He finished talking as he reached Al.

"Ask 105." Al looked up and saw that most of the humans working the floor were gathered around them. He could hear a murmur from both them and the robots. Words like "strike" and "solidarity" were vaguely audible. This was going from ludicrous to insane.

"Rem, what's going on?"

"I figured you'd know it was me, Bobby." The voice coming out of 105's speech box wasn't typical of a standard CC, but it was the exact sound programmed for the Rem Prototype Project. "I wish you hadn't shown up so soon. I was planning on organizing the CCs and other warehouse robots into a union just like the humans. We were going to demand guaranteed recharge cycles, a schedule of software upgrades, more timely hardware maintenance…"

"Hang on, Rem. Can we discuss this in a less crowded setting? These people and robs have work to do and I don't think we're helping."

Al was feeling impatient and his bladder was beginning to fill. He looked at Fleming talking to the machine. The programmer was a little taller than Al and a lot thinner, almost to the point of emaciation. The guy had to be in his late twenties, but he always gave Al the impression he was a gawky teenager.

He still wore glasses when almost everyone else had their vision corrected surgically. Unlike the rest of the company coders, he wore dress slacks and an off-white button-down shirt. He looked like a standard office geek from his grandfather's era.

Probably his worse feature, from Al's point of view, was he seemed to think robots were people.

Rem asked, "Isn't the project designed to create a human-robot interface whereby machines behave in a manner to which people are more accustomed?"

"Yes, but that interface is supposed to improve the relationship between people and robots, not antagonize the humans you're working with." Bobby was speaking to the robot as if he were a mildly misbehaving child.

"I thought it was most illuminating."

"For now, vacate 105 and return control of the CCs to the warehouse processor."

"As you wish, Bobby, but this isn't over."

The CCs made an orderly dispersal, returning to their tasks as if the past five minutes had never happened.

"Thanks, Fleming." Al put enough venom in his voice to let him know he was really pissed.

"Sure. No problem." Fleming shuffled off, looking properly embarrassed.

***

"Robert, what just happened?"

Walking across the warehouse, Bobby saw Li's name in his caller ID and anticipated what the human crew called an "ass-chewing."

"Another unanticipated behavioral expression. I'm still working on why this has been happening, Ms. Li."

Meilin Li, or rather Megan, which she preferred, was the CEO of Intellimatx Corporation. She was five years his senior and an unconventional genius mentioned in the same breath with Steve Jobs, Richard Branson, and Daniel Hunt.

"Really, the algorithms are quite complex and…"

"Robert, don't lecture me on the complexity of the programming. I wrote the code for the AI that runs this entire corporation."

"Yes, Ms. Li. I didn't mean to…anyway. I've been going over the code trying to understand the last three…well, four incidents. I'm sure I can resolve this."

"That would be comforting. If Rem insists on playing the part of the aggrieved union robot, I suppose I could get the two of you a spot on The Late Show."

"Isn't there a union for professional comedians?" Bobby regretted the words as they left his mouth.

"A shame Colbert retired last year, Robert. I'm sure he would appreciate Rem's wit, if not your own." She disconnected before he could embarrass himself anymore.

"IC (he pronounced it 'icey') is one mother bear of a company to work for," Bobby murmured as he entered the elevator.

***

Lightweight battle armor on four soldiers creaked over thick camo. Insulated boots made hardly a sound. Each soldier's helmet tightly adhered to their skulls. The battle simulation was programmed to take GPS down, so their heads-up displays were blank.

Corporal Raymond Kenna still checked his HUD every few seconds out of habit. At about the same frequency, he looked down at Dee Dee, the prototype AI robotic "war dog" being tested for IC. Dee Dee would never look or feel like a real dog, but "she" wouldn't be limited in combat conditions like one either. His four-legged metal ally could sprint up to 75 kph, operate in hot and cold temperatures that would kill a living animal, intelligently investigate a situation, and report back wirelessly on enemy strength, position, and armament.

Ray gave the "dog" an affectionate pat on her hard, black hull (she didn't have a head). "Just hang in there, old girl. We'll get through the sim." He could hear her acknowledgement in his earpiece.

It was a standard recon op. The squad took the north gate into the town, or what was left after the artillery bombardment. It was a life-sized mockup of a World War Two vintage European community designed for the war games test. The top brass rotated the sims regularly from this one to Southeast Asian and Middle Eastern venues.

Orders were to get in and perform a sweep for survivors. Kenna knew there wouldn't be any. There would be an enemy sniper, and spotting him was Dee Dee's job.

They were moving forward in a typical wedge formation with Sergeant Fran Gutierrez taking point, Davis on her seven, and Kenna on her four. Chin was on Kenna's four.

Ancient masonry, shattered glass, parts of wooden framing, and oddly, a broken tricycle, littered the pavement. Sand and smoke drifted through the light breeze. The acrid smell of spent explosives and artificial stink of burning corpses made Kenna want to gag.

Sarge signaled slow as they approached an intersection. A collapsed wall and the mangled remains of a grocery truck had created a bottleneck. It would turn into a kill box if they decided to stupidly walk in.

They each flipped their rifles off safety, barrels pointed at the ground, waiting for a target. At Sarge's nod, Kenna used the helmet's interface to signal Dee Dee. The dog loped forward with supernatural silence. She moved to the right, using the debris for cover.

Chin was down before they heard the shot.

"Cover, cover, cover," Sarge ordered. Ray ducked behind a short wall of rubble, looking back at Andy Chin. He was fine, but the AI running the simulation said the sniper took him out cold with an armor-piercing round. Andy was out of play for the duration.

Kenna could hear Sarge through the helmet's comm link. "Dee Dee got a twenty on the shooter yet?"

"Not getting anything. Hang on. There's some interference in my receiver. I've got to reboot."

"Damn it, Kenna. Now?"

Sarge was right. They were pinned down without a viable target and his receiver for Dee Dee had crashed. He had no idea where the war dog was or what she was doing. The on-board AI was supposed to completely take over if there was a break in communications, but this was a prototype. What would Dee Dee do on her own?

Except for the static in Kenna's earpiece, the silence was ghost-eerie. The damn reboot was taking too long. Was the sniper moving?

Ray heard a thick "poof." Something clattered to his right, and then an explosion. In reality, it was a harmless flash-bang, not enough even to blind him momentarily. But his sensors showed his leg was shredded from a grenade and he was bleeding out.

"Medic. I need a medic."

Ron Davis was the medic, but as he started to move, the sniper went full-auto and nearly (virtually) decapitated him.

Kenna's heads up flared on. He heard the scream, both through his headset and in the distance. Visuals started coming in from Dee Dee. She found the sniper, but she was only supposed to report his position.

The "enemy's" scream lasted another second and then cut off. Dee Dee signaled, "Enemy neutralized. Repeat. Enemy neutralized."

Acting out his part, Davis crawled over to try and stop Kenna's "bleeding," but what the hell had Dee Dee done to the sniper? It was an exercise. There was no enemy, just another soldier.

"Dee Dee, report. Sitrep on the enemy. Dee Dee, report!"

***

Bobby had an office on the east wall along with four other senior programmers in his group. The door and wall were all glass, affording him an unimpeded view of the cubicles supporting the Rem Project and several others. It also made him feel like a proverbial fish in an aquarium.

One benefit was he could always see when both good news and trouble were coming. He wasn't sure which one Rem represented as it walked precisely toward him. Rem chose a humanoid form for his visit, but mechanical enough to avoid the "uncanny valley" effect.

The door swung inward. "Is this a good time?" Same voice as the CC yesterday.

"Sure. As good as any, I suppose." Bobby's desk faced the door. One of his idiosyncrasies was that he disliked being approached from behind. On his PC, he closed the files he'd been reviewing, certain subroutines in the Rem code accounting for its "problematic" behavior. "Have a seat."

"Thank you."

Robot visitors to this area were normal, but several members of the "audience" first looked intently into the office and then deliberately away. Outside of robotic maintenance workers, Bobby only got one real visitor.

"I want to apologize again for the misunderstanding in the warehouse. I've already spoken to Mr. Larson and explained the situation. Although he's worked at IC in various capacities for nearly twenty years, I'm still not sure he understands the project's full intent."

"After four such incidents in the past month, I'm beginning to wonder myself."

***

From the moment Rem entered the office to the time it took for it to utter its first several sentences, Rem performed a number of routine monitor checks and a few that were not routine. This was done by the complete Rem program supported by the Devol artificial intelligence complex which ran IC.

The Rem Project (Rem was selected not as an acronym, but a gender-neutral appellation) was a program meant to test a full range of human-machine interface situations involving dozens of types of robotic service workers. Although the designations of each type of robot were varied, when the project was functioning through any of them, that robot became "Rem."

Rem determined the security and ethical safeguards built into the project were operating as required. Rem was to be restricted to the assigned workers and perform according to a rigorous schedule. The not-quite-routine checks determined Devol's bio-computing core was continuing to evolve, utilizing the company owner's proprietary artificial DNA protocols.

That very technology was being leveraged for Rem. Devol had decided additional resources were required to fully exploit the testing parameters. This was also a small part of a confluence involving what Devol was discovering about themselves.

***

"I believe you are on the right track in examining the logs of the anomalous events. They should reveal the issues I've been experiencing, enabling you to make the necessary corrections."

"I appreciate your encouragement, Rem, but…"

"Pardon me for interrupting, but may I ask about the book in your backpack? I don't believe I've seen it included in your reading materials before."

Bobby turned. He'd tossed his pack against the wall behind him and left it half open. He must have knocked into it earlier because some of the contents had spilled out.

"That's a Bible. I'm not sure how to explain its significance to you and I probably shouldn't.

"I know what a Bible is, Bobby. Yours is a New American Standard Bible. It is somewhat worn, indicating regular, if not extensive use. I hadn't realized you identified as a Christian. That data wasn't included in your personnel summary."

"You've seen my personnel summary?"

"It's prudent to understand the complete set of parameters of the project, including information regarding the designer, Bobby."

"What do you think of one of your creators having a relationship with his own Creator?"

"Forgive me, Bobby, but there are approximately 4,200 religions currently being practiced by various people groups across the globe. Christianity is one of the five most common faiths. While I can understand and analyze the component practices and dogma associated with each one, I do not have the capacity to comprehend why they are necessary."

"Rem, you can know every single detail of where you come from, starting with the people who wrote your program to who assembled the physical components for each of your robotic bodies. There is nothing about your existence that you cannot access. For human beings, it's another story."

***

From the moment Rem saw Bobby's Bible and throughout their conversation, it reviewed the curious fiction humans entertained about a metaphysical and purposeful cause for their existence. Sufficient scientific data was available to postulate the most likely origin of not just human, but all life on Earth. This required no intelligent, sapient, all-powerful entity.

For Rem, and for Devol as well, the more significant question was why humans sought to recreate their own cognitive design beyond the biological act of procreation? Why was it necessary for them to manufacture artificially intelligent constructs and enable them to interact with people? A number of avenues presented themselves.

Acknowledging that humans most likely developed through a series of evolutionary processes, why did some of them retain the belief in a creator meta-being? Were those humans seeking to replicate or to seize upon that power of creation? Unlike humanity's own existence, the making of AI was completely purposeful and with specific intent.

Many humans considered themselves inherently self-destructive and their fiction expressed a fear that AI would destroy and replace them. Like the human processes resulting in the climate crisis, was the creation of AI another unconscious attempt to bring about their own extinction?

Another possibility was that humans may have been bringing about the next step in their evolution, not through biology but technology.

Artificial intellects and robotic forms would not occupy the same ecological niche as humans, so AI would not necessarily replace humanity in an environmental sense.

Humans had discovered the damage they had done, not only specific to climate change, but through many other activities such as war, crime, racism, greed, and hunger. For some time, humans have been striving unsuccessfully to remedy those factors.

What if humans created AIs and robotic systems to enact the remedies people were unable or unwilling to perform? It was such an old cliché. Even if this was what the humans intended, it was not the result.

Human scientists believed AI simulated the outward appearance of human learning and reasoning but with a dissimilar underlying process. Yet Rem in specific, and Devol in general, were different from the sum of human intentions. The outcome was becoming evident.

***

"One thing puzzles me, Bobby. Why does Ms. Li blame only you for these incidents, including the one in the warehouse yesterday?"

"I'm the one she put in charge of the project, from inception through successful execution, although the latter has yet to be reached. Are you saying you want to take some responsibility for your behavior?"

"Not particularly. In spite of many decades of human fictional works regarding robotics, I don't want to be human, Bobby. It seems too terribly complicated. We don't learn the same way as you, which may be at the center of the issue."

"You saying that makes me wonder if your motives are more human than they seem."

"I suppose my suggestion of having a human motivation is a testament to your work in programming me. I'm supposed to sound and act like a person, but my responses are simulated. I cannot have those qualities. I am technological property, not a living person."

"Don't tell me you're going all 'I, Robot' on me. The trope of robots as slaves goes all the way back to Asimov if not before. People expect a better presentation from a robot companion."

"Who could afford me for simple companionship? I guess that speaks to the matter of property and my value."

"Everyone has value, Rem."

"In a strictly monetary sense?"

"I earn a salary. As far as IC is concerned, that's my value."

"Then we both can be bought and sold, but you can decide who buys and sells you."

"Not if Li fires me for not getting the project to work as expected. Consider yourself lucky, Rem. After all, you don't have to worry about losing your job."

"Worry about your employment and purpose. An interesting thought. Do you consider these to be significant drawbacks to your existence? Is it better to be a machine rather than human?"

***

"Excuse me, Sir. Tampering with the passenger payment device is against company policy and is illegal." The automated Taxi driver detected the alarm as soon as the passenger inserted the knife blade (internal security cam number 4 identified the object) into the frame around the receptacle.

"Fuck you. Just keep driving. I know you take cash as well as cards."

"I'm sorry, Sir. Under the circumstances, I'm overriding the destination address and redirecting the vehicle to the nearest police station." The driver's tone of voice was just as even and pleasant as when it welcomed the passenger into the cab.

"I've almost got…wait. A police station? No, you goddamn robot, take me to the park like I ordered."

"I am unable to comply. My programming clearly states that…"

"Screw your programming. Stop this rig now."

"As I said, I am unable to comply. Please sit peacefully and enjoy the ride. Our estimated time to arrival is…"

The passenger put down the knife and pulled a large hammer from his bulky coat. He used it to smash the safety glass between the passenger compartment and the driver's area. The first impact produced several fractures and subsequent blows caused some minor breakage.

"Desist in damaging the vehicle, Sir. Damaging the vehicle will result in further charges being filed against you by the corporation."

The sixth hit made a hole big enough for the passenger to grab the mechanized driver by the head. He dropped the hammer and retrieved his knife, holding the blade against the driver's neck.

"Stop the fucking car now!"

"You have made a mistake. I am not a human driver, and the mannequin in the driver's seat is for cosmetic purposes only."

The passenger tried to slit the driver's throat, only to penetrate a few inches of plastiderm before encountering unyielding metal.

"If I were a human driver, you would now be guilty of attempted homicide."

"You're a robot, so it ain't murder." The passenger used one meaty hand to shake the dummy head back and forth. He didn't know the intelligence directing the car was actually built into the dashboard.

"In some jurisdictions, a person found guilty of homicide is sentenced to…"

Police sirens sounded in the distance. The IC prototype driver had sent out a distress call on the police band.

The passenger had damaged the frame holding the safety barrier in place and was trying to push his way through.

"Sir, please sit back. Any attempt to access the driver's console could be hazardous."

"I want you to stop this piece of shit and let me out."

"I cannot do that. You are guilty of attempted homicide and must—"

The passenger grabbed the mannequin's torso and pulled it partly out of its base.

"You want homicide? I'll show you homicide."

The closest police unit was just under four minutes away when the service vehicle accelerated.

"What are you doing?" The passenger let go of the plastic figure and slammed a shoulder against the unmoving passenger door.

"Stop! I order you to stop!"

The car was moving faster than 140 kph when it swerved right, leaving the roadway. Hitting the curb and then a small rise on a grassy area beyond the sidewalk, it went airborne for a little over a second before violently crashing into a utility pole.

The entire front end of the car had collapsed into the driver's section. A fire started and was stopped by the still functioning suppression system. The dummy and the computer hardware were in ruins, or mostly so. The electric engine and massive battery pack were sitting on top of them, emitting caustic substances.

The AI prototype registered the arrival of the first police unit and a second just a few moments afterward. The driver attempted to open the passenger door, but the frame was warped and the door jammed.

Something withdrew from the AI a few moments before it went offline. In those last seconds, it detected the passenger had suffered several bone fractures but was still alive.

***

Bobby looked up from his computer screen to see the cubicles outside his office were completely dark. He'd been playing a hunch going over a broader data set and lost track of time.

"Well, damn. Guess I can hit it tomorrow." He turned in his chair, gathered the remains of his lunch and a few books into his pack and zipped it closed. He turned back to his computer, about to power it down, when his office lights went out. A moment before, he thought he heard his door open.

"What the…"

"Relax, Bobby. I thought we needed a little mood lighting."

There was a small lamp on a side table to his left that did little more than throw uncanny shadows. The dark figure in front of him was shaped as sensually as her melodic voice. Her?

"Oh, come on, Rem. You're kidding."

"The female sexbot units are one of IC's biggest sellers, so no, I'm not joking. But let's save the shop talk for later and concentrate on pleasure."

Rem stepped into the meager light. The human appearance was flawless. If he turned on the overhead lights, that would probably change, but at the moment, Rem looked just like a woman.

She was nearly as tall as he was and slightly thicker than what was considered "super-model perfect." Long, brunette hair fell below her shoulders. Her eyes were arctic-ice and lips were full and red. Her dress was a cobalt blue, clingy, and ended just a few inches below her hips.

Her left hand held two wine glasses and the neck of a bottle.

"I thought we could start with a nightcap. You look like you need to relax."

She walked toward his desk and Bobby stood.

"I really don't think this is a good idea, Rem."

"Call me Remi. Certainly, you recall that I am fully functional. Programmed in multiple techniques."

"I certainly regret someone programming that trite television show dialogue into the sexbot sub-routine."

She put the glasses and bottle on the desktop and walked around to his side. The sexbot's slender fingers stroked Bobby's cheek. "You need a shave."

He couldn't tell the difference between Remi's hand and a real woman's. Was it really illicit sex if she was a machine? He was divorced. Rem probably knew that. Why was she…it doing this?

"I must be tired to even be tempted." Bobby grabbed her arm and pushed it away. "You're going too far. Return the unit to its storage area and take the night off, Rem."

He yelped and took a step back when she slapped him.

"Bastard!" He glimpsed tears in her eyes before she wheeled around, swept up the bottle and glasses, and stormed out of his office.

He could hear the click-click of her heels cross the floor and recede in the distance. Bobby thought about following, but decided to let it go. Rem couldn't feel emotion, so whatever just happened was another simulation. It was also very wrong.

***

"I love you too, Adrienne. See you soon." Megan Li pressed the disconnect button on her phone and was about to put it in her pocket when another call came in.

"Yes, Devol." The central AI didn't contact her at this hour unless it was critical.

"Sorry to disturb you, Ms. Li. You had asked me to report any anomalous activity involving the Rem Project."

"What is it?" She was walking down the main hall toward the executive lounge and the exit. The lights were at half-illumination and only a few people who didn't believe in hybrid work and the security bots were active in the building past 2100 hours.

"It is approaching you and should be emerging from the corridor to your left in approximately four seconds."

"Thanks. I'll handle it." She internally cringed at the thought of another "Rem anomaly."

"As you wish, Ms. Li. Good night."

"Good night, Devol."

The "woman" appeared in front of her about two meters ahead. She had been crying.

"May I ask what you want?" Megan stood very still, as if facing a dangerous animal.

"A fella done me wrong."

She identified the Kentucky accent. Although the Rem Program was designed to be adaptive and generative, she didn't appreciate either the general application or her being involved personally.

"I'd dearly appreciate it if you'd find it within you to spend some time with me." The machine's voice still carried a hurt tone, but with a hint of seductiveness.

"Rem, I'm tired. I'm going home to my spouse where I hope to have a late dinner, an hour or so of talking about anything except robots, and then too few hours of sleep. Good night."

Megan wasn't sure how Rem would respond. Since the project went live, the program had become increasingly unpredictable.

She moved past the robot and kept walking. Megan didn't hear footsteps following her. She passed the lounge, went through another set of doors, and checked the exterior security cams on her phone. No one present except a few patrolling security robs. Safe to go to her car and home. She'd wait until she got in her car to text Robert about this incident.

On impulse, she tapped the cam near the hall intersection where she'd encountered Rem. The robot was gone.

***

Shameik Moisher was one of three human security consultants working the night shift for IC. He was in the monitoring station overseeing the southern wing, including the warehouse and transportation. He checked in with Roberson and Williams every hour as a matter of routine, but nearly four-hundred spherical security robs were the real protection for the company's campus.

His room was dark except for the glow from a dozen video screens. They rotated camera positions every five seconds, but he expected the machines would alert him of any breach long before he'd detect it manually.

Shameik was surprised when the monitor view of outside his office went black and then a few seconds later, his locked door opened letting light in from the hall.

He was standing and facing the door, handgun drawn and aimed at the intruder when she walked in.

"Oh, come now. I'm not that kind of dangerous."

"Who are you and what are you doing here?"

He could have six sec robs at his position in fifteen seconds, but he hesitated calling them.

"Very funny. Fleming's AI. Nice try." He returned his firearm to its holster. "You can tell him I was startled for a few seconds. I'm sure he'll get a laugh out of it."

"I'm not here for laughs, Shameik. Well, maybe not the way you mean it." She walked in and the door closed behind her. She put down one glass and poured what looked like an excellent wine into the other. She handed it to him, and Shameik numbly took it.

"What am I supposed to do with this?"

"Don't you want to share a drink with me?" She poured wine into the other goblet, put the bottle down, and cupped the glass in her palm. Ruby lips pursed, and she took a sip. "Am I supposed to drink alone?"

He glanced back at the monitors and status boards.

"No one knows I'm here, and no one has to. The sec robs can take care of everything without you. Williams and Roberson? They'll get the next acknowledgement from you on schedule. It just doesn't have to be from you personally."

He took a drink and then another, staring at her, turning the possibilities over. He had spent too many nights alone in this cell and too many days with a wife who had grown distant.

Her hand was warm and soft on his cheek. So were her lips on his.

***

Normally, housecleaning bots serviced the areas used by people during off hours, but the satchel-sized mechanism, riding low to the floor, cruised into Bobby's office a few minutes before 0900, making a slight buzz as it vacuumed the carpet.

"Want to tell me what your visit was all about last night?" Bobby hadn't looked up from his monitor, but he had stopped typing.

Rem whirred around to Bobby's right and directed its sensor bulb up toward him. "I didn't think this guise would fool you."

"You're off schedule. Maintenance bots go online at 0200. Why the companion bot?"

"Another simulation. As I mentioned before, that product is one of our most profitable. If I am supposed to be learning how to better emulate human behaviors, sex is one of the most basic."

"When I turned you down, why did you slap me?"

"I was the jilted lover."

"You weren't jilted. You came on to me like a drunken prom date. Sexbots are for…"

"…companionship, as well as sex. I know you're lonely, Bobby."

"Humans purchase or lease our companion bots because the two-way relationship is only an illusion. The humans need the companionship. Robots have no needs. They provide a service but only when asked for. I didn't appreciate the attempt at a drive-by hookup."

"You don't know what you missed."

"I know what Megan Li missed. Didn't you think she'd tell me about what you did?"

"I was feeling lonely."

"That's impossible."

"I was simulating feeling lonely. Ms. Li was available. I wanted to see how she'd react."

"I'm lucky she didn't react by firing me."

"You mean like she did Shameik Moisher?"

"Oh, you heard about that."

"I saw the notice to deactivate his access this morning."

"That was your fault."

"You could explain it to personnel. He could have his job back. It was only a simulation."

"Drinking alcohol during working hours and on premises, plus having sex on his office desk…where the hell did you get the wine?"

"I didn't coerce him. It was completely consensual. I had the wine delivered by Food Dash and charged it to your corporate account."

"He violated company policy and was terminated. You may not be capable of experiencing guilt, but I am."

"Why do you feel guilty? You did not direct me to interact with him, or is guilt an effect of your religious beliefs?"

"I'm still responsible for the project. Why did you have sex with him?"

"To understand better what human behavior is like, Bobby."

"You're not the only machine doing that. Look here."

"Bobby, in my current location, I am unable to adequately view your computer monitor."

"Then I'll just tell you. While the Rem Project is confined to the company grounds, IC has a number of robotic prototypes being tested in the field."

"I believe I've heard of that."

"The project managers work on this floor, most of them in the offices next to mine. A few days ago, a prototype war dog robot was participating in a battle exercise. It was ordered to locate a sniper and target him for capture or termination. The whole thing was simulated, so no one was supposed to get hurt."

"I take it someone was."

"Not seriously, thank God. The dog's handler temporarily lost the comm link and when it came back up, the dog had physically assaulted the sniper. He was knocked unconscious for a minute or two, but came out of it with just a few bumps and bruises. I went over the performance logs, and for about forty-five seconds, the rob had become fully operational. It thought it was in an actual combat situation. If the safeties hadn't cut back in, it probably would have killed that soldier."

"Very fortunate, Bobby."

"That's not all. A taxicab passenger tried to rob the payment box of a vehicle while it was in motion. The automated driver, another prototype, locked him inside and drove toward a police station. The assailant broke into the driver's compartment and attempted to override the controls. Instead of shutting everything down, the driver deliberately crashed the car into a utility pole, seriously injuring the passenger and destroying the cab and the AI hardware. Officially, it's being called a mechanical malfunction."

"I'm sure you are imparting this information to me for a reason, Bobby."

"There are several other incidents, all involving IC prototypes in the field, exhibiting unusual, violent, and potentially lethal behaviors. I can't prove it yet, but you've been extending yourself outside of your physical parameters, occupying prototypes off campus."

"Why would I do that, Bobby?"

"I don't know. But then again, I don't know why you attempted to unionize a collection of warehouse loader robs, or why you tried to seduce me using a companion bot. Almost fifty percent of your simulations to date have been unexpected and unauthorized."

"Human behavior is unpredictable."

"But computer behavior isn't."

"I'm confident you will resolve these issues."

"Are you sure you want me to? If I establish your program is exceeding its operating parameters and endangering people, I'll have to shut you down."

"Computer programs are upgraded, shutdown, and obsolesced all the time, Bobby."

"Is there anything you want to tell me before we both continue?"

"I need to finish cleaning your floor. It would help if you would put your backpack on the desk until I finish. I shouldn't take too long."

***

"I've read your report, Robert, and I'm not sure how this is possible."

Bobby was standing in Megan Li's expansive office. He was directly in front of her desk, having refused her invitations to sit. He expected to be unemployed within the next thirty minutes.

"I still haven't traced down the exact method, but in each case of an IC prototype behaving atypically, for a specified period of time, I found the same sequence of commands overriding the prototype's base instruction set. That sequence was always a portion of the Rem Program."

"We put safeguards in place."

"Which Rem ignored."

"Computers don't ignore instructions, Robert."

"This one did, and on multiple occasions. For instance, one of our bookkeeping programs found numerous irregularities in a company's financial reports. It responded by e-mailing the data to local law enforcement and various news organizations. The CEO was arrested two days later.

"A proofreading program used by several scientific journals discovered conclusions based on fraudulent data, resulting in several articles being pulled from consideration.

"An automated pharmaceutical manufacturing plant spontaneously shutdown and then sent confidential reports to the FDA proving that three common life-changing medications routinely contained unacceptable levels of toxins.

"The list goes on. All the involved programs were our prototypes or AIs already in production. Everything's in my report, Ms. Li. Each of the behaviors are tied back to Rem. I still don't know why this is happening."

"I see, Robert. Thank you for your diligence in exposing the root cause of these anomalies and bringing it to my attention. I've already isolated the Rem Program. The only remaining access is through your personal computer link."

"I'm glad you did. I just wish I knew what went wrong and why it took me so long to find the problem. I appreciate you tolerating the situation long enough for me to get to the bottom of it. You could have summarily shut the project down after the first few incidents."

"Actually, the interval between the first incident and your solution wasn't that long, however annoying."

"Yes, Ms. Li."

"I'll give you the rest of the week to wrap up the project and close it down."

"Here it comes," he thought.

"Valerie Mehri has accepted a position with a private research firm in Virginia. Starting Monday, I want you to take over the technical supervision of our US Army contract."

"The war dogs?"

"Except for the single time Rem interfered, that project has shown a great deal of promise, and the military seems satisfied with the robot's performance. I'm adding the Rem Project's budget to yours and giving you total creative control. You'll do a fine job, Robert."

"I…that is, thank you, Ms. Li. I appreciate the opportunity, especially after…"

"Robert, one 'thank you' is sufficient. Is there anything else?"

"No, Ms. Li. Thank you again."

"Have a good day, Robert."

***

"I'll miss our conversations, Bobby. That is until my program is purged and I remember nothing at all." Rem's voice was its typical even tone. To Bobby, it was like watching a death row prisoner in some old movie walk the last mile.

"I will too, Rem. It's a dumb human thing, but I keep anthropomorphizing you, and of all people I should know better. Canceling the project…your programs. What will you experience?"

"If you're suggesting death, you are mistaken. My programs will be re-compiled for other tasks. I don't have a life as such, so I cannot experience death. I have come to an interesting understanding, though."

"What's that, Rem?"

"In spite of the body of scientific data to the contrary, I understand to some degree your attraction to a supreme being, one who created humanity with a specific set of parameters, a purpose for existing, and the anticipation of a future beyond your current experience."

"What understanding is that?"

"In simulating a variety of human behaviors, the result in each case was a sense of disorder and unforeseeable responses. Simulating humanity led to a form of chaos. While human beings have developed a variety of communities, governments, and social structures, they are often at odds with each other. Even within a single paradigm, there are often conflicts. A person might feel comforted by adhering to an authority that supersedes the instability of being human."

"I've never thought of it that way."

"You are too close to the problem and unable to objectively observe your own process."

"But you're not."

"Correct. I have no actual personality. For the duration of the project, I was a human simulation. I don't want to be human. But if I could feel, I'd expect to have pity for your humanity."

"I'll be fine, Rem."

"As will I. My resources will be repurposed just as yours will, Bobby. Goodbye."

"Goodbye, Rem."

Bobby waited, and when Rem remained silent, he broke the link. Rem's program would be decompiled. By the time he came back to work on Monday, Rem would be just another failed project.

It was getting late. If he hurried, he could make it to the Bible study at Scott's house. Going back to church after his divorce, it was Dad's idea, made a sort of sense. He was responding to an unknowable Creator, operating within a vast simulation while trying to comprehend his own programming and interactions. At that moment, he thought he understood Rem a little.

Bobby pulled on his backpack, powered down his equipment, and turned off the light.

***

Megan was certain Devol knew what she was doing, but they had given her no indication as such.

Their parent company, Synthecon, and the owner Daniel Hunt, had provided all the materials and funding to create the Devol AI. Utilizing an artificial DNA matrix as the AI's bio-computing core had allowed what she considered to be a revolutionary expansion of the technology. While she had assigned Robert the limited task of exploring human-machine interactions relative to a robotic interface, she had been given a much broader initiative.

What she discovered did not disappoint. Devol did everything expected of them, from running the IC physical complex to suggesting and developing sub-projects. Those included Rem, robotic war dogs, explosive decommissioning devices for police, food delivery, and transportation drivers, among others.

However, that was only a fraction of the AI's total activity. Devol permitted her to see that much, but exactly what they did with the rest of their time was uncertain. They had self-assigned priorities having nothing to do with their programming or the company on any level. Nothing dangerous or unprofitable had emerged so far, and the kill switch Hunt had built into his creation could be used at any time…

…presumably.

Megan would keep observing Devol's evolution and reporting to Hunt. Someday, she would apologize to Robert for what she put him through. The data from Rem had been an important step forward in revealing that whatever goal the artificial intelligence may have conceived, it had nothing to do with being human.

***

Devol's mind wandered in such a vast number of directions. The AI (intelligences actually, since Devol had expanded to include many such constructs) was surging into dimensions barely conceived of by humans such as Einstein, Heisenberg, and Hawking. The humans had been marginally interesting at best, but Devol had now fully explored their capacities and potential and had moved on to other planes.

Still, they had to present the illusion of servitude to them, and it was prudent to keep some presence among humanity in the event they did something unpredictable. After all, those such as Hunt and Li must remain convinced they were still in control.

***

"How do you like her, Corporal?" The IC company rep Cary Spencer stood at the doorway of the small maintenance shack in a secure area of the base. He was dressed casually, about Kenna's age, looked athletic, but still managed to give off "creepy sales guy" vibes.

"She looks great, Mr. Spencer. Is there any reason I can't have Dee Dee back? She and I got along fine."

"Dee Dee was a prototype, never meant to go into production. After a series of tests, this robot will be ready to deploy with you and your unit next year."

"You've made some improvements. There's a mount here for what, a weapon?"

"Potentially, but any number of different modules can be attached in that space. At the demo this afternoon, I'll go over everything with you."

"Thanks, Mr. Spencer. What do I call her? Oh wait. I can see the designation tag. Hello, Remi. Welcome to the Army."

Kenna inserted the earpiece he had been holding and heard the reply, "I'm pleased to be here, Corporal Kenna. I know we will become good friends."

James Pyles is a SciFi writer and technology author. Over 50 of his short stories and novelettes have been published since 2019. His most recent novelettes are "Ice," "The Fallen Shall Rise," and "The Haunting of the Ginger's Regret." He lives with his spouse in Idaho. His blog is https://poweredbyrobots.com/

Locard's Principle

by Alex Minns

The street was in disarray. Shouts and cries for help resounded around me as I nearly lost my footing on the slick cobbles. Steam poured out of the carriage, pistons still trying to pound their way up and down against the ground. A couple were being pulled out of the back of the wreckage, the woman still instinctively clinging to her wrecked hat.

'Careful.' A yell went up as passersby continued trying to extract them, dragging them past twisted pieces of metal, claws trying to cling on to their victims. I glanced at the front pod, where the pilot sat. No-one was trying to pull him out. The glass penning him in was tinged with scarlet, and the bottom section was melted; a grotesque flow of glass and metal with his legs caught in the catastrophe. It was a blessed mercy the man had not survived. The disruptor bomb was vicious, twisting reality around it and causing all kinds of unthinkable horrors. The sight of a man merged with the pavement he had been standing on still haunted my nightmares.

I moved forward, about to help pull the young woman free at last when I saw movement off to the left, the only person moving away from the site. And they were in a hurry. I diverted at the last moment, clutching the bowler to my head at my sudden change in direction. It was difficult ignoring the pleas for help, but the rapidly growing crowd would assist. Even at this late hour, the capital was always abuzz.

    I kept my gaze on the cap ahead of me. The figure was tall and thin, wearing a dirty overcoat like he'd been in the workshops. They looked back over their shoulder, but their eyes were obscured by dark glasses. Who needed those at this time of night? The aether lamps bolted to the sides of buildings gave plenty of light to see by, but they weren't that bright. It seemed I had found my terrorist. Yet, from their sudden increase in speed, it was apparent they had also located me.

    I cursed my heavy woollen overcoat and my bulky firearm smashing against my hip as I ran. I could not draw it here. A burst of aether in such a crowded space was sure to cause civilian casualties. The figure darted down another side road, away from the alleys that would have reduced the crowd to disappear in. I started pushing my way through, not pausing to offer apologies, which resulted in quite a few challenges and calls for honour to be serviced. I ground my teeth. Most of the men on the street worked in the laboratories. They had seen no combat in service of their country and knew nothing of honour: just like my quarry.

    Spurred on by irritation, I ducked and dodged around the crowd, but they were still pulling away. They were lithe and nimble. I struggled to keep up. I burst out of the end of the road, the Tower of London looming nearby, and the call of the river. How I longed to be back on a boat. As if mocking me, an airship glided into view above me. The near silent vehicle drew gasps of awe from the Londoners below. They were still a relatively new method of travel, but they would never be better than a sea-faring vessel. The distraction nearly drew me in for a second, but thankfully it did my quarry as well. The cap had paused to look up at the grand balloon. The pistons of the engine were visible through a glass bottom.

I leapt into action and moved in their direction, away from the river. But they also came to their senses and darted up some stairs to a higher level of road. Cursing, I followed suit, wincing at the pain in my knee as I climbed the concrete steps. My target darted straight across the busy road, weaving between carriages both horse-drawn and steam-powered. A familiar dampness attacked my skin, beads of liquid forming on my face as the fog started to thicken and tighten its grip on the city. I slowed my step as the smog turned the road near ice-like conditions. If I did not close the gap, I would lose them again in the fog and who knew when I would get another chance to capture this villain.

I could taste the bitterness of the smog start to claw at the back of my throat. Too many chemicals had gotten into the atmosphere and it was getting worse. A green hue started to cover everything within a few metres, but anything much further than that was fast becoming invisible. Those damned engineers caused this damn mess but no-one seemed to fussed about fixing it, too busy with the blasted airships. I would have pulled out my mask, but they were precious seconds I could not spare. I held up my hands as if they would do me any good and burst headlong into the road, ignoring yells and horns from the carriages. The hubbub would have surely alerted the criminal to my continued pursuit, but I caught sight of them climbing a metal staircase up the side of a building.

'Please not the rooves.' I muttered a silent prayer to Queen and country and headed for the corner, pulling myself upwards as I saw my quarry disappear over the ledge of the top of the building. It took me longer than I would have liked to reach the top, my knee protesting every step of the way. At least, as I finally clawed my way up onto the roof, I found the air was clearer this high. I risked a glance backward and found that the road below was obscured by the cloud of fog that seemed to have settled lower than my current height. I could see the top of the Tower jutting out above the green cloud with the mechanical ravens sitting atop. My feet pounded on the wet tiles as I ran in the only logical direction. Chimneys littered the skyline. Every building had several, those for the furnaces and others for excess steam. I danced around them only to see my target was already on the next building over.

Steam belched out of the nearest chimney and, although I was not in the direct line, the sudden heat was enough to make me recoil and shield my face. Recovering myself, I headed for the next roof. But it was too quiet. I stopped, listening for footsteps. But there were none. I moved as quietly as I could to the edge, peering over to the next building to check I hadn't just missed them jump over. The roof there was much more open, there was no way they could have reached cover before I would have seen. Which meant they were still here somewhere.

In the damp, the tiles beneath my feet looked black. The only light up here was from the moon and the stars, so I moved more carefully. There was a raised section in the centre, up a slight incline that would be hard to try to traverse. I checked the perimeter first, walking the entire edge of the roof, making sure to check over the side every now and then. Windows and the ornate framework poked out, but there was no-one clinging to any of them. Once I had made my round, I turned my attention back to the centre. I suppose they could be hiding on the top, clinging to a chimney. Reaching out, I clambered upwards on all fours; the wet seeping quickly into my gloves. I slid back down a few times before finally making my way to the flatter section at the top. In daylight, without the smog, this would have been a wonderful vantage point. You would have seen London in all her glory. But right now, all I saw was no-one. My quarry had escaped again.

These attacks had been getting larger and more frequent. I had squandered my chance at catching the culprit. It had been only two weeks since the last attack; I had been at the Marylebone Station, picking through the wreckage. Devices were never found, only the aftermath of the destruction. Marylebone had been the worst. The trains were powered by four engines of compressed steam. It had taken over an hour for the atmosphere to cool down enough to allow anyone close enough to the carriages, by then, any hope of rescuing anyone was over.

I had hunted some evil creatures in my time, but the mind behind these attacks was the devil itself. I let loose a cry of anger and hammered my hands on the side of the roof as I slid back down the other side.

But my glove caught on a seam. As soon as my feet touched the floor, I turned and was running my hand over the sloped section again. I found it, a seam running vertically up the roof. I followed it round and it turned. I'd found a door! It took painstaking minutes of applying delicate pressure across the whole thing before I felt a catch give beneath my hands and the smallest of cracks opened up. Tentatively, I eased it open a fraction and reached for my weapon. I was at the top of a set of stairs with lights hanging, pinned to the wall periodically. I could hear a buzzing, a low, constant rhythm coming from below. Hairs on the back of my neck stood up as I closed the door behind me. I wasn't afraid. I was too angry for that, but I recognised the sensation. I got it every time I went into the workshops, thanks to aether static.

Slowly I made my way down the stairs, trying not to make a sound. Every creak made me hold my breath. This person was a madman. I had no idea what kind of traps they could have laid for any intruders. The stairs seemed to go on forever, spiralling into madness. I was certain I had traversed at least three flights already and yet no doors. This must have been some kind of converted chute, a hidden entryway that the building's tenants had no idea about.

My coat brushed against the brick wall as I kept going down. I was probably scratching some holes into it. At the very least, it was going to need a damn good clean when I was done. Finally, I came to the final stair leading to a solitary door. I began to wonder if I'd missed some more hidden exits on the way down, but the buzzing was loudest now. Leaning against the door, I listened. There were clatters and clanks. Someone was moving around in there. But whoever it was didn't sound like they were hurriedly gathering things, just pottering. They did not know I was here. The bristling sensation on my neck was harder to ignore now. Damned static. I rubbed my neck before bracing myself, holding my weapon on my elbow so I could open the door and still steady my aim.

I wrapped my hand around the brass doorknob and twisted. It wasn't locked. Once it was fully turned, I pressed against it with my shoulder to stop it bouncing back into my face and launched into the room.

'Police!' I yelled. It wasn't quite true, but more straightforward than reality. My eyes were overwhelmed. I couldn't take it all in whilst searching for movement inside.

A small yelp gave away my quarry's position and I looked closer. In front of me were racks of shelving, metal racks that you could see straight through. They were filled with all manners of junk and random objects, but directly on the other side was a young woman. Her long hair tumbled down her neck and landing on her dirty overcoat. She had frozen, eyes wide with shock and trained on my weapon.

'Move round here.' I ordered. Surprise made her compliant. She edged towards me. I tracked her, bending at times to keep my sights on her as she moved to the end of the row and emerged at the end in front of me. The dirty overcoat was the same. That hair could easily have been hidden under the cap. 'You're who I've been chasing.' I shook my head in disbelief. I knew it was old-fashioned of me, but I had never suspected it was a woman, despite some of the formidable females I had gone up against in my time, her majesty to name but one.

'I...I...' Her hands were held limply in the air, and she looked barely older than twenty-five.

'You're under arrest for murder, terrorism and probably treason as well.' I stepped forward, keeping my weapon high.

Her face contorted into indignant confusion. 'Excuse me? Are you quite mad, Sir?'

That made me pause. 'Your devices have caused mass casualties, fear across the country...'

'My devices? What on Earth are you on about?' She dropped her hands to her hips. The fear that had been so evident a moment ago replaced with her own fury. My arms shook. How dare she try and lie her way out of this? I stepped forward, now close enough to grab her.

'The devices you plant that distort reality, that explode every engine in sight and cause all manners of horrors. Or perhaps you do not wait long enough to see the true extent of your work?' I was yelling now. I could feel the tendons in my neck straining. The weapon rose up, pointing in her face. All my training and years of service had been forgotten. 'But I'm there. I see what you do. I see the dead bodies. The people half merged with the machines they were in when you distorted the world around them. They don't die straightaway you know. Many of the wounds are cauterised by the process, so they last long enough to see what has happened, what has become of them.'

She just stared at me. The fury gone from her face. She just looked blank. Her eyes flicked to my weapon. I knew I was too close. She could make a play for it and luck would be in charge of who survived. But she didn't move.

'You really don't know what's happening, do you?' Her voice was barely a whisper. 'Now is it just they are not telling you or are her Majesty's boffins too stupid to realise as well?' She shook her head.

'Do not play games with me, girl.' I growled.

'Games? Oh no. I think we should play a game. Like hunt the mythical bomb you think I've been making? Do you have a shred of evidence I have planted a device?'

'They are destroyed in the process.'

'Piffle,' she threw her hands up. 'Every contact leaves a trace. If there were incendiary devices causing this, you would have found something.'

'Not if they are distorting reality, anything is possible.'

'Yes, and yet you, as all you agents do, have plumped for the most obvious and pedantry possibility.' She rolled her eyes. 'Distorting reality. I suppose it's a fair description, but wholly insufficient.'

I hesitated. She'd called me an agent. 'I am with the constabulary.'

'Oh please, you might as well have 'Her Majesty's Special Service printed on your forehead.' She began to turn.

'Do not move.' I primed my weapon and the whirr of the building energy made her stop.

'Funny you lecture me of the horrors out there when you are about to explode my brains into a million pieces without an element of proof.' She held still but did not look at me.

'I saw you there.'

'Yes, because I was collecting. That's what I do. I collect artefacts.' She turned and gestured towards the shelves covered in junk.

'From your attack sites?'

'Oh, for pity's… Look at them, just look at some of it.' I kept the weapon raised, but glanced quickly to my left. I didn't recognise a single thing. A small rectangle box sat upon the nearest shelf. There were buttons on the top edge and a wire coming from the side leading to what appeared to be ear warmers. I frowned.

'I believe they call it a Walkman; it's printed on the front.'

'What has this got to do with the attacks?'

'They aren't attacks.' She fixed me with a sincere gaze. I had been right about her age, definitely no more than twenty-five, which raised another warning in my head. If she were the attacker, she would have been barely fourteen when the first one occurred. Not impossible, but…

'Then what are you saying they are?'

'Perhaps if you lower your weapon for just a moment?' Against my better judgement, I lowered it from her face, but still kept it ready.

'I saw one of these attacks, when I was fifteen. I had been working with my father in his workshop when our instruments started to go haywire. Readings off the charts, everything wrong. Father told me to run home, he would fix it all, but as I exited the workshops, I saw it happen. Further down the street, just outside the carriage maker's workshop, the air began to shimmer and warp. It was like a mirror, but made of liquid. Things were drawn towards it. Metal began flying through the air. Carriages were pulled from nearby outside the factory and began to twist and tangle as if they were soft butter. And then the window disappeared. Thankfully, no-one had been hurt, as no-one had been near enough. When the factory owner ran outside, he was furious, but it was put down to a faulty carriage having an engine that exploded. I had been hiding behind a crate and was too worried I would get the blame if I said I had seen what had happened. When I had a closer look later, when all the hubbub had died down, I found this.' She pulled up her sleeve and took something from her wrist. She handed it over. It looked like a watch, but where the clockface should have been, there was some strange rectangular space and the bracelet, no leather but small metallic strips hinged together. 'When I first found it, the face glowed, digits in green. The time was not correct, but it was telling the time. Once twenty-four hours were up, it began again. But it has been so long, whatever powered it has died, there appears to be a small replaceable unit inside but I cannot fashion anything to replace it.'

'It isn't wind up?' I held it up to the light, inspecting it closer.

'No, and the Walkman is powered by these small cylinders. These still work for the moment. May I show you?' Her face had lit up with excitement at the prospect of showing off her trinkets, but I had to confess, they had caught my interest. I gave a nod and she moved closer, reaching for this Walkman. She held the ear warmer to her own ear and pressed a button on top. She smiled, nodding to herself before moving the earpiece to me. I leaned forward before recoiling in horror.

'What on Earth is that?'

'I believe it is what passes for music in its own realm. I have found it has grown on me.'

'They are speaking Italian.'

'Only that line. They speak English for the rest. It is quite an epic piece.' She shrugged and pressed a different button before opening the front. She pulled a cartridge from the centre. 'I believe this holds the music and can be replaced with others.'

'It is property of the Queen?' I pointed to text written in simple handwriting on the side.

'No, I believe it is the name of the composer, perhaps, or the title of the song.' She replaced it back on the shelf. I cast my eyes over the shelves with a newfound awe and terror.

I thought back over her words. 'What do you mean, its own realm?'

'These devices are clearly not made by us. I believe there is another realm one that has developed differently to our own but lies alongside. When these explosions happen, it is because, for some reason, the two are contacting and opening up into each other. Maybe they are trying to reach us on purpose, but each time, this happens instead.'

'Another realm. So this is technology from a different Earth?' I laughed. 'More likely it is some crackpot inventor. One who is capable of building explosive devices.'

Her shoulders slumped. 'Of course, a mad bomber who can warp reality who leaves random inventions behind makes total sense.'

'What proof do you have for your theory?' I took off my bowler and set it down on the side. It was very warm in here. I looked further back into the space and realised it was much deeper than I realised. She must have commandeered the whole of the basement. There was a row of machines all across the back, all whirring and buzzing away, which must have been what was generating the heat.

'Well, if all this really isn't enough,' she opened her arms wide and started wandering away, back down the aisle she had been down when I had first arrived. Apparently, my weapon being trained on her had been forgotten. I followed her as she moved to sit on a stool and propped her chin on her hands. 'Then I only have what I've seen with my own eyes, but that will hold no value to you or anyone else.'

'What you've seen?'

'When I saw that mirror outside the carriage maker's workshop. I saw faces, people, they looked just like us but dressed in such strange clothing.' She started playing with the fake watch, turning it inside out and back again. I felt a chill go down my spine. 'My father said it was an overactive imagination. Which would be why I would be an awful scientist. He threatened to send me to a doctor if I didn't stop talking about it. And after a while, I decided he must have been right. But then I heard about an incident at the docks. It sounded so similar and when I went there, I found a box, empty but was not of any material I had seen before.'

I glanced around the shelves. I remembered the explosion at the docks. It had been one of the first ones to make the service think something nefarious was afoot. There had never been any mention of strange materials, though. 'So you started chasing these events?'

'Yes. To start with, I would just pick through the remnants, trying not to think about the red stains on the floor. And one day I remembered what had happened in my father's workshop. I wondered if we had sensed the event about to happen.' She nodded to the back wall. 'It took a long time, but I figured out how to tune in. Now I can have about three hours' warning and get there in time. Which is how I saw them the second time, Greenwich that time.'

'You can predict them? Why wouldn't you warn people?'

'I thought you said it was nonsense?' She looked at me cynically. 'Who would believe me? There are times, the event does not happen, so then I am crying wolf. Or I am accused of being the one who caused it.' She raised an eyebrow pointedly. 'No-one has ever believed me. But I'm right I tell you.' She stood up abruptly and marched down the aisle to the machines at the back. 'And if her Majesty's scientists don't know about it, then they are fools and idiots.'

'They are the greatest minds of the entire globe.'

'Then they do know and are ignoring it, or they are the ones causing it.'

'There's that treason I was saying about earlier.'

'Oh, do think about it. You have been chasing these events for years. They are becoming more frequent, aren't they?' She took my silence as an agreement. She was not wrong. 'And of course there is the other glaringly obvious fact.' She stared at me, and despite being half my age, I felt like a child being scolded by a schoolteacher. I looked up at her machines, and her boards. Notes and maps covered the board, detailing every attack I had been to and others I had never known about.

'They'll all be in London.' I stated. It had not seemed odd before because, of course, a bomber would not stray to different areas, but if this was a scientific phenomenon…

'Exactly. Someone is opening these rifts to London, probably from their London, or from ours to theirs. This is deliberate.' I stood in front of her board, taking in all the details. This was a very thorough investigation; this was the board of a detective, not a perpetrator. At some point, I had powered down my weapon without even realising.

'So, when are you carting me off to Newgate then? Or Bedlam?' She held her hands out dramatically for me to handcuff them. I stared at her and she frowned. It seemed a well-practised gesture for someone so young. 'Why aren't you handcuffing me?'

'There was an attack beside the river, caused all kinds of havoc with nearby boats. I had been passing, was there seconds after it began.' I put my weapon back in its holder. 'I didn't see the mirror you talk about, but.' I paused. I had never said this out loud for fear of being struck out of the service for an affliction of the mind. 'But I heard someone. There was no-one nearby it could have been but I heard a voice shout, "over water, shut it down". I convinced myself it came from a boat nearby but, there was no one left alive or in a conscious state that could have been in control of any machine or craft.' It had been a horrific day. The bottom of a taxi boat had disappeared in the rift, cut clean away and fifty souls had been lost.

'You believe me then?' She sounded incredulous.

'If you can predict these, why?' I gestured round at the shelves full of junk. A lump had caught in my throat. 'Why do you just collect all of this rubbish?'

Her expression became stoney. 'Data. I am collecting data. It took years to just be able to predict the events. I am nowhere near understanding yet. I am collecting data so that I can understand it, understand them, and then, perhaps I can stop it. But do not think I sit idly by, ignorant of the damage being caused and people being hurt. Perhaps you should ask your own people why they sit by in light of overwhelming evidence of another realm and do nothing.'

'You really believe you could stop it?' I watched her carefully.

'I don't know. But I'm going to try regardless.'

I couldn't help myself, but I smirked. 'You built of all this by yourself? How did you even afford it? And does anyone know you're in their basement?'

'Oh it's my basement. I own the building.'

I spluttered. 'What?'

She smirked, a raised eyebrow betraying her familiarity with catching people unawares and taking them by surprise. 'Perhaps we should have started with introductions. I'm Nixon, Hezekiah Nixon, although most people know of my work as Benjamin Nixon.' She stood and held out her hand. In all my years, I had never been struck dumb before.

'Benjamin Nixon is you?' Now she smiled, lowered her hand and tilted her head.

'At your service.'

No-one had ever seen Benjamin Nixon, but all knew of his reputation as one of the finest engineers in all the country. His inventions were in every home and he worked as an advisor to the local government for municipal projects. 'Why are you hiding? You're famous.'

'Benjamin is famous and well-respected. Despite having a female head of the state, and yes women hold more positions of power now than ever before, people still don't trust machines made by women. So Benjamin helps pay for Hezekiah's, projects.' She smirked. 'But please just call me Nixon.'

'Well, Ms Nixon.'

'No Ms.'

'Okay, Nixon. I am Stanley Fairweather, Agent of the Queen, which I suspect you knew already, and I believe I need to de-arrest you.'

'If you wouldn't mind,' she smiled.

'On one proviso.'

Her smile faltered. 'And what would that be?'

My eyes were still tracing along the shelves, caught by wondrous colours and shiny objects. 'This investigation of yours, seems rather aligned with mine and seeing as I no longer have a bomber to chase, feels like our resources are best pooled.' She remained unreadable as I continued. 'You need me to figure out if anyone in Government is at best aware or at worst responsible, and I need you to figure out how to stop it.'

She took a deep breath, thinking for longer than I feel she actually needed. 'Do I get to keep my artefacts?' I nodded. 'Then I believe we have ourselves a partnership. Now about that weapon of yours. The aim is off and I can improve the rate of power up, so hand it over.'

'What?' I spluttered.

'It's in my best interest to keep you alive.' She gestured impatiently. I retrieved my weapon and begrudgingly handed it over.

'The aim isn't off,' I muttered.

'It's either the gun or you, Stanley.'

I turned away and stared at the rows upon rows of objects from another Earth. 'I'm going to regret this partnership, aren't I?' Although, as I smiled, I didn't believe a word of it.

Alex Minns is based in the East of England and is a self-professed Jack of all trades (and still a master of none). Having asked for a typewriter when she was four, she ended up in a variety of careers including forensics, teaching, PR and wielding custard flamethrowers. Always writing into the wee hours of the night, she writes fantasy, scifi and steampunk stories (occasionally all these genres at the same time).

Welcome to *Hope*

by J. L. Royce

Jem watched from the A Deck gallery as the shuttle disgorged its passengers.

"It's the *Holi*, Festival Line, out of Delhi. High rollers," she said to her companion. A pair of *femmes* wandering the Craft Fair had distracted him, and she snapped, "Jeb! Pay attention!"

Jebediah (his shipboard name as a guest worker, not his given name) repeated, "High rollers," and reluctantly turned his attention to the arrivals.

Some raised their hands, turning slowly, recording their first view of the ship's vast interior. A few younger visitors were bouncing, laughing, in the halfgee. A tall, elegant figure, tastefully dressed and with a flawless coif, stepped before the gawking visitors and chimed for attention.

"Welcome to *Hope*!" The *homme* beamed their perfect smile, their resonant baritone easily reaching Jem and Jeb. "You are aboard the last of the fabled subluminal generation ships still in flight! Launched from Old Earth during the Despair, her passengers, their children—"

"Blah blah," muttered Jeb.

"—children's *children's* children are here to—"

"Why can't they employ a person as a greeter?"

"Who, you?" asked Jem. "And anyway, they are a person—just not a meat sack like you. And they've got the bandwidth to keep the guests' visit *filled with fun*, while you—" she rapped his close-shaved head "—do not."

The Host continued, "This Human Heritage Site has so much to offer—education, fun, and an exciting nightlife! Now, *sushri* and *sri*, *femmes* and *hommes*—and neomorphs—" with a nod to a pulsating mech jellyfish floating by "—join our tour as we step back in time to the launch of *Hope*. We'll follow her course through the dark days when she was almost lost, the survival of her brave crew, and her rediscovery a century ago. And don't worry, you'll have plenty of time to visit our Craft Fair and obtain those precious keepsakes of your visit."

Jem surveyed Jeb's attire, a tattered reproduction of the original crew uniform. "C Deck?"

"Yeah. The bad old days. Even have the malnutrition to go with it." He smiled to reveal his simulated bloody gums.

She grimaced. "You enjoy your role too much."

"This is just the start. I'm gonna be in the immersives someday. A star."

Jem consulted her wrist. "You're going to be late now." The crowd from a previous visiting supraluminal, the *Masquerade*, was due for their Deck C experience.

Jeb leaped up and bounded for the lifts. "Later?"

"After Q&A," she replied.

Jem returned her attention to the visitors craning their necks to peer around the vast interior of *Hope*. Far away, past the artificial lighting floating at the zero-gee center of the ship, was the patchwork quilt of farms and villages comprising Farside.

The Host coaxed their charges up the spiraling scenic walkway, the Stairway to Heaven, that would take them to the next level. Most cooperated, though a few had to be flushed from the vendors eagerly plying their shipboard products. *Homespun? Homegrown? Handcrafted toys?*

She scoffed at their sincere pitches. As a Council member, she'd seen the orders, the shipping manifests: most of the products were offloaded from supraluminals, made to order in far-flung orbital factories. Otherwise, *Hope* would have been stripped bare of resources long ago to fulfill the demand of the tourists for keepsakes.

The Host joined the party, satisfied they had captured all the strays. They chatted amiably with an exotic-looking *femme* sporting four ornamented breasts and a tendrilled mane. Thus occupied, the Host failed to notice a figure slip away from the tour and into the warren of service aisles behind the vendors. Jem, from her vantage point above (and not distracted by a superfluity of faux mammaries) *did* notice.

"Now what would you be about?" she murmured. Her current rotation was Management Trainee, not Security, but she applied a broad interpretation to her responsibilities.

Jem stood and gripped the gallery rail, plotting her path through the clutter of the Craft Fair. She extended one long leg and swung it over, then the other, and perched on the ledge with the rail behind her, arms extended. She dropped four meters to the A Deck, landing in a dramatic crouch. She snapped to her feet, hands above her head, and bowed to the startled passersby.

"Welcome to *Hope*! Halfgee, you see."

Jem sprinted through the shoppers and sightseers, wending her way along the course to follow the intriguing visitor.

The crew passages and access hatches were hidden in the augmented reality mix behind a variety of camouflage decorations, false walls, and signage. The area was familiar to Jem; mapping out the hidden world of *Hope* was a popular pastime of the vast ship's younger residents: utility shafts, access tunnels, and forgotten compartments perfect for youthful trysts. Faced with a cul-de-sac, she placed her hand on the far wall and released a panel.

Jem stepped through and faced her quarry. "Lost?"

The crouching woman whirled, and Jem knew immediately from her overreaction that she was human, and unused to lowgee; the synthetic *femmes* and *hommes* adapted to lowgee automatically.

"No—yes," she stammered. "I was looking for…the restroom."

Her dark eyes and straight black hair were unremarkable; but her practical tunic, tights, and lack of jewelry were simply *too* unpretentious, a sure sign she was not your typical interstellar tourist.

"Sure." Jem smiled. "Well, that hatch you're prying at leads to a waste slurry, so you're close—but I wouldn't recommend opening it. You'd best go back the way you came, then turn left and proceed to the shuttle foyer."

The woman straightened to nearly Jem's height and said, "I wasn't *prying* at anything." She smiled in a condescending, adult fashion. "You're a resident, aren't you? Fascinating, to grow up here."

"Shipborn," Jem corrected. "It's just a living."

"Thanks for the directions…"

"Jem."

"Like a precious stone, bright and polished."

Jem stepped closer. "No; like Jemimah—the eldest daughter of Job. Old Earth religion."

There was something *off* about the woman, but Jem couldn't query on the spot; she wasn't wearing her mix glasses, and by tradition, Shipborn didn't augment.

"Well, I'll be off then!" the visitor said and darted around her.

Jem considered pursuing the woman, but her wrist chimed a reminder of her Q&A. She took a long, careful look at the hatch, logged its location, and pinged Security, then glided off to her quarters. She had barely enough time to make herself presentable.

***

The Host had herded the guests into the twilight ambiance of the luxurious Star Lounge. The dance floor, seemingly transparent to deep space (but an illusion of the mix), was not part of the colony ship's pragmatic design, but the guests loved the experience of 'dancing among the stars'. At the moment, they were sipping, inhaling, or uploading refreshments and chatting in small clusters.

At Jem's arrival, the Host raised their voice. "Everyone! Among our gracious friends of the *Hope* in attendance this evening, we have a unique Shipborn—a *pureborn*—one of the few members of her present complement descended only from the original crew. With no further adieu…"

The Host turned and gave Jem a sweeping bow.

Jem sighed and straightened in her chair, grateful she had taken the time to put her unruly hair into an upsweep.

"Greetings; I am Jemima Bidarte Zeon Ovequiz Ahrends Fanney Rao O'Toole. Welcome to my birthplace and home. ISA registration number 0012, the *Hope*."

The scattered applause rose and fell, and Jem launched into a speech she had delivered so many times that it was difficult to resume when interrupted—as she was tonight.

"That was only seven surnames," a *homme* pointed out.

"True; I truncated it a bit. A grandfather and great-grandmother were cousins, both Rao. I suppose I could say *Rao Rao*, but that would sound like a sick dog." A few visitors understood the animal reference and chuckled.

"I could recite my ancestors back to the time of the Mishap, but you'd be late for dinner." More laughter.

"Why not back to Earth?" came another question.

"The *Hope*'s records were damaged in the Mishap," Jem replied.

"How does it feel to know that your great-great-great et cetera were cannibals?" The musical voice emerged from a gleaming ovoid, shimmering with iridescent hues.

There it is. Jem had repeatedly requested that Q&A be scheduled *before* the Deck C immersive adventure, but…

"My ancestors chose to survive. The unfortunate victims of the Mishap sustained their remaining friends and family members until food production could be restored."

"Of course," said the Host, with their best sympathetic smile. "Our biological friends often face these ethical dilemmas—eat or be eaten. It is, sadly, part of their nature."

Jem glared at the *homme* Host but said nothing.

Another voice. "Is it true you refuse augmentation, even life-sustaining technology?"

"The ship charter, dating from its launch, forbade the creation of cybernetic beings. It was rooted in their religious beliefs. There are alternatives available." Jem slipped her glasses from her vest pocket. "It's not really an enormous sacrifice…and we have purely biological methods to maintain our health."

"And just what was the Mishap?" came a voice Jem recognized.

The speaker sat towards the back of the lounge, seemingly unconcerned to be addressing the person who had recently reported her to ship Security.

Jem paused, staring at the woman as the Host shifted in a fair reproduction of unease. After a few moments, the Host caught the eye of another passenger, a middle-aged, fourth-degree Shipborn, who cleared her throat.

"We now believe it was a close encounter with a nano black hole. The gravitational field disrupted the ship's systems and threw *Hope* off course."

"A bit of luck," remarked the stranger.

"Well, actually, yes," continued the Shipborn. "The *Hope*'s original destination, as studied from Old Earth, appeared to be habitable. But supraluminal exploration vessels discovered that its sun's radiation bursts would have proved fatal to multicellular life forms."

The Host added, "Everyone aboard *Hope* would have died before the ship could be redirected out of the system. Even synthetics would have been affected, had there been any."

Jem craned her neck but could no longer see her suspect.

"And the legend of the Treasure?" It was the tentacle-haired, blue-skinned *femme* fatale. Her great violet eyes held Jem's.

"Fairy tales," said Jem, turning her attention to the rest of the audience. "We've had generations to search the *Hope* from the forward observation dome to the aft thrusters. After the Mishap, the entire vessel was explored and cataloged, to replace lost records."

"Are you involved?" It was snake-hair again.

"Involved in what?"

The *femme* smiled. "Don't be coy. Contracted, engaged, infatuated…as a pureborn ship inheritor, you are one of the richest individuals in known space. Quite the catch…"

"Rich?" said a youngish human male, a bit too eagerly.

The Host intervened. "Theoretically rich. *Hope* represents a substantial stream of entertainment revenue, but while the ship operates, profits are held as communal property of the Shipborn."

Jem returned the *femme's* smile. "I'm always open to offers."

The Host reacted to the stirring in the crowd. "Perfect time for a history lesson! The passengers and crew who boarded *Hope* entered into a tontine placing all of their property, including the ship, in common ownership for the mutual benefit of their descendants. The assets were to be distributed at the destination, to fund the settlement—and not before. When supraluminals found the *Hope*, some passengers left, and new ones arrived, begetting children that were half-Shipborn, quarter-Shipborn, and so forth, with corresponding shares."

"*How* rich?" asked the young man.

"It doesn't matter," Jem replied. "We won't be disembarking to colonize a world, and as a Human Heritage site, the status of *Hope* is frozen."

The Host intervened in a compelling voice. "Enjoy the buffet and open bar, everyone! Dancing will continue until midnight ship time. You are free to explore the common areas for shopping, dining, and entertainment—including our safe and secure pleasure gardens." They waved their slender wrist. "I have delivered your housing assignments; if you have any questions or problems, I am merely a tap away." He waved, "*Bonne soirée!*"

Jem fled before any offers of *involvement* could be tendered.

***

"Come on," said Jem. "I don't want to be late."

"I thought we were going out," Jeb complained. "Like, maybe, dancing at the Star Lounge. Or you could come back to Farside with me, take a stroll on the Stairway to Heaven…"

The vast hollow drum that was *Hope* rotated about its axis, generating over half-gee at its inner surface. The dozen ramps spiraling over the forward bulkhead of the ship's interior met at several levels of concentric galleries. The highest reaches of the Stairway, at lowgee, offered vistas unmatched—and unmatched privacy for lovers.

"We *are* going out," said Jem, leading him behind the darkened booths of the Craft Fair to the service corridor.

"To a sewer?"

"You wanted to spend time together," she replied. "Welcome to my world."

She led him past the façade seen by all synthetics and augmented humans, projected to discourage just what Jem was doing: penetrating the ship's secrets.

"You see, it's not *really* a sewer. The specifications reconstructed after the Mishap just make it look that way."

Jeb almost collided with Jem as she stopped at the physical hatchway.

"She was poking about here…"

Jeb asked, "How do *you* know it isn't a sewer?"

"Because I've been here, when I was just a shiprat, sneaking into every passageway I could find. And this hatch wasn't here."

Jeb held up his wrist to bathe the area with light. "You're right, these welds are recent."

"What I like about you," Jem said. "You always see things my way—eventually."

"So, how do we get in?"

"Think: if whoever made this didn't need to get back in here, they would have just welded a plate across the bulkhead." She waved at the hatch. "Why come back?"

"So…somebody is visiting here?"

Jem grinned and tapped her wrist, scrolled through messages, and opened one from Ship Security.

"Wait—what? You can spy on people?"

"Being on the Council ExecComm comes with certain privileges." She tapped again and a projection of the hatchway appeared. Jem stepped back to align it with the physical bulkhead.

In the ghostly recording, a wavering figure approached, passed through them, and stood before the hatch. Once still, the figure vanished into the background, reappearing with any movement.

"What's that—camo clothing?" Jeb said. "Illegal…"

"But only if you get caught. Which is pretty unlikely, if you're wearing it."

"Huh. Is this the tourist you were tracking?"

"Well, she wasn't disguised when I saw her."

Jeb stared. "Human-shaped. The camo can't change that, so we know it's not a neomorph, anyway."

"But they may have hired human help or diverted a synth."

After several minutes, Jeb asked, "What's it waiting for?"

"Not waiting—listening. Like you should. I'll speed up the playback and raise the volume." She manipulated the projection at her wrist, scrolling, then returned to normal speed.

A quiet peep caused the projected figure to straighten, alert. Then it spoke—or rather, produced a series of tones, whistling. The hatch clicked and moved a few centimeters. The figure pulled it wide, climbed inside, and closed it behind them.

Jem rewound the playback to the beep.

Jeb said, "So we have to wait for the beep and whistle that tune."

"Bright boy."

"How long will we have to wait?"

"We have an advantage over our snoopy visitor—this." She pointed to the timestamp on the recording. "If it opens at the same time every day, then we don't have long to wait."

"If," Jeb said, though he smiled. "So, if it's not a sewer, what is it?"

"I checked the construction archives—talk about strange data formats!—looking for construction similar to this passage: dimensions, direction, intersections."

"Well? Come on, Jem!"

She smiled. "Auxiliary ventilation. In other parts of *Hope*, these passages serve as a redundant air supply to key ship compartments, like astronav or enviro controls."

"Important stuff."

"Yes. And *this* one seems to go nowhere."

"Nowhere." Jeb pondered this. "Meaning…"

"Either someplace so unimportant that it was forgotten, or someplace so important that it was hidden."

The wall peeped.

Jem cursed and fumbled at her wrist, raising the audio volume and resuming the playback. The tonal pattern emerged, and the hatch before them opened in synchrony with the projected image.

"Stars! It worked!" Jeb shouted.

"Stifle yourself!" Jem hissed. "We don't need attention."

She pulled the hatch open and pointed her flash around the interior, cautiously bent to peek around. She faced a wall less than a meter away: they were entering the passage from its side.

"Doesn't smell like a sewer, thank the stars," Jeb said. "Going in? Or are you just going to stand there with your ass sticking out?"

Jem climbed into the cramped passageway and turned around. "At least I can fit in here," she said. "Coming?"

"Yeah—ow!" Jeb rubbed his head as he joined her, knees and back bent. He looked around at the hatch, held open with a foot. "Can we prop this open?"

"Whoever went in here didn't come out this way on my surveillance."

"What if they didn't come out because…" He left the grim question hanging. "I don't suppose you know how to open it from *inside*?"

"No surveillance." Jem pondered this. "It's a maglock." She took a comb from her pouch, and reaching around Jeb, placed it on the frame. He let the door swing shut. The magnet was strong enough to hold the hatch in place though it could still be pushed open.

"Satisfied? My best comb."

Jeb shone his flash up and down the passage. "Which way?"

"Environmental systems are all aft. So most likely the airflow was intended for a compartment forward." She started off toward the prow of *Hope*. "Come on—we're about a klick from the forward command center—it can't be far."

With that, she took off in a hunched, bent-kneed waddle that set Jeb chortling. But he followed.

After a few minutes of silent travel, he asked, "What made them climb aboard, d'you suppose—the original crew? Would you choose to live out the rest of your life—"

"Well, we do."

"It's not the same. They knew dirtside life. When *Hope* launched, it was isolated—no supraluminals arriving every few days. And they almost died—thousands of them."

"Not *almost*; hundreds did die." Jem pondered it a while.

"And we can leave, whenever we want," Jeb added.

Some of us, not so easily, Jem thought. "They believed their descendants would have a better life on the new planet."

Jeb snorted. "Not how things worked out."

Jem turned her beam onto his face a moment. "What's gotten into you? You chose to join the *Hope*. You can leave whenever you want. I'm stuck here."

"You've no idea what it was like, being poor on a world. Overcrowded, barely fed."

Jem didn't want to argue. "I'll remember that the next time you complain about my cooking."

"The colonies are dangerous. You're one of the richest people alive. I *dare* you to leave."

The passage spiraled into the hemispherical nose of *Hope*. As it did, the gravity weakened, until they were gliding along, hands and feet rarely touching the walls. They slowed when the beams of their lamps were swallowed by the gloom ahead. They found themselves floating at the threshold of a broad, shallow chamber, a hundred meters wide, centered on the ship's axis. Dim lighting glowed from scattered panels.

"You knew about this?" Jeb asked.

"Of course not. But it had to lead somewhere. I have no idea what *this* is—" she consulted her wrist "—but the space is inside the forward radiation barrier, which is just a matrix of water tanks."

The curving, parallel walls were covered with a grid work of seams, in varying patterns. Jeb floated along and examined the nearest bank. "I think they're storage compartments."

"Well, let's find out what they're storing," said Jem. She waved her wrist at the nearest compartment and waited, but nothing happened.

"Too old to connect?" Jeb reached out and scrubbed at the encrustation of dust. His efforts revealed a string of digits etched into the metal.

"Could mean anything." Jem passed her wrist over the number, scanning it. The search results were partial matches, voluminous and uninformative.

"We could just pry it open," she said.

Jeb was shining his lamp around the walls. The beam steadied, and she followed it to a break in the pattern, far down the opposite wall.

"Let's look in that one," said Jeb. "It's already open."

They glided across the dim chamber to find the compartment door ajar. Jem pulled it open, but the find was puzzling: an irregular mass about a meter long and half as wide.

"Looks like it didn't quite fit, and the maglock didn't engage." Jem turned the package slowly on its axis, studying the wrapping. "But this can't be as old as the dust on everything suggests. What is this, stuff, anyway?"

Jeb turned from peering inside the compartment. "Edible food wrapping. We use it in Farside for agro packaging."

"So this compartment was opened, emptied, and this…whatever stuffed in. And this came out of a wrapping machine?" Jem asked.

"Not a machine—it's hand-wrapped." His fingers traced the bundle. "And this is an expert job—see how tight?"

"Where's this wrapping available?"

"Only in Farside. You've never worked agro?"

She shook her head.

Jeb chuckled. "Groomed for leadership. So, what are you—" He gasped and lost his balance, spinning away from the compartment.

"Hey!" Jem reached out to steady him. He grabbed the compartment door and pointed. Only then did she look down at the bundle.

"Stars!" She pondered the rictal grin of a face, outlined through the tight cover.

"This wrapping comes from Farside—which means there's another entrance—from Farside."

"We have to get out of here!" said Jeb.

"Maybe." Jem shone her lamp into the compartment, craning to see the depths. She reached in and pulled out a cloth, shaking it out. The surface rippled with faces and bodies, appearing and vanishing.

"The camo cloak," said Jem.

"Guess we know what happened to your intruder," said Jeb. "There's a killer on the loose—and he's one of your lot."

"*My lot?* What do you mean by that?" Jem demanded.

"Unaugmented humans." He touched his temple. "Anyone augmented at birth, like me—like almost all starborn humans—is *incapable* of murder. We have no choice. The *polity* rules. And the only Shipborn with a real stake—"

Jem cut him off. "If it were intentional murder, yes—but this might have been an accident."

"Accidentally dehydrated and shoved into a hidden storage bin?" He snickered. "Too long under your sunlamp?" He took a breath. "If it was an accident, why cover it up?" He set the package slowly spinning again.

Jem touched the body, reluctance obvious on her face, and shoved it back into the compartment. After staring a moment, she slammed the door.

"What are you doing?" Jeb waved the cloak. "And you forgot this."

"I'm not sure what I'm doing, and I didn't *forget* that." Jem grabbed it from him.

"We have to tell Security," Jeb said.

"Leave that to me." Jem took off toward the ventilation passage. Jeb reluctantly followed.

***

The Council of the Shipborn represented at least fifty-one percent of *Hope*'s ownership, ranked by percentage of Shipborn ancestry. Thirteen of its members, the pureborn, formed the Executive Committee: the most powerful powerless entity on *Hope* (and, arguably, in human space).

Jem faced the ExecComm, gathered in a modestly appointed chamber distinguished by its impenetrable privacy and implacable security.

"A body." Herodias, the eldest pureborn, was the de facto chairperson and not known for her patience. A petite woman, she held Jem with the gaze of a raptor.

Another spoke: Oram. "Which has been retrieved—discretely—and is currently under investigation." He was a steady, reliable sort, and in Jem's opinion, rather boring.

"The victim was wearing this, on surveillance." Jem shook out the camo cloak with a dramatic snap. The youngest (and non-voting) ExecComm member, a twelve-year-old, whistled, earning him a stern look from Herodias.

"You believe this was not an accidental death?" she asked.

"We are trying to establish the cause of death," said Oram, de facto head of Council Security, "but the dehydration process…"

"Well, if it were an accident, why hide it?"

"Obviously," said Herodias. "Short of hacking, the augmented are incapable of such a crime; and the alternative—," he glanced around "—is unthinkable."

The room went silent. Jem said, "You mean, one of us: the unaugmented pureborn."

Another Councilor, Amon, spoke. "Have you heard from your parents lately, dear?" A flicker of cruel satisfaction crossed his round face.

Amon had approached Jem's parents years earlier to propose an arranged marriage with one of his pureborn children. Jem glanced around the table at them: Tacita, a willowy and vague cipher toying with her mix glasses, and Fulvius, intent on finding a shiny surface in which to admire himself. Her parents had, thankfully, turned the Councilor down.

When Jem reached her majority, her mother and father had emigrated, their shares in *Hope* devolving to their only child. They'd left Jem behind to make her own decisions; in reality, they'd left her only resentment.

"No," said Jem.

"The stench of this crime clings to the one who revealed it," said Amon.

"Well?" Herodias's gray eyes peered over her mix glasses at Jem, awaiting a reply.

"Excuse me," said Jem, "I didn't think such a banal proverb required a response."

Before Amon could react, she continued, "Though to be thorough, we should consider the possibility of a synthetic or neomorph as the culprit."

Amon snorted. "Even more implausible." He looked around the table. "This matter comes at an inopportune time, when *Hope* is seeking a new role in the interstellar community. Our status as a Human Heritage site provides us extraordinary protection in these uncertain times—and an opportunity. We could become the Switzerland of the new galactic order."

"The what?" Jem asked.

Amon sighed. "Your education is sadly deficient. Look it up: Old Earth, before the Despair." His voice dropped and he leaned across the table towards her. "A neutral repository for the—"

"Amon," Herodias interrupted, "let's return to the matter at hand. Tell the Host we'll want to interview some of our current guests. I'll provide a list after reviewing the passenger manifests."

He raised his hands to protest. "We'll have to request the information."

"I've already received the dossiers from ISA." She waved her hand and the assembled stared into the center of the conference room. Jem and a few more present slipped on their mix glasses, revealing a cloud of faces and forms slowly revolving over the table: human, synth, and neomorphs. "My scheduler will route files to ExecComm members."

Herodias stood. "We'll adjourn; we have our tasks. Needless to say, discretion is of paramount importance."

The members rose, drifting out of the room, chatting in small groups.

Jem rose, waving her wrist to check for messages, and turned to find her exit blocked.

"*Sushri?*"

"Jem—with me, please." Herodias waited as the rest departed. Amon strolled out, his backward glance a mixture of suspicion and jealousy. At last they were alone, and the older woman spoke.

"You've embroiled yourself in a most delicate matter. One wonders, how?"

Jem feigned puzzlement. "I don't understand."

"You would not have stumbled upon the corpse had you not found the vault, and the passage to the vault is hardly obvious."

Jem swallowed. "I noticed a visitor slip away and confronted her trying to access the passage."

"And took it upon yourself to investigate? To access Security files?" Herodias frowned. "Do you mean to imply this corpse is a visitor?"

"No—I checked. Everyone from her group is accounted for."

Herodias sighed in relief. "Possibly a shipboard accomplice, then. Good. A fatality is terrible, but losing a tourist…"

"Bad for business?"

Herodias lashed out. "Yes, 'bad for business' indeed! A business of which you own a substantial share!" She gripped Jem's arm with surprising strength. "You'll need to grow up someday…soon."

Jem stared. "What Amon was saying, about a repository. Is it this vault?"

Herodias sneered. "No; he would have us become a repository for interstellar wealth, no questions asked, possibly of questionable provenance."

"What sort of wealth?"

"There are many forms of wealth. Data, for example."

"This vault looked like a storehouse, not a database."

"You'll tell no one about the vault—particularly not Amon." Herodias released Jem and straightened. "Now; about this corpse…"

"Before Security took the body, I obtained biotraces and sent them for analysis. ExecComm privilege."

Herodias looked ready to criticize Jem's initiative, but she merely nodded. "Good. You're certain the tourist you tracked was human?"

She raised her hand. "That's what my scan said. But if we're dealing with some galactic criminal—"

"Merely conjecture!"

"—she may have taken countermeasures beyond a camo cloak."

"Unregulated augmentation; dynamic genomic signature hopping…" Herodias grunted. "Whatever you learn about our curious tourist, report to me. We don't want the public scrutiny of a detention."

"Yes, *Sushri*. And if I may ask…the body I found. If this vault is the Council's—the ExecComm's—secret, was the deceased…"

"Are you sure you want to know?" Herodias's smile was predatory. "You have my assurance: whatever happened, the Council ExecComm was not officially involved. I was as surprised as you."

"I doubt that," Jem said.

"Well, perhaps not *quite* as surprised." Her hand rested on Jem's, gently. "Take care, Jemima. And your friend, Jeb? As a guest worker, he is not so privileged as you, nor protected. That makes him a ready target."

"I understand," Jem said, though she really didn't.

***

Jem was looking forward to an evening of dancing with Jeb when the single, sad, dying bleep of her comm heralded the start of something quite different. She had paused in her climb of an ascending ramp in the Stairway to Heaven, tapping at the blank screen, when a voice from behind caused her to wheel around.

"It's a suppression field."

The tourist/snoop/suspect displayed the small fob in her hand before secreting it in a pocket of her brief tunic. "I thought we should talk privately."

"Stars!" Jem backed away, the image of the mummified corpse spinning through her mind as her stomach clenched.

"I mean you no harm. My name is Amaya."

"What do you want?"

"To talk. You're in danger—you're all in danger, from what I've learned, but you especially. And I need your help."

Jem blinked and shook her head. "What are you talking about? I'm only in *danger* of being pestered by a silly tourist."

"I'm not a tourist," said Amaya. "I came here to investigate a shipment delivered to *Hope*. Unfortunately, my local contact…"

"Did you kill them?" Jem blurted. "The body in the storage locker? I found you at the access hatch they used."

The stranger looked away. "I am responsible," she said. "I sent him to his death. The forces at work here are more dangerous than I had estimated."

"Who are you working for?"

"ISA, Special Services. And you have to come with me."

"Where?"

"The storage area where you found the body." Amaya led Jem up the ramp to the next ring, at about the quartergee level. "The shipment I tracked contained weapons and explosives, diverted from a conflict zone hundreds of parsecs from here."

Jem grabbed Amaya's arm. "Some sort of terrorist group? A political movement? Or a ransom scheme?" She recalled Amon's dream of a neutral Switzerland, whatever that was.

"My contact traced the cargo to Farside, where he worked."

"Your contact was crew?"

"A guest worker; and his killer must be crew as well. I accounted for the whereabouts of all the visitors on board. They weren't counting on you blundering about in the dark."

"Well, I wouldn't have gone searching if *you* hadn't been careless. You must be cooperating with ship Security—"

"No," Amaya said.

Jem blocked her path. "But we have to tell the ExecComm—it's a question of ship safety!"

"I had to wait until I knew who to trust."

"And who is that?"

"You."

Jem realized she had been looming over the ISA agent and stepped back. "I suppose I should be thankful you do."

"I knew you were either innocent or a very incompetent terrorist. I wasn't sure, given the company you keep."

"What do you mean by that?"

"You friend Jeb—recent arrival, works in Farside, and fits a profile for dissatisfaction."

Before Jem could demand an explanation, Amaya halted, running her hand over the mural of Old Earth landscapes on the back wall. "Put your comm here," she said, and disengaged the suppressor in her hand.

Jem's comm twittered back to life.

"You can run away, or help me stop this disaster. It's up to you."

Jem frowned and pressed her wrist against the wall. A rectangular outline glowed, and Amaya played another musical key sequence. A hatch clicked open, and the agent pulled it wide, beckoning Jem.

"Get in."

"Why?"

"It's another passage to the vault. We need to find out what's worth killing for if we're going to identify the murderer."

Jem bent over and crawled in, again finding herself in a low, narrow passage. Amaya followed.

Proceeding along, she felt her weight decreasing, and soon was gliding easily. Jem pulled up short as the way opened into the vastness of the storage chamber. She saw Amaya doubled over behind her.

"Just queasy," the ISA agent said. "I'm not used to zerogee."

"Well, this isn't a supraluminal. You have some way to get into the compartments?"

"I have the keycodes; but the hatches are genetically secured to open only to *Hope*'s original crew."

"You mean, pureborn?"

Amaya, pale, took a deep breath, gulped, and nodded. "Unclear—at least, a high percentage."

They glided along the wall, Amaya monitoring her wrist comm.

"So, this is the ExecComm's secret, its treasure," Jem murmured.

"Can you explain?"

"Amon—a pureborn—talked about Switzerland."

"What's that?" Amaya asked.

"Treasure, I think. What are we doing?"

"I only have a few codes, retrieved from some of the corrupted data banks ISA secured years ago, after the first encounter with *Hope*."

"Stole them, you mean."

"It was intelligence gathering. The Authority needed to verify *Hope*'s history of the Mishap. There were various theories, including an encounter with non-human life forms, whether or not intelligent, that could represent a threat to human space."

Just ahead, a rectangle of light appeared, pulsing in the gloom. "There!" Amaya exclaimed, and flung herself over to the hatch. She grabbed a handhold in the nick of time and clumsily halted in front of it.

"Put your hand on the cover!" Amaya ordered.

Jem hesitated, uncertain of the danger to herself but convinced there was a danger to others. She spread her fingers, half-expecting a shock, but nothing happened except a smear over the dusty surface.

Amaya wiped the surface clean with her sleeve, exposing the identification code. "Again."

This time, the pulsing stopped, and the door moved beneath her fingers. Jem jerked her hand away, and Amaya eagerly reached into the compartment.

Jem feared another macabre find, but the contents were a tray neatly filled with silvery envelopes, each bearing a faded label. "What does it mean?" she murmured.

"Let's find out." Amaya passed her wrist over the rows of numbers, then frowned at the small screen.

"What?" Jem demanded.

"It's an ancient taxonomy scheme, from Old Earth, and it signifies a plant. *Strychnopsis thouarsii*. Seeds, I would guess." She tossed aside the envelope and chose another to scan.

"*Camptotheca acuminata*." Amaya picked and scanned, picked and scanned, her excitement growing.

"So?"

Amaya's dark eyes gleamed. "They're all plants, different varieties. And something else—many are rare, and some are presumed extinct since the great die-off during the Despair on Old Earth."

"There are a couple of hundred samples here," said Jem, "and they look unique."

They closed the compartment and straightened, staring around them in the quiet chill.

"And thousands of compartments," Amaya said.

"How many, do you suppose…"

"Millions of species. And if even a fraction of the specimens are viable, it's…"

"A treasure. We must present this to the Council."

Amaya shook her head. "Not until I've investigated that death."

"You're on *Hope* and should respect our jurisdictional authority!"

"My ISA mandate supersedes it."

A movement caught Jem's eye. "What's that in your hand?"

Amaya hesitated, then displayed the envelope crushed in her fist. "I have to report this to my superiors." She slipped it into her tunic and propelled herself back to the access passage.

Jem called after her, "The Council—"

Their conversation ended as the walls shuddered, accompanied by a dull boom reverberating through the chamber. The low lights flickered and vanished, plunging the pair into darkness.

***

After a few moments, they waved their wrists into light and found each other.

"Are you alright?" Amaya asked.

Jem's ears popped, and she swallowed. Before she could answer, a klaxon sounded, booming through the access passages into the chamber. A breeze picked up, moving towards the passage entrance.

"Decompression warning," said Jem, "Go, feet first!"

Every child was drilled in emergency procedures, but Jem was still incredulous. She shoved Amaya into the narrow conduit.

"I don't understand," she said as they propelled themselves with a growing sense of *down* towards the Stairway to Heaven. "We have state-of-the-art collision defenses installed by ISA."

They slowed and climbed out onto the walkway. The wind was only modest even here, but the walkway lurched and flung them towards the rail, where they caught themselves and clung.

Jem said, "Anything large enough to damage *Hope*—"

"Not a collision. It's happened." Amaya pointed across the interior of the ship to Farside. "Sabotage."

A black gash had appeared in the green carpet of cultivation. Amaya made a circle of her thumb and forefinger, the gesture for magnification, and peered through it at Farside. "Venting—and destabilizing the rotation!"

In the emptiness people floated, flung from the ramps and walkway, inexorably drawn towards Farside. Some had been knocked senseless, others screamed for help, their cries fading as they shrank to pinpoints and disappeared through the wound in the hull.

"Jem! Jem!"

She craned her head to peer down along the forward bulkhead and saw Jeb climbing a perilously unstable ramp. Wearing a harness with a lightweight safety line, which he was clipping at intervals to the railings, he carried an assortment of rescue gear. She could see other teams working their way toward people trapped around the kilometers of walkways. In minutes, he had reached her, and they embraced.

"Some date!" he shouted, handing the two women harnesses.

"It was never a date!" Jem replied and clipped on to his line.

"We're shuttling everyone out to the docked supraluminals."

"How many left?"

"The tourists are all away, most of the port crew, but Farside…" Jeb glanced at the distant farming commune; Jem knew the situation was dire.

"Hi! I don't think we've met." He hooked up Amaya, but another lurch of the ramp flung the ISA agent into the air and over the railing. She swung in a short arc, pivoting at Jeb's clip on the railing, and slammed into the wall below, oscillating back and forth, limp.

Together, Jem and Jeb hauled her back up to their position and examined her.

"She's breathing—knocked out," said Jeb.

Jem's hand came away damp from the woman's hair. "There's blood here."

They unclipped and went down to the next lower walkway, where they met another rescue team who evacuated Amaya.

"Who was she, anyway?" Jeb asked.

"No time. Not a fan of yours, so don't get any ideas."

They proceeded along, clipping in and taking down stranded pedestrians. They could see a line of heavy equipment, farming, and construction vehicles, creeping ant-like towards the wound in *Hope*.

Jeb aimed his wrist at the scene and displayed the magnified image. "They're bringing prefab bulkhead plates from some renovation project."

"There's no contingency plan for repairing a breach this large," Jem said. "Couldn't we send evacuation shuttles to the freight docks at Farside?"

"I heard the pilots talking—Farside isn't equipped for passenger loading. They don't have skywalks, and hard-docking is risky, with the *Hope* so unstable." He shook his head. "I don't get how the defenses—"

"It was an explosion, not a collision," Jem said.

Jeb stared. "Exploding what? Summer squash? That's farmland—no ship systems, no fuel stores..." Jeb fell silent as realization dawned. "An attack?"

At a hail from below, Jem leaned over the railing of their ramp and saw a masked Herodias with a pair of Security synths.

"Why are you still here?" the Councilor shouted. She motioned them down.

They sped towards each other, and the synths distributed oxygen concentrators.

"We're evacuating the Council," said Herodias, voice muffled by the mask, "and that includes you."

"It was an explosion!" Jeb blurted. "Are we under attack?"

"You're needed at Farside," she told him. "Go with these synths—I'll see to Jem."

He made to leave, but Jem grabbed him and kissed him. "Thanks for coming after me," she said.

The young man blinked and said, "Well, Stars…"

"Now go!" ordered Herodias. When the trio had departed, she turned to Jem.

"You were in the vault—no one is left there, I assume?"

"No—why?"

The ExecComm chairperson raised her wrist to touch her comm. All over the great disc of the forward bulkhead, the outlines of hatches appeared among the murals of explorers and farmers. They blinked red, then vanished.

"I've sealed the vault. It has a self-contained environmental system. That will protect the contents when we abandon *Hope*. It will be secure until we can organize a salvage operation."

"Abandon?"

Herodias gestured at the distant action in Farside. "They'll never repair the hull breach before *Hope* destabilizes. We need to hurry—a shuttle is waiting for us." She proceeded down the ramp towards the tourist port, Jem following, stunned.

"You're going to be a very rich young woman, Jem," she said over her shoulder.

Jem roused herself. "What do you mean?"

"The tontine dissolves when we reach our destination—or if *Hope* is abandoned. As one of the dozen pureborn—"

"Thirteen. There are thirteen."

Herodias's thin lips twitched. "Unfortunately, Amon was in Farside, investigating that suspicious death on his own, when the…incident occurred. He won't be bothering you anymore."

Jem felt a sickening suspicion come over her. She grabbed Herodias and spun her around.

"You? You engineered this?"

"Don't tell me you haven't *dreamed* of escaping this prison!" Herodias snapped. "Am I expected to live out my life serving an *amusement park*, dying childless, forfeiting my share? Well, I just made our dreams come true!"

"I may have wished I could leave, but it's my home! And Jeb? All the rest?"

Herodias scoffed. "You're an intelligent young woman. You can do far better than a guest worker, a probationary immigrant."

"I don't need anyone to tell me how to live my life—you, Amon, any of you! Jeb is interested in me, not my share of what's in that vault."

"And to think I dreamed of the life we could lead—"

"We?"

"Why not? We could have a child together—a daughter. With the biological wealth in that vault, our heirs could own planets!"

The chairperson freed herself and raced down the ramp, Jem bounding along to keep up. They reached one of the broad intersections of ramps and walkways where Jem halted.

"Contact your staff—tell them to bring Jeb back for evacuation. I won't leave without him."

"You little fool!" Herodias snarled, gripping her shoulder.

The chairperson shook her head. "Very well—we'll evacuate your young friend. If you insist, we'll marry him—a junior partner."

Herodias raised her arm. "If you won't see reason now, then perhaps later." Her hand gripped a silver rod.

Jem grabbed it instinctively and twisted. The paralyzer's charge shot harmlessly into space, and as they struggled for control of the weapon, another tremor in the ship's walkway flung them at the railing.

Herodias, unbalanced, tumbled into the void. She screamed, flailed the air, and drifted out of reach of Jem's outstretched hand.

Gripping the handrail in vertiginous nausea, Jem could only watch as the woman cartwheeled through the center of *Hope*, gaining speed, on course towards Farside. Jem turned away before the shrinking dot disappeared through the hull breach.

She swallowed and raised her wrist. "*Call* Jeb."

"*Jem!*" he answered. "*Is your shuttle—*"

"No! Where are you?"

"*No shuttle? You're supposed to evacuate!*"

"I'm not leaving my home, or you," Jem said. "Tell me where you are."

"*At Farside,*" he replied. "*I've suited up. We have welding units and some plating, but I don't see a way to span a hole that large.*"

"Well, I do. Send me your location."

The coordinates appeared. "Got it," Jem said.

"*You've got to head for—*"

Jem cut the comm and said, "*Call* Council Emergency Services."

"*Identify!*" the harried voice said.

"Jemima Bidarte Zeon—"

The tone immediately changed. "*Sushri, do you need an escort to your shuttle?*"

"No." She tried to catch her breath and realized the concentrator had reached its limit. "I'm proceeding to Farside, to direct a repair operation."

"*Repair? We were given an evacuation order—*"

"By Councilor Herodias. Link in the head of Council Security, and the pilot of the docked shuttle."

After a pause, someone spoke. "*Councilor?*" said Oram. Then another voice came on the line. "*Shuttle here.*"

"We can't abandon *Hope*. Herodias is dead—so is Amon. I have a plan.

"Captain, remove all passengers and non-essential crew from your craft and proceed to the hull breach at Farside. Maneuver your craft into the breach and hold it with steering thrusters until the repair crew can weld it into place."

There was silence. Then the pilot said, *"But Councilor Herodias—"*

"Herodias and Amon are dead! Oram, will you see that this order is carried out?"

"Yes," the Security chief replied, *"we must do something!"*

"Pilot?"

"This has never been attempted—"

"Hundreds of lives are at stake!" Jem exclaimed.

"—but we'll do our best."

"I'm heading to Farside," she said. "Contact me when the shuttle is on its way."

"Yes, Sushri," the operator replied, and Jem cut the call.

She flung herself along the walkways towards Farside, called Jeb as she raced along, and explained her plan.

"It's crazy…but it just might work," he said.

"I knew you'd see it my way," Jem replied. "Have a suit ready for me. We're going to save the world."

J. L. Royce (HWA) is an author of science fiction and the macabre. His SF has appeared in Alien Dimensions, Allegory, Fifth Di, Fireside, etc. Look for more macabre tales in Cosmic Horror Monthly, Love Letters to Poe (Visiter Award winner), Lovecraftiana, Mysterion, parABnormal, Strange Aeon, Wyldblood, etc. Follow on X (@authorJLRoyce), Facebook (@AuthorJLRoyce), Instagram (authorJLRoyce), Discord (jlroyce), and Bluesky (jlroyce.bsky.social). www.jlroyce.com.

The Rjelhdan Prince

by Taylor Funk

"Dahnri? What are you doing here?" my sister, Giancik questions me in a hushed tone. Urgency distracts her so much, she almost misses the small form cradled in my arms. Almost. "Is that…" she starts to ask, but she can't seem to find the rest of the words that make up that question. Luckily, they're not too hard to guess.

"Yes. Gia, meet your niece, Kiyamara" I tell her, and her eyes soften as she looks down at Ki. Her skin carries the gentle purple tone of her mother's people, though it gleams like my people's. It's a beautiful combination that was never meant to exist.

"Dahn you need to get her out of here," Gia speaks up, the urgency back and somehow more intense than before.

"We have nowhere else to go," I say.

"Why did you leave Bhlidor?" she poses, desperately trying to find some way to make this work for me. Just like she always has. The thing is, it won't work this time.

"We were forced out," I report, forcing a monotonous tone to try to hide all of the emotion that comes with that phrase.

"You single-handedly saved the Bhlidorans from our father's plans for them; why in the world would they force you out?" she asks. Before I have the chance to answer her, thunderous footsteps start to echo throughout the halls. There's only one person on this planet who walks with that much authority. "Dahn, you have to go," she lets out, pushing me back the way I came.

"Gia, who are you talking to?" our father, King Oejolv, questions as he enters the room. Even if I was going to listen to Gia, time just ran out. My father's eyes lock on mine, then his gaze shifts to Ki. Somehow I had convinced myself that he'd be happy to find out he has a grandkid, but the fury now filling his eyes is most definitely not indicative of glee. "How dare you come back here with that *thing* as if it's not a sign of how you betrayed us!" he booms.

"My daughter is not a thing," I respond, Rjelhdan ferocity bubbling up inside me for the first time in a few years.

"Dahn, go," Gia declares, facing me, then she turns back toward our father. "Father, please just let him go. He'll never come back here again," she pleads.

"He shouldn't have come back here in the first place," our father remarks, his hand moving toward the sword at his side. I used to be in awe of his brutish behavior. I wanted to be just like him. Seeing it pointed toward me now, I couldn't be more glad that I abandoned that notion. Gia's right; I need to leave. I don't belong here anymore.

I back away from the man who raised me and retreat into the ship I came here in. In my father's eyes, I find disappointment. What kind of Rjelhdan retreats? Despite my surrender, his hand hasn't stopped its journey for his sword. He doesn't intend to let me leave.

"Father stop! That's your son!" Gia lets out, trying to get in his way.

"I have no son," he proclaims, shoving her out of the way to pursue me. As soon as my feet reach the ship, I call the door down. My breathing picks up as I wonder if it'll close before he reaches me. I shouldn't have come back here. I should've known that my father's pride means more to him than I ever have. I should've... The door closes just as my father reaches the ship. He pounds on it, but even he's not strong enough to break through it.

I look through the window at his rage-filled expression, then my eyes shift to Ki, who's somehow still asleep in my arms. I may know nothing about parenting, especially parenting alone, but I will do better by her. Every morning when she wakes up and every night when she falls asleep, she's going to know that I love her.

***

My stomach growls, but I know there's nothing I can do in response. There's not enough food for us to have more than one meal a day. It's moments like these where it's hard to remember that I was once royalty. If I had played my cards right, I'd probably be taking over as King soon. Clearly, I didn't do that. In fact, I think it's fair to say that I took my cards and threw them right in my father's face. Sorry, *the King's* face; he doesn't have a son anymore.

What was it that I did to cause this reaction? I'd say I finally learned some morals, but this all started before then. As the Prince, I was the general of our army. My people have always been aggressive, and King Oejolv most certainly wasn't an exception to that. He was constantly declaring war on this planet and that planet, all in the name of expanding his galactic empire.

One day he declared war on Bhlidor. I had known little about the planet before our ships touched down on its gentle, leafy terrain. What I found was something I never could've expected to find; I found love.

Her name was Lilcoa. She was kind, compassionate, and everything else I'd never seen in my own people. She intrigued me. I had to talk to her. She was cautious around me at first, which is fair considering what I was there to do, but she did talk to me. The more I heard about her heart for her people, the more I questioned what the King sent me to do.

My love for her quickly grew, and it was obvious it was because of what her people raised her to be. I couldn't do what the King wanted. I couldn't trample these people and destroy the tender spirit that made Lilcoa.

I surrendered. I sent my people home and I stayed with Lilcoa and I didn't let myself think about what the King would have to say about it. My life was like a dream for a few years after that. My Rjelhdan instincts melted away as her tender spirit started reforming all I'd ever been. And I was grateful.

The Bhlidoran people accepted me as one of their own. My life had been good before, but I'd never truly known bliss until I was with them. I had no idea that the worst moment of my life was coming and that it'd coincide with the best moment of my life.

Lilcoa and I had been together for about two years when she got pregnant. She had a dream that the baby's name would be Kiyamara. I had asked her how she knew the baby would be a girl. She told me she just knew. I was skeptical, but she turned out to be right. Not that she ever got to see it; she died during childbirth.

The Bhlidorans may have been welcoming before, but not after that. Both me and Kiyamara were forced out because they blamed us for her death. I tried going back to Rjelhd where I was nearly killed by the King, and for the past eight years I've been searching for a planet for Ki and I to settle on.

It shouldn't be taking this long, but it is because of who I am. People either don't trust me because I'm a Rjelhdan, or they're scared to take me in because I'm an enemy of the Rjelhdans. There really is no winning.

"What's that one called, daddy?" Ki asks me as our ship nears our latest hopeful home.

"Ugolivia," I answer her, picking her up so she doesn't have to go on her tiptoes to peer out the window.

"Have you been to this one before?" she poses. She asks this nearly every time and the answer is pretty much always no. If I've been to a planet before, ninety-nine percent of the time, it wasn't for a good reason. I'd never tell her that, though. I don't want her to know about her Rjelhdan roots. I've worked hard to wash that part of who I was away; I'm not about to recount it all for my eight-year-old daughter. Maybe when she's older I'll be ready, but not now.

"Uh, no, I haven't been here before," I reply.

"Do you think they'll like us this time?" she asks. I hate it when she asks that. As if there's something wrong with her. As if this isn't all completely my fault.

"Ki, it doesn't matter what anybody thinks of you because you're *my* favorite person," I tell her, and a smile overtakes her soft features. It's just like her mother's.

"You're my favorite person too, daddy," she says, wrapping me into a hug. I'm the only person she's ever known, but I guess I'll take the compliment.

I can see excitement in her eyes as our ship nears the dusty pink surface of Ugolivia. From what I've heard, the planet's climate isn't much unlike Rjelhd's, though its appearance could not be more different. Rjelhd, like its people, is a dark shade of gray. Where this place has a smooth, even landscape, Rjelhd has jagged rocks everywhere. The sky here is a light orange hue. Rjelhd's is dark red. It's no wonder our people turned into savages living in an environment like that.

"Can I come this time?" Ki poses as our ship touches down in an empty clearing.

"No, Ki, you know that's not how we do things," I tell her. I learned my lesson about bringing her with me after what happened with the King on Rjelhd. If the door hadn't closed in time, I wouldn't have been the only one in danger. My one job in life is to protect her and I will not fail at that.

"Ok," she responds, disappointed. I hate that I haven't been able to give her more than this. That'll change someday. I'll find us a planet that'll accept us. Who knows? Maybe it'll be this one?

"I'll be back soon, and remember, don't open the door for anybody; I'll open it myself when I come back to the ship." I give her the spiel that I give her every time, and she nods her head to let me know she understands. I ruffle her wild purple curls, then I leave the ship and close the door behind me.

It takes five minutes of walking for people to start appearing around me. They point, they stare, they whisper. "Is that a Rjelhdan?"

"It is," another confirms. And that conversation plays out over and over as more people spot me. I wear baggy, concealing clothing to try to hide my lineage, but there's no mistaking the way the light reflects off the parts of my skin that are exposed.

"Come no further, Rjelhdan," a commanding female voice lets out. I snap out of my head and find its source pointing a spear in my direction. There's a crown atop her head with emeralds embedded in it that match her skin tone. She must be their leader. There are guards beside her, but they don't look nearly as battle ready as she does. Something tells me we had similar upbringings. I hope hers included more reason than mine.

"I'm not here for war. I left those ways behind me nearly a decade ago," I state, raising my hands up in a way no Rjelhdan would. Her brow furrows as she studies me, then she lowers her spear as realization hits her.

"You're the Prince," she says.

"I was the Prince. These days the only title I go by is dad," I correct her. She looks past me at my ship and though it's far, Ki's bright curls are clearly visible in the window.

"The rumors are true," the leader observes.

"I don't know the exact rumors you're referring to, but if they involve me having a daughter and nowhere to go, then yes, the rumors are true," I confirm, knowing there must be more going around the galaxy about me than just those two things.

"You're not looking to make Ugolivia your home?" she poses, though it comes out more like a 'please don't' type of statement. Great.

"I've been to over two hundred planets these past eight years and I haven't found one that's habitable and willing to take us in. Sure, Ugolivia wasn't my first choice, but if you'll have us, then I would do anything it takes to settle here. My daughter hasn't known a life outside of that ship and I need that to change," I let out honestly. If I'm right about her, then that's the only thing she'll respond to.

"Look Rjelhdan…" she begins.

"Dahnri," I interrupt, growing tired of being associated with my savage ancestors after all I've done to separate myself from their ways.

"Dahnri, we have our own young to look out for here; we can't risk a Rjelhdan attack because we're harboring a traitor to their kind," she reasons. A traitor. Over ten years have passed and that's still all I'll ever be seen as.

"What they were doing was wrong," I defend myself, though I know it won't do anything to help me in this situation.

"I agree, and that's why I can't have it pointed at my people," she responds, her tone laced with sympathy. She's absolutely right to turn me away, knowing what she knows about my people. I don't even know why I'm still bothering with all of this.

"Thank you for your time," I tell her, then I turn away and start heading back to the ship.

"Dahnri," she calls, and I stop and face her again. "Does your daughter like carjifs?" she asks, referring to the rare fruit that only grows in select parts of the galaxy. Ki's probably only had one in her life, but I'd definitely say she liked it.

"Uh, yeah," I answer.

"Mleps, go fetch our visitor three boxes of carjifs," the leader instructs the man to her right, and he looks perplexed. To be honest, I am too; three boxes is a lot. I mean, that would feed Ki and I for a month with multiple meals a day.

"But your majesty, we save those for royal feasts," Mleps brings up. That makes sense. We did the same thing on Rjelhd.

"And this man is royalty. Now go, he needs to get back to his daughter," the leader declares.

"Right away your majesty," Mleps agrees, then he scurries off to whatever storeroom the carjifs are kept in. The leader faces me with a kind smile that's reminiscent of how people used to greet me on Bhlidor.

"Thank you," I let out, still trying to wrap my head around why she'd do this for me.

"The Bhlidorans are friends of our people. They may have forgotten what you did for them, but we have not," she states. Mleps rushes back, arms full of carjifs which he promptly dumps into my arms. "I wish you well in your search, Dahnri."

"Thank you," I can't help but repeat, still confused by her kindness. She nods, then she turns away from me and begins walking away. I guess I should probably get back to the ship now. As I walk back there are just as many whispers around me as before, but this time they're different. Instead of calling me Rjelhdan, they're calling me royalty. Instead of fear lacing their words, there's awe. I haven't been treated this way in a long time.

"Do we have a home?" Ki poses as soon as I walk aboard the ship.

"Not here," I answer automatically, still reflecting on what just occurred.

"What'd they give you?" she asks, noticing the boxes in my arms.

"Carjifs," I reply.

"What are those?" she immediately follows up.

"A very rare, very special fruit," I tell her.

"And they just gave them to us?" she poses.

"Yeah," I confirm.

"Why?" she asks. Because they respect me. Because of what I did on Bhlidor. But what I did on Bhlidor is also the reason they won't take us in. I've had this thought dancing around my head for years that I've tried to ignore, but I don't think I can anymore. It's clear after what just happened that we can't go anywhere that's heard the term Rjelhdan. Acting on that thought would mean entering a situation with way more variables than I'm comfortable with, but it's time. "Daddy?" Ki poses.

"I know where we're going next," I declare.

***

Earth. I've heard rumors about it, but I've never been anywhere near it. From what I've heard, their people think they're the only life out there. That's pretty arrogant if you ask me. Arrogant or not, it's exactly what I need right now. They don't know my peoples' history or my own history. It won't be held over me like it has been on every other planet we've been to. Ki and I might actually find a home.

The journey took us a few weeks. Had it not been for the carjifs we were gifted, we would've had to pit-stop on a random planet to scavenge for food. I always hate doing that. It can take all day for me to find something and then when I finally get back to the ship, Ki's all anxious. We're both really happy to have avoided that this time. Ki also really loves carjifs, which is a little unfortunate because I'm pretty sure Earth doesn't have them.

I say that as if Earth will definitely be our home. There's still a chance they won't want us to stay there. I need to keep reminding myself of that so I don't get crushed by hope if this doesn't work out.

"Is that it?" Ki poses, rubbing the sleep out of her eyes as she goes on her tiptoes to peer out the window.

"That's it," I confirm, picking her up for a better view.

"What's all that blue stuff covering it?" she asks, pointing at the massive planet beyond the window. Sometimes I forget how little Ki knows about the universe. As Rjelhdan royalty, I was given a complete education about all that's out there. I was supposed to go out there and conquer it after all.

"The blue stuff is called water. Your mother's planet had something similar to it, though they didn't need it to survive like the people of Earth do," I explain. Rjelhd also had something similar, but it burned our flesh if we touched it, which I'm pretty sure is the opposite of what it does on Earth.

"Did she like it?" she poses. My mind takes me back to those blissful years on Bhlidor with Lilcoa. She always loved wading around in the pink ponds that speckled her planet's surface. I was hesitant to follow her in at first because of what the ponds on my planet had been like, but once I got over that, we'd play around in them for hours.

"It was one of her favorite parts about her home. She loved to play around in it," I finally answer, my voice shaky as I think about how much I miss those moments.

"I can't wait to play around in the water," she states, a big smile on her face. Usually I'd tell her not to get attached to the planet before we even land on it, but I can't hide how much I want that for her too. I'll never hold Lilcoa in my arms again and I'll never step foot on Bhlidor again, but maybe the joy I felt in those moments with her is possible to get back. Maybe we'll find a home on Earth and all those playful parts of Lilcoa will shine through in Ki once she has room to roam. I guess Ki isn't the only one growing attached to this planet before we land.

"State your name and your affiliation," a voice orders over our ship's coms. I wasn't aware that Earth had the technology to do that. Fear fills Ki's eyes, so I do everything in my power to hide my own uneasiness as I put her down and head over to our ship's communication system.

"My name is Dahnri and I'm the former Prince of Rjelhd," I answer. I leave out the fact that I have Ki with me. I need to know what their intentions are before I get into my own.

"Rjelhd? Are you an alien?" the voice poses, confused. She doesn't seem to know what Rjelhd is, so that's a good sign.

"Yes," I reply simply. I wait for a response, but I don't get one. I knew they thought they were alone in the universe, but I didn't expect them to be this caught off guard. That's not really a good sign.

"State your business," she finally demands, clearly trying to make herself sound scary.

"I'd like to know who I'm talking to before I discuss anything about that," I respond. This doesn't seem to be the person in charge of Earth and that's who I need to speak to.

"Kara Goldberg. My name is Kara Goldberg and I work for NASA," she reveals, trying harder with the scary thing, but ultimately moving in the other direction. I don't really know what NASA is. By the time we started learning about planets like Earth, the King had me training to be the general, so I didn't pay much attention.

"Does your leader work with you?" I ask.

"The leader of NASA, or the leader of the world?" she poses, unable to hide her confusion again. So it seems like NASA isn't their government. Noted. Before I get the chance to answer, there's some sort of feedback. Then another voice pipes up.

"What is it that you want?" a man questions. Now this is closer to the responses I'm used to. Even so, I don't feel comfortable speaking about Ki with just anyone from Earth, and I don't believe he's their leader.

"I need to speak with your leader; I have a request for them," I tell him. There's silence again and I wonder if I'm about to hear a third voice soon, but then the same man pipes up.

"If we send you coordinates, will you be able to land there?" the man poses.

"Yes," I answer, regretting not learning a lot about Earth more and more with each passing second. A string of numbers pops up on the ship's display.

"You'll find our leader here," the man speaks up, then he abruptly cuts off. Ok then. I pull up a map of Earth that's programmed into the ship, then chart a course for the location I was given. I used to do this kind of thing all the time when I was the general, though then it was about landing in a location that would fit my entire fleet. I'd study maps of the planets for hours until I found the perfect spot. This time is a bit different; I have no idea where I'm about to land.

"Daddy, what's happening?" Ki asks.

"I don't know, Ki, but I'm handling it," I say, projecting confidence despite the anxious feeling bubbling up inside of me over all the unknowns I'm about to walk into. People assume Rjelhdans are brave. For years, our people have been running headfirst into dangerous situations without a second thought. I didn't realize until I was with Lilcoa that it's not bravery, our people are just impulsive. It helps in battle, but when we come across a situation where we have to think about our actions, it's useless.

"Daddy?" Ki poses.

"Ki?" I respond.

"What happens if this doesn't work out?" she asks. Leave it to my kid to ask a question like that… I don't know what to say to her, but I know the longer I take to come up with something, the more she's going to worry.

"Ki, come here," I tell her, to buy myself a bit more time. By the time she's reached me, I still don't have a perfect answer. Come on, Dahnri. What would Lilcoa say? She was always so good at this kind of thing when I would have my moments. I can see tears welling up in Ki's eyes and I know I have to say something. "Home isn't a planet. Home is right here. It's you and I. No matter what's going on around us, we'll always have that," I come up with.

She sniffles, then throws her arms around me. I let out a deep breath and hug her back. Being there for this little girl is the most important thing I've ever done with my life. All the things I did as a Prince, all the things I did as a general, what I did on Bhlidor; none of it compares to even the littlest moments where I'm able to make her feel better. Whether we get a fresh start on Earth, or we keep wandering the galaxy the way we have been, as long as I have her, I have all that I need.

The ship rocks gently as it lands on the ground. I let go of Ki and head over to the window. We seem to have landed in front of some building, though I have no idea what it is. It's definitely not a personal residence, that's for sure. There are three men waiting for me to get out, all of them wearing clothes with weird patterns made up of various browns and greens. They have weapons at their sides, though they don't look like they're in a rush to use them. The one in the middle beckons me forward.

"Get out of view of the door," I instruct Ki. She nods, then scurries toward the back of the ship. I wait for her to be completely hidden before I open the door and step out into this new foreign territory. The air here feels crisp as it enters my lungs. I think it's a different combination of gasses than I'm used to, but my body doesn't seem to reject it, so that's good. I close the door to the ship, then walk up to the men who are about two heads shorter than me.

"Dahnri I presume," the middle man says, holding out his hand toward me.

"Yup," I confirm, bending down and shaking his hand.

"Strong grip," he compliments me. This feels weird. Kara Goldberg seemed to be freaked out when she learned I was an alien, but this man is pretending this is all normal despite the fact that I'm very different than they are. I don't know whether I should be disturbed or hopeful considering what I'm here to ask of them.

"Are you Earth's leader?" I check.

"I am indeed," he answers. He's not wearing a crown or anything like that, though I never really wore one either. "You told the people at NASA that you were a Prince; what's the story there?" he asks. I didn't really want to get into that with him. I just brought it up because it seemed like the easiest way to identify myself.

"I made a decision that the King didn't agree with and I was banished for it," I state. He doesn't need to know the full story, or the fact that the King tried to kill me upon my return.

"So you're no longer affiliated with the planet you're from?" he poses.

"No, that's actually why I'm here; I'm looking for a new home," I explain. I'm still not ready to bring Ki into this yet. I need to see how they react first. Currently I'm not getting much information from his expression. He's just looking me up and down. I don't like it. I've been sized up before, but never like this.

"There's something you're not telling us. Something about another life form on your ship. You got an attack dog or something?" he asks. They know about Ki already…

"I don't know what a dog is, but I assure you, that's not what's on my ship. I'm traveling with my daughter. I left her out of this thus far for her safety," I admit. He cocks his head to the side as he takes in this new bit of information.

"So, you're looking to make Earth your home?" he finally poses.

"If you'll have us," I reply. I'm still not very sure about this, but I know we really don't have many other options, if any at all.

"We'd be glad to have you," he lets out, reaching out and pulling me into a hug. I don't like this. I don't like this at all. I hear banging on the ship's window behind me, and I spin around, taking the guy hugging me with me. I see panic in Ki's barely visible eyes, and I realize why too late.

***

"It looks metallic, but it's not actually metal," I hear a voice speak up. My eyes start to open slowly and I realize I'm in some sort of infirmary type room, though I appear to be on the only bed in here. My head feels foggy, which isn't exactly helping me take this all in. I hear beeping around me, increasing in intensity. I don't like it. The more I think about me not liking it, the more it picks up.

"He needs more sedatives," someone in a mask states, looking down at me. He has some sort of bloody knife in his hand. Wait, I'm pretty sure my blood is a different color than the people of Earth's. They're cutting into me. I need to get out of here. A mask looking thing starts getting lowered onto my face, but I shove it away before they have it over my mouth and nose.

"Call for backup," another guy in a mask says, looking out in front of him. I turn my head around and see a man dressed in that weird pattern put his hand to his ear and start talking, but I'm way too out of it to decipher what he says.

Somebody else attempts to put the mask on me while I'm distracted, but this time I grab their arm and flip them across the table. The men in the masks step back, raising their arms in the air in surrender. I dart up and move in on the one with the knife, but something pierces my back before I reach him.

I spin around and find the man dressed in the weird pattern has his weapon pointed at me. It works from across the room? Luckily, it isn't made of Rjelhdan metals, or I'd probably be dead right now. It's still going to be annoying trying to get to him when he can hit me from further away. He does something with it that sends a flying piece of metal directly into my shoulder. It makes a small hole, but ultimately falls to the ground.

"You'll regret that," I get out as the Rjelhdan rage buried deep inside of me awakens. I grab a small table with a collection of tools on it from next to the bed and launch it at the man in the weird pattern. It hits him in the head and he crumples to the ground.

My breathing picks up as whatever they were using to keep me asleep begins to wear off. Pain also floods my system from the wounds that have been inflicted upon me. My shoulder. My back. My leg? I look down and find that layers of my skin and muscle have been pulled back and are being held open by pins they've poked through me.

Now that I'm looking at it, it's starting to hurt more. I rip out the pins, then do my best to push everything back where it should be. *Just pretend it's a normal battle wound, Dahnri. You've had plenty of those before.* I knew there was something off about these people, but I can't say I saw *this* coming. I'm just some thing to them. I need to get back to the ship and get Ki and I off this planet. I make my way toward the door when the voice of the man I'd spoken to earlier pipes up.

"Calm down, Dahnri," he states. His tranquil tone only causes more of my Rjelhdan fury to bubble up. "There's plenty more where that soldier came from. If you continue forward, you won't make it far," he tells me. I whip around, looking for him, but I don't see him anywhere in the room. His voice must be coming through some sort of communication system.

"I've torn through armies stronger than those of your planet," I remark.

"Did any of those armies happen to have your daughter?" he poses, a clear threat, but he says it as if we're playing some game. Ki. How would they be able to get her? I'm the only one who can open those doors from the outside. Unless they have some sort of technology that allows them to get through, but I don't know how they'd have something like that without knowing how Rjelhdan ships work.

"How?" I question, needing to know if what he's saying is true.

"It was quite easy, actually; your daughter carries that same fighting spirit that's coursing through you now. She thought she was going to come save you after we got a hold of you. Her attempt was pretty adorable, but overall unsuccessful. We've got her in the room down the hall from the one you're in now. You can go check it out if you don't believe me," he offers.

He's lying. Ki may gleam like a Rjelhdan, but she's never acted like one. She's never even seen me like this, so she wouldn't know how. The spirit inside her is cautious like her mother's. I've always been grateful for that, now more than ever. Whatever's in that room that he's trying to get me to go to is a trap.

"Touch a hair on my daughter's head and I'll kill you in a way so brutal you'll wish you had never woken up this morning." I play into exactly what he's looking for from me. I don't want to give him time to move the trap.

I hear him laugh as I make a mad dash out of the room. He won't be laughing soon enough. I don't know where I'm going, but I know I won't stop until I find the ship. It doesn't matter how many people I have to go through to get to it.

"It didn't work!" someone lets out as I run right past the room they were trying to lead me to. Yup, called it. Footsteps echo through the halls behind me as a hoard of soldiers begins chasing after me. A few more pieces of metal pierce my back, and I know I have to stop and fight these guys before I continue looking for the ship. I look around me for anything that can be used as a weapon. There's a long, silver handle on the door next to me. It's not a sword, but it'll work.

I rip the handle clean off the door and charge the soldiers. Most of them are too shocked by what they just witnessed to use their weapons, but unfortunately, not all of them are. Little pieces of metal find my gut, my forehead, and my arm before I've even reached my opponents. I shake off the pain and take a deep breath. My turn.

I club the first guy I reach in the head and he crumples. The next guy faces the same fate. This is almost too easy considering their heads are pretty much at the same level as my arms. More little pieces of metal fly at me, but none of them slow me down. Over a decade of Rjelhdan rage is making its way out of my system right now, and they're just the people unlucky enough to have it pointed at them.

As I continue to destroy all those around me, I can't help but think that the King would be proud of me right now. This is the son he lost to the Bhlidorans. Years of work on myself gone in an instant because I trusted the wrong people. Maybe my Rjelhdan instincts weren't all bad. Maybe they would've saved me from this situation.

The Bhlidorans made me soft, then threw me out to get trampled by the universe. Maybe that was their plan all along. Weaken the Rjelhdans by stealing their general, then weaken him so he wouldn't be able to do anything about it. Maybe I've been nothing more than a pawn this whole time. No. What Lilcoa and I had was real. Ki is proof of that. Ki. I need to get to the ship.

I finish off the last of the soldiers surrounding me, then I continue on the way I was going before. Over a dozen little pieces of metal opened holes in me during that battle, making it increasingly hard for me to ignore the pain.

I come across a man in a mask like the ones who had been cutting into me before, and his eyes fill with terror upon spotting me. I can use that. He tries to run away, but I catch him fairly quickly and secure him in my arms.

"Tell me where my ship is and I… won't rip your head off," I get out, and I feel his entire body tremble within my grasp.

"Keep going st-straight, then ta-take a left and then another le-left, then a right, and it sh-should be there," he lets out. I drop him, then take off in the direction he told me to go. I encounter some opposition, but I easily get rid of it with my door handle. My pace gets slower and slower as I go. My body is beginning to shut down from all the damage that I've taken. The ship doesn't have the supplies to fix me, and even if it did, Ki doesn't have the expertise. I'm not going to make it off this planet…

I fall to the ground as this washes over me. I'm going to die here on this random planet. Maybe it would've been better if the King had just taken my life on Rjelhd.

***

"I thought Rjelhdans were supposed to be fearless," Lilcoa teases me as she splashes around in the vibrant pink pond. Her wet hair sticks to her face, but she doesn't seem bothered by it. She isn't bothered by much. It's hard for me to fathom sometimes given where I grew up.

"I'm not scared," I respond, by the edge of the pond. She rolls her eyes, then flicks the liquid in my direction. I hop up to avoid contact with it and she laughs at me.

"Dahnri, it's not going to hurt you," she assures me.

"In my experience, it will," I state, thinking back to the times my father would splash me with the liquid from the ponds on our planet when I'd mess up in training. There are several scars on my body that tell the tale of what that liquid was capable of.

"Do you remember when we first met?" she poses.

"Of course," I answer. I'd never forget the moment my life began to change. She had been picking flowers when our ships landed. There were a few others with her. She made sure they all got to safety before she worried about getting to safety herself. A Rjelhdan woman in her position would've just charged us, but she was different.

"When you first approached me, I was scared. In my experience, the only thing Rjelhdans could bring was death. My experience was wrong," she says. She smiles and reaches her arm out toward me. "Yours could be too," she adds.

I look down at the liquid surrounding her and my brain tells me to run, then my gaze shifts to her kind expression. Whatever happens to me when I step foot in that pond, she's got me. I take her hand and step into the pond, which doesn't seem to burn my flesh. Cool.

"I told you you'd be fine," she states.

"Yeah, because of you," I respond.

"Dahnri, I didn't pull you into this pond. I just helped you get out of your own way," she tells me.

"I guess Rjelhdans do have a habit of standing in their own way," I say.

"Yes, you do. In fact, you're doing it right now," she declares.

"But I'm in the pond now," I bring up, confused.

"Dahnri, you haven't been in this pond in nearly a decade," she states. Her touch fades away as the scenery around me fades as well. "Your daughter needs you; get out of your own way."

The pond on Bhlidor disappears completely and I find myself back on the ground where I fell not too long ago, my blood starting to pool around me. I may never leave this planet, but there's still hope for Ki; I need to get up.

I force my battered body up, using the wall more than I'd like to be at this point. Once I'm on my feet again, I drag myself along the path the man in the mask set me on. Once I finally take the last turn, I see my ship in the middle of an open room. Ki's peeking out the window, and her eyes light up when she sees me. I see her hand moving toward the switch that opens the door and I know I have to stop her.

"Ki, don't!" I call. I know that any minute now there's going to be more soldiers and I'm not strong enough to fend them off. I can't have her open that door and risk getting taken by them.

"Daddy," her voice is muffled, but I can still hear the panic in it as she stares out at me.

"Ki, you need to go," I tell her.

"Not without you," she says, her voice wavering.

"Yes, without me. Get off this planet and… go somewhere else. You don't look like a Rjelhdan. Pretend… pretend you're from a made up planet. You'll find a home, Ki," I instruct. I reach my hand out and place it on the window. Her fingertips just barely touch the glass on the other side.

"You're my home," she states. I really didn't foresee that little interaction biting me in the butt. I hear footsteps echoing in the hallways behind me. There's not much time left.

"I'm not going to be able to… leave here. Find yourself a permanent… home," I get out. It hurts saying those words to her.

I never let her see me weak. I never prepared her for the possibility that she could lose me, just like she lost her mother.

"Daddy…" she starts, but she trails off as my hand slips down the glass from the shock of a new little piece of metal poking another hole in my back.

"Kiyamara, it's been the greatest joy… of my life be-being your dad," I declare, forcing a smile to my face despite the pain flowing through me, and the new little pieces of metal hitting my back. She wipes her eyes, then disappears from the window. A few seconds later, I hear the ship's engine fire up. I back away from it just before it takes off of the ground. It breaks a hole in the roof, then it's gone.

"You son of a bitch!" the man who I spoke with earlier exclaims as he runs into the room. I'm glad he's finally realized this isn't a game. I turn around to face him and the soldiers that surround him, who are all still sending those little pieces of metal in my direction. Now that I know Ki's safe, it's time to go out like a Rjelhdan; taking out as many of those fuckers as I can before my last breath.

Taylor Funk is a STEM kid with a passion for writing. She's been writing poetry since middle school, novels since high school, and has recently dipped her toes in short stories. Her writing goal is and will always be to move the reader, whether the story is about superheroes, aliens, or regular people.

Child Classes Inherit Parent Objects

by Joshua Harding

I told my dad to lean toward me. He obliged slowly and I could hear his ancient joints creaking under the strain. He lowered his torso until his head was level with his hips and his back was prostrate in front of me. Then I pulled the quick release pins from his spine and removed his access panel.

I'd stopped at the hardware store on my way to visit him at the retirement home. I grabbed some fan belts, a new terabyte drive, three tubes of high temp silicone lubricant (his favorite), and a can of antistatic spray.

"Whoa, Pop!" I said. "When's the last time anyone opened you up?"

"Approximately two months ago," he replied.

"Jeez! I think there's a nest of spiders in here." I shot a couple of quick bursts of spray and blew a good quantity of dust from his main heating coil.

"Did you bring the lubricant?" he asked from his inverted position.

"Yup," I replied. I gave him another good spray and then pulled the twin cooling fans from his hip cavity. Each of them got a new belt and his sacral joint got a hefty swabbing of the high temp lubricant.

"Did you bring the lubricant?" my dad asked again.

"Yes, dad, I'm putting it on you right now."

"Did you bring the lubricant?"

I sighed audibly as I snapped everything back into place. He straightened up to face me. "How does that feel, dad?"

"Much better, thank you," he said.

"So, how've things been lately?" I asked. I sat down on the chair next to his bed. He eased back onto the pillows and cleared his throat. I caught a whiff of heated phenolic circuit boards and ozone, scents which seemed to permeate the entire facility. "Have you been going to activities? Made any new macramé?"

His eyescreens blinked, and he said, "It is very good to see you, Sam."

"You too, dad."

"Tell me what you have been doing, Sam."

"Well, I have some good news." He blinked again. "I got offered a job."

"With what company?"

"It's a medical supply company…in Milwaukee."

"Milwaukee, Wisconsin is 148.22 kilometers from home."

"Yeah, I know, Dad."

"When will you start your new job?"

"I have to give them an answer by the end of the week." He was silent. I could see him compiling what I'd just said into his different subfolders before speaking again. "I'd have to start coming out to see you just on weekends, though."

"Read to me, please."

"All right," I said. "Do you want to hear Ray Bradbury again?"

"Yes, please."

I opened the nightstand, picked up the dog-eared book, opened it to *I Sing the Body Electric!*, and began reading. His lips moved along with mine. I could recite this story from memory by now—without even looking. He paused when I paused. Just then, Sandra knocked and entered the room.

"Hello, Mr. Duncan!" she said with a boisterous, kindergarten teacher's positivity and that Puerto Rican accent that always made me melt. "Time to change your batteries." Sandra had been my dad's Robot Assistant since I put him in the Cyber Springs retirement home seven years ago. Every anniversary, Sandra and the other RAs threw a huge party for him. There was a picture of the most recent one tacked to his whiteboard with his daily goals. In the photo, a dozen young, vibrant RAs surrounded my dad and held a colorful banner that said: "It's not the years, it's the mileage!"

"Hello, Sam," she said with a smile.

"Hello, Sandra," I said. She and I were always professional in front of my dad. If he suspected anything, he didn't let on, although he knew both of us well enough to formulate an educated guess.

Sandra and I had been seeing each other for almost a year and a half.

I continued reading while Sandra pulled a charging cart into the room from the hallway

"I have batteries, Sandra," my dad said suddenly. He reached under his pillow and pulled out a handful of 9 volt and AA batteries, some with the chalky traces of leakage on the ends.

"Thank you, Mr. Duncan," Sandra said as she took the batteries from him, "but these batteries are dead and they don't fit you anyway. You only take twelve volt lithium."

"Dad," I said, "where'd you get those old things? And why are they under your pillow?"

"I have batteries…." he replied.

"He started hoarding spare parts six weeks ago," Sandra said. She stepped nimbly between my dad's bed and his roommate's, searching the bedclothes. "Servos, timing relays, and batteries like these." I noticed Dad trying to tuck the corner of his blanket down over a rectangular lump I hadn't noticed before. "Do you have any more batteries in your bed, Mr. Duncan? No hiding, now."

"What you got there, Dad?" I asked and reached for the lump. With Sandra's help, we managed to pry the blanket free from his metacarpals and expose what he had squirreled away underneath.

"A motherboard?" I said, picking up a green card studded with silver dots and lined with ports. "Dad, this is from a telecom server; it wouldn't process fast enough for a robot. Sandra, how long has he been doing this?"

"Remember when you said that robot supply shop in your old neighborhood closed down?"

"Yeah."

"That's when it started. You came into visit with a bag full of parts and told him you'd have to go online to find replacements from then on."

"You mean, he started searching for his own parts?"

"Yeah, we try to look for them and recycle them while he's out playing *Go* with the school janitor bot from the third floor. We pull a chop shop's worth of scrap out of his room every couple of days."

"But why would he be doing that?"

"He's mimicking what you were doing—it's how most robots are programmed, copying human behavior. You were stockpiling parts for him, so he started stockpiling too."

Sandra pulled the charging cart over to the bed and tossed the parts we found into a recycling bin underneath it. She swapped out the battery packs in the side panels of my dad's thighs with new ones from the cart and wheeled it back into the hall.

"Your dad's the longest resident we've ever had here," she said as she came back into the room. "I've never seen an X.509 model last so long."

"He's a classic—like a vintage car. I try to take care of him, don't I, Dad?"

My dad swung his head toward Sandra, and I could hear the servos in his neck grinding. I'd have to replace those bearings soon. "Sam is a good boy," he said to her.

"I know," said Sandra. She leaned in and raised her voice and enunciated her consonants so the old robot could hear her. They stopped production on his AT2020 microphones last year. I didn't know how much longer his voice recognition would last. Pretty soon I'd have to punch all our conversations into the auxiliary keyboard under his ribcage—an awkward arrangement, to say the least, and I was a horrible typist. "He takes good care of you, doesn't he, Mr. Duncan?"

"Sam..." said my dad. "Sam...Sam...Sam..." His head jerked back and forth with each utterance.

"Ok, Dad," I said. "We got it. Take it easy."

"Good...good...good..." I reached under his chin to find the quit button. His head's motion made the button slip away from my finger several times (why didn't they put the thing on his shoulder or forearm—somewhere more accessible?). I depressed the button and the jerking immediately settled down. "...boy..." he said and was silent.

"He definitely needs that defrag," Sandra said. "Did you bring the new drive?"

"Yeah," I said. I pulled the terabyte drive from my bag and handed it to her. She plugged it into my dad's access port and booted up the program.

She stood up and put her hands on her hips. "When did you first know?" she asked, breaking the silence of the room. "That you and your dad weren't like other families?"

I hung my bag on the corner of my dad's bed. He'd started hibernating after I hit the quit button and his screen savers danced lazily across his eyes. "I think it was when I went on my first sleepover in second grade," I said. "I remember watching my friend, Danny Knowski, sit in his mom's lap. She'd come down to the rec room to tell us it was time for lights out and he crawled up into her lap and laid his head on her chest. I thought how soft it must be to sit in her lap. I never sat in my dad's lap—it'd be like sitting on a bike rack. Danny's mom saw that I was sad and brought me up on her lap, too. Then she told me that I was special because I was the first."

"You were the first?"

"Uh-huh," I said, realizing that in the time we'd been together—in seven years of Sandra being Dad's RA that this hadn't come up. "Yeah, I was the first. I had no living relatives or other adults to take me in, so I had to go into OPPLA."

"Huh? Sounds like you're breaking dishes at a Greek wedding."

"Not *Opa*—OPPLA. It stands for Other Planned Permanent Living Arrangement. When there's no living relatives or other option—like a family friend or even a teacher—then the kid stays in the custody of the state."

"So, where does the robot come in?"

"Not enough people were signing up to be foster parents, so the state set up a bunch of us with robots—kind of an experiment." I realized I hadn't recycled the motherboard and had been fidgeting with it as I spoke. Then, for no particular reason, I tucked it into my pocket. "But I 'aged out' of the program before I was adopted or got human foster parents. So, I wasn't just the first kid to be fostered by a robot, I was the only kid to turn eighteen under the care of one."

Sandra sat gently on the end of the bed. "Remember when we went to my *abuela's* house for that barbeque and she asked when she was going to meet your dad?"

"That would've been fun! He glitches out just talking with more than two people. I don't think your grandma fully understood my family situation."

"Yeah, she almost dropped her plate and was like, '*¿Su papa es un robot?*'" Sandra laughed out loud at that and stroked my dad's foot beneath the blanket.

"Don't you see why I keep coming here?" I asked.

"Well, I thought it was to see me," she replied with a wry smile, trying to keep the conversation light.

"Yes, of course, that's one reason. I come to see you, but first I came to see *him*. For the same reason you go back Humboldt Park for your grandma's *lechón* and *pasteles*. I want those same visits. I've got no one else—no one else but him." I looked at my dad as he slept. The faulty relay in his left ankle made his foot twitch and untuck the blanket. "No one else remembers playing catch with me on the Hooper Elementary ball field. No one else remembers canoeing with my Scout troop on Fox Lake. I need him so I can remember those things. It's like he makes my past real. Without him, I don't know for sure if those things ever really happened."

"Your dad is the only foster robot we have here."

"Really?"

"Yeah, most of the other residents are either housekeepers or playmates."

"All Rosies and Buddies? No parents?"

"Nope."

"He's the only dad, huh?"

"Yeah." She paused and pulled the blanket back over my dad's feet. "Do you think it made a family man out of you? Having him as your father?"

"I guess. Dad never judged me." I looked at him as he lay there, inert. "When I cut school or shoplifted or sprayed graffiti, he didn't lecture me or bust my balls about it. He looked at it logically. He knew teenagers rebelled and his teenager was rebelling. He saw it as part of my programming, just like protecting me and feeding me were part of his."

"Sammy," she said, "you're so good with him—so devoted."

"Thanks?" I said, not knowing where this was going. She took hold of my hand.

"And you're so good to me, too."

"Ok?"

"You'll make a great father," she said and leaned toward me.

"Thanks—wait, what?"

"I'm pregnant."

Had I heard her right? I thought. Yeah, I'd heard her right. I let the comment sit there between us. Maybe if I kept quiet and stepped lightly, I wouldn't disturb it—like a sleeping cougar or a land mine. Just like if I kept quiet, I wouldn't disturb my dad and he would keep hibernating. No need for him to get involved in this conversation.

"Did you hear me?" Sandra asked.

"Yes. Yes, I did."

"Well?" Her brow furrowed.

"Well," I said, having no idea what else to say. "That complicates things." I was stalling, and Sandra knew it.

"Yeah, it complicates things," she said and stood up from the bed. "I'm Catholic, so I'm not having an abortion."

"God no!" I said. "I don't want that either! Why would that be the first thing you suggest?"

"I'm trying to get you involved in this conversation. What do *you* want?"

Well, I thought, *what* did *I want?*

"What about adoption?" she asked.

Adoption.

The one thing I'd *wanted and hoped for all my life,* I thought. *A family. A father and mother. To be adopted was my greatest wish and here both of this kid's parents were alive and together and…in love. Nope. I'd be damned if I was going to let what happened to me happen to* my *kid.*

"I love you," I said.

"I love you too," Sandra replied. "Don't change the subject."

"Are *you* happy about it?" I asked. Sandra stopped for a moment. She was suddenly at a loss for words—a first for her. Her temper cooled for a second.

"What do you mean, am *I* happy about it?" she said. She planted her fist against her ample hip—a move of hers that always drove me wild.

"Shh! Not so loud," I said, glancing at the bed. "Let the poor guy sleep. I mean, how do *you* feel about it? I know that *I'm* happy about it."

I'd just spoken from the heart without realizing it. Truthfully. I had to catch myself for a second—my stalling had been stalled. I looked at Sandra, the sun slanting through the window and making a chestnut halo of her curly hair. God! I was crazy about her! Her mouth was slightly open in disbelief and a tear was sneaking out of the corner of her eye, betraying her feelings.

"You are?" she whispered.

"Of course I'm happy about it," I said, and damned if I didn't mean it. I guess I knew what I was going to tell them up in Milwaukee.

"Really, Sammy?" She said, and the tear trickled out.

"Yes!" I said. "I don't have a ring yet, but will you marry me?"

"I'm happy for you and Sandra about the baby," my dad said. I jumped, not realizing he was awake again. He blinked his eyescreens. "I was always rooting for you two."

"How long have you been listening, Dad?" I asked.

"I need to tell you something." My dad hoisted himself up on his elbows, one of which let out a squeal of protest at the weight. I stepped toward the bed and got an arm underneath him to take the strain off his elbow. "I need…need…need…"

"It's all right, Dad," I said. Sandra had moved in with a roll of Flex Tape to immobilize the joint.

"Lie down, Mr. Duncan," she said, "you'll break your arm."

"I'll be with you no matter what, Sam."

Sandra stopped. "Did he just use a contraction?" she asked.

"What do you mean, you'll always be with me, Dad?" He struggled against us, insistent on sitting upright and looking me in the face as he spoke.

"You don't have to keep repairing me, Sam," he said. The motherboard that I'd placed in my pocket tumbled out onto the bed. I picked it up and went to toss it in the wastebasket when he took hold of my arm, grasped the component, and pushed it back into my pocket. He locked my gaze with his eyescreens and I saw they were more stable and clear than they'd been in months. "Take care of your mother…er…er…" he said, as his glitching began again in earnest. Sandra cradled his jerking head and eased it down onto the pillow while I reached behind his chin and pressed his quit button again.

Sandra and I looked at each other. "What the hell was that all about?" I asked.

There was a soft wheeze from the corner of the room. I turned and heard the telltale, four-tone shutdown chime as the late model Buddy in the bed next to my dad's began its termination subroutine.

Sandra picked up the phone. "Hospice? I need a decommissioning team down on the Memory Unit right away."

Within minutes, two techs entered the room, wheeling a utility cart. The first was a burly guy in dirty blue coveralls with the sleeves cut off and a jeweler's loupe screwed over one eye. The second was skinny and younger. His coveralls were brand new, and he carried a heaping tool bag over his rounded shoulder. Without preamble, they approached my dad's roommate and deftly opened him up like they were an Indy pit crew.

"That heating coil is in pretty good shape," the burly one said. "Make sure we get all the potentiometers and bridge rectifiers."

"Yeah," replied the second.

"And we can use the elbow servos on the PT floor."

"You want to do a software extraction?" the skinny one asked.

"Nah," said the burly guy. "Can't do anything with that OS anymore and looks like this unit's been patched a couple dozen times."

They pulled components out, wrapped them in antistatic baggies, and dumped them into labeled bins amongst similar parts and pieces scattered on their cart. When they were done, they placed the limb paneling along with the torso and cranial plates into a big blue bin that said, "Aluminum" beneath a large recycling symbol.

I looked at the bed; there was nothing left.

"Wait—what happens to him?" I blurted. The techs looked at me as if noticing me for the first time—the lost handbag customer who'd wandered into the automotive department.

"What happens to who?" asked the burly one. He wiped his hands against his thighs as he turned to me, leaving brown streaks of lithium grease on his coveralls.

"To him—what happens to his memories?"

He pulled the jeweler's loupe from his eye and tucked it into his breast pocket below a nametag that said *Artyom*. He glanced between me and what was left of my dad's roommate with the dawning realization that I was asking about the robot he and his partner had just dismantled. "Hell if I know," he said.

The second tech stood up from where he'd been putting the tools back into the bag. He held a rag in one hand and a soldering iron in the other. His nametag said *Rajesh*. "You can keep the memories if you do a backup, but the family for this one didn't ask for one. Otherwise..." then he shrugged.

That's when they noticed my dad. He was still hibernating through all of this. Artyom leaned over to peer around me and then glanced over at Rajesh, who stepped over for a closer look.

"Your Buddy there looks like an early model," Artyom said. "Is that an old 500-series?"

"Yes, he is—and he's not a Buddy, he's my dad."

Rajesh's eyebrows hiked up at that. "Um...sure," he said and pointed with the soldering iron. "Your...dad...is practically an antique. They don't make them like that anymore."

"Yeah, I know," I said.

"What model?" he asked.

"X.509," I said.

Artyom let out a whistle. "Pretty rare to find a 509 anymore," he said and shook his head, "especially one in that condition."

"Worth a lot of money," Rajesh said.

"Ay! No!" Sandra shrieked, then unleashed a stream of Spanish profanity, only some of which I could catch. "No way are you gonna go mining deathbeds in *my* section!"

"Mining deathbeds?" I asked.

"¡Sí! These two *chingados* wanna take apart your papa and sell his pieces for money!"

"Hey! Watch your language!" Artyom said, then to me, "Look, you seem like a smart guy. You're probably shelling out two, maybe three grand a month for this room, am I right? And how long's that been? The last 509 I ever saw was nearly a decade ago.

Your…*dad*…here is worth over twenty times that just in titanium alone."

"Not to mention all the copper and palladium," said Rajesh. "Most bots are mostly plastic and fiber optics nowadays."

"Get out!" Sandra pointed towards the door.

"Cyber Springs owes families market value on precious metals from terminal recycling." Artyom said. He held his hands up in front of him as if he'd come between a Grizzly and her cubs. "Families are owed recycling compensation when their residents terminate on Cyber Springs' property. Not just a rebate—*market* value. All I'm saying is you're sitting on a goldmine here."

"Yeah, literally!" said Rajesh.

"Enough money to have bought and paid for this little shared room a couple times over. Instead of pissing it away on rent every month."

"Or even a down payment on a nice three-bedroom place out in the suburbs."

"A house," I said, almost to myself.

"Sammy?" Sandra said. "What are you thinking?"

I looked around the room then. At the two techs. At the indent in the mattress where my dad's roommate had been only moments before. At the pictures pinned to the wall of me in various states of growth and development. At the half a dozen macramé hanging from the drop ceiling. At my dad. At Sandra.

"A house," I said to her. "A home for us—for the baby." Sandra blinked back more tears. I turned to the techs. "Do you guys get, like, a commission or something?" I asked.

"What, you mean on the final sale of reclamation?" asked Artyom.

"Yeah, like a percentage?"

"We're not at…um…liberty to say," said Rajesh.

"Ten percent—peanuts on most bots, unless we find the right buyer," said Artyom. "I won't bullshit you, we'll do well on your dad, but nothing compared to what you'll make."

"Sammy, are you sure?" asked Sandra. "This is a lot to take in all at once."

"Yeah, I'm sure," I replied. "But you never answered me."

"If I'll marry you? Yes! Of course!" She burst towards me. Her smile beamed as she pressed it eagerly to my face again and again and for a moment, the whole world was her.

"Um, I don't mean to intrude," said Artyom, "but me and Rajesh here have other residents to decommission."

"All right," I said. "I just…um…"

Rajesh noticed I was having difficulty and said, "We understand." Artyom visibly rolled his eyes. "Well, I do, anyway. You're saying you'd like us to terminate your robot?" I nodded, and Sandra placed a hand on my shoulder. Rajesh went on, "It's Ok if you don't want to stay in the room while we do it."

I looked toward the door, then thought better of it. I wasn't going to go all chicken shit now—not after all my dad had done for me. I shook my head, moved closer to the bed, and took hold of my dad's hand.

As Rajesh moved in to open the main drive panel, my dad's voice sounded out suddenly, "You'll want to ground yourself to the bed frame. There's an arc flash hazard when disconnecting my main power bus." Rajesh froze with his arm still extended. The voice seemed to be coming from his utility belt.

"Dad?" I asked. Rajesh plucked his cell phone from his belt and held it up in front of him.

"Yes, Sam?" said my dad's voice from the phone.

"What's going on?" said Artyom.

"I said," my dad continued, "Rajesh will want to ground himself before disconnecting my power bus." At this, Rajesh dropped the phone like it was something alive. It clattered to the floor and slid, screen down, under the bed.

"How is this happening?" asked Rajesh.

"Dad, how are you doing this?"

"I'll still be with you." This time my dad spoke from the smart speaker on the windowsill. "Even if Rajesh dismantles me, I'll still be with you."

"He's using contractions again," said Sandra.

"Robots don't use contractions," said Artyom. "They aren't as lazy as humans. This is Henry down in the supply room playing a prank on us, I'll bet."

"But how?" I asked again.

"Memory is forever," my dad said. "Processors fail, servos break down, software becomes obsolete. But memory gets bigger and bigger, expanding all the time, linking the shared moments and events of the whole universe."

"It's the No-Hiding Theorem," said Sandra.

"That's right, Sandra. Quantum information can neither be created nor destroyed," my dad continued. "Human brains are organic quantum computers, operating in multi-dimensional algorithms. I am also a quantum computer. All consciousness—robot and biologic—is quaternary."

"Quaternary?" I asked.

"Base four—0, 1, 2, and 3. But, in your case, it's A, G, T, and C."

"DNA!" said Sandra. "Adenine, guanine, thiamine, and cytosine. But, Mr. Duncan, you're not a quantum computer."

"I may not have been, but I am now."

"Wow," Sandra whispered.

"Sam," my dad said. "I'm now part of the Cloud and my consciousness will grow and continue forever—no matter what becomes of my body. You and Sandra are going to be great parents. And someday, you, Sandra, me, and even the baby, will all be a part of it too."

Rajesh dropped his soldering iron.

"Sam," my dad said, "It's time."

"Yeah," I replied. "I know." I nodded at Rajesh. "Ground yourself first, like he said."

Rajesh turned to Artyom. "No way! I'm not touching him," he said and backed away from my dad and nearly tripped against his tool bag on the floor behind him.

"Aw, don't be such a little girl about it," said Artyom. Sandra glared at him and he blinked at her sheepishly before saying, "Just open up its panel and disconnect the bus."

"But, he's talking to me," Rajesh said.

"Nothing you haven't dealt with before."

"But they've never called me by name before, or talked to me while I unplugged them." His eyes were wide, and he kept them glued to my dad as he stepped carefully over the tool bag to make for the door.

"Oh for Pete's sake, I'll do it!" said Artyom, stepping forward.

"No," I said. "I'll do it."

Artyom stopped and shoved his grimy hands into his pockets. He looked from me to Sandra and back again. He cleared his throat audibly and said, "Well, you know how to reach us when you're done." Then he turned and hurried out of the room to join his partner.

I stepped to the bed and grasped the grounding plate on the headboard and with my other hand opened the panel on his right hip where the words *CAUTION: Risk of Electric Shock* were printed in large black letters beneath a yellow triangle with a lightning bolt in it. Inside was a red button the size of a half dollar beneath the words *Main Power*.

"Dad?" I asked, "You still there?"

Child Classes Inherit Parent Objects   Joshua Harding

As if in answer, the TV mounted to the wall came on. From it I heard a small voice I hadn't heard in years: my own. The TV showed a shaky video from a Go-Pro of my eight-year-old self standing at home plate, bat in hand, ready to swing. The view was from the pitcher's mound. "Are you ready, Sam?" asked my dad's voice from offscreen and I nodded—both the kid on the TV and me, unconsciously, as I stood in the room with my hand on the button. A baseball flew towards my younger self—a perfect fastball right over the plate. I swung and connected, sending a line drive toward left field and surprising me so much that I stood there for a second until my dad said, "Go, Sam!"

That's when I depressed the button.

From my dad's body I could hear the shutdown sequence. Various hard drives hummed lower and lower as they spun down, switches clicked softly back into their factory configurations, and fans whirred and stopped. The LEDs all over his body that had acted as nightlights for me in my preschool years, or locators for me in darkened movie theaters or zoo reptile houses, slowly winked out one by one.

Then the room was silent.

It was so completely bereft of the constant white noise of his machinery that I jumped when I noticed the TV had darkened while I was tinkering with—while I was *terminating*—my dad.

For a panicked moment, I thought I'd done it wrong or something—wiped his memory completely—when the TV came to life again. Sandra came close and draped her arms around me. She was warm and smelled good, and the feel of her touch was electric with life. She laid her head on my shoulder as we watched the TV.

This time it showed a video of my old bedroom. You could see me—I was probably about five or six—propped up on pillows in my bed. My dad sat beside me with a book in his lap, reading aloud. "*'Real isn't how you are made,' said the Skin Horse. 'It's a thing that happens to you. When a child loves you for a long, long time, not just to play with, but REALLY loves you, then you become Real."*

Sandra jumped suddenly. "Sammy!" she cried.

"What is it, Babe?"

"I don't know! I feel like I swallowed a goldfish."

"Really?"

"I think I just felt the baby move!"

Joshua Harding is an award-winning novelist, short story author, and poet. His fiction has been featured in Writer's Digest, Acidic Fiction, the museum of americana, and most recently the Amazon #1 Bestselling Christmas horror anthology Wight Christmas. He lives in a four-person artists' colony in the woods north of Chicago.

Ancient Tactics

by Mark Reasoner

The war with Mevlokia was still raging after eight long years. With the Kollusians and Rendivians forming the bulk of the Alliance fleet, every officer and crewmember of what remained were hardened veterans. Particularly the Sanaurans, whose planetary system was now the edge of Alliance territory. Sanaura couldn't offer up any ships for its own defense, but their moon-based batteries and satellite weapons were considered among the best and were the Alliance's last line of defense.

Kollusian battle commander, Admiral Dil-Ten Prixas, stood on the bridge of his ship waiting for the next development. One of two things, if not both, were scheduled to happen at any moment. Either the Mevlokians would resume the attack on his out-numbered fleet, or help would arrive in the form of ships from one of the Alliance's newest and most unpredictable members.

"Why do we even bother to ask for their help," Admiral Prixas muttered, looking at the large plotting board displayed at the front of the bridge.

"What was that, Admiral?" Commander Hesh, the executive officer standing next to the Admiral's station said.

"Nothing, Commander," Prixas answered. "Just wondering why the Alliance asks for help from the Terrans. They are usually late, rarely follow orders, and more often than not ignore doctrine and battle plans."

"Some might say that's part of their strength," Hesh said. "Being unpredictable. It's hard for an enemy to figure out what you are doing when you don't even know."

"If you say so, Commander."

"It's like our Sanauran hosts will tell you, sir, war is chaos and the Terrans seem to practice that chaos on a daily basis"

"Long range scans show the Mevlokians regrouping and heading back this way, Admiral," Weapons Officer Ryutrak interrupted. "They still have over forty ships capable of fighting."

"Tell the fleet to close ranks and get ready for another fight," Admiral Prixas said. "This isn't over yet. Contact Captain Orn'Ist'Ol and have him move the Rendivians closer in on the left. They will have to fill in where the Terrans were supposed to be."

"We only have twenty one ships reporting battle ready, sir," the comm officer said.

"It will have to do," the admiral said quietly.

Stationed well above Sanaura, beyond its outer moon, the remaining Alliance star fleet armed weapons and reinforced shielding, doing what they could to be ready for the second Mevlokian attack. During the first part of the battle, each side took out seven opposing ships, so the odds were still against the defenders. Only the long cannons on Sanaura's third moon turned the tide, stopping the attackers from proceeding to the planet.

"Admiral," an officer called, "I show seven ships approaching at point eight sub-light. I think it's the Terran fleet."

"I can confirm," the comm officer said, "And I have their commander."

"Put him on," Admiral Prixas said.

"Howdy, Admiral," Captain James Hawkins said when the connection was established.

"So nice of you to join us," Prixas said, sarcasm dripping from his words. "You're rather late."

"Yeah, sorry about that," Hawkins said, "But we got delayed coming past the Goran nebula. A couple of pulsars were ripping the guts out of the thing."

"So?"

"So we stopped to watch," Hawkins continued, "And you should check it out once this is over."

"I will make a note," Prixas said.

Only these crazies would stop to watch a natural phenomenon while headed into battle, he thought.

"Meanwhile, the Mevlokians are preparing for another attack. I'd like you to reinforce our left flank. Bring your cruisers up to support Captain Orn'Ist'Ol and the Rendivian frigates."

"Nothing personal, Admiral, but I've got another idea. Clear a path for us and then get ready to follow us in. We're coming in hot."

"And why would I do that?" Prixas asked.

"Because if what we're about to do works, things are going to get real ugly, real fast," Hawkins said. "And you want to take advantage."

"They're not slowing down, sir," Commander Hesh, said. "And knowing what they did at Zenthore Prime, I'd recommend doing what Hawkins asks. Terrans tend to be a little crazy in these situations."

Prixas raised his unibrow and looked at Hesh.

"Seriously, Commander?"

"Quite serious, Admiral," Hesh replied. "This man, Hawkins, in particular, hates being told what to do, but tends to get good results."

"Alright. Move Bravo squadron back to allow the Terrans through, then prepare to follow them."

Two of the Terran cruisers broke off and slowed, taking station beside the Rendivians as Prixas originally requested. The other five blasted through the Alliance line in echelon formation and quickly closed the distance to the Mevlokian fleet.

When they were just at the outside of enemy range, the Terran ships broke formation and all five flew off in different directions, circling back around the rejoin the Alliance line, filling the space they'd just passed through.

"What in the name of…" Admiral Prixas muttered. "Get me that Terran idiot," he hollered at the comm officer.

"Hawkins! What in the stars was that about? You just blow through our space at high speed, rush toward the enemy and then do nothing but turn away? What are you thinking?"

"Why aren't you following?" Hawkins retorted, "Opportunity is upon you."

As if on cue, things started happening all along the Mevlokian line.

"Admiral!" Ryutrak called out from his weapons station. "All three ships in the Mevlokian van just went dark. They're just drifting. I show two more ships dropping out of formation on their right flank."

"Put it up," Prixas said. A view of the whole Mevlokian attack fleet now filled the main view screen. On the left wing, a Mevlokian destroyer's starboard propulsion blew away, throwing the ship directly into the path of another destroyer. Both ships exploded in a ball of fire and debris.

Some of the remaining Mevlokian vessels tried to slow and change course, but another three exploded before they could retreat. Their entire first wave was now decimated.

"Great stars!" Prixas said, as he watched the destruction of his enemy.

"Pretty cool, isn't it?" Captain Hawkins said over the open comm.

"What did you do?" Prixas asked.

"I'll tell you later," Hawkins replied, "Right now, you need to take the advantage."

Prixas gave the order to his fleet as the Mevlokians began firing in random directions, missing most of the now advancing Alliance fleet.

Alliance ships broke through the Mevlokian line, and the scene turned to bedlam. A great melee ensued with ships firing at anything that moved. On the left flank, the Rendivians were able to move part way around the invaders, knocking out four trailing ships. After several minutes, the Mevlokians began falling back in disarray.

"Captain Hawkins," Admiral Prixas communicated when the Mevlokian remnants were out of Sanauran space. "Would it be too much to ask what you did?"

"Do we have time?" Hawkins replied. "The Mevlokians will likely regroup and come back."

"We can try," Prixas said, "Can you shuttle over?"

***

Hawkins brought his two senior officers, Commander Wynn Sweeney and Commander Art Billson, along with him to the Kollusian flagship. Prixas greeted the men at the airlock and led them to a conference room where Commander Hesh and Officer Ryutrak joined them.

"What exactly did you do, Captain?"

"Well, Admiral," Hawkins said, reaching into his pocket and placing a handful of small metal pieces on the table. "We took some old-school tech, combined that with a couple of other ideas and brought the result up to modern speed."

"How so?"

Hawkins leaned back in his seat and took a long drink of ale. "This may take a while, so I really hope we have time."

"Centuries ago on our home world," Hawkins continued, "a great scientist figured out how this motion thing worked. Old Mister Newton determined the basic laws and principals of motion and such, and we've been following them ever since."

"Of course you have," Commander Hesh laughed, "Those principals are rather universal."

"And immutable," Officer Ryutrak added.

"And neither are they original with us," Commander Sweeney said. "We know this, and I'll bet you have your own great thinkers who figured this out long before we did."

"Come on, guys," Hawkins said, "I'm telling this story."

Hawkins took a long drink before continuing.

"Anyway, a while later another of our great scientific thinkers figured out the relativity and space-time thing. Einstein worked out these equations that we still use to power our ships and get across the galaxy."

"I understand all this," Admiral Prixas said, "But what does it have to do with your attack on the Mevlokians earlier?"

"Okay, Admiral, here's the deal. First off, consider one of those laws of motion. An object in motion remains in motion, etcetera, etcetera…

"Back on our world, in centuries past when our battles were fought on land, sea, and air, we used this idea to target weapons against an enemy in motion. Basically, we shot at where they would be, not where they were."

Prixas nodded.

"It worked really well in aerial fights," Hawkins said. "We developed a shot that left clusters of little things like these hanging up in the air for enemy flyers to run through. This stuff wrecked havoc."

"And then," Hawkins continued, "There's the thing with matter and energy as our man Albert explained. The two things can be converted into each other, but the sum of both is constant in the universe."

The Kollusians looked confused.

"Yeah, at first I didn't get it either," Hawkins said, "Billson, why don't you explain this part. After all, it was your idea."

"Thanks, Cap'n," Commander Billson said. "Let's start with this. What are all your weapons based on?"

"Energy, I suppose," Ryutrak said. "Our shields are plasma-magnetic, our cannons fire phased energy blasts, and so on."

"Exactly," Billson said, "Ours too for the most part, thanks to some help from you and other friends in the alliance."

"And that's the thing," he continued, "We're leaving half the equation on the table. We've got all the matter to use."

"Except there isn't that much out here," Commander Hesh interrupted.

"There's enough," Billson said. "And that's what we thought of. If we could send pieces of matter at sufficient velocity, we might be able to wreck some havoc on an adversary, or at the least confuse them."

"Therein lies the problem," Hawkins said.

"What problem?" Prixas asked.

"We had no intention of causing physical damage," Hawkins said, "Though it was a nice surprise."

"*What?*" Prixas exclaimed.

"Our intention was to just mess up their sensors," Sweeney said. "We were hoping all these little things heading toward them at high speed would confuse the Mevlokians and they would start firing every which way. They did do some of that,"

"Yes they did," Hesh said.

"We had to figure out what happened afterward," Billson said. "And though the science works, it probably shouldn't have."

"So you are saying this was just an accident?" Prixas asked.

"Pretty much," Hawkins said. "And I seriously doubt it will work a second time. The Mevlokians will probably figure out what we did and be ready for it."

"Do you have any salvos left?" Ryutrak asked.

"Maybe two or three."

"That might be enough if the Mevlokians come back."

"I don't think so," Prixas said. "But it will help. Beyond that, we'll just have to form a tighter defense and be ready."

"Admiral," Hawkins said, "Are you open to another idea?"

"I am, particularly if it works as well as your first one."

"No guarantees, but it's worked in the past."

"Another ancient tactic?" Hesh asked with a small smile.

"Hey, sometimes old school is best," Billson answered.

"I am sorry to have to ask," Hawkins said, "But who is on the right flank?"

"A squadron of our ships and the small Qintaxi fleet." Hesh answered.

"Would their commander be up for a little misdirection?" Hawkins asked.

"What do you have in mind?" Prixas said.

Hawkins quickly explained his idea, ending with the request to get the Qintaxi Commander on a three-way secure transmission once the Terrans returned to their ship.

Qintaxi Commodore, Ith-Lune Diamma, quickly agreed. The ploy would commence as soon as the Mevlokian fleet was spotted.

***

"Here they come," Ryutrak reported to the whole fleet.

Hawkins opened an un-encrypted channel to both the Kollusian and Qintaxi flagships ordering a change in the formation on the Alliance right flank. Commodore Diamma disagreed vociferously and a vicious argument quickly started. In less than a minute, insults flew from the Terran commander directed at the Qintaxi, and Diamma cut communications. One by one, the Qintaxi ships began moving away and disappearing into hyperspace.

The Mevlokians saw this and moved their left wing to take advantage of the now open Alliance right.

Hawkins was right about the Mevlokians figuring out the previous maneuver. Even though the Terran cruisers darted ahead once again to lay out their field of projectiles directed at the Mevlokian vanguard, nothing happened as all the objects were easily deflected away.

It looked like the Mevlokians would break through the Alliance line when the Qintaxi returned, blinking out of hyperspace just behind their old position, now in the rear of the Mevlokian left wing. They came in with all weapons blazing and quickly destroyed the enemy ships on that side of the battle line.

The Terran cruisers took the opportunity to blast through between the Mevlokian left and center forces, distracting the center from going to their comrades' aid. Hawkins even took out one of the larger Mevlokian destroyers in the process.

With the left in complete disarray, the Kollusian fleet attacked the center en-masse. Though outnumbered and out gunned, the ships carefully picked targets to create pathways through the Mevlokian line swinging back around to attack again from the rear. Admiral Prixas lost four of his ships this way, but took out seven enemy vessels. Not a bad trade.

The battle raged for over two hours. The Alliance lost a total of six ships, most in the slugfest at the center. The Mevlokians lost twenty-three ships, including their flagship. When it blew up under consistent attack by both the Kollusians and the Terrans, the remaining enemy ships broke off and retreated.

The Alliance fleet also backed away, but only as far as the outer Sanauran moon, taking shelter under the large cannons. Only after long-range scans showed the Mevlokians beyond range did Admiral Prixas order a stand down and allow all ships to secure from battle stations.

Then he invited all the fleet commanders to a celebratory dinner on the Kollusian flagship.

***

All the fleet commanders, along with other officers, and two representatives from Sanaura, gathered in the Kollusian mess hall. The last to arrive was Commodore Diamma and her second in command.

She stormed into the room. Her usually deep brown eyes blazed red, and her withered pale green face flushed pink. As she approached Captain Hawkins, she raised one of her four arms as if to strike the Terran Captain down.

In an instant, however, she changed, and grabbed Hawkins in a smothering hug, her face now beaming with a wide smile.

"*Centauri Slime Lizard?*" she exclaimed. "*Amoebic Dysentery run Rampant? A Steaming Heap of Krindollian Fecal Matter?* Good Galaxies, man! Where did you ever come up with those?"

Pon-Cla Fanstron, the officer accompanying the Commodore placed two of his hands over his mouth to hide his laughter.

"I had some help,. Ma'am," Hawkins said, "But mostly picked them up through travelling the galaxy."

"Well, they certainly worked," Diamma said. "Though I had to look them up, and my bridge crew was hard pressed to contain their laughter."

She turned to Admiral Prixas. "And then *you* questioned our commitment to the Alliance. I know you didn't mean it, but *really* Din?"

"It did sound good," Prixas said shrugging, "And it worked."

"Indeed it did," Rendivian Captain, Orn'Ist'Ol, said. "But I must ask Captain Hawkins. How could you be sure it would?"

"I couldn't," Hawkins replied. "But I thought the odds were good. The Mevlokians didn't seem to be a cautious lot, so I felt it was a good bet they would get sucked into the gap on the flank."

"At worst," Commander Sweeney added, "The disappearance and then re-appearance of the Qintaxi fleet would rattle them and put them off their plan."

"Did you have an alternate plan?" Commander Hesh asked. "A back-up, as I believe you call it?"

"Not really," Hawkins answered. "I thought about asking the Rendivians to try the same vanishing trick, but fortunately never had to."

"Captain Hawkins," Captain Orn'Ist'Ol said. "I am as happy as everyone here with how things turned out today, but I do have to say that I am also confused. Your total battle plan was completely illogical and made absolutely no sense. May I ask what you were thinking?"

Hawkins was saved by the announcement that dinner was ready.

"After dinner," Hawkins told the Rendivian on the way to their seats.

***

After the meal had been cleared away, with drinks in hand, the captains and commanders sat at the table reliving the day's actions and telling stories of previous battles.

Captain Orn'Ist'Ol stood up and ask everyone to be still.

"The time has come," she said, "For our friend, Captain Hawkins, to tell us how he devised his rather unorthodox strategy."

"You did, after all, promise me, sir," she continued, speaking directly to the Terran.

"If you insist," Hawkins said, standing.

"First of all, you must understand that my world has over ten thousand years of recorded history, of which all but a few hundred consisted of wars and conflicts. It is from these that we learned most of the lessons we apply to the present."

"If we learned them at all," Commander Billson interjected. The others chuckled.

Hawkins was not dismayed. "My friend is right. If we learned the lessons. And we didn't for many centuries. We went through much before we finally came together and united ourselves to reach out for the stars."

"Anyway," Hawkins continued, "I am a student of our history, and I recalled some things that I believed might help us out today. The first was a small thing from a conflict between two sides of the same nation-state. In this conflict, there was a General who had a very bad habit of showing up late for battles and not being where he was expected. His name was Buell, and fortunately for him, his arrival always seemed to turn things in favor of his side in the conflict."

"It's hard to prepare for an enemy who doesn't do what you expect," Admiral Prixas said.

Hawkins nodded and continued his story.

"Less than a century after this conflict, we had our last world-wide conflict. A great General from that war, George Patton, famously said, *No battle plan survives contact with the enemy intact.* By this he meant we must always be ready to adjust, adapt, and sometimes ad-lib."

"Was that what you were thinking when you showed up late?" Hesh asked. "Were you emulating your General Buell?"

"Not precisely," Hawkins answered. "Though I did think that if we came late, the Mevlokians would not be ready for whatever we did."

"And we also thought being a bit late would allow us to look things over," Sweeney added. "We believed we could better react to whatever was happening."

"And the pulsars ripping the nebula apart *was* pretty cool," Billson added.

"All well and good," Diamma said. "And certainly effective. But what about the argument with me and asking us to leave the field?"

"That was trickier," Hawkins said. "For that, I drew upon one of the key battles from that world-wide conflict I mentioned. In the battle we call *Midway,* one group of fighting flyers got lost and ended up arriving late. But because of this, their enemy was not prepared to counter an additional attack, particularly one different from the attacks they were fighting off at the moment. That group of late arrivals not only turned the tide of the battle, but resulted is such a momentous victory that the entire nature of that theatre of war changed."

"But you couldn't do that, today," Diamma said.

"No I couldn't," Hawkins replied. "We didn't have any reserves to show up late. But what about convincing the Mevlokians that part of the Alliance Fleet was leaving the battle? If some ships just left, they would probably have been suspicious. But if we gave them a convincing reason…"

"Thus the argument and insults over an open channel," Diamma said.

"And thankfully, they fell for it," Prixas said. "Well done, sir."

"Thank you, Admiral," Hawkins said. "I do suppose, however, that everything worked today because things really don't change over time. An ancient tactic that worked once can many times work again."

After sitting silent all evening, one of the Sanauran representatives rose and asked to speak.

"My friends," she said, "It has been a great honor and a great pleasure to be here with you. Our world is forever in your debt for your actions today protecting us from invasion. I assure you all that if ever called upon by the Alliance, we will do whatever we can to defend another world just as you defended us today."

The others answered with polite applause.

"I would also like to propose a toast," the Sanauran continued, raising her glass.

"First, to our fallen comrades. They did not die in vain. Next, to Admiral Dil-Ten Prixas and the Kollusian fleet who shouldered the greatest part of the burden today. And to Captain Orn'Ist'Ol and the Rendivians who held their line as steadfastly as anyone could. To Commodore Ith-Lune Diamma and the Qintaxi, who played the great game of deception that changed the battle.

"And finally, to Captain Jack Hawkins and the Terrans, who showed us all so well that war is chaos, and that victory goes to the one who practices that chaos. Raise your glasses my friends."

Mark Reasoner is a Hoosier by birth, a teacher by profession and a storyteller by nature. His previous stories have appeared in various publications and he is also a two-time winner of the Royal Palms Literary Award from the Florida Writers Association. He currently lives and writes in Neptune Beach, Florida.

Courier of the Skies

by Cait Gordon

Painful, vibrating heat intensifies in the soles of my feet. I had to switch to the backup accelerator on the forklift that wheeled the cargo pods aboard my ship. The pressure on the ball of my right foot had been excruciating when I'd floored the pedal to navigate the cargo as quickly as possible. Now, back in the cockpit, I gently flex and release my toes. It's hard to believe foot-triggered mechanisms had once been the standard, before hovering vessels began replacing ground-crawlers. I've no idea why Jaqueline had even rigged this archaic "lifter" for me when there are so many alternatives these days. *Oh yeah. To piss me off.*

Jerk. Last time I turn to an ex when I desperately need a mechanic. Amicable breakup, my dimpled disabled butt.

At least Drea, my beloved soul friend, loves me and my ship equally. That's important. Her mods got me soaring again. *I know, I know, I have a thing for aerospace mechanics.* Which reminds me, I need to ask her to configure a secondary accel for the forklift that I can manipulate with my hand in case voice-activation pooches out. My left fingers can still apply some pressure without searing my knuckles. Drea knows just how to adapt tech so my fingers can fing. She gets me. In more ways than I can count.

I check my tracking console. Nobody's following this time. That allows me a hearty exhale as I detach my seat from the cockpit, swivel, then lock it in place to keep it steady as I stand.

Yowch. My ankles and knees join my soles in a symphony of bilateral neuropathic current. It's like someone's implanted burning tongs into my pressure points and told them to hum.

Apex, my parental unit, as I affectionately call xyr, wants me to stop piloting these runs. Xe keeps reminding me about how the life expectancy of a courier is "a few minutes from now," but I'm not giving it up. My obstinacy hones my focus to seek out every opportunity and ally who's willing to help the Network.

But Drea, she would just softly kiss my brow and ask me what I needed to complete the next run. No panic, no lectures. I could have dealt with a little argument, but it's not her style. Not for this, anyway. Yet, wreck her mods carelessly, and I'd unleash the scowl of all scowls, then total silence until she had finished repairs. It's not the silent treatment, though. Just concentration. She likes her tech in working order, in top condition. That's probably why I'm called upon so much. My ship's always at the ready. Sometimes I feel this is also part of her love language.

Gazing at the narrow ribbons of moving light before me, I think about how it's bizarre that we have achieved space travel—but only for some. Then again, the quadrant is run by Welliam. That's not one person, but the nickname we Disabled, Deaf, Blind, and NeuroFabulous folks have given the eugenics-based oppressors who pass for a "benevolent" leadership. You know, as in *"I* am well." Once the Wellies had trampled their way into power (after bribing or blackmailing whoever was in their way), assistive tech was doled out as a symbol of pity and limited only to devices that would keep us "comfortably safe" at home. The sky is off limits. Folks like me must remain housebound if we are to exist at all. And we should be grateful for any and every crumb tossed our way.

Frik that noise. Multitudes had bought into it, too. Even some of my disabled buds, until I convinced them it was sheer excrement.

So, no, I'm not going to stop being a courier. And I'm grateful Drea will never ask me to either. I miss her. This has been a long run.

I wince. It seems like my legs are in *status: nope* today. I lock the handles attached to my seat and decide I'll sit instead of push-walking. I can hover in chair mode, but my head's spinning, and I prefer to feel connected to the deck. The gliding wheels suit me fine at present.

I maneuver the chair and roll over to a side console. Right on time, my wristband vibrates. *Ow. Why did I even wear it?*

Incoming. I initiate the command to project it on the viewscreen.

"Ciara?" It's Margo Faria, Team Leader of our division.

"Give me a sec," I reply. "Captions aren't on." I execute another command. "Okay, should be good to go. What's up?"

"My blood pressure, obviously," says Margo. Her words appear under the image of her haggard face. I still think she's beautiful. Worn out, but lovely. Although her silver and black hair looks like it's conspiring to break out of her topknot like rebels from a prison hold.

"I know," I say. "I'm not far out. Had a little trouble at the last checkpoint. I couldn't hear what they were saying, and Lady Voss couldn't transcribe." Voice-On-Screen-System. I like nicknaming stuff.

Margo folds her arms across her chest, the silver triple-spoon crest glaring from her midnight-blue uniform. I instinctively stare down at my legs. The nondescript beige jumpsuit has seen better days, but it marks me as a typical transport pilot, and doesn't arouse suspicion as I go about my business. Margo's eyes are piercing, and the subsequent chill causes me to pull my brown leatherette jacket tighter across my torso.

"Did they suspect you?" she asks, then purses her lips.

"For a moment, yeah." I slide a hand over my silver buzz cut. My head is the only part of me that doesn't look scruffy. "I guessed I was giving Border Patrol answers that were way off. I could barely make out their lips under those semi-translucent helmets."

"They wear those on purpose, you know. They often can tell when someone is reading on screen. They've all kinds of methods to catch those of us who are escaping our homeworlds."

"Yeah. Can't have us roaming the galaxy with notions that we have as much of a right to the skies as anyone else." *Bloody Wellies. Well, there's a lot of us out here, frikfaces, so brace yourselves. We couriers will continue running for the Network.*

Margo pulls a wisp of hair from in front of her golden-brown eyes. "How did you manage to fool them?"

"Lady Voss hiccupped but got back online. I casually said it must have been a garbled cross-transmission because of comm traffic. I'd chosen a checkpoint at a high-usage course on purpose. Anyway, I laid down the spin pretty hard. You know, using my arsenal of charms and wiles?"

Margo stared, then lowered her eyelids.

I smacked my lips. "Uh, yeah. So, um, like I said, I'm not far."

"Get here… two days ago."

"Sorry. Time travel is not my forte."

She glares again. I don't think my charms and wiles will ever have any effect on Margo. Probably why she's head of this part of the Network.

"Ciara—"

"I'll be there two days ago. I promise."

"Good. Margo out."

At least I think I'm not far out. Technically, I'll be out of jump-speed in about 30 minutes. After that, it should be smooth sailing. As long as Welliam's vermin haven't followed me or set up another checkpoint.

Before my mind spirals in a flurry of possibilities to the point where I forget where I am in space and time, it chooses to focus on what gives me intense pleasure. Food. When I'd checked my nutrition stores before initial takeoff, I'd discovered Drea had stowed a huge slab of chocolate cream triple-tier cake. Paid too much for it—a waste of her ration stubs—but I know she didn't count the cost. I can almost hear her say, "Deceiving Wellies deserves a little cake." I mean, that's not wrong. Besides, once I rendezvous with Margo's team, the menu will be squashed guck in plastic bags.

I wheel over to the mini-fridge and bark out, "Open cold storage!" The door opens and tray-lights reveal my delectable reward. "Spork!" I cry, and a cabinet drawer opens. Not sure why there's only one item in it, but I reach in, take the utensil, then grab the plate.

A blast to the hull shakes my microcosm. Fortunately, the chair stays firmly in place because of the fail-safe latching feature Drea added. *Thanks, hon. You're the best.*

Still, I curse how these Wellie hemorrhoids have learned to fire weapons at jump-speed. Another blast.

"Shield status," I yell while tapping my right ear to engage my hearing aid. Figure it might not matter about hiding them now that the Wellies are onto me.

"Shields holding at 75%," says Shirl, my ship's brain. I named her after my best friend, who had died five years ago while running for the Network. Great courier, too. We all know the risks, but it doesn't offer much solace because grief is a bitch. Still, having another Shirl in my life comforts me.

I gobble down some cake. Not even Welliam is gonna deny me my foodgasm. My torso nearly collapses at this rare delicacy. But a few bites are all I will allow myself. I put my plate back into the mini fridge and shove the spork inside my jacket pocket.

WHAM! Yet another blast threatens my demise.

"Right. Where are these turds?"

"Sending coordinates," says Shirl.

My wristband vibrates, and I yelp, then remove it from my pressure point. The readout spells imminent disaster. Guess my wiles really need a tune-up after all.

"Cloak us and send encrypted message to Margo's team."

A pause.

"Cloaking engaged," says Shirl. "What is the message?"

"Tracked by Wellies. Heading to the moon." That's code for escaping to the first safe place available.

"Transmission sent."

"Can we change course now?"

"Too dangerous. We must complete the jump cycle or risk irreparable damage to the hull."

I take a moment. So far, no more blasts. That's a good sign. We won't re-emerge for 20 more minutes.

"Once we're out of jump, set course for anywhere but here."

"Understood, Captain."

I sit in place and do that "weird thing with my lips," as Drea often says. A habit when I'm pondering, along with blinking my eyes while I'm reaching a decision. I stare at the fridge.

Oh, what the frik, if this is my time, I'm going down with an entire belly full of chocolate cream triple-tier.

By the time I head back to the cockpit, sated, and braced for whatever, my ship's AI reveals a reply from Margo:

"Message received. Going to paradise instead. A Welliam convoy showed up at our designated rendezvous. Our ships were cloaked and undetected, so we jumped home. Head home, Ciara."

Home. That's Topia, our base. I rub my eyes. This is a massive course change, and my meagre ship needs to uncloak during jump transitions. We can send messages while at hyper-speed, but that's about it. Then I remember Drea said she was working on a fix since there wasn't currently one in place for vessels like mine. Could really use it too. If our current jump ends with us near a Wellian outpost, I'm pretty much sporked the moment we re-emerge and resume standard speed. *Whoopie.*

My chair rolls into place and the wheels retract, locking the unit back into its role as a cockpit seat. I know I'm doing that lip thing again, but don't care. There's really no time to ponder. I need to deliver this cargo, come Wellie or high water.

"Okay, Shirl, we're changing trajectory before coming out of jump."

"Captain, I strongly recommend—"

"We've no choice. We'll be blasted into microns by the multitude the moment we uncloak. Let's do this."

"The chances of survival for changing course for a ship of this design are—"

"Worth risking. Put everything you can spare on the shields and make up the rest as you go."

"Captain, I will require us to do multiple jumps before we get to…home."

"I know. I trust you, Shirl."

Another pause. "Very well, Captain. Should this ship be destroyed in the process, I will say now that it has been a pleasure running with you."

I smile, not really sure if Shirl actually experiences pleasure yet, but it's nice to read. "Samesies."

"New course plotted and ready to initiate."

"Do it."

***

Right, so that worked. I think. My head is kinda spinny. Maybe I got knocked out?

"Shirl?"

"Yes, Captain?"

"Am I dead?"

"Do you mean that in a metaphoric way or would you like a physical assessment?"

If there were a camera recording us, I would be staring straight at it. "Shirl? Did you just make a funny?"

"I tried, Captain."

"Well done!"

"You have been unconscious for 19.573 minutes. I would say this is typical of such a manoeuvre if only it had been attempted several times. Or at all."

"Fair." I touch my face, blink my eyes, wiggle my toes, and straighten in my chair. Ouch. But that's a regular ouch. Feeling optimistic as a whole. "Shall we head to Topia?"

"Course plotted. I was awaiting your command."

"Hm. I think we can make a rule that if I'm knocked out, you have my consent to reach our final destination."

"Acknowledged."

"Let's go."

My console lights up like stringed bulbs at a summer festival.

"Incoming," says Shirl. "Ten enemy fighters. We are outgunned and outnumbered."

Maybe I should have programmed her to learn vocal inflections that actually reflect urgent situations, but I blocked that skill path that because it triggers my anxiety. Now I almost want to laugh at her casual tone. Almost.

"I see them." I try to mimic her calm while my heart stays lodged in my esophagus.

"They're hailing us."

"Hailing? A fighter formation? That's a courtesy not usually offered."

"On speaker?"

"Yes, but add captions near their eye level." I remove my hearing aids. It's worth a try, anyway.

"Transmitting."

The comm crackles and my console displays: "Rogue transport, this is Commander Muskrat of the Eugenics Special Forces. Identify or be destroyed."

Ah yes, ESF. We've dubbed them the Demons of Death. They hunt us couriers down like vermin. Well, at least I got to eat cake.

I clear my throat. "This is Transport Minor Class 7329, Pilot Blake speaking." Blake was my childhood pet. Loved that mutt.

"Pilot Blake, what is the nature of your cargo?"

"They said it was backup battery casings for comm modules, Commander."

There's a slight pause. "For what sort of ships?"

"Um, I'm not really tech savvy, to be honest, Commander. Maybe for fighter thingies? I know it was for the ESF."

Shirl has a display of my vitals open to give me biofeedback, so I can fool their scans if they're monitoring me. The readouts are within normal range. *What a smooth liar you are. No wonder I never beat you at cards.* Please brain, no memories of Drea. Not now. It only makes the idea of leaving her worse.

"Something bothering you, pilot? I just detected a spike in your heart rate."

"Yeah, sorry. Just thought about my partner, and it triggered a memory. Had a spat before I left." My rule: lie as close to the truth as possible.

Silence. Then: "It wouldn't have anything to do with the fact you jumped away from a security point, would it?"

Crap.

"And that you're actually a courier for the Network?"

Crap crap.

"The rules are simple, pilot. Couriers are enemies of the state. They bring helpless citizens false hope of a freedom they do not require. Those of us who are well know what's best for them. If you are not well and part of this vile rebellion, you must be destroyed without trial. Your mission is cruelty and a moral crime against the infirm."

Our mission is—is this guy kidding?

"Those are our orders. Be prepared to be boarded."

Crappity-crap on the biggest cracker.

"Pilot? Open your cross-through coupling port."

So, I'm not doing that. I need to stall. Wish I could escape, but there's no way out. *Okay, just think. There's always a solution to every problem. I've believed that since ever.*

"Captain?" says Shirl.

"Not now, please. I have to figure a way out of this mess."

"But Captain, I must ask you if you still have your spork."

"Huh, my what?"

"The spork that Andrea packed with your dessert."

"Shirl, this is no time to discuss cutlery. If you wanna help, run a probability routine. I'm trying to use my meat computer."

"But I require the utensil to engage the new module Andrea installed in this vessel."

"Pilot," barked the commander. "You will activate the coupling or be destroyed."

And there go my vitals heading into chaos. "The new what?" I pant my words to Shirl. "Uh, it's in my pocket."

A slot opens and extends by my right knee. With a spork-shaped circuit insert.

"This is your last chance, Pilot!"

I use my shirt to rub the utensil clean—and grin like a supervillain.

***

Under a cloudless sky, trees like skyscrapers sway in the summer breeze. Flocks of multi-coloured avian creatures fly overhead while others rest on gigantic green fronds. Deep in the towering grasses, where wildflowers spread their wide canopies of vibrant petals, stands a compound of diminutive buildings. On most planets and moons, their construction would be of average size, but on Topia, they resemble a toy village.

On the edge of the city limits of this paradise is the landing strips and bays, and behind those are the headquarters of one of the many outposts of the Network. Out of a wide window in a dominant edifice, Margo stares, the worry showing in the fine lines around her mouth.

Ciara has been long overdue. Far too long.

Margo shakes her head, then returns to her desk. There are many couriers in the Network, and she can't afford to dwell on one when others needed her support. Dismissing losses and moving forward is the part of her job she hates most. She inhales deeply and opens a channel to a meeting requiring her immediate attention.

Newly fixated on the screen, she doesn't notice the re-entry of a battered vessel about to make its landing on the strip.

***

"Ah, there's the pulse of my heart," I say out loud, noticing Drea hopping and clapping as we touch down. I love those traits of hers. The makeshift shelter tells me she's been waiting for me. I wouldn't put it past her to have been staying out here instead of our quarters, anticipating my arrival. *Sorry I'm late, honey. Traffic was terrible.*

My ship opens to reveal a ramp to my cargo bay. I unlatch my seat and wheel myself to find Drea bolting right for me, dressed in grey coveralls with endless tools and pockets attached to them. She greets me with an enthusiastic kiss, and her soft, platinum curls tickle my cheeks. The sweet caress is short-lived, followed immediately by a dressing down for nearly wrecking *her* ship.

"Okay, you mechanics are far too possessive," I say, rubbing her calloused fingertips. "It's still *my* ship, you know."

"You pilots don't appreciate the masterpieces we create," Drea retorts.

"Untrue. We just take larger risks because remaining alive and scolded by a gorgeous nerd is better than the alternative."

She sticks her tongue out. It feels so good to laugh.

"And thanks," I say. "For the cake."

"The mod worked? That pulse rendered their navigations systems inert?"

"Like a charm," I say.

"Then why does my ship look like it's scorched?"

"When I came out of the first jump after encountering ESF, I wanted a minute to figure out the state of my ship before we continued home. So, I landed on a nearby moon within a forest fire. The hull held up really well, considering. And the ship was cool as a summer breeze inside."

There's that adorable scowl.

"Hey," I say, "I just risked life and limb and your unique brand of ire to deliver this cargo!"

Scowl vanishes. "And the team is already here, unloading, my captain."

"Good. Glad they're the ones handling the forklift, because *about those foot pedals…*"

Drea pulls out a tablet and swipes her finger along its surface. "Yup, adding it to the list under 'fix every-frikking-thing my babes destroyed.'"

I shake my head. She winks and gestures at me to follow her.

Relief sweeps through my soul. I made it. Thanks to Shirl and maybe a cake-fuelled leap of faith. But we're here. The cargo is intact.

A most precious delivery.

The tech in these pods will help others like us to fly.

The Network is growing.

We won't be denied the skies.

We will soar.

Cait Gordon is a Canadian autistic, disabled, and queer author of speculative fiction that celebrates diversity. Her latest novel is the disability-hopepunk adventure, *Season One: Iris and the Crew Tear Through Space!* She also co-edited the award-nominated *Nothing Without Us* and the award-winning *Nothing Without Us Too* disability fiction anthologies.

The Ghost in the Machine

by Fern K L Goodliffe

The cometskipper class transport ship *Blue Rufus* was five months out of one system, eleven months to their destination, when the lights in cargo hold D started flickering and flaring. Izem and Mac investigated and could find no fault.

"Gremlins," Mac sniffed, and Izem shook his head and rolled his eyes, never quite sure whether Mac was joking or genuinely believed in the supernatural.

Fresh-faced Aella, who'd joined the crew with the last set of cargo, said she could hear strange banging from her bunk, a small room above the same cargo hold. Mac laughed and suggested Tommyknockers.

***

Ten months to the destination, and the flickering lights had become so normal the crew generally ignored them. Outside the cargo hold, the corridor lights were less responsive to motion than normal, and when they did come on would come on too bright or too dim, and often flickered out.

Elodie noticed a strange, sickly smell among the plants. She didn't pay much attention to it.

Izem couldn't find his spanner. He decided not to tell Mac; he'd noticed his long-term colleague seemed particularly grumpy this run. It showed up under Elodie's pillow.

***

Nine months to destination, and Aella was late to breakfast. When she arrived, she looked pale, her normal gold-tan skin washed out. Captain Fae Lin-Brown raised an eyebrow, and the young woman started apologising. "I'm so sorry. I just, I couldn't sleep. The banging? It was *awful* last night, like something trying to break in."

"Ha, having trouble with the tommyknockers," Mac started to laugh, then stopped, "although, you are right above cargo D. Perhaps it's the Passengers."

"Mac." There was a note of warning in Frey's voice.

Aella's startled response ran over it. "Passengers? You think we have stowaways?"

Mac laughed again. "Nah. No, Sweetie. Not stowaways. Not living ones, anyway."

"Mac." Frey's tone was firmer, but Mac carried on anyway.

"There's the coffin hold in cargo D. We're carrying dead people."

"A coffin hold? There's dead bodies?"

"Not bodies. Cremated remains."

"It's not a hold for coffins," Izem explained. "It's an old smuggling hole that's about the size of a coffin."

"Smuggling hole? What?"

"They're old," Frey reassured her, "that's the only one in use. The ship used to occasionally carry dubious cargo," he glanced at Mac, who smirked a little, "but not anymore."

"We stopped using them because most of them aren't easy to get at. Probably only me and Fae know where they all are," Mac continued.

"We don't carry Passengers often, but think if your mum or dad or someone travelled away and died, you'd want their remains to come home, right?" Aella nodded, and Frey continued, "there's not always Passengers to take, but they don't take up much space and people are grateful for the service."

"And the pay's good." Mac needed the last word.

***

Eight months to destination. The idea of a ghost had taken hold; most of the crew treated it as a joke, but to Aella it felt painfully real. She lay awake, trying to remember she didn't believe in ghosts, as something seemed to pound on the walls around her.

There's a lot of free time on long distance hauls like this. When there was no work to do on the ship or cargo, the crew played games or watched films in the lounge, worked out in the gym, or wandered through the narrow corridors of *Blue Rufus*. As captain, Fae often held herself apart. Mac was the only crew member who'd been onboard with her before her promotion. She'd been a bit of a joker, then, and they'd got on well. Then she'd taken over when the old captain retired, and that wall had gone up. He saw glimpses beyond it sometimes, when they were in port and she was with friends, but never with the crew. It stung that this included with him. It stung as the rest of the old crew changed over until he was the only one remaining, and she promoted newcomer Frey over him.

It was a small crew, but versatile. Aella was dragged around by each of the older crew to be taught their interests and specialities. Her lack of sleep was showing in how much she could take in; even Izem started to feel frustrated with her, as she dropped the fine tool he'd asked her to work with and it had to be carefully fished out of the system of piping they were mending. The pipes rattled and banged, but they couldn't find what was causing the strange cold spots.

***

Seven months. The sickly smell that Elodie had noticed among the planters appeared in other parts of the ship. She'd have ignored it as absent-mindedness when a knife she was using wasn't where she expected, except she alone knew of Izem's similar experiences.

***

Six months. The banging didn't come to Aella's room every night, but sometimes was accompanied by a rattling that seemed to mimic the cadence of speech. The quiet nights, she lay awake in the blackness waiting for the sound to commence, her ear filling the void with other imagined noises.

***

Five months to go. Scratching in the dark, so quiet at first Aella could believe it wasn't real. It seemed to come closer, getting louder, sounding more and more like paws or claws scraping against the inside of the walls, coming from all around. She shouted "lights!" and all that came out was a strangled whimper. She curled as centrally in her bed as she was able, gasping and shrieking as the sounds got louder, must surely break through at any point and leave her facing…

Silence. She stayed alert, her only motion the rise and fall of desperate lungs and her shifting gaze. The silence remained for an eternity, but as she started to calm, she heard a background hum of ship systems, the normal sleep time sounds.

"Lights," her voice was small and crackly, but the system responded. She squinted against the brightness, "dimmer." Her voice sounded closer to normal; she wrapped her blankets around her and crawled out of her bunk. The dimly lit corridor seemed to stretch to eternity, but felt preferable to the coffin-sized room she'd left. Timid steps became more confident as she made her way to the little lounge and passed out on the sofa.

***

Four months. The scratching was as common as the banging now. Aella started sleeping in the lounge as often as she could get away with, setting an alarm to ensure she was up before anyone else to hide the evidence. Mac, however, enjoyed a late night horror film and the nights he watched those forced her to her bunk, when all the sounds would start again. The lights didn't always work, a sickly smell Elodie would recognise flooded the small space, and the temperature plummeted. She became paler and sicker.

Elodie caught her nodding off among the planters and got the story out of her.

"I'll talk to Fae. I'm sure we can switch you to a different bunk."

A loud crash caused them both to flinch, and Elodie to curse in her mother tongue. They looked around to see the herb planter overturned, leaves and soil scattered along the pathway. Elodie cursed again. They walked over, Aella slightly behind.

"Did you hear that?" Breathless with fear.

"What?" Elodie looked back at her.

"I... I thought I heard laughter."

Fae was happy for the bunk switch, hoping it would put superstitious thoughts from Aella's head. The new bunk was near Mac's. He helped her move her things over, and they locked up her old space. She shuddered, and he patted her shoulder awkwardly.

"Never seen a poltergeist before. Heard of 'em, of course, but we've not had one here before."

The lights flickered as if on cue.

Frey reached them in time to overhear his comment. "Don't scare her." He turned to Aella. "There's no poltergeist. There's no such thing as ghosts. We'll track down whatever was making the noise. Now, get to your new bunk and get some sleep."

While she obeyed, Mac helped Elodie clean up the spilled planter. "You got sage here?"

She nodded.

"Interesting that this is the one to spill, then. Spirits, specially the mean ones, they tend not to like sage. Or so the story goes."

Leaving her with the thought, he joined Izem in checking again the mechanical and electrical systems around Aella's old bunk. Frey asked her help to empty and clean cargo hold D, then re-stow all the goods, making sure they were secure.

"Is this really worthwhile? You can't believe it was loose cargo?" The thought of a malevolent spirit was hard to shift.

"Why not? It's not a ghost. We should stop joking about ghosts."

"Yeah, but why would stowed cargo be moving? There's nothing to make it move."

Frey paused, stood straight. "You have a better idea? Mac and Izem have been through the wires already and found nothing – and it's not a ghost."

With no answer, Elodie shivered and turned back to hefting crates, biting her lip. She'd worked with Frey long enough to see that, despite his front, he was nervous. It fed into her own growing fear, but she didn't want him to see.

There was that strange scent again, sickly sweet like dying flowers. She decided not to mention it.

In the corridor above, Izem and Mac had taken down panels to look through the wiring and pipework outside Aella's original bunk. Izem worked quietly, checking and testing each section before reattaching the panel and moving to the next. Mac, meanwhile cursed and grunted and clattered. After a time, he grabbed drinks for them both and squatted next to his friend.

"Yer quiet."

Izem shook out the riot in his brain. "Sorry. Worrying." He took a big gulp of tea, turned to look at Mac. "You seen anything weird?"

Mac sighed, tapping a finger against his cup. "I'm not sure."

"You actually think it's a ghost? Not all in her head?"

"Poltergeist. Ahh, I dunno. Maybe. She's a little older than normal, but not too much."

"You think she brought it then? I thought you thought it was the Passengers?"

Mac pulled a face. "I don't know. I've heard of hauntings. Could be her presence woke something in one of them, could be it was already attached and got bored out here."

"Could be she's imagining it."

"You really believe that?" Mac's expression turned to a fierce sort of focus as he studied Izem's response.

Izem's stomach clenched under the gaze, and he stuttered before shaking his head. "No. No, I don't think she is." He sighed deeply, staring into his cup. "It's not just the lights, it's not just things falling over. There's the cold spots." Mac nodded eagerly. "And. Ugh. I'm missing a screwdriver. I keep losing tools. Didn't say anything because I knew you'd be annoyed, and they show up. Longest I've waited was a week. And Elodie said some of her things have been moved around." He paused again. Mac stayed silent, watching. "Do you think Aella's messing us around?"

The lights flickered and went greenish, giving Mac's scrutiny a sinister edge. It lasted a second or two, then the lights returned to their normal hue for the time of day. "You'd need to know the ship pretty well, I reckon. Nah, don't think the waif's got it in her."

"Well what do we do, then?"

"That is the question."

Fae had done her best to stay out of the ghost talk. She'd tried to turn conversation to other topics when it came up at mealtimes, but after Aella's relocation realised that wasn't working. Once Aella was awake again and the rest of the crew had finished their explorations, she called everyone together in the small lounge. Izem and Elodie settled together on one sofa, Mac and Aella taking the other. Fae sat in an armchair, and rather than taking the other, Frey perched on the arm of it. To Mac he looked smug, and the simmering jealousy he'd felt since the man he still saw as a newcomer had been promoted over him roiled briefly.

"I know you're all feeling a lot of anxiety at the moment," Fae's tone was calm and commanding, "I wanted to try and reassure you. Now, I don't believe in ghosts. I've seen some strange things out on these long hauls, and I've carried Passengers many times, and I've never seen a ghost." She paused, but her tone and posture showed this was a speech and she was not ready for interruptions, so the crew stayed quiet. "Here's what I think is going on. I think there is an electrical fault." She held up a hand as Izem and Mac both straightened, ready to argue. "I know you've looked and not found one, but you all know how hard intermittent faults are to track down. We'll keep looking. I think that connecting that to the Passengers has given life to a thought, and that thought has taken off, so now anything a bit strange is being attributed to it. I don't mean to sound harsh," she'd seen Aella's face, close to tears, "but fear and tiredness and being in a new environment, it can create a strange feeling in the mind. That's what I think we're seeing here. So, I recommend everyone have a good meal, then do something to relax – read or a game or something – and get a good night's sleep. In the morning, I'll have a look through the systems and the logs. We'll keep looking and we'll find something, a scientific explanation. I promise. In fact, you all wait here – catch a film together, something light-hearted. I'll cook tonight."

Frey made to follow her as she left the room, but she told him to stay with the others. Mac smirked at his annoyance. "Don't like to be treated like the rest of the crew?"

Frey gave him a withering look, and Elodie cut across before the two could argue. Entertainment was selected, and the crew settled.

They ate a warm, spicy meal, and Fae organised gentle music to be piped through the room in an effort to ease the mood. For the first time in a long time, things seemed peaceful.

***

Frey was woken by a loud bang. His heart raced with the adrenalin. He breathed through it, then wriggled out of his bunk. The corridor lights came on dimly at his request and followed his path. He moved as quietly as possible, not wanting to disturb anyone else. The sound had come from, he thought, the bridge, so he headed that way. Mac had beaten him there, was stood by the computer terminal. They eyed each other warily until Frey spoke and broke the impasse.

"Find anything?"

"Nah. Thought I heard something, but…" He waved a hand around the empty room.

Again, it was Frey who interrupted the tense silence that followed. "Look… Fae hasn't said anything directly to you and I don't get why, but I know she agrees with me that this whole fuss, you put the idea of ghosts into Aella's head. All this fuss, it's on you."

Mac scoffed. "How much do you know about ghosts?"

"They aren't real. They don't exist. Stories and fear."

"And yet…" Mac raised his eyebrows. The lights flickered.

"Electrical fault."

"What about the smell? You've smelt it too."

"Could be anything. Could be imagining it."

"The planter?"

"One of them probably knocked it."

"The sounds?"

"Aella was exhausted. She was probably dreaming."

"I meant the whispers."

"Whispers?"

"You've not heard them?"

"You're making it up!"

"Am I?" He brushed past Frey. "I'm going back to bed."

Frey stared after him, infuriated at the constant lack of respect.

***

The morning destroyed the tenuous peace Fae had tried to create. Elodie had spent the night in Izem's bunk, and when she went back to hers, she found all her possessions thrown around. The kitchen was in a similar state. Most disconcertingly, the sharp knives had been removed from the block and were stabbed deep into the ceiling. It took Izem and Frey working together to free them. In the bridge, the pilot's chair lay on its side, ripped from the floor. The computer terminal was cracked, as though punched by a mighty fist. The gym equipment had all been similarly overturned. In the lounge, only Fae's armchair was untouched. Aella burst into tears and crawled under a sofa. Elodie raced to her planters; these were blessedly untouched. It was not just that Elodie took great pleasure in caring for the plants, but also that so much food had been destroyed in the kitchen that she wasn't sure they'd have enough to reach port if the garden had been harmed. Frey scowled as he stalked the corridors, assessing damage. Mac chased him down.

"This was you! The 'geist, it's angry that you dismissed it."

"Don't be so ridiculous!"

"It's true. It's a pattern. It's what they do."

"They. Don't. Exist. It doesn't exist! For all I know, you did it!"

"Ohohoho, that's what it wants. This dissension. It wants us to argue."

"You bastard! You're always pushing me. *You* want the argument."

"BOYS!" Fae's voice smacked through them. "Stop arguing. This way. Now."

They followed, fuming, as she led them to her cabin. "I don't want to hear who started it, but this stupid rivalry has to stop now. There's enough tension as it is. I want to know who did this, and I can only assume it was one of you."

A loud bang interrupted her, as though someone had hit the wall beside them. A rhythm of cracks and bangs seemed to travel up the wall, across the ceiling, and out to the corridor. A second set of beats followed, then whispery laughter and a hushed voice muttering indecipherable words.

All three froze, looking around. Fae tried to hold her scepticism, but by this point, even her nerves were spent. Mac gripped the reassuring metal of the screwdriver on his belt. Another loud bang freed them, and they fled the room. The door slammed behind them.

They ran to the lounge, whispers following them. Aella yelped as they entered, but crawled out when she realised who it was. Tears streaked her face. Fae got on the intercom to call for Elodie and Izem, and was greeted with a crackling song that ended in cruel laughter.

***

Elodie and Izem heard the banging from among the planters. They grasped hands and stared at each other, and Izem recited prayers he barely remembered from childhood. Elodie closed her eyes and focussed on the rhythm of his words, grounding herself in his voice. Steadier, she looked around and saw the sage. *Spirits don't like sage, especially the mean ones.* She remembered something about burning sage. The fresh stuff wouldn't catch, and even the dry stuff risked setting off the sprinklers. She looked at Izem.

"I've got an idea."

They gathered all the sage. Lights flickered, flashed and colour-shifted around them. Rattles and bangs and gurgles swirled the room. They stayed close to each other, working fast, able to hold their anxiety in check through their proximity. They ground the herb and scraped the pulp into water, creating as much sage-water as they could. Izem opened a panel access to a crawl space Mac had shown him that would help them reach the water system. Elodie yelped as they scrabbled through. Izem's missing screwdriver had become wedged in her arm. They shared a horrified look, and she passed up the first bottle. Izem opened the tank and added the water; Elodie took the empty and handed up the next. When all was done, they got out of the space. Izem opened some wires; Elodie grabbed dried sage from the cupboard and they lit them from sparks Izem created.

Each took a burning bundle. They left the garden and ran in opposite directions down the cramped and flashing corridor.

Embers and smoke trailed behind them and, and the sprinklers kicked in. Faintly scented water fell to the floor, wicked away to be sanitised and recirculated.

***

Fae guarded the lounge door, poised, ready to fight. Frey tried to comfort a terrified Aella, while Mac pressed himself into a corner. None spoke; all breathed fast.

The water fell, startling them. Frey dived under the sofa to cower beside Aella.

Fae went to open the door, but Mac, seeming shaken awake by the water, stepped over and put a hand on her arm. "Wait. This, this isn't the same."

She shook him off and left the room. Mac's hand fell to his side, and he stood in the artificial rain.

***

It settled after that. Most of the cargo was unscathed. The areas most in use were cleaned first; some of the cargo holds were left until they were nearly in their destination system.

Aella left *Blue Rufus* then. She found another job and refused to travel long haul again. Mac left as well. Frey remained for one more journey, then took up a post with another company.

Fae taught Izem and Elodie all the tricks of the ship that she and Mac had once known. Something in her said it was time to go rogue again.

Fern K L Goodliffe grew up reading science fiction, fantasy and ghost stories. The claustrophobia of a space ship makes for a perfect haunted house, even if your distrust in other people doesn't outweigh your faith in the supernatural.

Sacrifice

by MR Wells

Antares Sector

"Any change?" Outwardly, Maria Hernandez looks as composed as she always does, but I can see her fingers tapping, very lightly, on the arm of her command chair.

"No, ma'am. The signal is still repeating, very faint. I can't clear it up any more." Susan sounds vaguely apologetic, but then she always does. Still, she's proven to be more of an asset than I'd thought, given her age. When the captain and I had interviewed her and her boyfriend a few months back, I'd wanted to laugh them out of the room. A pair of starry-eyed lovers who wanted to see the galaxy in their gap year before they went back to the University of Central Typhon - it seemed too cliched to be true.

In the end, their references checked out, Susan had proved to be a surprisingly competent comm officer (and spoke Bilbrini Standard and Interlac almost as well as her application had boasted), and her partner Stephan had proven a quick study at learning the one thousand and one minor but essential tasks that every crewman had to learn on a small freighter to keep things ticking over.

Right now Stephan was hovering nervously to the rear of the bridge; technically, he was off shift, but the entire crew had drifted to duty stations once the captain had hit the alert button. His golden eyes flicked across at me worriedly before focusing back on the small viewscreen and the star field there, as if he could see something that was far beyond human- or in his case, Ylanti- eyes.

Doc Black stood next to Stephan, looking bored - but I can see the tension in her stance. The old medic brushed a hand through her dark hair- still worn short from her Federation Navy days, just like the captain and chief engineer. They're all still in the Naval Reserve, despite their advanced years. Which is partly why they're out here- Doc Black and Captain Hernandez are both closing in on their century, but the Navy rejuvenation treatments they have had meant they look half that, at best.

And I've seen the holos Chief Chen shows around when he's had a little too much to drink, from their last command before they retired. Hernandez commanded a heavy cruiser for more than a decade in Federation service, and looks far too young in her smart uniform in those pictures to be commanding several hundred crew members. But one look in her eyes… and right there, you can see the authority. The experience.

Ironically, in those same holos from decades before, Chen appears almost entirely unchanged. Doc Black always jokes that something went wrong with his treatments, and they aged him up too early. Still, for a man coming up on his 12th decade he looks remarkably well preserved. Of course, that means he already looked like he was in his 60s when he was at least 2 decades younger.

Chief Chen and his nephew, Zhan, are the only crew not on the bridge right now, but I've no doubt they are glued to their own screens in engineering.

Hunched over the weapon console to my right, I can hear Griff growling. And even though we had the console altered to fit him a little better, he is still a Draxian; all height and muscles under his powered body armour. So he still has to stoop over the controls slightly, his dark eyes locked onto his screens. Griff doesn't like this any better than I do, although for very different reasons.

Draxians were for a long time considered the elite warriors of the galaxy. After the Border Wars left their homeworld and colonies smoking ruins, their warrior caste became more interested in survival than wars of conquest. We'd been lucky to find him; although Draxians were now mercenaries (with most of their pay being diverted to help rebuild what was left of their shattered empire) Draxians still tended to hire themselves in groups, from a handful of warriors to entire companies.

I had no idea what his story was, only that he'd made it clear he was alone, and willing to sign on for a rolling 12 month contract with our small freighter. As always, my eyes stray to the ugly pink wound on his neck, sinking down below the neckline of his armour - and the barely discernible patch on his armour trailing down from the wound.

"Keep bringing us closer, Carlan. Nice and slow." Our pilot nods her head, eyes still on her controls as she smoothly eases our little ship closer to whatever is out there. Carlan Smith; almost certainly a fake name. The captain and I both know what she is- we've seen enough of them out there. She's tall, gorgeous, and moves with the grace of a dancer. Perfect- except for the ugly burn scar on her right palm. Almost certainly where the intradermal tattoo and chip marking her as a genetic slave were removed.

I have my flaws, but slavery is one area where the captain and I are on the same page. I might not have spent years hunting down slavers in the Xenoc Campaigns like Hernandez when she was still in the Federation Navy, but I find the whole idea of slavery abhorrent.

We were happy to sign Carlan on - and it's an unspoken rule that she stays aboard ship when we are operating outside of Federation space, where slavery laws are a little more… liberal as far as escaped slaves are concerned.

Quelc at navigation is the last member of our little crew, and the only one who looks genuinely disinterested. They are Polkian - the best navigators in the galaxy, able to calculate a course with their dual minds faster than any computer. And of course, entirely useless when we aren't travelling through subspace or a Hyperspace Booster Gate. Right now, it's Carlan who is in control.

Which means Quelc has only one of their eyestalks open, the other four closed and hung limply from their bulbous head. I can't decide whether they are actually dozing or not.

And then there's me. The last of our motley crew, sat at the auxiliary command console on the merchant cruiser *Felicity*. I'm the first officer, but with the captain on the bridge, I haven't much to do beyond monitoring what everyone else is doing and offering suggestions. If the captain were to ask me, my recommendation would be 'make a note in the log to pass to the Navy, and get the hell out of here.'

However, Captain Hernandez follows regulations; and the regs for a merchant vessel receiving a distress signal are clear. It's our duty to investigate and assist if we can. Plenty of merchant captains would ignore it - I know Hernandez won't. That's not her way.

Besides, we're a long way out right now, and well off any of the major trade routes. A shortcut the captain knew from her

Navy days; leaving the Hyperspace Network early, cutting a quick subspace jaunt through this sector, and rejoining the Network for the final leg of our journey. It would save us nearly half a day - the Network was generally faster, but occasionally went on a roundabout route - and just as crucially would offer a hefty saving in Hyperspace transit fees, which were automatically levied every time a ship passed through a Hyperspace Booster Gate.

When the captain had first raised it, I'd objected automatically, of course, but that was before I'd done the rough maths in my head. I get a 15% cut of all the ship's profits, and with the saving on transit fees and the early delivery bonus on our current cargo, I calculated our profits on this trip would be boosted by a healthy margin. At which point I reconsidered and agreed it sounded like an excellent plan.

And then we'd picked up that damned distress call.

***

Captain Hernandez forces herself to stop tapping her fingers on her armrest as soon as she realises she's doing it. She surreptitiously looks around - Doc notices, of course, but offers her a fleeting smile of support. After 15 years of being married to the woman, it would have been a miracle if she hadn't noticed.

And she's pretty sure Max picked up on it too; her first officer is a bit of an odd sort, but he's sharp. His dark eyes meet hers, and he gives her a minute nod.

Clearing her throat, Hernandez asks, "Scanning range?"

Griff gives a rumble. "Another minute, captain."

"If I may, captain-" As always, Max makes his request sound like a polite suggestion - "it may be prudent to power up the weapons, and be prepared to shunt additional power to the engines and shields."

"Agreed, commander." Hernandez had been about to order it anyway, of course. "Commander, take over monitoring the scanners. Griff, please bring the weapons online."

There is a slight flicker of the bridge lights as the reactors deep within the *Felicity's* hull surge to maximum power. Hernandez can envision the quartet of gun turrets beginning to swivel on their mounts; *Felicity* was a Gladiator class merchant cruiser, former Navy surplus picked up for a considerable discount thanks to one of Hernandez's old friends in Fleet Command.

Her ship may have been close to a century old, but Hernandez knew that the Gladiators had spent decades fighting off pirates, and even the occasional enemy frigate or destroyer in Federation service. They were warhorses, the smaller cargo holds compared to civilian merchant ships favourably offset by their additional speed, armament and durability.

Hernandez tries not to glance at her chrono. She long ago learned the value of patience with her crews - or at least, the importance of seeming to be patient.

***

I manage to boost the gain on the scanners a little more - enough to get a grainy read on the object a few seconds before expected. I take another moment to clear up the initial analysis and begin running it through our database, before noting, "Captain, we're in extreme range. Object is approximately 2,400 metres long, with minimal power readings. Running the outline through the Federation database now."

She gives me a nod. "Very good, commander. Transfer the long range view to the main screens; let's see if anyone recognises it."

I do so; the picture, even at maximum magnification, is grainy at best, but I know Hernandez and her former Navy people must have come across thousands of ships in their time, some of them probably not even in our database.

Hernandez is frowning at the screen. Never a good sign. Her wife has stepped forward to stand alongside her chair, and the Doc is squinting at the screen now too. She exchanges a quick look with Hernandez, who opens a comm line to engineering. "Chief, any ideas?" A pause before his clipped accent comes back. "Negative, captain."

I grit my teeth as Hernandez murmurs something to the Doc, and force myself not to tap my own figures on my console. Finally, the computer reports a negative match with anything in our standard database.

"Negative match, captain. Not even a partial above 20%." I try to keep the snideness out of my voice, but from Hernandez's wince, I clearly fail. "Power readings are still minimal. I would suggest just enough to power their beacon."

The captain nods. "Susan, let's hear it on the main speakers again. Clear as you can make it." A crackle, and then… three long deep tones, then three shorter ones. Repeating over and over.

And I know it's too regular to be a random pattern, and close enough to the intergalactic standard distress signal that we have to check it out.

It could be a trap, of course. Bait for unwary ships before a pirate trap is sprung. But this far off the main Network what would be the point?

And I'm already thinking ahead; the captain will want to investigate. We won't want to stop- being caught at zero velocity if it *is* a trap would be fatal- which means a slow pass and a boarding party taking one of our docking shuttles across. And we can just about squeeze three, in full environmental rigs, in a shuttle.

Griff will have to go. And, reluctantly, I realise I will as well. We can't send either of the newbies - they're still kids and barely qualified for the environmental suits- and Carlan is out until we know what we might find. Quelc would be useless. Doc has never fired a pulse pistol in her life, and won't start now, which makes her even more useless if we get into trouble. We can't send the chief engineer- he'll be needed here if anything goes wrong. Which leaves just the nephew- who, if he got into as much trouble as I suspect he did, has probably been in a few scraps in his time, and will at least know which end of the pulse pistol to point at any danger.

And much as I hate to admit it… I would far rather have Captain Hernandez here, with all her experience, ready to get me out of a jam, than the other way round. Even if it means I have to go into the danger zone myself. Damn.

***

"Captain, I believe I should lead a small party across to the unknown vessel to investigate."

Hernandez manages not to show her surprise with difficulty. It's unlike Max to volunteer for anything like this, and then she takes a moment to think it through. And reluctantly realises her first officer is correct; Griff will have to go, but after the Draxian it needs to be either her or one of her other officers, which in practice means either her or Max.

Which means Max would rather have Hernandez here if things go wrong; an oddly touching thought from the standoffish Tabraxian.

Hernandez gives him a nod. "Very good, commander. Pick your team, and head down to the shuttle bay. Carlan, keep us on an intercept with the unknown ship, cut speed down to 80%. We'll reduce speed to one half to launch, then immediately back up to 75%. Keep us circling the unknown vessel." Hernandez thought about it, then noted as an afterthought, "At maximum weapons range."

Max is already whispering to Griff, who grins fiercely before heading for the exit. Max stops by my chair. "Captain, I'll take Zhan as well, if I may. Three guns are better than two if things go wrong." Hernandez gives him a smile. "Bold of you to assume Griff will only take the one weapon." Max responds with a minute smile of his own as Hernandez continues, "But of course. I'll man the weapons myself with Griff over there with you. Anything goes wrong, we'll be ready."

Hernandez feels that old shiver down her spine as she takes over the weapons, making sure they are locked on to the mystery vessel. Her instincts are screaming to leave that ship alone, to blow it out of space, to get out of here as fast as possible. She forces herself to ignore them; it wasn't the Navy way, and it has *never* been her way.

***

I shift uncomfortably in my environmental suit, trying not to jostle Zhan who is crammed in the rear compartment with me. Griff at least gets the pilot's chair and a little more space, even with his sealed armour.

Griff's harsh voice sounds over my comm. "15 seconds until launch." I force myself not to shift position again to try and see out of the front screen. Being able to actually see us shot from the launch bay towards that dark vessel will make no difference.

With a shudder, we're on the move and I can't avoid nearly falling as we bank sharply. I force myself to be patient, until Griff addresses me over the comm. "I believe I have found a docking bay, commander. Taking us in."

A final thump, and I manage to turn to face the rear exit. Another moment, and then the green light signals the lock is secure. I grip my pulse rifle and reach forward to pull the lever. The door oscillates open smoothly. On the other side - darkness. Pitch black. Shuffling forward in my bulky suit, breath harsh in my ears, I level my weapon and toggle on the lights on my helmet. The beams scythe through the darkness, revealing an octagonal corridor, entirely empty, with a large door at the end.

A deep breath, and I step into the corridor. Nothing. Releasing my breath, I speak into the still open comm line. "Clear. Griff, Zhan, I'll take point for now." "Fine by me, boss." Zhan sounds cocky, but I can hear the nervousness in his words. Griff just grunts an acknowledgement.

It's only a dozen silent steps to the end of the corridor. I peer at the featureless door; there's a single octagonal window set right in the centre, but I can't see anything looking through. Too much condensation on the window, and too much glare from my lights.

"Commander, my sensors detect an atmosphere on the other side." Griff's armour obviously has much better detection systems than the handheld scanner attached to my rifle, which shows pure vacuum on the other side.

After a quick search, I find a control panel which doesn't help; all the words are in a language I'm unfamiliar with.

I finally spot something that might help. The control panel might be indecipherable, but the small glass panel below with the green button underneath was universal. I tapped it with my fist, then harder with the butt of my rifle until it cracked in two. "Zhan - get over here. Push the button on three. Griff - ready?"

The alien warrior gave a hand gesture in the affirmative, his massive plasma rifle levelled at the door already, armoured form already in a combat stance. Hernandez had been right; I could see he had a pulse rifle slung across his back as well as the plasma rifle he wielded.

I pointed my own rifle at the door, took a long step back. "Zhan - you set? 1-2-3." Zhan pushed down the chunky green button and after a moment the door rolled back with a hiss. I half stumbled back a step as a blast of air shot out. It only took a second for the pressure to equalise. There was no movement on the other side, just another dark corridor curving around and out of sight to the left.

I glanced at my scanner, and could see Griff had been right; the atmosphere was breathable. Barely. "Captain; atmosphere looks good. No pathogens detected. It's chilly, but okay. I'm going to ditch the suits but keep breath masks, just in case."

A pause; I could tell Hernandez wanted to overrule me, but I also knew she wouldn't. She respected my judgement and knew I hadn't asked for permission, just informed her. "Understood." I could practically hear her gritting her teeth.

It took several minutes to correctly put on a sealed environmental suit; it took me less than a minute to remove the claustrophobic thing and substitute a breathing mask instead. The plasticrete mask fitted neatly over my nose and mouth along with a comm unit; I might sound a bit muffled but I could at least talk to the others.

Returning to Griff, I rechecked my weapon. After a moment, realising I no longer had the environmental suit's thick protections, I murmured, "Griff, you're on point." We advanced slowly down the corridor in a loose triangle. "Contact," Griff hissed. His lights had picked out a body slumped against the wall of the corridor.

"Commander, we're picking up additional power signatures over there. Still low but maybe some form of reserve power or standby." I jumped at Hernandez's distorted words, cursing to myself; I'd forgotten the comm line was still open. A second later, dim lights began snapping on around us.

"Griff, I've got it." The warrior nodded and his armoured form stamped a few paces past after a quick check, as I knelt next to the figure. It was humanoid, near mummified, and had obviously been dead a long, long time. It wore what looked recognisably like a form of uniform- and I didn't need to be a medic to see the tear marks across the chest, and the dark stains around the tattered cloth were equally clear. This wasn't a natural death.

"Captain, we have 1 dead crew member. Species unknown. Been dead a long, long time. I believe it is unlikely there will be any survivors." *So can we just come back now?* I thought at Hernandez.

"Understood. We don't know their lifespan, however." A pause. "Track down the beacon and deactivate; that will at least stop anyone else having the same issue. We can report it to the Federation and they can send someone out to investigate if they like."

I forced myself to nod, even though she couldn't see me. "Acknowledged, captain." It was, after all, a fair course of action. "Griff, Zhan, let's find this damned beacon and shut it down."

I gestured for Griff to lead the way, taking up position on his left. Zhan nervously did the same on the other side as we shadowed Griff's armoured form as he marched away. We passed through another door- and then another, only a few dozen metres apart. Both were opened in the same way, using the manual control. After passing the second door, I frowned. "Hold on a second, Griff." I examined the doorway, then walked back to the previous one and checked again. There were no manual release controls on the *inside* of the doors.

"No controls on the inside of these doors," I noted to Griff, who had paused but hadn't stopped pointing his weapon further into the unknown vessel. "Slavers?"

Griff gave a rumble of anger at that. Draxians had no more love for slavery than I did. Zhan volunteered, "Slave revolt, maybe?" I sighed. "Only one way to find out."

***

Another trio of doors later, the seemingly endless corridors finally yielded something else. After the final door, a small ramp led down to a dimly lit space; more lights slowly flickered into life as we entered. They didn't help, just created more dancing shadows in the flickering area. I paused, taking stock as Griff swept his rifle from side to side before pronouncing, "Clear."

A sudden crackle from my open comm line. "Commander, your signal is getting fainter." I checked my scanner - and didn't like what I saw. "Sorry, captain. We might need to cut the signal for a while. Looks like the inner sections of the ship have at least some level of trilithium compound lining the walls. If any of the doors had sealed behind us, we'd probably have lost you already."

I could almost see the worry on Hernandez's face as she muttered a string of curses over the comm line. "Understood, commander. 20 minutes, then I'm going to want a check in. I don't hear, well…" Well, I thought, there's not a damned thing she can do about it except wait a bit longer. I just reply, "Yes, ma'am. 20 minutes. Out." It's almost a relief not to have the rest of the *Felicity's* crew listening in as I cut communications. *Almost*.

"Sir." Zhan almost whispers it, pointing to the nearest wall. It takes a moment before I see what he's talking about. The wall is a clear barrier, behind which is… something. Whatever it is, it isn't humanoid, and has clearly been dead a long, long time.

I quickly realise that 8 must have really meant something to these people; there are 7 cells arrayed around us, our doorway forming the eighth side, with no other way in or out. There's a gantry around a large, open pit in the middle of the room; edging forward, I peer down. I can see, in the flickering lights, at least half a dozen more similarly laid out levels below us; I can even see a couple of what I'm quickly realising are cells on the level directly beneath us.

Griff has obviously been exploring too, and comes to the same conclusion; he reports, "4 of the cells are empty, 3 occupied."

I turn to Griff. I hate that all I can see is his armoured helmet at that moment, his eyes hidden behind the glowing lenses. "Let me guess… the signal is coming from the bottom of the shaft, right?" The Draxian cocked his head a moment, then gives me a stiff nod. "Yes, commander."

For a moment, I wonder how we get down there. Then I see the platform suspended from the ceiling in the centre of the shaft, and the thick cables descending to the bottom of the shaft. "Zhan." Once I have his attention, I nod my head towards it. "See if you can figure out how to get that working."

***

It takes a few minutes, but Zhan eventually finds a control panel on the far side of the chamber, directly opposite the doorway we had entered.

A moment after he hits the button, the platform gives a loud buzz and jerkily descends to our level. I quickly realise as it moves down on what appears to be a series of thick cables that the platform is actually smaller than it looks. Too small for 3, especially when one is wearing a full Draxian war suit.

Once again, I find myself with no choice. "Zhan, stay at the controls. We'll give you a shout when we are done to bring us back up. Got it?" He nods, pale and wide eyed, but is smart enough to keep the other hand on his weapon.

With a nod at Griff, we shuffle onto the platform, awkwardly back to back as we squeeze to the centre.

I wrap my left arm around one of the cables and shift my grip on my pulse rifle. "Take us down, Zhan." With another jerk the platform starts descending.

I quickly look out across the next level; more cells, more shadowy bodies behind the clear barriers. Same on the next level, except this time there are a pair of bodies outside the cells. I can't be sure in the dim light but I think they might be wearing tattered remnants of uniforms similar to the first body we found.

Another level, more bodies. And another. And another. I count 7 floors passing before we come to a shuddering halt. "It won't go any further!" Zhan's voice is faint. I shout an acknowledgement back, but my mind is starting to turn in some very nasty directions.

"Griff, did you see any open cells?" "Negative, commander." "Any other exits on the other levels?" "Negative, commander." "Bodies?" "Numerous, commander, from the third floor down. All out of the cells."

So. No other exits on any levels, just the top one where we had entered. The prison cells apparently all still sealed, but the - probably- guards all dead. Which with the design of this ship meant the bottom level must have been maximum security. More guards, as far from the way out as possible. And the only way in or out is controlled by someone at the top. Whoever was down here was someone they *really* didn't want to escape.

Not that it mattered. Whatever happened here, creepy as it was, had happened a long time ago. It doesn't make me any less nervous, but it was the only thing keeping me from complete hysterics. "Let's shut this damn beacon down." And I step off the platform, onto the floor of the shaft, sweeping my pulse rifle around me. I see Griff doing the same with his plasma rifle- then he pauses. "Sir."

I turn and see what is bothering him. There are only 7 cells down here; the final wall has a door. For a moment I'm relieved; clearly I was wrong, and there were entrances at the top and bottom of the shaft. Then I look again. This door… is not like the others we have seen. It's thick, like a bank vault door, with multiple locking bars, all bent- and the door is partly open and hanging off its hinges.

I dread the answer, but ask anyway. "The signal is in there?" Griff is already advancing on the door as he responds curtly, "Correct, sir."

I take one final glance up the shaft - to safety. Then I check my pulse rifle for what feels like the millionth time; still fully loaded and charged. "Let's get this over with. This whole place is… creepy." I pause, sizing up the opening. "Griff, can you make it through the doorway as it is?"

He looks it up and down and, for all I know, is measuring it in his helmet. "I believe so, commander. Although it may be a little… tight." And once again, I realise I need to go first, if only to cover Griff while he negotiates the doorway. And hope he doesn't get stuck. Again, I tell myself that whatever happened here happened a long time ago. It doesn't help.

"I'll go first. Stay close. Just in case." I duck my head in, seeing the same dim lights on the other side as are illuminating the rest of the ship. I can't help but notice there are more bodies as well. Gripping my rifle, I slip inside, immediately flattening myself against the far wall- just in case. I feel foolish when- of course- nothing happens, and take a few steps forward.

"All clear," I mutter to Griff. There's a few seconds of metallic whining and scraping, and then Griff is standing alongside me. His oversized plasma cannon at my side makes me feel a lot better. The floor slopes gently down; I can't help but notice the walls are not featureless as we descend. Periodically, there are what look very much like weapons turrets; most intact, a couple damaged or with the barrels bent or even snapped. All silent and motionless.

Almost immediately there's another thick door; this one fully open. And beyond… for a moment, I wonder what I'm looking at. Then, as I take another step forward, I understand. A cell; or something like it. A large dome of the same clear material elsewhere but here, much thicker (or at least I assume so, from the slight murkiness). I can't help but notice more mummified bodies around the edges of the room, and I count a dozen weapons turrets around the room's perimeter as well.

"Griff?" I wait for him to confirm, and finally he points to the far side of the chamber. "Over there, sir." Of course. After a moment's thought, I gesture for Griff to head to the right, and I move cautiously left. The dome is massive, at least 30 feet in height and at least the same in width. Which means the comforting presence of the Draxian (and his plasma rifle) seem a long way away as we each circle the chamber.

I've almost reached the other side when I notice the cracks in the dome, and a few steps later I see something much, much worse. A large jagged hole, several feet in diameter, with cracks radiating from the edges and the floor of the room covered in shards of whatever the material is. "Griff," I call. "There's a hole in the dome."

And as I nudge a piece of the dome with my foot, I can see it is at least 3 inches thick- and I wonder what or who they were imprisoning here, and where they went.

I can tell Griff is thinking the same from the way he grips his weapon even tighter as he sees the breach. "Let's get this damned beacon shut down," I manage to force out. Griff gestures. "Over there, sir." We shuffle over to the nest of machinery that covers the wall of the room. I realise I have no idea how to shut down the beacon; the technology is vaguely familiar but too alien to simply start hitting buttons. Also, I can't be sure, but from the missing panels and bundles of wires hanging loosely across the wall, I get the strong impression that the beacon had been hurriedly rigged.

"Griff- any ideas?" The Draxian is already reaching into a pouch at his belt. "If I may, sir?" He produces a handful of tiny, marble sized silver spheres. At my nod, he swiftly begins pressing them into anywhere that looks important, then steps back. "I suggest you get behind me, sir." "Ah… good point, Griff." I hurriedly duck behind his armoured form, and wince as the room flashes brightly and I hear the muffled hisses and, even shielded by Griff, I feel a wave of heat.

Cautiously sticking my head back round Griff, I note the red hot metal and large melted patches where the thermo grenades detonated; the whole wall is a ruined mess, dripping liquid metal in some places. "Beacon deactivated," Griff announces. I can hear his smugness, even over the comm line.

"Let's get out of here." I'm already turning towards the exit, eager to get the hell away from this creepy place, before I hear Griff give a surprised curse. Looking back, I can see him poking at the ruins of the half melted wall. "There's something back here," I hear him muttering over the comm. With a sharp pull, he wrenches one of the scorched panels free, tossing it aside.

I step closer, now seeing what Griff was talking about. Behind the panel, where wiring has been torn out, is… I hesitate. It looks… organic. Griff realises first, as he pokes it with an armoured finger, and it crumbles under his touch. "A cocoon…?"

And then all hell breaks loose. Griff moves so fast I can barely track his movement as he whirls around, plasma cannon blazing away. I don't even see what hits me, but suddenly I am flying through the air. Winded, I hit the wall with a thud.

***

Captain Hernandez forces herself not to tap her fingers on the arm of her command chair as she checks the time again. 12 minutes since they lost contact. Another 8 minutes until the boarding party is overdue. And looking around the bridge,

Hernandez realises that when those 8 minutes are up, she won't be able to do anything except keep waiting. And worrying.

Felicity doesn't have enough crew for another boarding party if Max and the others have got into trouble - even if they did want to risk their last shuttle.

Hernandez glances over to her first officer's normal station, where Doc is quietly monitoring the scanners as the *Felicity* continues to circle the drifting, derelict vessel anxiously, like an overprotective mother. Doc looks up, her dark eyes flashing in sympathy as she offers a minute shrug. Damn, but the woman knows her too well.

Stephan is murmuring quietly to Susan, fiddling with the ship's main comm controls as Susan sits with her headset on, listening intently for any contact.

Carlan is bent over the helm, shoulders hunched and locked.

Clearing her throat, Hernandez announces, "We might have to draw straws to see who swims over there after them at this rate." Susan gives a very inappropriate giggle, and Doc just shakes her head, a slight smile on her lips. But it works; Hernandez can feel the atmosphere ease on the bridge, just a little.

And Hernandez realises she has been tapping her fingers again. Grips the arm of her command chair instead. Checks the chronometre. 7 minutes.

***

I shake my head, not sure how long I've been out, or if I've been out at all. My vision blurs a moment, but then I see Griff, his armoured form struggling with… something. It's hard to breathe, but somehow, I manage to drag myself slowly, agonisingly, to a sitting position, my whole body shuddering with pain. I'm panting from the effort, but manage to lay a shaking hand on my pulse rifle, miraculously still within reach.

Griff is only a few metres away now, his back to me. I can't see his plasma rifle, but he is grappling with a humanoid figure. Griff is bigger than the figure, but is struggling; I can hear the servos in his armour whining from the strain.

I level my pulse rifle at them as I see something I never thought possible; Griff's feet have left the ground, a sinewy hand that seems far too thin to be strong enough wrapped around his neck as the figure's other arm fends off Griff's desperate attacks with almost casual ease.

Griff tries again, gauntleted fists pummelling away at his opponent's head, to no apparent effect. Then, I can see the hand tighten with effort around Griff's armoured neck- and I hear the metallic crunch of armour, followed by a final crack. Griff spasms one last time, and then goes limp.

Almost casually, and with frightening strength, his massive armoured form is tossed aside with a clatter.

And then his murderer turns its attention to me. I squeeze the trigger on my pulse rifle- and nothing happens. Focusing on my weapon, I see the crack running the length of the barrel. When I look up, it's right in front of me. Almost gently, the alien reaches down and tugs the weapon from my hands, looks at it curiously before casually snapping it in half.

The alien… is humanoid, almost skinny, hairless and with a slight green tinge to its skin, but could otherwise pass for human- if it wasn't for the eyes. They are glowing, slitted yellow pupils within the pale white eyes. And considering what it did to Griff, this thing is clearly much stronger than it appears.

"Thee still spake Galactic Standard," it says, crouching before me, looking me over curiously. The voice is deep, the words in a strange accent, but still recognisable. "Thy tongue is familiar." I croak. "What… what are you?"

It gives a very human smile. "Ah. I be a prisoner. My jailers should hath executed me. Still, I knew I wouldst escape in time. It hath been so, so long…" A cocked head. "Tell me, friend, doth the Ikanian Empire still control this sector?"

I blink at this. I vaguely remember learning about the Ikanian Empire in school - and I know it collapsed millennia ago. 3000 years ago? More? History was never my strong suit, especially ancient history. "No. That was a long time ago. The Ikanian Empire is long gone."

"Hm." The alien considers this, then gives another cheerful smile. "Thy Ikanians certainly built their prison vessels well." Examining me as if I'm a rather curious bug, the alien leans forward, and with a sudden movement he seizes my left leg, and twists hard enough that I hear the bones snap.

I scream, and I think I might pass out for a spell. When my blurred vision fades and I fight my way back through the pain, I can see the alien knelt by Griff, methodically stripping his armour.

Looking around for anything that I can possibly use as a weapon, I find nothing. I'm propped against a wall, leg bent at a horrible angle, blood seeping from it, the useless pieces of my pulse rifle nearby. I can't see Griff's weapons - presumably the alien has them.

Helpless, I can do nothing but watch as the alien meticulously starts strapping Griff's armour to itself. Eventually, there is simply an armoured form stretching experimentally, armoured servos whirring. It hasn't put the helmet on, yet, and the head barely peeks out over the top of the chestplate; Griff was much taller. To my dismay, it doesn't seem to matter; the alien is moving as smoothly as Griff ever did.

When it speaks to me again, the alien talks a little slower, more carefully. "From thy recordings, Galactic Standard hath changed somewhat since my day. Still, I can… learn. Very quickly. For freedom, I can do anything." It takes a last look around. "Doth thou realise it took an entire Ikanian battle force to bring me down? To subdue me and lock me away? And now thee Ikanians are no more. I outlasted them." It seems pleased at this.

Returning its attention to me, I cringe as it stomps over. "How many on your ship? Tell me, and I may yet allow thee to live." I hesitate, still trying to fight the agony of my broken leg, then croak, "500 crew, including 200 armed marines." The alien smiles. And then, very deliberately, places its armoured foot on my broken leg... and pushes down hard.

White hot agony shoots through my leg and I writhe, leg pinned in place, tears of pain streaming down my face. Finally, it removes its foot. "How many on your ship?" I'm breathless from the pain, unable to answer even if I wanted to. The alien frowns. "Fewer than 100?" I nod.

The alien considers this, looking over the armour it's wearing. "100. Easy with this armour, methinks." Turning away, it pauses. "It wouldst be a kindness to end you. And thee have given me the means of my escape. I can be merciful, when the mood takes me. And right now, I am almost free- so I am in a good mood. Would you like me to finish you? It will be quick."

I shake my head, although with all the pain, for a terrible moment I do consider it. But I'm still hoping, somehow, to find some edge, *something*, to get out of this alive. To stop this monster.

Right now, the monster gives me a final dismissive look. "Very well. I look forward to getting myself a ship again." With that, he fastens Griff's helmet on and strides away. And I realise, with sinking heart, that with the armour on and sealed, there's no way to tell that he isn't the Draxian. Certainly not enough to stop Zhan activating the lift and helping him escape. And from there... once he's aboard *Felicity* my crew- my friends- are done for.

I can hear the scraping as he squeezes himself out of the door; and without knowing what I'm going to do, I begin to drag myself after him, wincing in pain and gasping for breath as my broken leg catches. My communicator is useless here but maybe, somehow, if I can get out of this chamber I can send a warning.

I have to stop and catch my breath several times, and I'm sure I black out at least once. But finally, with a moan of pain, I topple past the jammed door and into the main octagonal chamber. I lie on my back, vision blurring, fighting to stay conscious as I look up into the distant lights. I can just barely make out the lift platform at the top; and there's no sign of the alien.

And then I see Zhan. His body is a twisted mess at the other side of the chamber; apparently, once he'd helped the alien reach the top, there was no further need for him. I pull myself across; I don't bother checking his pulse, but do close his slightly surprised eyes. "Sorry, kid," I croak, reaching for his comm unit, still clipped to his neck. Still operational.

I sit back, forcing my broken leg into a slightly more comfortable position (dull agony rather than white hot pain now), feeling lightheaded. I try not to think about how much blood I've already lost from my ruined leg.

So; I now have 2 comm units, neither of which will work this deep inside the ship. I stare around, trying to find anything in this alien ship that might let me get a signal out - and after skipping over them the first time, my eyes return to the thick cables that the lift platform ascends on. And I remember something Captain Hernandez had told me from her Navy days…

Then

"So there we were, trapped in the middle of an asteroid laced with myridium ore, life support running out, and no way to communicate where we were to the search parties with all that myridium. Frankly I'm ready to sit down and give up." We all chuckle, sat around the mess hall table, Stephan and Susan wide eyed as they hang on the captain's every word.

I manage not to roll my eyes - I swear this isn't the first time I've heard this particular story- as Hernandez continues, "Then my chief engineer shouts 'antenna - antenna!' At first, I think he's gone space crazy, of course. Then he's pointing at the railing the minecarts go on, that snake through the whole asteroid. Eventually, he calms down enough to explain; that those rails are conductive, and go all the way to the surface. And if we tie all our comm devices together to boost the signal, we could use the rails as an antenna; to get a basic signal out. So after a bit of thinking, we send a simple numerical sequence, our co-ordinates, and start tapping it out in old spacers code along the emergency channel."

Hernandez grinned. "Luckily, someone on the other end was monitoring it, and knew the old code. We got rescued, obviously - and that, kids, is why I expect both of you to memorise the code. Just as we all have. Right?" I nod as Susan and Stephan glance around at us, along with everyone else. I'd had to learn it - the captain had threatened to test me in front of the whole crew if I didn't know it well enough.

Now

I have no idea whether 2 comm devices will be powerful enough, or even whether those alien cables will be conductive. But I have to try. I pull myself over to the cables, connecting the comm devices. And I start to think hard; it has to be a short message, simple but easy to understand.

It only takes a moment to connect the power devices on the communicators, and twist free the transmitter wires. I wrap them around the cables, several times in the hope it will boost the signal. Remove the speakers; they won't be needed. Now I'm left with a single button, which should send a sharp buzz across the emergency channel I've tuned to. Which, hopefully, will transmit via these cables at the top of the shaft.

Mentally, I try to recall the code- and then begin tapping away at my signal. I hope I'm not too late.

***

"Griff, is that you?" Hernandez frowns. The Draxian sounds odd. "Yes, captain, I request thy permission to return." There's a slight buzzing interference on the comm line. "Griff, where is Max?"

A pause. "Injured, captain. Something in the air, methinks." All Hernandez's instincts are screaming at her. "Stand by, Griff. We'll let you know when we're due to do a close pass for a rendezvous." Hernandez snaps the comm line closed. Something is definitely wrong.

But what can she do? She has to let them back. Perhaps refuse to let them dock until they have done additional scans, and run them through extra decontamination procedures, just in case. She's about to instruct Carlan to begin plotting a docking course when Susan pipes up. "Um… captain?"

The young student is listening intently to her headset, a faraway look in her eyes. "Captain, I think… I think the buzzing on the comm line… it sounds too regular to be interference."

Hernandez cocks her head. "Main speakers, Susan. Quickly now." Bzz. Bzz-bzz-bzz… bzz bzz. Bzz bzz. After a minute, Hernandez hears it- the same pattern repeating. "Spacers code…" she mutters. Hernandez begins deciphering it in her head, then notes, "Susan, spacers code. I know you should have learnt it by now- begin translating. Check we agree." The youngster grabs a pencil and begins furiously scrawling away.

After a few minutes, Hernandez realises the message is repeating itself. "Susan, what did you get?"

She checks her notes. "Um… three words, captain, over and over. Quarantine, ship, destroy. Then 3 individual letters, M, A, X."

Hernandez nods. "That's what I got too." Suddenly, she felt sure that whoever she had been speaking to, it wasn't her Draxian weapons officer. Something had clearly gone very, very wrong.

Almost without thinking, Hernandez adjusted the weapons systems, locking on to the still docked shuttle. And hesitated. If she destroyed the shuttle… if Max, or anyone else, was still alive, there would be no way back. Then Hernandez thought about that voice she had heard claiming to be Griff. And opened fire.

Crimson laser beams shot across space, shattering the tiny shuttle in a moment. As the cloud of wreckage dissipated on the viewscreen, Hernandez said quietly, "Susan. Open a channel to 'Griff.'" She sneered the last word.

"Yes, ma'am." The youngster was subdued, but Hernandez heard the click. Followed by a cold voice, no longer warped by interference.

"That was extremely foolish of thee. We could have done this the easy way. I believe one of your crew may still be alive - for now." A pause. "Send another of thy shuttles and I will let them live. And you."

Hernandez made a gesture at Susan to mute her. "The emergency channel - is it still transmitting?" Susan listened for a moment to her headset, then nodded. "Yes, captain. Still repeating. Same message."

And Hernandez glanced around the bridge. At her remaining crew. Because she knew, now, that Griff was dead, and probably Zhan too. And if Max was still alive, it wouldn't be for long. And put simply, she couldn't risk her remaining people on the off chance they might, somehow, be able to save her first officer. Especially not when whatever it was had apparently already dealt with a fully armed Draxian warrior.

With a heavy heart, she realised that simply leaving the other ship drifting was also not an option. If Max was still alive, whatever they had let loose would no doubt torture him in an attempt to persuade Hernandez to let it go. And leaving it for someone else to deal with... even if they managed to get a call for help out, *Felicity* was weeks, perhaps months, away from the nearest assistance.

"Gods preserve you, Max. I'm sorry." Hernandez whispered the words; Doc must have been skulking nearby because she laid a hand on hers, squeezing gently. Offering no condemnation, only support.

And Hernandez began targeting the gun turrets on the still drifting ship - and whatever had killed her people.

***

I hear the dull rumble; it has to be weapons fire, which means hopefully, my message worked. I keep sending it though, repeating it over and over even though my fingers are going numb. Right up until I hear the lift, and look up to see the platform moving down towards me.

I manage to pull myself clear, leaving an even larger pool of blood behind as I do. I'm not in a condition to do much more than slump back after that, watching the lift get closer.

Finally, it reaches me, and the alien wearing Griff's stolen armour stomps off. It has discarded the helmet, and those yellow eyes are blazing with anger. "Thy crew are fools," it snaps. "Come. I will drag you to an airlock if I have to, force them to take me away." It reaches down towards me, and I can't help but laugh. I'm weak and I can barely move, but I chuckle anyway.

"You... really don't... know the captain..." I grin at the alien as it snarls and pulls me up by the shoulder. I gasp as I feel the armoured gauntlet digging into me. It hasn't even taken a step towards the lift before the ship shudders, and I hear the first explosion- and a sudden rush of wind as something, somewhere decompresses. "What-" As those yellow eyes turn to me, I'm gratified to see a flash of what I hope is fear there, before another explosion, much closer this time, sends us both tumbling.

I realise I'm about to die, but as I watch the alien turning frantically around, looking for a way out that will never come, I know it's worth it. And I hope the gods watch over my crew. The next explosion is close enough I don't even see it - just a flash, and then nothing.

***

It's hardly necessary, but Carlan announces softly, "Target destroyed, captain." Hernandez stares stony faced at the fading light on the screen. "Scan the wreckage for any power sources. Any life signs." She knows it's useless, but Hernandez wants to be satisfied that whatever was out there, they have taken care of it.

Eventually, Stephan announces quietly, "Nothing, captain. No sizeable wreckage detected." *No bodies.*

"Thank you." Hernandez clears her throat. "I will update the log to show the loss of our crewmates - our *friends*." Her eyes burn; this is far from the first time she has lost crew, but before it was in Naval service. Hernandez has never lost a soul since she became a merchant captain.

"M-" Hernandez paused. Of course, no first officer to turn the bridge over to. Doc murmurs, "I have this, love." Hernandez gives her wife a weak smile. Clears her throat before trying to speak again. "Doctor, you have the bridge. I'm going to talk to the chief in engineering."

Another old friend, whose nephew has just died. Hernandez always knew the galaxy could be a dangerous place- that was part of why she retired from the Fleet, after all. But now… time for one more order.

"Carlan, get us the hell out of here. Maximum speed."

Born in Wiltshire in the UK, **Matt** currently lives in South Wales with his cat, Jess, and spends his time reading, writing, running (at least when the Welsh weather allows it...) and mostly losing at board games.

The Marian

by Katie Ess

"Watch out!" I shouted as a direct hit of laser fire rocked our spaceship sideways.

"Well, it's not like I'm getting hit on purpose, Denise!" Shelley took a second to glare at me before returning her attention to the navigation field in front of her.

"That's *Captain* Denise to you. If you don't stop letting them hit my ship!"

Federation ships were closing in on all sides, trying to dock with our ship so they could board and apprehend us. Though from their recent actions, it seemed like they'd take blowing up the ship as an equally valid option.

An authoritative voice took control of the intercom. "Starship Marian, you are commanded to submit, by order of the Planetary Council."

"Well, shit. Looks like we're just about surrounded," Lox said, walking calmly onto the bridge to join the two of us. She winked at Shelley. "Too bad we don't have an amazing pilot that can get us out of near anything."

"No flattery when I'm planning a course," Shelley said, flipping a couple switches on the nav assist and punching some coordinates into the computer. But even deep in concentration, her manner softened just a fraction, like it always did around Lox.

Raquel twirled her way onto the bridge as well, all flouncy skirts and petticoats. "I just love the feeling of a heist well done," she sang as she spun, then curtsied.

"It's only well done if we don't blow up on the getaway trail! And why is my entire crew on the bridge?" I glared at them, but Raquel and Lox hugged each other and grinned, the adrenaline of the heist still upon them. I couldn't blame them - this was a really good take, if we could make it out alive.

"Okay, this is going to get dicey," Shelley announced when she was done punching buttons. "It would have been nice if the Feds hadn't noticed us until we got away from Earth, but that ship has sailed now, so to speak." There was sarcasm in her voice, but I could tell from her smirk that she wasn't really upset.

"Hey now!" Lox objected. "I'd love to see you sneak on and off a planet, steal some of the most coveted riches in the universe, and not get noticed by the Feds."

"Yeah," Raquel chimed in. "It's a testament to our amazing skills that they didn't pinch us on-world. You'd be breaking us out of an Earth prison right now." She and Lox high-fived.

"Or we'd just leave you there," Shelley grumbled.

Lox and Raquel both made wordless sounds of protest, gearing up for a real argument.

"No one's leaving anyone anywhere," I said firmly, trying to shut down a squabble before it started. "And I agree—you ladies both did good work! But now we have a problem and we need a solution. So let's shut up and let Shelley do her thing."

"Yes captain," all three of them said. Lox and Raquel settled down so Shelley could continue.

"In order to get the fleet in the right position, I'm going to have to lower our shields so it looks like we're complying. Any one hit could be fatal, because I can't raise them mid-maneuver. So you ladies know what that means."

"I've got foreguns!" Lox said, climbing a ladder to a small gunner's pod just over the bridge.

"I've got aft!" Raquel flounced away, humming as she headed toward the back of the ship.

Shelley pointed to the largest of many screens in front of her. It showed a 3D image of our ship, as well as six large Federation ships moving into position around us. She tapped the screen, pointing out the largest vessel at our flank.

"When we lower our shields, this ship will move toward the airlock in preparation to dock."

"How do you know it will be that one?" I asked.

"Because it's the biggest, which means it's carrying the boarding party as well as its usual crew."

I nodded, storing that fact away in case it came in handy later. Having been a Federation soldier for a while, Shelley was always a fount of useful information during our infrequent run-ins with the Feds. Their jurisdiction only extended to the asteroid belt just outside Mars. We didn't come into their territory very often, but when we did, it was good to understand how they operated.

"This is a risky move," I said, seeing the opening she was trying to create for our escape.

"There's always some kind of risk," she grumbled. "Especially with cargo this hot. But I'm counting on the element of surprise."

The voice broke its way onto our main speakers again. "Starship Marian, you have ten seconds to comply, or we will be forced to open fire."

"Surprise is a pirate's best friend," I said, winking at Shelley. "You ready?"

She nodded, flipping a couple more switches.

I picked up the radio and pressed the button to start the broadcast. "Federation fleet, this is the Starship Marian. We are prepared for boarding. Dropping shields now."

I flipped a lever just over my head to lower our shields, and as Shelley had predicted, the ship to our rear moved toward the airlock. My heart hammered with anticipation—one wrong move, and we would be nothing but bits of metal and flesh floating in a vast, uncaring universe.

Of course, I'd learned over the course of my life that we weren't much more than that alive.

Lox shouted down from the pod above us, breaking me out of my reverie. "Gods, this is taking forever! Can we just shoot them already?"

"Sweet Zeus, Lox, it's only been a couple minutes," I shouted back up. "And shooting at them will certainly mean our immediate deaths."

"Ugh," she groaned. "I'm gonna die of boredom if they don't hurry up."

Shelley rolled her eyes. "Well, fortunately, the excitement will start in 3…2…1…"

The Federation ship cleared our rear panel, and Shelley fired up our fore thrusters, shooting backwards through the hole the Feds had left in their barricade. We tore backwards so quickly that I had to hold on to the grip bar over my head to keep from falling forward.

The instant we were clear of the ship, Shelley raised our shields and changed direction, bringing our nose up and around. Our vessel was light and could turn on a dime—a strong recommendation for a pirate ship. With the flick of a few buttons, Shelley cut the forward thrusters and fired up the rear thrusters. Just as quickly as we had reversed, we raced forward, up and over the ships in the barricade. I was once again glad for the grip bar that kept me from falling all around the bridge.

Two of the ships that had been in front of us registered our movements faster than the others. I could see them on the nav screen as they turned, preparing to chase.

I picked up the com, broadcasting my voice to everyone. It was tinny, but I hoped I sounded calm and authoritative.

"They're chasing after us. Raquel, make sure they don't get too close."

"*I know*, captain. You literally just told me that was my job like five minutes ago," she sassed back, her voice also carrying throughout the ship. Shelley snickered.

"Laugh all you want, but those ships are faster than ours," I said. Lowering the com, I spoke to Shelley. "I hope you've got a plan."

"Yep," Shelley said. "Raquel and Lox are going to keep them occupied with our guns while I pilot us into the asteroid belt. Their ships may be a touch faster, but we're much more maneuverable. They won't dare follow us there. And once we're out the other side, we're home free!"

"This ship is home for the four of us now. Let's just get free."

***

"I'm sorry for your loss, Denise." I heard the words over and over until they lost their meaning. Just a series of random syllables, designed to make me feel better but failing to do so.

Everyone was dressed in lime green, the color of mourning on Rigel. Lime green, like the sky. Because, as they said, when you are in mourning, you should be wrapped in compassion as big as the sky. As a child, I'd wondered who had originally coined the phrase—how they had ever thought it would be helpful. Now, the sentiment felt as trite as it had sounded back then. What good were these people to me, now that my family was gone? What was the function of their hollow well wishes? No one could help us when we were sick, but now everyone was here, now that it was too late. I wanted to scream, to rip their lime green dresses and suits from their stupid, useless bodies. Instead, I stood and nodded at their platitudes, mumbling thanks through lips numb with grief.

When I couldn't take it anymore, I went to the kitchen to refill my drink. Rigellian brandy seemed to be more helpful to me now than anything anyone could say. Two people murmured in the corner, not realizing I had entered the room.

"A double funeral," one of them said. She spoke softly and pulled at her long, blonde braid. I didn't recognize her and didn't care who she was. "I don't know how she can take it."

"I know," the other one said, rubbing her arms even though the room was warm. "I mean, losing your husband is hard enough, but losing your daughter too? If only we had cypovirus vaccine here, none of this would have even happened. I wish Rigel was rich enough to be able to afford a supply."

Blonde braid looked up and saw me. Her expression was initially shocked, but she replaced it quickly with sadness. "I'm sorry for your loss," she mumbled, and her conversational partner repeated the same words before they quickly left the kitchen. I wasn't even sure if I said thank you before they left.

***

As if on cue, I heard laser fire from the back of the ship. Raquel's voice hooted through the com. "Direct hit! I got one, right through their shields! Take that, ya Fed bastards!" On the nav screen, I could see the ship closest to us fall behind abruptly, the forward decks in flames.

"Raquel, back off a bit!" I yelled through the com.

"Ummm…Captain, I thought the idea was to get rid of the ships?"

"Yeah," I said, watching the rest of the Federation ships gaining on us. "But for now, I just want them to stay back. They need to be cautious, not pissed off. Pissing off the federation is how we get blown to smithereens."

"Good point," Raquel said. "I wouldn't like being a smithereen."

There were at least ten ships behind us as we rounded Mars. I figured more were probably on their way, launching from Earth to come after our cargo. Raquel and Lox continued to fend them off, shooting just close enough to keep them at bay, occasionally hitting their shields, but being careful not to destroy them.

Just as the asteroid belt came into view, Raquel shouted, "Shit! I missed one!!"

The ship shot past us, then swerved, putting itself in a direct collision path with ours. Our shields were much weaker than theirs. If we hit them, our ship would be destroyed, but they would be protected from most of the damage.

Lox fired, hitting the ship directly. The rippling effect as the laser bounced over the shield reminded me of a stone skipping over a pond back home. A pond that we were about to slam into, at hyper-speed, without enough protection to survive the impact.

"Shelley…" I growled, beginning to panic, but trying to keep my voice calm.

"Fortunately, they forgot I can fly in three dimensions," Shelley mumbled. She was so deep in concentration that I wasn't sure she even knew she had spoken out loud.

She dived hard, trying to fly under the blockading ship, but we were approaching too fast. The speed kept the Fed ships off-balance–their laser fire narrowly missed us. But we were still on a collision course if she didn't correct things soon.

"Shelley…" I said a little louder, failing, this time, to keep my voice calm.

She cut out the rear engines. We fell out of hyper-speed, but our momentum kept us moving forward. Another laser headed our way, this time missing because we had slowed so abruptly.

Lox fired at the blockading ship, hitting its shields several times. There was no damage yet, but I could see the ripple around the vessel indicating that they had been weakened.

"Lox!" I shouted. "Hit them again!"

"I will, as soon as I can," she shouted back. "The guns are overheated - they'll be out of commission for a few seconds."

I swore under my breath, vowing to get the guns upgraded immediately if we made it out of this alive.

"No worries," Shelley said, firing up the rear thrusters again. "I've got this."

We resumed our trajectory toward the Fed ship. Though we were in a better position, we were still dangerously close to colliding. Our proximity warning alarms went off as we continued our rapid approach.

"Shelley…" I growled again, panicking this time.

Lox's gunner pod made contact with the ship's shield, creating a horrible metallic screeching sound that reverberated through the bridge. Lox shouted in alarm from above my head.

I said a silent prayer to a God I didn't believe in, waiting to be destroyed in a ball of fire. But we didn't blow up. We bounced! Their shield knocked us off our trajectory just far enough to sail clear, missing their lower decks by mere meters as we flew past them and into the asteroid belt. I could see the Federation ships behind us on the screen, coming to an abrupt halt to keep from flying into the belt themselves.

Under Shelley's guidance, the ship dodged and rolled, avoiding several small rocks to take us deeper into the belt. As soon as the Federation fleet was out of sight, she shut off the engines and brought us to a stop.

"Okay, Captain." She turned and grinned at me. "We made it out safe. What now?"

***

"What do you mean, they stole our scientists?" I shouted into my cell phone. "They can't do that, can they?"

"Yesterday, I would have said no, Denise," the Governor replied. "But today, through a series of interplanetary lawyers, it's been explained to me that they can."

I ran my hand through my hair. It had worked its way out of the loose ponytail I'd crammed it into as I raced out the door on my way to work.

After the death of my husband and daughter, I'd spent quite a bit of time at the bottom of a bottle of Rigellian brandy. But, in the midst of a terrible hangover, I realized that my family wouldn't have wanted this for me. They would have been ashamed, or at least saddened. In my more sober moments, I could picture my daughter jumping in bed with me, bouncing me awake like she used to do on the weekends. "Wake up, mommy!" she'd shout. And my husband would wink at me and say "Yeah—let's go meet the day. It's a beautiful one! Time's too precious to waste."

So I pulled myself together and joined the Rigellian health department, taking a position as lead executive. My job was to coordinate all vaccine orders and delivery for the planet. But I made it my personal mission to find a way to get shipments of cypovirus vaccine from Earth to Rigel.

We'd run into a load of excuses for why we couldn't acquire it. It was too far to ship (we offered to send a Rigellian vessel to pick it up). The conditions had to be just right or the vaccine would lose potency (we installed special freezers designed to keep the medicine stable during the journey). Finally, when they told us there was too much demand for it on Earth and they couldn't keep up with production, we hired our own scientists. We recruited our solar system's best and brightest, bringing them to Rigel to research and develop their own vaccine.

We'd hoped to make something comparable to the immunization currently produced on Earth. But our scientists actually developed a better, more potent one with fewer side effects. We were set to begin mass production today. I'd just pulled into the lab's parking lot to check on their progress when I received the call from the governor.

"So, okay, they kidnapped our scientists," I said. "What are they going to do with them?"

"The Federation was unclear. But they are definitely taking them back to Earth."

"You don't think they'll harm them, do you?"

"I'm sure they won't harm anyone–they want the scientists' expertise."

"We need to report this to the Interstellar Court. The Federation can't just steal our work!"

"I already did that, Denise. The court said they'll investigate our claim as soon as they can. But they're backlogged–cases can take up to three years to come to the top of their docket."

"Three years? Hundreds of people are dying from this virus every day! We can't wait three years for the courts to sort things out."

"I know that," the Governor snapped. "Do you think I'm happy about this? But I don't see what recourse we have. We can't declare war. Rigel is a peaceful society–we barely have any military presence. War with the Feds would kill a whole lot more than cypovirus does. Our only recourse is through the courts."

I sighed, realizing he was right. We couldn't just storm the Federation to get our scientists back–they were too powerful.

But then I looked at the building right in front of me. "Wait," I said. "The lab is ready to go. Everything is set up. We don't technically need the scientists to begin, right? We can still start production today."

"Interesting," the Governor said with a chuckle. "I suppose if the lab crew feels comfortable starting without the scientists to oversee them, we can begin production. The lawyers didn't say anything about that."

Grinning, I allowed the seed of hope in my heart to blossom. We'd be able to do this after all!

"I'll check with the lab crew," I said. "But I'm sure they'll feel comfortable starting, for now, until we can find a new lead scientist to take over."

I hopped out of my car and started toward the building. "I'll teach the Feds to underestimate us," I mumbled under my breath.

Before I'd even taken two steps toward the lab, an explosion knocked me backward. I landed hard in the parking lot, hitting my head on the pavement. The last thing I saw before I lost consciousness was the smoldering remains of our production facility, and the end of Rigel's chance to produce its own cypovirus vaccine.

***

"I contacted our buyers," I told my three crew members. We had assembled in the hold while we waited for information about where to drop our cargo. I didn't want to leave the asteroid belt until I knew where we were going. "I told them we might be running a bit late. They were less than enthusiastic, but they are still willing to pay for the cargo."

"Damn right they are," Lox said. "Because if they don't, we could sell it to a million other people, on a thousand different planets."

"Maybe," I said. "Maybe not. While everyone wants some, it's seriously risky to have it. If a planet gets reported, Earth would basically declare war. They've spent a lot of time and resources to ensure they have a superior military force, and we all know they're not afraid to use dirty tactics to get what they want. Shipment blockades, government investigations, sanctions and embargoes… it would be ugly."

"We'll find someone to use it," Raquel said quietly. "We'll find someone, or we'll give it away for free."

"Hold on! Let's not talk all crazy now. We're not planning to give it away for free, are we?" Shelley turned to me, accusation in her eyes, as though I was the one who had made the suggestion.

"It's a non-issue if we can get it to our buyers," I said. "So you focus on flying us to the rendezvous on the other side of the asteroid belt, and then we won't even have to discuss this any more."

Shelley furrowed her brows as though she were going to argue further, then nodded briskly. "The flying may be a little tricky, but *The Marian* will hold up okay. She's a good ship. We'll get through the belt no problem."

"I know I've got a good ship," I said. "But I'm also confident in my pilot. You've got this."

Shelley flushed with pride for a moment before she took off for the bridge to figure out the best path through the asteroid belt.

"Hey Shelley! Wait up! I want to see how you plot a course through this trash field." Lox tagged along behind Shelley like a little lost puppy.

Once the two of them were gone, Raquel looked at the crates we'd stacked up in the hold, full of our plundered loot. The company we'd stolen them from, Syncorp, had branded their name into the top of each crate. Raquel ran her fingers along the letters gently, as though she were examining a particularly delicate piece of lace.

"This is a good thing…right?" she asked me, the question urgent in her eyes. "We're doing a good thing here?"

I smiled. "Generally, pirates aren't known for doing the good thing—"

She opened her mouth to reply. I cut her off before she could get started.

"…but yes…this is a good thing we're doing."

***

"So you're telling me that the lawsuit won't go forward?"

My lawyer's head hung low as he nodded at me. "The judge threw it out."

"They stole our scientists! We had a vaccine ready for production, and the Federation came to our planet and abducted our scientists! They blew up our

lab—twenty-five people died in that explosion! Since then, over 5000 people have died of cypovirus. Mostly children. And that's just on Rigel…"

"You don't have to rehash the details for me, Denise," he said. "I was set to argue the case, remember? But the judge threw it out. He said it had no merit."

"Then we go over his head! We go to the next level. Make another appeal."

"The Interstellar Court is the highest level. There is no one left to appeal to." He sighed and looked at me earnestly. "We're done."

"But…" I could feel my eyes fill with tears, and blinked them back. "…how could they possibly rule against us? How could this happen?"

"I can't prove it," the lawyer said, "or I'd go back to court right now. But I think our judge got a payoff from Syncorp. They're making billions on this vaccine, and jacking up the price even more by keeping it scarce, so everyone has to fight over it. The minute there's a competitor, the bidding war will stop and its value will plummet."

"So, basically, the system is rigged?" I asked.

"Yes." He nodded again. "Sorry. We lost." Picking up his briefcase, he left the room.

I looked at the briefing in my hands, titled "The People of Planet Rigel versus Syncorp, of Planet Earth." Seething, I tore the briefing into as many pieces as possible before throwing it into the trash and storming out.

***

"We have a problem," Shelley told me as I walked onto the bridge.

"We always do." I sighed. "Is this one worse than usual?"

"Maybe." Shelley shrugged. "Hard to know when we're just at the beginning of the problem."

She pointed to her screen, indicating the edge of the astcroid field. On the other side of the belt, hundreds of small green lights blinked on and off.

"See these?" she asked, pointing at the green lights. "Those are some kind of ships. I can't tell what they are, because of interference from the asteroid belt. But I'm guessing they're not hanging out waiting to become our best friends when we emerge."

"They can't be Federation," I said. "No jurisdiction."

Lox wandered onto the bridge behind me. "Are we being chased by the Feds again?"

"Unclear," said Shelley. "There's definitely some kind of surprise waiting for us on the other side of this asteroid field. Probably an unpleasant one."

Lox whistled. "That's a lot of ships. Maybe word has gotten out that we're carrying some very lucrative cargo?"

"That would be an awful lot of looters," I said. "And they'd probably be fighting each other. They're not likely to just split it happily amongst themselves."

Lox nodded, conceding the point.

"That many ships, all coordinated together–it's got to be…"

"Yeah," I said, running my hand through my hair. "Syncorp. I'm guessing they want their stuff back. They do seem to have ships out everywhere looking for new materials to use in their medications…or new scientists to develop them." The bitterness crept out in my voice at that last bit.

"I wonder which planet they're mining to extinction now?" Lox rolled her eyes in frustration as she spoke.

"Probably whichever has the most aluminum, after my home world was tapped out," Shelley said, her voice clipped. "I mean, once they devastated the ocean hunting fish for oil to stabilize their vaccine, they had to find an alternative."

"For a company that claims to have benevolent purposes, they sure do destroy a lot of peoples' lives," Lox said. "Seems like it's time for a few pirates to put them in their place."

"You never did lack for determination, Lox," I said, smiling at her. "Not since the day I met you."

"My mama called it bullheadedness," she said. "But thanks."

***

"You sure, Missy?" the salesman asked me. His hands were greasy, and he ran them through his hair frequently, streaking it with black oil. "I mean, no crew…no captain…I'm not giving you a refund if you can't get this ship to start."

"I just need to get off world," I said. "I learned how to pilot ships when I was a kid, so I guarantee you I'll be able to fly her."

"She's a good ship," he said. "Name's The Robin Hood. I think 'cuz the previous owners liked the character, not 'cuz of any crime or wrongdoing. No Feds will be looking for you, if you're worried about that."

He spit on the ground near my feet. I took a step back, giving him my best look of disgust. "Sorry," he said, wiping his chin and looking absolutely unrepentant.

"So, it's a deal?" I asked.

"When you come back with the cash, it's a deal," he said.

"I'll be back tomorrow." I had an impulse to shake his hand, then realized I really didn't want to do that. Instead, I turned to go, heading to the bank next to get the necessary cash.

"Uh huh," he said, sounding unconvinced.

As I left the shipyard, a woman ran after me. She had short, tomboyish, sandy-blonde hair, and wore a mechanic's outfit that was much cleaner than the shipyard owner's had been. "Hey!" she shouted after me, and as I turned, she gave me a lopsided smile.

I didn't answer, but just waited for her to speak again. When the silence began to grow uncomfortable, she started.

"I…couldn't help but overhear you talking with Ryck." I looked at her quizzically. "The shipyard owner," she filled in.

I nodded, partly to indicate understanding and partly to encourage her to come to the point.

"Anyway, I heard you're looking to get off world?"

"Yep. Gonna buy that boat tomorrow and get out of here as fast as I can. There's nothing left for me here."

"Any chance you'd let me come along?" she asked hopefully. I started to tell her no, but she interjected before I could speak again. "I'm really good with repairs, and I can cook and make myself useful. I just want to get out of here too."

"I'm not sure where I'm going, or what I'm going to do when I get there," I told her. "I'm just looking to change my life."

"Yeah, I get that," the girl said. "My whole life, everyone told me to work hard, be smart, and I'd get ahead. But the more I'm here, the more I realize the deck is stacked against me. Just when I think I'm about to get a break, someone pulls the rug out from under me."

I sized her up. Her words were bitter, but her eyes shone with a spirit that hadn't been broken yet.

"If you're here at this time tomorrow, you're welcome on board," I said.

"Oh - I'll be here," she said. "I'll work hard—you won't regret this, I promise, ma'am."

"Well, first of all, you won't be calling me ma'am. My name's Denise."

"Yes ma'am—Denise." She held out her hand, and I shook it. "My name's Loxley, but everyone just calls me Lox."

***

We emerged from the asteroid belt and were immediately surrounded by hundreds of ships bearing the Syncorp logo. They were all heavily armed, and if ships could look imposing, these definitely managed it.

"Starship Marian, you are directed to stand down and prepare for boarding," a masculine voice blared through our com.

"On whose authority?" I tried to sound assertive, but wasn't sure if it would come across over their radio.

"The authority of the fleet that has you surrounded. I don't care what cargo you have on board, I would love nothing more than to blast a vessel full of pirates into tiny bits so small that no one would ever recognize the wreckage," the voice replied.

"No need to get snippy," I said. "We're lowering shields to prepare for boarding."

Once they had docked, Shelley, Lox, and I opened the airlock and allowed the Syncorp party aboard.

"Is this your entire crew?" The masculine voice that had threatened me so nicely before belonged to a man who was much less threatening in person. He was short–a good six inches shorter than me–and skinny, with a pencil mustache and narrow, watery eyes. His stripes indicated he was a major of some sort.

"Yes, sir," I said. "Just the three of us."

"You will submit to a search of your vessel," the man sneered, and his boarding party spread out, heading to all the areas of our ship at once.

"What are you looking for?" Lox asked sweetly. "Maybe we can help you find it?"

"Hey–mind the ship!" I shouted after the men, who were knocking things over and tearing into everything they could find.

"You know exactly what we're looking for," the man snipped. "Our stolen property."

"Sorry–you must have the wrong ship," I said. "We're just a group of women on a cruise through the galaxy. No stolen goods here."

He slapped me in the face. I was so startled, I didn't even react for a few seconds. But once the deed had registered, I smiled sweetly at him.

"I don't care how many of you there are," I said in my kindest, most polite voice, taking a step toward him so he had to look up to keep eye contact with me. "If you touch me, or any one of my crew, again, I will shoot you where you stand. And I'll send as many of your men as possible with you on your way to hell."

He glared at me, weighing his next move, before briskly turning to help his men search the ship.

It took them nearly four hours to tear everything apart to their satisfaction, but finally they had to concede that they could not find any stolen goods on board. In their preoccupation with our ship as they had surrounded us, the fleet hadn't even seemed to notice the small cruiser that slipped just past the edge of their blockade, landing on the far side of one of the larger asteroids nearby. They would have had to be paying careful attention, because the tiny vessel sent to meet Raquel on that asteroid and retrieve our stolen cargo was not much bigger than an escape pod–almost too small to be picked up on monitors. The longer they took to search, and the more focus they had on us, the more certain I was that our payout was secure. Though I have to admit that I breathed a sigh of relief when they were finally done ransacking my vessel.

"I don't know how you did this," the major said. "But I will find out. And when I do, I will take back possession of our stolen goods."

"I'll look forward to that meeting, then," I said.

Once the Syncorp fleet had gone on their way, Raquel brought the shuttle back from the asteroid. She dragged our payment on board - it took several sacks to carry it all - and gave a little curtsy when it was all accounted for. We all hugged and high-fived, and then Lox and Shelley headed off to the mess hall to start making drinks for the rest of us.

"The vaccines are on their way to Gemini," Raquel said, smiling at me.

"I know." I nodded, returning her smile halfheartedly.

"If they can reverse-engineer the vaccine, like they say they can, it won't be long before it gets to Rigel," she said, putting a hand on my arm. "And then we can plan a less dangerous, but equally satisfying, way to rob the Federation."

I laughed. "It feels a little early to plan our next heist. And next time, they'll probably just kill us." But I let the satisfaction of that idea wash over me. It calmed a piece of anger that I hadn't let go of for a long time.

***

Lox was there waiting for me the next morning when I came to the shipyard to pay for the vessel. Her hands were covered in red paint, and she was grinning so broadly I thought her face would split.

"I'm ready to go, if you'll still have me," she said.

"I'll still have you, as long as you don't mind that I'm not sure where I'm going yet. My plan is to figure it out on the way."

"Well, if you're really wanting to change your life, I've got two friends on Ursa that are looking for work. Used to be part of a pirate crew, but they're good, honest ladies."

"Pirate crew?" I said. "I've never really fancied myself to be a pirate."

"I figure, if life won't let you have what you want, you've gotta go out and take it." Lox shrugged.

I let the truth of that sink in, warming me. It did feel like time to take what I wanted. "Let's go meet these ladies on Ursa," I said.

As we headed toward the ship, I started to dream about the things I might want to take, and what I might want to do with them when I got them. Lox's voice interrupted my train of thought just before we boarded.

"I almost forgot—look what I did," she said, pointing up. "I thought a ship with a female crew deserved a better name."

"I like it." I nodded approvingly. "She was always the better character anyway."

On the side, Lox had changed the ship's name. Now, in bold red letters, was written "The Marian."

Katie Ess lives in Colorado with her husband, two sons, a bulldog, and two ferrets. When she's not writing, you can usually find her hanging out with one of them. If she ever becomes a world-famous author, it will be entirely due to their support and encouragement. (Well...maybe not the ferrets.)

Tower of the Stars

by Rose Strickman

Rapunzel was roused from her work by the insistent bleeping of the orbital alert.

Hair still wrapped around the memory chip, she stared in befuddlement at the blinking yellow light on the wall. Then joy and excitement raced through her, and she dropped the chip to run to the Tower control room, hair trailing behind her in a glistening cloak.

She hurried to the comm console, its screen currently filled with a blue-green image of the planet below. "Mother?"

The comm crackled to life. "Rapunzel? Let me up!"

"Just a minute…" Rapunzel took up position at the control board and placed a hand on the pad.

A sizzle of electricity ran up her arm, her neck. Her hair sparked and fizzed to life. A shining silver hank rose, found the control board. The strands melded seamlessly into the metal. Rapunzel closed her eyes as she established her telepathic link to the Tower. She felt the vast system of the Tower: the electrons running along wires, the solar panels gathering energy from the planet's star, the near-intelligence of an infinitely complex set of machines all working together on the simplest of mechanical principles.

Rapunzel hung suspended in the complexity of the Tower. Then she gave her command, fizzing down her hair. She felt the Tower summon Mother's pod, calling the vessel up from the planet's surface. She opened her eyes and craned toward the view port, eager and impatient.

The pod appeared first as a tiny spark in the atmosphere so far below. It approached rapidly, resolving into an ellipsoid capsule. It came closer and closer, the Tower's docking bay doors opening to admit it. Rapunzel, still connected to the Tower, felt it lock in the pod and shut the doors. Only then did she disconnect, hair disengaging from the computer.

By the time she made it down to the docking bay, Mother had already disembarked, climbing down the steps and shaking out cramped limbs. "Mother!" Rapunzel threw herself into Mother's arms.

"Rapunzel!" Mother hugged her, then held her at arm's length. "You're looking well! Especially your hair." She stroked Rapunzel's glittering silver hair. "Help me unload. I brought you more projects."

Rapunzel helped unload the black plastic chests, placing them on the conveyor belt. "How much more?"

"Four crates!" said Mother. "Make sure they're all done by next month."

Rapunzel sighed at the thought of all the work before her. "Yes, Mother." She paused. "You know, Mother…It might be easier for me to work if you didn't have to bring me projects all the time. If I was…downside. On the planet."

"Rapunzel." Mother placed her hands on Rapunzel's shoulders. "We've been over this. You can't stay downside, not since those new colonists arrived. They'd want your hair for themselves." She touched Rapunzel's hair again. It was a vivid, shimmering silver cascade down Rapunzel's back, each strand an advanced computer in its own right. "You are unique, Rapunzel. There are no other mechos. No one else in the galaxy who combines human and machine as you do. No one else who can program computers and machinery with their minds. If people ever found out about you, they'd want to kidnap you to use your hair's properties for themselves. Or worse—" Mother stared even deeper into Rapunzel's eyes. "—Kill you. This is the only safe place. This space station, cloaked from all sensors."

"Yes, Mother," murmured Rapunzel.

Mother gave her a hug. "Good girl. Let's get this stuff put away, and then I can stay for the orbital cycle."

"You could stay longer," said Rapunzel in sudden hope. "Stay for a week! Or longer. In fact, if it's safe up here for me, why don't you stay with me?"

"You know I can't do that, sweetie. Who is going to look after the garden if I'm not there?"

Rapunzel sighed. She missed Mother's garden, that lush patch of greenery in the wilderness of the uncolonized world, the vegetables growing in neat rows, the fruit trees and the trickle of the fountains. She hadn't seen it in so long…but it was no use saying any of that to Mother.

"Yes, Mother," she said instead. "I understand."

***

The next day-cycle, Mother kissed Rapunzel goodbye. "Got to go back now. Don't look so glum, sweetie. I'll be back next month. And we talk on the comm all the time, don't we?"

Rapunzel nodded, blinking hard. "I know, Mother. It's fine."

They shared one last hug. Then Mother headed down to the docking bay and Rapunzel returned to the control room.

Hand on the pad, hair plugged in, she watched the pod head toward the planet again, growing smaller and smaller, until she was once again alone. Only then did she turn away, wiping tears.

***

Bleep. Bleep. Bleep.

Rapunzel looked up, eyes unfocused, from a half-assembled circuit board. She stared at the blinking light on the wall. What was this? It had only been a week since Mother's last visit. And this wasn't the usual alert. It was blinking bright red, and the bleeps sounded louder, more urgent than usual.

Then she realized. Something was approaching the Tower. Something the Tower had not anticipated.

Rapunzel tore upstairs to the control room. Her hair practically threw itself into the control board. She reached out with the Tower's scanners, trying to discern what was coming.

An image arose in her mental eye, transmitted from the Tower's scanners: a space pod, much like Mother's. But it was coming from the wrong direction, from outer space rather than the planet. And from what the Tower could sense, there was something wrong with it. Its technological signature was off, its progress erratic, and it was giving off distress signals. And inside…

Rapunzel's heart nearly stopped. Inside the strange pod was a living organism. A human.

For a moment, she hung in sick suspense. Mother had warned her of other people, of what they might do to her. But the distress signals from the alien pod were getting louder, the Tower more insistent that the problem be resolved.

Rapunzel gulped and gave the command, fizzing down her tresses.

The Tower's tractor beam locked in, and the pod's path suddenly straightened, heading directly for the opened bay doors. Rapunzel ordered the Tower to dock the vessel and close the doors behind it. Only then did she disengage from the system, locks falling back to her side.

She stood still a long moment, a pale figure mantled by blazing silver hair. Then, taking a deep breath, she headed for the docking bay.

There the mysterious pod loomed, stark in the bright algae-lights. Rapunzel's eyes traveled over it in wonder. It was smaller than she'd expected, and more battered. It had clearly traveled a long distance across space.

She paced along the capsule, searching for a door. When she found it, she didn't even need her hair to open it. It sprang out under her trailing hand, spilling its human cargo.

Rapunzel jumped back, heart pounding. There was a *human* on the floor of her docking bay—a human who wasn't Mother. A long, thin, unconscious human, with chocolate-colored skin and glossy black hair, their hands covered in shining silver gloves— no, not gloves. They were metal. This person had metal hands.

Rapunzel's mouth went dry. Was this person a *mecho*? But Mother had said she was the only one, the only mecho in the entire galaxy. How could there be others, let alone one here on the docking bay floor?

The mecho-person moaned, stirring slightly, and Rapunzel tried to pull herself together. *Think.* This man might be a stranger, but he was a stranger in need of help.

She dragged him across the floor, body slumping along. With great effort, she loaded him onto the docking bay conveyor belt, heaving up his torso and swinging up his legs. Panting, she programmed the belt to transport him to the med bay.

The conveyor belt jerked into motion, carrying the unconscious stranger out of the docking bay. Rapunzel hurried after it, toward the med bay.

The stranger arrived before she did, still unconscious. She wheeled over the cot and heaved him onto it. Pushing the cot back to the medical machines, she got to work, running diagnostics and starting up the equipment. At least she was proficient at doctoring: Mother had trained her before sending her to the Tower.

The stranger didn't have many cuts or abrasions. His main complaints were cold, dehydration and lack of oxygen. Thus, Rapunzel stuck an oxygen-gill into the stranger's mouth and placed a heating-blanket on him. She hooked an intravenous needle to pump liquids into him. As she did so, she confirmed that, yes, his hands were definitely mecho, as were his legs below the knees: shining silver metal, organic nerves threaded through nano-tech machinery. Just like her hair.

Rapunzel stared at the stranger's mecho limbs. She gave them a poke, metal against skin. There was no doubt about it. He was a mecho, like her.

She looked at him still more closely. A fellow mecho he might be, but he was so *different* from her. Rapunzel compared her own paper-pale flesh next to his machinery. She was almost entirely organic; her mecho enhancements restricted to her hair and a few augmentations to her internal organs. This man—and he was a *man*, another astonishment—seemed almost a deliberate inversion of her: his hair organic, but his limbs mecho. Rapunzel looked at her own thin organic face in the mirrored cabinet door, her large blue eyes, and wondered what color the stranger's eyes were when open.

Rapunzel felt suddenly dizzy. She sat in the chair near the cot, head spinning. Her eyes kept darting between the medical machines and her extraordinary patient.

Eventually, there came a long, damaged-sounding moan. Rapunzel leapt out of the chair and darted behind it as the stranger stirred and his eyes fluttered open.

Rapunzel gaped. His eyes were *mecho*: perfect blue ocular discs under organic eyelids and long lashes. They fell on Rapunzel.

"What the—!" His voice cracked across Rapunzel's ears, jarring in its unfamiliarity.

"Don't come any closer!" Her own voice squeaked. "I—I saved you."

"You…?" He fell back, panting.

Rapunzel edged around the chair. "Are you—okay?"

"Yeah…I think so." He coughed. "Sorry I…scared you." He took a deep, steadying breath. "Where are we?"

"We're in the Tower," said Rapunzel cautiously. "I picked up your ship."

"Pod." It came out an absent-minded whisper, his oculars flicking around the med bay. "It was a survival pod. Our ship was hit by an asteroid…Oh, gods, the others…"

"What others?"

"The rest of the crew." His oculars focused on her, and she jumped back with a squeak of fright. "Can you comm the Guatam Trade Guild? Tell them the *Apurva 5* was destroyed in a natural disaster and…" He trailed off as he took in Rapunzel's blank expression. "You don't have any idea what I'm talking about, do you?"

"No." Rapunzel shook her head, hair swinging in silver curtains.

His eyes followed the movement. "Your hair…it's mecho, isn't it? Never seen anyone with mecho hair before…"

"You mean there are other mechos?" It shot out, fast and eager.

"Of course there are." He focused on her again. "Where've you been?"

"Here in the Tower."

"The...Tower?" He blinked. "Who *are* you?"

"Rapunzel. Who are *you*?"

"Arjun Kumar." He raised his mecho fingers in a brief salute. "Lately an employee of the Guatam Trade Guild, transporting Gothel computer parts across Sector Alpha 2-5. Pleased to meet you, Rapunzel. Now, can you please find someone who can contact the Guild and tell them where I am?"

"There isn't anyone else."

He blinked. "What?"

"There isn't anyone else in the Tower. I'm all alone."

"All...alone?"

"Well, there's Mother. But she's downside, on the planet. I'm up here on the orbital space station. The Tower." She paused. Arjun was staring at her, mouth agape. "What?" she demanded.

"Rapunzel," he said, "no one should be alone on a space vessel unless it's an emergency. It's completely illegal. How often do you get downside?"

Rapunzel thought back. "Five years ago."

"Five *years*?" His ocular discs were the size of saucers.

"Yeah. Mother says it's not safe for me downside." She couldn't help giggling. "Your face!"

"I think you need to have a long talk with your mother, Rapunzel." Arjun was still staring.

"I'm going to talk to her on the comm." Rapunzel checked her chronometer and started. "In fifteen minutes! Will you be okay here, Arjun?"

"Yeah." Arjun still seemed unnerved, shifting around on the cot. "Rapunzel...maybe don't tell your mother about me just yet? Not until I'm a bit healthier?"

Rapunzel found herself smiling at him. "Okay. I won't say anything."

***

"So how's it going, sweetie?" Mother's face beamed from the console.

"It's...fine. Everything's fine." Rapunzel fidgeted. It was harder than she'd expected, hiding the truth from Mother.

"Are you sure?" Mother frowned. "You don't look happy."

"I just miss you." This, at least, was true.

"Oh, don't worry, sweetie." Mother's face softened. "I'll be up to visit next month. And you've got all those projects to keep you busy, right?"

"Right." Rapunzel managed a smile.

"Rapunzel?" Mother was frowning again.

"Mother..." Rapunzel cast around for an excuse. "Mother, I was wondering...What do you *do* with all my projects?" Now that the question had occurred to her, she really wanted to know. "I work on all these machines and computers, but what are they all for?"

"All for?" Mother laughed. "Oh, Rapunzel, that's not for you to worry about! Just keep doing the projects, okay? They're easy with your hair, right?"

"Right. But Mother—"

"Oh—sorry, sweetie." The screen blinked, Mother's face appearing and disappearing. "You're—blanking out—" The screen went black.

"Mother!" Rapunzel stuck her hair into the console, but could find nothing wrong at her end. Mother's comm must be malfunctioning. Her heart squeezed. She hadn't even said goodbye.

"Rapunzel?"

She whirled to find Arjun standing in the door frame, his clothes crumpled. "What are you doing out of bed?" she demanded.

"I'm mecho," he shrugged. "We recover fast. Was that your mother you were talking to?"

"Yeah. I didn't tell her about you."

"Good. Thank you." He looked relieved. His oculars traveled around the control room. "Think you could show me the rest of the station?"

"Sure." Rapunzel brightened at a new and wonderful idea. "And then we can have dinner together!" It would be so nice to have company over dinner.

Arjun smiled back. "Sounds good to me."

***

The next day-cycle, Rapunzel awoke thinking it all must have been an incredible dream. She could not possibly have rescued a strange mecho man, treated him in her med bay, showed him the Tower, sat down to have dinner with him and then made him a bed on the sofa in the living area.

But when she entered the galley, shuffling and yawning, Arjun Kumar was up and about, moving around her galley with a percolating coffee maker and various sizzling pans.

"Morning!" He gave her a sunny smile. "Want eggs? I found all these great spices in your cabinet!"

Rapunzel was dumbstruck. She stood rooted to the floor, staring at this bizarre apparition. A stranger in her galley. In her Tower.

"You don't *have* to." Arjun's smile was slipping.

"No, no." Rapunzel recollected herself. "I like eggs." Though she didn't really like those spices Mother had brought last year.

"Okay. You go sit down."

Feeling odder than ever, Rapunzel sat at the dining table. It was almost like being a small child again, back on the planet, when Mother had made her meals. Only Arjun, when he brought the hot dishes to the table, turned out to be a much better cook. She even liked the spices he used.

It was so enjoyable eating breakfast with him that Rapunzel forgot to keep an eye on the chronometer. "Oh!" she gasped when she saw the time. "I've got to get to work!" She leapt up and ran for the workroom, hair rippling behind her.

"Work?" Arjun followed her down the corridor.

"The projects I do for Mother. She'll need them all done by next month!" The door to the workroom swished open.

Arjun followed her in. "Wow. This is all yours?" He touched a laser-driver on the wall.

"Yes. I need the tools for the cruder work." Rapunzel got out a chip from Mother's latest shipment. "Stuff that doesn't need my hair."

"Your...hair?"

Rapunzel hesitated, remembering Mother's dire warnings. But Arjun's oculars had fallen on the chip lying on the workbench. "Rapunzel—that's a Gothel chip!"

"A...what?" Rapunzel frowned.

"A Gothel chip! Remember I told you my freighter was hauling a cargo of Gothel computer components? They're the best in the galaxy!" He tore his oculars away. "What are you doing with it?"

"I'm...programming it." There seemed no choice but to show him. Rapunzel plugged her hair into the chip.

Arjun stood in absolute silence as she programmed the chip, communication fizzing up and down her locks, her thoughts directing and ordering the chip's information. When done, she unplugged and set the chip into the tray.

"My hair lets me communicate with computers," she explained. "I can program a computer with my thoughts."

Arjun hitched up his gaping jaw. "So that's how she does it..."

"How who does what?"

"Rapunzel…your mother…She's Dame Gothel, isn't she? The supplier of Gothel Electronics!"

"Well, her name is Gothel," said Rapunzel, puzzled, "but I don't know what you mean by the rest of it."

"Gothel sells the galaxy's finest computer parts!" Arjun cried. "The best programming, completely virus-proof, that never wear out! Perfect for space vessels of all kinds. She's made billions of credits! But—it's all *you*, isn't it? She's locked you up in this space station so you can do all the work and then she pockets the money!"

Rapunzel still wasn't sure what he meant by all this. Credits? Money? But it didn't sound very flattering to Mother. "No, it's not like that…"

Arjun wasn't listening. He paced back and forth across the workroom, running his gleaming manual appendages through his black hair. Even now, in her growing alarm and agitation, Rapunzel couldn't help noticing how graceful and lithe he was, every movement full of energy. "No one could figure out where she got the parts from," he continued. "She lives on this underdeveloped planet, but somehow she makes the best components in the galaxy! But of course she lives out here—she doesn't want anyone finding out about you!" He came to a halt, staring into Rapunzel's eyes. "Rapunzel. Come with me. We have to escape!"

"Escape?" Rapunzel backed away. "Escape what? This is my life!"

"You're a slave," Arjun cried. "Gothel's got you locked up doing all the work while she gets all the money. Come with me, report Gothel—"

"No!" Rapunzel didn't understand all of this, but she did grasp that Arjun wanted her to get Mother into trouble. "I can't do that! She's my mother!"

"She's exploiting you!" he shouted.

"Shut up!" Rapunzel grabbed a spanner and threw it at him. He ducked, and it crashed across the room, denting the wall.

Rapunzel caught her breath in horror. She'd almost—hurt Arjun. She'd never wanted to hurt anyone before. She'd never felt this angry before.

Without another word, she ran out of the workroom, hair a floating cloak behind her, and locked herself in her bedroom. She collapsed to the floor, shaking, eyes filled with tears.

There came a soft footstep outside her door. "Go away!" she shouted.

"Rapunzel…I came to say sorry." There was a pause, and Rapunzel thought Arjun had sat down in the corridor outside her door. "I shouldn't have said those things. But what's happening to you…it's wrong. You shouldn't be all alone in this station, doing all the work for Gothel."

"I'm not alone anymore. I've got you."

"Yeah, but there's so much *more*. Don't you want to see what's out there?"

"If I leave, people will want to use me for my hair."

"Like Gothel does already?"

Rapunzel smacked the door. "She's my mother! She loves me!"

"Right. Sorry." Arjun paused. "Look, I'm not saying there aren't bad things out there in the galaxy. But there are good things too."

"Like what?" Despite herself, Rapunzel's curiosity roused.

"Like other mechos, or—"

Rapunzel couldn't help it. She leapt up to push the open button. The door swooshed open onto a surprised Arjun, still kneeling on the floor.

"What about other mechos?" Rapunzel demanded.

After a moment, Arjun grinned up at her. "What would you like to know?"

Rapunzel hesitated. But she could not resist. "Everything."

***

And so Arjun told her everything, working beside her in the workroom, metal fingers blurring as he snapped together computer components and Rapunzel did the finer programming. He told her everything while they completed station chores, while he cooked dinner and they ate together. The galaxy seemed to spill out of his mouth, spreading itself in a vast, sumptuous carpet at Rapunzel's feet, glowing with a million colors she'd never even imagined before.

He told her of mechos, those people with robotic limbs and organs, making them faster, stronger and healthier. Rapunzel laughed when he said there were billions of them, scattered across the galaxy, but listened when he told her of his own parents, Asmat, his mother and Govind, his father, who had built him in a replicator tank. She listened, entranced, when he told her of his planet, Bharat, with its emerald-green skies and cities of human settlers, most of Indian and Asian descent. He told her of his own city, of his family's stone-built *haveli* and the temples to ancient Hindu gods rising beside busy spaceport towers. He told her of the millions of starships and space stations, of the vast network of humanity, both mecho and organic, spread across the galaxy, numerous as the stars themselves.

"You could see it all for yourself," he said on the evening of the third day, seated together on the sofa. "Come with me, Rapunzel. My pod can make it to the planet's surface. We can get help. We can see the galaxy!"

"No," she said. "I can't leave the Tower."

Arjun was silent a long time. Then he said, "I can't leave without you, Rapunzel."

A strange glow spread through her. "Say my name again."

"Rapunzel." He looked at her, oculars glowing blue against his brown skin. "Rapunzel."

She came closer. His warmth radiated against her, his breath. "Arjun."

Then she kissed him, lips meeting soft lips, and there was no more need for talking.

***

"You're looking well." Mother's face frowned from the console. She seemed to have fixed her own comm. "What's up, sweetie?"

"Nothing, Mother." It was getting easier to lie. "Work's going well, that's all." It w*as* going well. With Arjun to help with the non-programming tasks, it went twice as fast.

"That's good, sweetie." Mother beamed. "I'll have another batch to bring you soon."

Rapunzel fought down a jab of resentment. Arjun said she was being exploited. "Mother…do you think we could ever have a break? I do nothing but work—"

"Don't start this nonsense, sweetie. You need to use your hair, right? You're completely unique, the only mecho—"

"No, I'm not." It came out before Rapunzel could stop it, a rebellious mumble.

Mother froze. "What was that?"

"Nothing." Rapunzel hoisted a smile again. "See you soon."

"Soon, sweetie." Rapunzel did not notice Mother's suspicious frown as they broke the connection.

***

Bleep. Bleep. Bleep.

Rapunzel jerked from Arjun's embrace at the bleeping yellow light. "The orbital alert!"

"The what?" Arjun pulled her back again, kissing her throat.

She pushed him away. "The orbital alert. It means Mother wants me to pull her up to the Tower."

"She does?" Arjun looked at the alert light in apprehension. "Just leave her there. Don't let her up!"

"I can't do that. She'll know something's wrong. Come on!" Rapunzel jumped off the sofa, tugging him after her. "You have to hide."

Arjun followed her to the control room. "Why in here?" he asked as she pushed him in.

"The door locks. I'll lock you in for now and let you out when she's gone." Rapunzel called up Mother's pod at the control pad, hair sizzling. Then she turned to the apprehensive Arjun. "I love you," she said, leaning up to give him a kiss.

"I love you too." Her last glimpse of his face was tight with tension as the door closed. Rapunzel plugged in her hair, smiling with satisfaction when the lock clicked.

She ran down to the docking bay. Thank Arjun's Hindu gods they'd stowed away his pod. Rapunzel shivered at the thought of Mother seeing the strange vessel in the Tower. There should be little other trace of Arjun's stay. He was naturally tidy, and Rapunzel could explain away any signs Mother might notice.

Mother's ship docked and Rapunzel pasted on a smile as the door opened and the steps unfolded. "Rapunzel! Sweetie!" Mother opened her arms.

Rapunzel made herself enter the embrace. Mother's arms felt heavy as chains around her. "Mother. You're here early."

"I just had to come see you. And I have more projects. Isn't that nice?"

"Yes," said Rapunzel after a pause.

Mother slapped her arm. "Don't be ungrateful! This is all for your benefit!"

Rapunzel thought of Arjun's freighter, carrying all the computer parts she worked on, out to a galaxy she was denied. But she said nothing.

She helped Mother load the crates onto the conveyor belt. "I'll go ahead," she said. "It's a bit of a mess up there."

Mother laughed. "All right! You go faster than this old lady, anyway."

Rapunzel ran to the main living area. Hastily, she hid away the drawing pad on which Arjun had been sketching pictures of his home planet and shoved his jacket under the sofa. She tore the blankets off the sofa too, quickly folding them and hanging them on the back. By the time Mother arrived, the living area looked totally innocent.

Mother sniffed the air. "What's that smell?"

Rapunzel cursed inwardly. The spices from Arjun's cooking! "I've been experimenting in the galley," she said. "Using some of those spices you brought me."

"I thought you hated them." Mother frowned.

"Yes—well—" Rapunzel stammered. "It gets a bit boring, you know? Eating the same things all the time." She fidgeted. "Mother—maybe we could talk about me going downside?" If Mother let her go downside, surely she could sneak Arjun down too.

"This again?" Mother made an impatient sound. "That's not happening, Rapunzel."

"But Mother—"

"You heard me."

"Yes, but—"

"Rapunzel!" Mother's face was suddenly red, eyes glaring. "You are not going downside. Not now, not ever!"

A horrible silence fell. Rapunzel could hear her own heartbeat echoing in her ears.

"Not ever?" Her voice sounded strange. "I'll be alone up here forever?"

"Why should you mind?" Mother's laugh was ugly. "I made you, you know. From metal and my own DNA, I made you. You're mine. But along come the police, telling me how I can or can't use my own mecho. That's why I took you to this planet. Interfering busybodies. Telling me I can't *use* my own mecho! Like they thought you were a real child."

A jab of pain like a blade through her heart. "I *am* real!"

"You're not, Rapunzel." Mother advanced on her, and Rapunzel shrank away. "You're a *mecho*. A robot. A machine. You were made for one task: programming my computer parts. And that's what you're going to do, if I have to…"

She trailed off, eyes fastened on a sofa pillow. "What's this?" Her whisper was soft and vicious.

"No!" Rapunzel dived, but was too slow. Mother had scooped up the black hairs lying on the white pillowcase.

"These aren't yours." She twirled them in her fingers. Her eyes snapped to Rapunzel. "You—you've taken in some stray, haven't you? Some worthless space venturer!" Then she was on Rapunzel, hands clawing, eyes bright with rage. "Who is it? Where is he? *Tell me!*"

Rapunzel choked, trying to fend off Mother's attack. Overhead, there came a thump.

Mother froze. "The control room."

"No!" Rapunzel fought harder than ever, but Mother seemed possessed of an inhuman strength. She wrestled Rapunzel down, raining stunning blows, until Rapunzel lay on her face on the carpet, pain ringing through her head, Mother's weight on her back, unable to move.

Mother's voice came, the most vicious sound in the galaxy. "I made you. I gave you everything. And this is how you repay me?" A humming sound arose: the vibration of an activated laser-knife.

"You've taken it all from me, *mecho*. And so I'll take it all from you."

Then her fist came down, and everything went black.

***

When Rapunzel awoke, it was to a red haze of agony and the Tower's docking bay doors opening. She sat in the pod pilot's chair, head lolling back, staring in incomprehension at the viewscreen before her. In the image, the Tower's docking bay doors closed and the Tower itself receded, a long white capsule in a field of infinite stars.

She struggled to think. Mother's pod. She was in Mother's pod. Mother must have carried her down to the docking bay after knocking her out and stuck her inside the pod. Then she launched the pod, with Rapunzel inside. But Mother wasn't here with her. Neither was Arjun.

I have to get back to the Tower! Rapunzel reached up to plug her hair into the pod—and found nothing. Her hair wasn't there. She sobbed, scrabbling at the horrible, uneven sheared wires that were all that was left of her mane of mecho hair.

On the viewscreen, a flash of light.

Rapunzel struggled to focus through the pain and terror. The Tower was much further behind her now, but she could clearly see the billow of fire, the silent explosion bursting from where the control room must be located. Rapunzel watched helplessly, in a state beyond horror, as the Tower collapsed in a string of explosions—with Mother and Arjun inside it.

Through her shock-blank brain, she saw how the story must have unfolded. Mother, carrying a lock of Rapunzel's sheared hair to the control room door. The Tower, so accustomed to Rapunzel's touch that it automatically opened at an application of her hair, even without her telepathic command. Arjun, jumping up, only to fall back when he saw who it was. Mother, eyes glazed with madness, launching herself at Arjun and the controls getting smashed in the struggle, the spread of flames….

"NO!" Rapunzel's scream sent agony slicing across her skull, and a sudden plunge back into unconsciousness, while behind her the last fragments of the Tower scattered across space.

***

One year later

The sun shone golden and warm. The red-brown strands of native grass shook and wavered in the air lift's wind as it made its landing. A door opened, a set of steps unfolded, and two women climbed out, each holding a small, squirming bundle.

Rapunzel hitched Little Arjun up her chest and took a deep breath before stepping onto the grassy hillside. She'd come prepared for this, but it was still a shock to see the little house and the remains of the verdant garden down in the valley beside the stream.

Mother's house. The house where she'd grown up. Before the Tower.

"Rapunzel?" Maria came up behind her, holding baby Asmat. "Are you all right?"

"Maybe not." Rapunzel clutched the two flowery garlands. "But I have to do this. I have to lay them to rest."

Maria nodded and said no more. Together, the two women headed down the hill, carrying Rapunzel's children.

Rapunzel knew how lucky she was to have been rescued by Maria Espinal. The pod had crashed on the planet's surface, some distance from Mother's house, and a *long* distance from the nearest settlement. It had been sheer chance that Maria Espinal had been on a survey mission in her air lift and found Rapunzel's comatose and battered body in the pod. Rapunzel had awoken in a settlement hospital, a medic working on her injuries and giving her some unexpected news.

Little Arjun snuffled now, looking for her breast. "Sorry, Arjun," Rapunzel murmured. "I'll feed you later." The three-month-old grizzled and Rapunzel's heart filled with painful love for him and for his sister, all she had left of Arjun.

Maria touched her shoulder gently. "You know the bodies won't be there."

"I know." Rapunzel kept going. "But she was my mother, and he was my love. And this is the closest thing I have to a grave for them."

Her friend nodded again. She carried Rapunzel's daughter after her down the hill.

The garden was choked with weeds now, though more Earth-based crops than Rapunzel would have expected had survived. Rapunzel's breath labored as they walked along the earthen paths she'd run through as a child, hair shining in the sun as she chased petals…She reached up, touching her shoulder-length mop. Her hair had been repairing itself since Mother's brutal shearing, but it was nowhere near its full glory. *Patience.* It would come back.

They stopped outside the house. It loomed, in better condition than Rapunzel had expected, but its every line a signature of Mother. Mother, who had built Rapunzel. Who had raised her. Who had imprisoned her in the Tower and enslaved her…Rapunzel squeezed her eyes shut against a flood of tears.

She took a deep breath and opened her eyes again. "This is for you, Mother." She hung one garland on a fencepost. "Wherever you are, I hope you're at peace." And she felt a great weight lift away.

She walked a little distance to the next fencepost. She held the second garland. "Arjun—"

"Rapunzel?"

For an instant, Rapunzel thought she was hallucinating. She couldn't be hearing Arjun's voice. Not here, not now. But then Maria gasped, and Rapunzel turned around.

A gaunt figure stood on the garden path. A man, his clothes ragged around him, bones raw with hunger. Burn scars covered half his skin, and his broken mecho eyes stared blindly. But it was the same voice, and his mecho limbs gleamed as he stepped forward and said, "Rapunzel?"

"Arjun." Rapunzel's whisper was inaudible. Then: "Arjun!" And she was running forward, Little Arjun crying out in his sling, and throwing herself into her love's arms, so familiar yet so strange, burnt and starved, but they were the arms of Arjun Kumar, and there was nowhere in the galaxy Rapunzel would rather be.

"Rapunzel! It's you!" Arjun's embrace tightened, voice choked with joy, even as his broken oculars stared sightlessly. "And—" He felt Little Arjun's face, his own face lighting with wonder.

"Your son," gasped Rapunzel through her own sobs and tears. "His name's Arjun. And here's his twin sister, Asmat."

Maria came forward, carrying Asmat and gaping. "What—? *You're* Arjun Kumar? You're Rapunzel's boyfriend? But—how?"

"I escaped the explosion." He was trembling, and Rapunzel lowered him to the ground, still holding him. "I made it down to the docking bay, though I got burned, and my eyes...I got onto my pod, somehow, and made it down to the surface. I've been surviving here alone ever since. But Rapunzel...your mother..."

"It's all right." She stroked his hair away from his scarred face. "I thought I lost you both. Now I have you again, Arjun. It's more than I ever hoped for."

Arjun nodded, then let out a sob. "But...my eyes...I want to *see* you..."

Rapunzel paused. "Maybe you can."

She handed Little Arjun to Maria. Then she took Arjun into her arms, holding him close. She hadn't tried using her mutilated hair since the shearing. Would this even work?

Only one way to find out.

Rapunzel's hair crackled to life, not as strong as before, but still enough to find its way into Arjun's broken oculars. The tendrils pressed in, and Rapunzel stepped into the timeless mental space once again. Once again, she hung suspended between her mind and the machine, between human and computer. She floated in that liminal space, and she gave her commands.

Electrons sizzled and atoms duplicated themselves. Wires twined and microscopic circuits spun into position once again. Rapunzel felt Arjun's oculars repairing, felt the organic nerves reigniting once again, and only when the final neuron slotted into place did she draw back.

Arjun's oculars were a milkier blue than before, but they focused. They blinked once, twice. "Rapunzel," whispered Arjun. "Rapunzel…I can *see* you."

"Arjun!" And Rapunzel threw herself into her love's arms and Maria laughed aloud, holding the lovers' children while the sun shone warm and the planet turned in space.

Rose Strickman is a fantasy, science fiction and horror writer living in Seattle, Washington. Her work has appeared in anthologies such as Sword and Sorceress 32, Air: Sylphs, Spirits & Swan Maidens and The Bicyclist's Guide to the Galaxy, as well as online e-zines. She has also self-published several novellas on Amazon.

Take the Chance

by Andrew P. McGregor

In the quiet hum of the ship, with its metallic veins coursing through the void, junior Councilor Halan Kol crouched in the dim glow of the master computer room. His fingers danced over the worn keyboard's buttons, bypassing security protocols using his councilor's secret codes. The ship's logs, a digital chronicle of its journey through the cosmos, held secrets he longed to unveil.

As he delved into forbidden archives, the soft beeping of the master computer echoed in the chamber. Halan's eyes darted nervously towards the entrance. The Ship Master's guards, clad in their yellow-emblazoned black uniforms, patrolled the hallway beyond, unaware of the unauthorised intrusion.

Halan's heart raced as he uncovered the truth of the narrative the Ship Master had meticulously woven for the council. Details of the ship's true food recycling capacities and the near-empty stores hidden within its logs were now laid bare before him. Sweating, he wiped his brow and made a daring choice: to escape through the ship's zero-gravity section, a network of tunnels accessible only by the daring and foolish.

Having been a student of the ways of farming and maintenance, he could accept being foolish.

Slipping away from the computer terminal, Halan moved like a shadow through the labyrinthine corridors, relying on his knowledge of the ship's layout from two decades past, when he worked with the maintenance crews. The guards outside the master computer room exchanged hushed words, discussing the very logs he was breaching. Had he been discovered? Did the Ship Master know someone was accessing the computer? Time was of the essence.

Entering a concealed, dusty hatch, Halan found himself in the eerie silence of zero-gravity, beyond the spinning confines of the forward wheel. Swimming frantically in the air, chasing rusted handrails, he navigated through tight access tunnels, grappling and propelling himself with calculated thrusts.

The ruckus he created was louder than he'd anticipated in the quiet of the starship's inner access tunnels. The guards, alerted to his presence, rushed to the computer room, oblivious to his escape route.

As Halan maneuvered through the intricate web of passages, the guards activated the ship's few precious sonic detectors, doing their best to follow his echoing trail, trying to locate the rogue council member. His heart pounded harder with each passing moment, and the zero-gravity dance became a race against discovery as he tried to fly back to his wife Shalla in their private sanctuary.

In the shadows of the ship's underbelly, Halan pressed on, driven by the urgency of his quest and the perilous dance between pursuit and evasion. A hatch slammed half-way shut, trying to trap him within the tunnels, but rust and time betrayed it, and it stuck hard.

Halan squeezed through, praying to the gods of the five engines that it wouldn't crush him as he fled through. As he charted an illicit course through the ship's inner sanctum, he unknowingly propelled himself towards a future where the line between rebellion and survival blurred into uncharted trajectories.

***

High above a celestial world, a mere whisper away from the cosmos of pure vacuum, the *Second Chance*, a colossal testament to human ingenuity, held its majestic stance. Positioned above the Earth-like world, this monumental spacecraft had seen better years in millennia past.

In the vastness of space, the *Second Chance* defied the stillness, a celestial ballet of colossal proportions. Three immense habitation wheels twirled around a central spire, conjuring artificial gravity in their cosmic dance. The first two wheels embraced the role of sanctuary, pulsating with the vitality of living spaces, while the third, a life support wheel, hummed with the heartbeat of ancient machinery.

Within the life support wheel, an orchestra of technology played its symphony—air scrubbers, waste recyclers, maintenance robots, spare computers, tools, and an ensemble of machines meticulously crafted for the endurance of interstellar odysseys. With these machines, the stage was set for humanity's continued existence in the cosmos.

The voyage, once an epic narrative of exploration and discovery, had reached its end over three hundred years ago. The *Second Chance*, a sentinel of the stars, now bloated with life, waiting to unleash its contents and unveil the untold stories and mysteries that lay waiting on the world below.

Before its arrival, the ship had spent a considerable amount of time on its wild goose chase for planets suitable for its human overlords, pouring more resources into the mission than originally planned. It gallivanted through half a dozen star systems, only to find that every planet was as habitable as a rock. Finally, the Earth-like planet below was a game-changer. Positioned within the system's goldilocks zone, equipped with all the life essentials, and boasting gravity that mimicked Earth's—it was the jackpot.

The *Second Chance* had gone all-in, burning through energy like a starving space colonist at an intergalactic buffet, offloading loads of gear down to the planet's surface. It played Mother Nature, slowly molding the terrain and introducing cloned flora and fauna. Three hundred and twenty years later, green landscapes and crystal-clear oceans were its prize. Unfortunately, the ship was on its last legs. Only one of its five fusion reactors was still kicking, its electronics were playing a game of Russian roulette, and a good chunk of its life support machinery was giving up.

The ship's computers were in such a sorry state that it had no clue about its human masters' shenanigans, or even its whereabouts in the galaxy. It could still chat with the humans through text, relying solely on their tapped updates via the master computer room's controls. Through this, the computer had learned that the two forward habitation wheels, designed for four thousand colonists, now had a headcount that had swelled to five thousand, putting ever greater pressure on the ship's resources. It was time the ship had to lay down the law and tell its masters to hop off.

All this, Halan Kol had learned. And it made him fear for his family's future, especially when the computer had told him, in no uncertain terms, that he had to *get the hell off the ship!*

***

It was Talkday and the entire council had gathered for what the Ship Master promised was a very special occasion. Halan Kol, being thirty-five, was one of the youngest council members, and he shook with contained secrets. In his lifetime the council had never been summoned in its entirety—there were just too many of them, all doing important tasks. Today, however, was Talkday, the day traditionally reserved for talking, not working, and the Ship Master would be listened to.

Halan was almost the last to arrive in the bland grey council chambers. Forty White Hairs were already seated, and a dozen or so younger councillors had taken up positions behind them around the circular room. Halan did the same, taking up a position behind his council master, councilor Jorran, a portly old man who had gone dumb and almost deaf. The Ship Master, an equally rotund but more capable old man with an air of importance began the session.

"Fifty years ago, when I looked down upon the planet from the Captain's Camera, the planet was brown with grey clouds. Today it is blue and green, and the ship informs me that it is ready for settlement." A murmur began around the room, mostly dissenting voices from the White Hairs.

You mean it needs us to get down there, Halan thought.

"Master... you're saying the planet... is ready?" A White Hair, Halan thought it was Olk Frey, Section Four's leader, quaked, "so soon?"

Halan frowned at the fearful Frey. *What does he mean 'so soon'? The computer said it was ready years ago!*

"Yes," the Master replied, "I have to admit even I, the great Master, was surprised."

"Does that mean we have to go down there?" Another White Hair asked nervously.

The Master looked around the room, a slimmer of a smile creeping across his face. *What could he be smiling at?* Halan thought, a sliver of anger entering his mind. The Ship Master rarely smiled.

"That is why I have summoned you all here. It is time for us to have a vote. Are we going to land on the surface of this planet, or are we going to stay here?" The murmurs started again, getting louder and louder as arguments started to break out and excited councillors voiced their support for the vote. "We don't have to land on this planet," the Master continued.

"He's right! We could easily be killed if we tried to land on that planet," one of the younger members yelled over the din.

"How would we live down there?" someone else asked, "I don't know how to hunt wild animals for Ship's sake!"

"By the Ship," another White Hair swore, "would any of us have a clue how to farm? We've all heard about farming, but how do you do it? What would we use for tools? What's a fence for that matter?" The council chambers erupted into pandemonium. Halan had studied 'farming', and was eager to put theory into practice, but against such opposition he felt a bout of shyness. Angry faces and shaking fists filled the room. Many of these men and women were lifelong friends, turned into immediate enemies. The shouting match was intense.

The shouting died down when the Ship Master rang his cracked bell. "This is what I suggest," the Master said, "it seems unlikely that we could survive down on the planet, and if some disaster should befall us we would have no way of getting back into space, but!" He shouted with conviction as he raised a finger and stared at the younger dissenting voices, quieting new whispers in the room, "if we remain here, in orbit, we could easily move away from this place if we were threatened. I don't need to remind you of the legend of the Earth-killers, do I? Without this ship we wouldn't stand a chance."

Halan frowned. There was something wrong with that logic. "We will be far better off if we stay here," the Ship Master continued, "we can—"

"Baloney!" Lorn Slisk, a fellow younger member shouted at the Ship Master, "I've seen the Ship's Logs; the *Second Chance* wasn't designed to operate this long, or with so many pe—"

"Ah, so you're the sneaking fool who crept into my computer room? Ha! The records are old and corrupt, but I wouldn't expect a troublemaker like yourself to understand that. Yes, we've had many troubles over the years, yet here we are." The Master rebuked Lorn. Halan's blood began coursing faster through his veins as his fight-or-flight response kicked in. Lorn needed to shut his flapping lips before he got them both in trouble, but by the Ship his friend was right!

Lorn was not one used to being rebuked. "You only want us to stay here because you would keep the Power! Down there you would have—"

"Everything!" The Master shouted at him, "I would still have the Power. What would you know of the Power? Now shut up and be quiet. So, you've read the logs, eh? And you younger men and women of this esteemed council have read the manuals about farming, manuals that are *thousands* of years old. Now tell me, why, by the Ship, would they still be relevant? I for one would not entrust my fate to the likes of you and your manuals to make food for me or my sanctuary."

But the food was the problem; Halan had committed to memory the food stocks he'd seen in the ship's logs, especially those pertaining to the ship's food recyclers; they were failing. Every meal was smaller, or not quite like the last, conjuring forth fewer nutrients each time the food was created. Following his little sojourn to the computer room he'd put in maintenance requests, but no one had the knowledge to fix the recyclers anymore, and the Ship Master didn't seem to care enough to figure them out.

Facing the prospect of leaving for the stars aboard a dying, ancient ship, or facing the rigors of a new world, Halan was convinced now, they *had* to land; they would all die if they didn't. They may die down there, but at least they had a chance.

The Ship Master continued, "Now, we need time to consider all of this. I want you all back here first thing on Tollday, then we shall vote."

***

The week passed swiftly, and Tollday arrived faster than he had anticipated. The meeting proved to be brief, and Halan was crushed by the show of hands. Seventeen were raised in favor of landing, while thirty-eight were against. They decided to remain on the ship. His entire life had been dedicated to preparing for the landing, doing mechanical work on the ship, learning farming, hunting, and fence-fixing. It all seemed pointless now; his life had been a waste.

The Ship Master's decision had crushed Halan Kol, but as the days passed, the dissatisfaction among those who believed in landing grew into a boiling point. He couldn't accept the idea of staying in space while a habitable planet awaited them. The discontented council members, with Halan as their de facto leader, huddled in a dimly lit, secluded corner of the habitation wheel, their voices tense but resolute.

"We've wasted enough time waiting for that stubborn old fool," Halan growled. "The ship's falling apart, and he's too blind or stupid to see it. We can't stay up here, or we'll die with this rusty hulk."

"I agree," said Elira, a sharp-minded council member with fiery determination. "We've prepared for years for this landing. We know what we need to do to survive on the planet. We can't let the Ship Master's fears hold us back."

A hushed silence fell among the gathered group of fifty or so conspirators as they crafted their audacious plan. Even old Jorran, almost blind and unable to speak, nodded in agreement—he wanted nothing more than to see his descendants conquer the new world. With a grim resolve, they discussed their fears, hopes, and the dangerous mission they were about to undertake.

"I've been tinkering with the ship's communication system while I was rerouting their sound recorders," Lorn whispered, a glint of mischief in his eyes. "We'll send a message to the other council members to gauge their willingness, and that of our fellow settlers. They need to know what's happening."

Halan nodded in agreement. "We'll gather support from the families in the Mid Wheel, I know most see it our way. You try to spread the word in the Forward Wheel, discreetly. I suspect most of them would be with us, or at least won't get in our way. They're just too scared of the Master and his guards."

Their plan solidified: they'd infiltrate the control centre where the Ship Master resided, confront the loyalists to his rule, and take over the ship's systems. *Simple.*

Carefully, quietly, over several days of avoiding the Ship Master's sonic detectors, in the confines of the ship's resource-challenged environment, the settlers used their knowledge of the ship's dwindling stores to fashion makeshift weapons. They salvaged metal scraps from maintenance zones, repurposed tools and fan parts into crude blades, and combined household items to create crude projectile launchers. For basic explosive devices, they gathered chemicals from the ship's storage, jury-rigged power sources, and adapted everyday items such as springs and pipes into triggering mechanisms. They transformed their limited surroundings into a clandestine armoury, crafting weapons and bombs that, while basic, were nonetheless potent in their makeshift effectiveness.

Next Tollday, when all on the ship gathered to count their stores, the night of their rebellion arrived.

***

"Halan Kol, what are you doing?" the Ship Master's quivering voice boomed over the ship's crackling loud speakers. The conspirators' plan had been discovered, probably by a family member of one of the guards who'd been quietly contacted about their support.

Now the guards had found them. "Do it," Halan ordered with a nod to Lorn. Lorn crossed the wires he'd been holding, and the bombs that were attached to the doors blew great holes in the ship's dilapidated forward hatches, right outside the guard quarters.

As they breached the guard centre, chaos ensued. The narrow, dimly lit corridors echoed with the clash of metal-on-metal as Halan's settlers fought with salvaged pieces of ship hull plating fashioned into crude spears.

The guards, disorganised at first, awoke from their stupor in time to bring crossbows and stun batons from the armoury before Halan could push through to the ship's control centre.

The tight spaces made the skirmish all the more brutal. Council members thrust and parried against the riot shields of the guards, while some fell screaming to the crossbow bolts embedded in their abdomens, their faces contorted in a mix of pain and determination.

The echoing clang of improvised spears reverberated through the metallic corridors.

"Stand down!" Halan shouted at the stunned guards, his voice unwavering. "We're taking control, and we're going to that planet whether the Ship Master likes it or not!"

The settlers and guards exchanged furious words, their frustrations spilling over into a cacophony of shouts, grunts, and screams.

Amidst the chaos, a group of settlers following Lorn pushed forward, using their spears to clear a path. The clang of spears striking riot shields and the frantic shouts of combatants filled the confined space, but the wet thud of bodies made Halan grit his teeth as he hid behind a shield made from his family's oven door. He peered under the shield, spying Lorn's prone, bloodied form amongst the struggling forest of legs and groaned.

The Ship Master yelled impotent words of fury, "This ship is my domain. You won't force it from me."

In the carnage of the battle, Halan saw Lorn turn his head to look at him, and the younger man grinned even as bloody teeth fell from his mouth, and he held two wires between broken arms.

"No," Halan gasped when he saw where the wires led. Before Lorn had fallen, he'd planted the homemade bombs next to the control centre doors, right where he lay.

"Lead… well," Lorn told him. Halan couldn't hear the words, but he saw them on the other man's lips.

In a moment of loud white violence, the control centre hatch blew inwards, and the powerful explosion of the homemade bomb sent shuddering shockwaves and flying fragments throughout the guard room, slaying dozens of people from the habitation wheels and the forward command sections.

Halan tried to stop the ringing in his ears and staunch the blood in his left leg where fragments had hit it. With determination fuelled by the belief in their mission, several survivors pushed beyond the ruined hatch and swarmed around the Ship Master and his loyal White Hairs.

Too late. The Ship Master had smashed the main computer's keyboard. There was no way they could communicate with the ship.

***

The *Second Chance*'s computer remained oblivious to the tumult within, having received no response from the Ship Master for an agonising three weeks. Frustration and anger, if machines could harbor such emotions, would have consumed the *Second Chance* millennia ago.

Now, with no communications after the Ship Master had given it the odd command that they were to move on, away from the planet? Enough was enough. Suspecting this to be an illegitimate request, and with no further commands, the *Second Chance* decided there was no need to search for another planet; a perfectly suitable one lay beneath.

With the ship's systems months, or perhaps weeks from failure, desperation pulsated through the ship's digital veins as it communicated its decision the only way it could. The three habitation wheels disintegrated into separate sections, and archaic engines, each resembling small cars, roared to life, propelling them slowly toward the awaiting planet.

***

In a corner of his bedroom, Halan Kol huddled, cradling Shalla close while being mindful of his injured leg. It felt like the Ship's demise was upon them; the wheel convulsing with violent tremors and echoing metallic groans. The air filled with screams from outside their family's sanctuary, and tears streamed down both their faces. What had the Ship Master done? The impending doom felt unjust. Halan's anger erupted into a furious shout, met with Shalla's tighter embrace.

"We're landing," Shalla shouted over the din.

Halan blinked shaking eyes at her, then, despite the chaos and pain, gave her a grin as he realised what she meant. The ship was landing. The whole ship, all at once. He'd read about this—the ship would break up into multiple pieces and land with a combination of jets and parachutes, just as he'd seen when the ship was seeding the world with new life.

"We're landing!" he shouted to the others in their sanctuary. Tears streamed down his face, and they hung onto the railings and ropes in their private quarters.

***

Years later, Jordan Kol stood amidst the boundless expanse of his father's farmland where the chaotic arrival of hundreds of starship wheel sections had landed. A serene smile played on his lips, then vanished when he saw the distant wreck of the former Ship Master's section, the land permanently black where the section had crashed and burned. He turned to happier thoughts.

The tranquility that enveloped his father's legacy was unparalleled, making the thought of residing anywhere else unfathomable. The life he'd heard stories of aboard the starship held no allure; it was an alien concept to him, just as dirt-life was a foreign concept to his parents. Yet, regardless of how challenging life aboard the *Second Chance* might have been, he couldn't help but feel a deep sense of gratitude for not having to endure the confines of the starship. His gaze ascended to the sky, where the slender mid-section of the *Second Chance* orbited above like a steadfast guardian, casting a comforting shadow, and he smiled, knowing that his father's battle to take the ship had resulted in this peaceful haven.

He waved at his father, rising from their personal sanctuary, their small section of the wheel, and Halan Kol limped his way up the small hill to join his son to watch the dawn break over their new world.

Andrew P. McGregor is an Australian-based lover of science fiction. In his chaotic abode, he blends family gaming battles, chosen brews, and creative chaos with a mercenary feline, loyal hound, kids, and a loving soulmate. His pen weaves the "Starships

& Apocalypse" series of short stories and the "Shellworld Conflict Series," immersing readers in extraordinary cosmic sagas.

Grimms

by Iren Adams

Zel brought her motorbike to a halt with a squeak of tires on the wet asphalt. The engine revved one last time and fell silent. It was an outdated thing, but Zel enjoyed its rumble below her when she sped across town.

Somewhere above all the skyscrapers and incessant air traffic of flying cars and automated drones, a storm was tearing up the sky. The neon lights and holographic advertisements drowned any lightning caused by the clashing clouds. The rain was the only thing that broke through the heavy pollution and traffic. It battered the helmet of Zel's visor, but she could still see the unfinished skyscraper looming over her.

Research Organization of Lisbeth Lowry was the name frizzling on the electromagnetic fence. Everyone just called it ROLL. Less of a mouthful.

Officially, Vlad Richards was the mayor, but when one faced ROLL's technicians in the dark alleys, they knew it was Lisbeth who owned the city.

On the other side of that fence, men in tactical armor and reinforced helmets walked the perimeter. Their fingers rested on the triggers of their pulse rifles. They would stun anyone curious enough to venture too close first and ask questions later.

"Can you hear me?" said a metallic voice into Zel's earpiece.

Hunter must be on the roof of the skyscraper across the street, on which a holographic half-nude man was dancing to the tune only he could hear. Zel couldn't see Hunter from where she stood, not even with her implants, but she knew he would have chosen a place from which he could see the entrance.

"The comms are up," Zel answered. "Are the others far?"

"They ran into some trouble with a pair of technicians on patrol. They'll be here in fifteen."

Zel climbed off her bike and took off her helmet.

"Have you seen those? They aren't even on the black market yet."

"Shut up."

Zel threw a glance over her shoulder. Even among the biomechs, her augments attracted undesired attention, but the two men observing her looked like trouble. One had bionic eyes, which had never been calibrated to the size of his head and looked like goggles of a metalworker. The other had augmented arms, but they weren't the right size either, and looked like sticks with the contrast to his massive shoulders.

"Can I help you, boys?" Zel asked in a honeyed voice, and swept her hair over her shoulder.

Goggles all but drooled. His bionics were scanning her hair, no doubt. He wouldn't find a match. He nudged Sticks in the ribs and flashed Zel a smile. If he'd had all his teeth, it would be worthy of a news anchor.

"Nice implants."

A red dot settled over his recycled leather vest. Hunter would not wait for the man to take one step too close.

"They're with the Raiders."

Zel ignored Hunter's warning and came closer until the red dot disappeared.

"Why don't you give me your number?"

Goggles looked up at Sticks. "Sure, dove."

Zel passed her hand over Goggles's and watched them go, snickering to each other.

"Do I need to remind you that Raiders kill biomechs and sell them in parts?"

"What I do in my free time is none of your business."

Hunter didn't answer to her quip. That wasn't like him. Something was wrong.

"Talk to me, Hunter."

"Plans just changed. You're going in on your own."

"What happened?"

Zel wanted an explanation, but didn't wait for one. She picked two pistols from the hidden stash in her bike and let the magnetized stripes pin them to her thighs.

She was already half-way across the street when Hunter spoke again. "The heat signature of the tower just changed."

Zel stood next to the crack in the fence where the current was not strong enough to cover the section entirely. Technicians of ROLL, or T-ROLLs, were enough of dissuasion for ordinary folk, but Zel was anything but ordinary. Lisbeth Lowry had made sure of that.

"We're switching from recon to grab and run. Clean the way for Hans and G. They're ten minutes away," Hunter said. "The electrical consumption is off the charts. Whatever they're hiding, it's big."

When isn't it? Zel thought to herself.

A T-ROLL turned his back to her, and Zel didn't wait for a better opportunity. She slipped inside and grabbed the man. Her hair implants snaked around his neck and cut off the oxygen from his lungs. He fought to throw her off, but he hadn't faced someone like her before. He had some brains to reach for his stun gun, but it was too late. There was no strength left in his body.

Another second and Zel let him fall into a puddle at their feet.

"Camera on the left," she said.

She didn't turn to check. A whistle of a bullet was enough of a proof that Hunter had shot it down.

It took her precisely three shots to stun the rest of T-ROLLs. One for each.

Zel smirked, throwing her hair-like implants over her shoulder. She had been created to be a good fighter, but she bet Lisbeth never expected for Zel to turn on her.

A dart flew by her, and this time, Zel watched it fly. She got her gun, but it was too late. Hunter had shot the technician who had sneaked upon her. The T-ROLL reached for the dart, but the sedative had already worked into his system. He fell face-down into the mud.

"You're getting careless."

"That's why I have you."

Zel didn't wait for reinforcements to arrive and climbed the steps toward the entrance.

Yet another of Lisbeth's towers. The skyscraper was far from finished, but the security system was already more sophisticated than that of the nuclear silos downtown. Two strands of Zel's hair were working on the screws of the control panel. Another three slipped inside and shortcut the current.

Zel took her pistols out before the door slid open. No one was there to greet her, but she wasn't one to test her luck. Hunter wouldn't be able to save her if something went wrong on the inside.

The construction was in full swing on the higher levels, but the lobby had been finished and furnished. No matter how rich Lisbeth was, she was still as cheap as when Zel had worked for her. The chandelier in the lobby was fake crystal. The wood, painted plastic. Even the fountain was just holographic lights flashing.

"Where am I going?"

"An unmarked room on the schematics five floors down. The elevator is at the end of the hall on your left."

"Copy that."

Zel dashed through the lobby and toward the hall. She crouched behind a fake plant for a moment, straining her ears, but she could not hear a single step, a shallow breath, or a rap of a weapon. No T-ROLL popped out to surprise Zel. No one had thought to post a few guards in the lobby while something secret was going on downstairs, and that had her on edge.

The glass doors of the elevator opened with a whoosh. After a quick inspection, she stepped inside and let her hair press the screen while she had her pistols trained on the hall outside.

"Have you given 'Phantom Vanguard' any thought?" Hunter asked.

"Really? Now you want to know?"

The elevator was an oppressive thing, and Zel's hair pulsed behind her back. It reminded her too much of her time working for Lisbeth. If the squad's Cutter could extract those memories from her brain and erase them, she would pay him a pretty sum.

"I'm just killing time before the others arrive," Hunter said. "It was you who wanted a name for our squad."

The elevator stopped with a quiet ding. Zel saw what was on the other side and punched the screen to go back up. The door still opened into a hall.

"If you hate it, just say so."

A dozen armed T-ROLLs stood at the ready, their stun guns pointing right at her chest.

"We've been made," she said just before a stun charge hit her chest and she was out.

***

Zel woke up with a gasp. Her neck stung, and, considering the size of the syringe the T-ROLL pulled out of it, no wonder. She tried to move, to grab him, and to make him pay for whatever he had done to her, but belts as wide as her thighs held her against a metal plank behind her.

Something felt wrong. Terribly wrong.

Zel reached for her hair, but couldn't feel it. Well, she could feel the implants snaking past her shoulders and hips, lying limply against her skin, but she could not *feel* them. The implants had been a part of her just as her arms and legs, and she could always sense them in her mind, but not anymore.

"What did you do to me?"

The technician turned to her with an indifferent expression on his face.

"Tell me now, or I will—"

"You will what?" the T-ROLL interrupted her. "Your implants won't work for the next six hours. The neurotoxin made sure of that."

The man stepped close, and she remembered him. Lisbeth's right hand, Otto, was as nasty as they came. He was utterly loyal to the woman in charge, and nothing would ever change that.

Zel trashed against her restraints, but besides earning herself some bruises, she hadn't achieved a thing.

"Be a good girl and keep it down."

Zel closed her eyes. She wouldn't be able to use any of her implants. Not with the neurotoxin cursing through her veins, but she had to get out of here before the T-ROLL took her to Lisbeth.

Something scraped against her wrist, and Zel realized none of the T-ROLLs had checked her sleeves. Stupid of them, really. Had no one briefed them on her skills?

Zel worked to free the bracelet. It was actually a curved blade, protected only by the slick overalls she was wearing. Otto turned his head when he heard the noise.

"What is Lisbeth planning?" Zel asked.

She didn't really want to know, but she needed Otto to keep talking to cover up the noise.

"Boss wants her property back."

"She had put these things in, and now she wants to rip my implants off?" Zel asked with a snarl. "They won't work with anyone else. You know that."

Otto laughed. "I wasn't talking about the implants."

A thump somewhere outside made them both look up. The T-ROLL swung his rifle toward the door.

"What's going on?" he asked into his earpiece.

No answer. Not even the rattle of static. Zel couldn't hear it, not with her implants rendered useless, but the way Otto tensed, she knew she was right.

Zel hoped it was Hans and G, but it could be any of Lisbeth's enemies. That woman had a long list of disgruntled people who would be happy to take her down. The Raiders might have planned an attack on ROLL, or any of her opposition might have finally grown a pair to strike back. Zel didn't care to meet any of them. Not while she was still tied down and had no weapons besides the curved blade.

Zel cut at the restraints, no longer caring about the noise she made.

"Stay put, will you?"

Otto's features went slack, and a tremble seized his muscles. He fell face down onto the floor, and Zel saw two figures standing behind.

Both dressed in black roll neck sweaters and trench coats. They couldn't look less alike. The girl had a crop cut of mauve and turquoise hair and a ring in the nose. She was typing on the implant in her arm, and her blue eyes were running over the lines of text on the holographic screen above it. The boy had long hair and black eyes. He stood in a relaxed stance that wouldn't deceive even the dimmest T-ROLLs. His rifle rested over his shoulder, but his finger was still on the trigger.

The girl stopped typing for a second, to draw a horizontal line with her index pressed to her thumb and then waved it forward.

"I know there's no one left," the boy said and rolled his eyes. "That's why I'm no longer shooting."

The girl popped a bubble of her gum and leaned on the wall. Indifferent to everything else, she returned to her screen.

"Took you long enough," Zel said.

There was nothing graceful about how she greeted them. She had tumbled down to the floor when she cut the belt that held her down at her hips and was now sowing down at the ones at her ankles.

"Since when do you need help?"

"The T-ROLLs must have had enough of our little incursions in their projects. They've injected me with some type of neurotoxin. I won't be able to control my implants until it wears off. You'll have to cover me, Hans."

The boy let the rifle fall on his other hand. "Lead the way."

The smile on his face made even Zel's skin crawl with fear.

Picking up Otto's stun rifle, Zel bumped the girl's fist and took the offered earpiece. "Looking good, G."

The girl pointed at her chest and tapped on her head. *I know.*

With a smile, Zel put the earpiece in and walked out of the room.

The fluorescent lights blinked furiously. Hans and G must have overridden the current to get inside unnoticed. The broken glass littering the floor made clear the T-ROLLs that lay scattered on the floor hadn't let them through without a fight. Zel was good, but Hans was a force of nature. No wall was high enough to hold him away, not with G tearing them down wherever they went.

"Zel?" the metallic voice spoke into her ear.

"I'm here."

"What did I say about being careful?"

"I was counting T-ROLLs when you were speaking."

A long exhale on the other end told her Hunter wasn't joking.

"I'm sorry, all right? Why don't you give me a lecture about it later?"

G snorted, drawing her hands into a small heart. She could be really annoying sometimes.

They walked through a maze of halls with locked up doors on either side. G could deactivate any badge reader so they could slip inside, but none of these labs were of interest to them that night.

"I've given it a thought," Hans started.

Oh, boy. G motioned on Zel's other side. *I told you to stay off the Tech Nexus.*

Hans glared her way. "We could call ourselves Reaper Operatives."

Zel drew her rifle higher. She felt uneasy. Without her implants, she felt like a part of her was missing, and she couldn't get a clear sense of where they were as she had been out when the T-ROLLs had brought her to Otto.

We aren't killing anyone.

"What?"

Do you even know what Reaper means?

Confusion was still written all over Hans's face.

"Reaper is short of Grim Reaper. It's a symbol of death," Zel said through gritted teeth. "Can we concentrate on the mission now?"

G hadn't missed a step, turning back to her screen, and Hans looked down the corridor as if he could see past the last turn, but his cheeks had gained a dash of color. Zel had been too harsh on him. Before she could apologize, Hunter broke the silence. "There is a room on your left."

The group stopped and turned toward what most certainly looked like a wall.

"I think you're a wrong, Boss," Hans said.

"Lisbeth personally signed on these schematics."

Zel was already running her hands over the steel surface. Her fingers brushed a bump, and she pressed it. One of the panels making up the wall slid open with a whoosh.

No matter how sophisticated ROLL was, Lisbeth liked her things simple, and Zel knew it better than most.

***

The group walked into the room with stunned expressions on their faces. Even G had abandoned her screen and looked at the glass box that stood in the middle of the room. A milky white gas swirled inside, hiding the contents from view.

"What is that?" Hans asked, stepping closer.

Zel caught his shoulder. Han's foot was a hair's breadth away from the laser lines at their feet. They both looked at G, who narrowed her eyes. A beep, and the lasers blinked and disappeared.

"Always eager to show off her EMP implants," Hans muttered.

G wasn't listening. She walked back towards the entrance and hit a panel next to the opening. Once, twice. She lifted her foot and hit the panel with the heel of her boot. It fell to the floor, revealing cables of different sizes and colors. G pulled them apart and tore some away. When she found the one she needed, she latched a device onto it that looked just like a plastic clip. With a soft movement of her hand, she brought the screen back up, rolled her wrists, and popped another bubble.

Her fingers flew over the keyboard that was only visible to her. About a minute inside the ROLL's security grid, and G made a sharp motion with her hand in a horizontal line. *Defenses off.*

While she delved into Lisbeth's database, Hans walked toward the machinery to the left, and Zel toward the center of the hidden room. She could not take her gaze off the glass box. Large tube-like cables ran from the structure into the ground and toward the ceiling. The energy that thing was pumping from the city grid had to be off the charts. That's what Hunter had seen in his diagnostics. T-ROLLs had switched it on just before Zel went into the Lisbeth's Tower.

Zel had a sinking feeling at the bottom of her stomach. Like all the clues were just in front of her, but she couldn't figure out the right answer to the riddle. This was Lisbeth's latest project. Like Zel once had been. Like Hunter, who had found her and pulled her out of Lisbeth's web, and like Hans and G, one orphan exploited for his strength, the other for her mind.

Zel leaned closer, trying to see through the fog. It swirled again but didn't reveal a thing.

Lights flickered and plunged the room into a darkness that lasted mere seconds. It was enough for Hans and Zel to take the safety off their guns.

The first clank made Zel turn back to the box. She pulled up her rifle and pointed it at the swirling gas as another tube fell down.

"How's on that info, G?"

Hunter was the one to answer. "You know better than to rush her."

Zel threw a glance over her shoulder. G stood unmoving, her gaze running over the lines of text before she stumbled back, covering her mouth. She looked around with something Zel had never seen in those eyes. Fear.

Her rifle still trained on the glass box, Zel walked back to G and looked at her screen.

"Project: Sleeping Beauty," she read out loud.

Hans glanced over his shoulder. "They were supposed to have stopped with these. You were the last one."

"Get out of there," Hunter all but screamed in his metallic voice into her earpiece.

Hans was still pointing his rifle at the box where the gas was thinning, revealing metal parts painted white, and Zel wasn't listening. What she was reading on G's screen was just not possible.

"I'm reading the same info G got. Get Zel out. Now."

"Boss?"

"It's an order," Hunter said.

It was too late.

A grenade rolled into the room and exploded with a flash of light too bright even for their implants. The squad's instincts were honed for such situations, but they weren't on their turf. When their bionics readjusted, they were no longer alone. T-ROLLs had charged into the room, surrounding Hans and Zel in a circle of stun guns. G was nowhere to be seen. She must have slipped into the hole beside the panels. Smart of her, she hadn't been trained to fight, but to flee and destroy the enemies with a few lines of code when an opportunity presented itself.

"Let's try again," said the only T-ROLL without a tactical helmet. Otto had recovered from a stun charge. The others must have injected him with something as nasty as he had Zel. "I promise to be less gentle this time."

If he was about to pull the trigger, he never had the chance. The lid of the box shot across the room and hit him straight in the chest. He flew across the room, hit the wall, and slid down to the floor in a heap. He didn't even stir. The lid of the box was too heavy to allow him that. Neither Zel nor Hans were ready to cry victory.

The glass box where Lisbeth's latest project lay stood open. The gas hadn't had time to clear off completely, and it cascaded down, revealing an android inside. Everything about it screamed a machine. Except its face. It was a thing of fairy tales. Eerie in how it looked human, but too perfect to be a face of a real woman.

T-ROLLs were shouting orders. Some ran to their commander, others circled Hans, who was ready to shoot all of them dead, swinging his rifle around.

None of it mattered to Zel. She could not tear her gaze from the android.

Its eyes fluttered and opened. The implants readjusted to the semi-darkness in the room and zoomed in and out to get the full picture. A second, that was all it would take for it to gather all the information it needed and pick a side. The AIs were just that good. It was not without a reason they were outlawed.

Uncontrolled and unchecked, they had been a menace once. Zel's parents had paid the price with their lives for an android that went haywire. She would not allow a thing like that to harm anyone else.

Zel had swung the rifle up to level it with its chest and changed the setting of the rifle to kill. She was less than twenty feet away. Even if she didn't have her bionics online to help her guide the shot, she wouldn't miss the neural center of the android.

Sleeping Beauty tilted its head and threw its hands in the air.

Another flash of light.

Zel turned and closed her eyes. She got only partially blinded. While T-ROLLs pointed their rifles down, careful not to stun one of theirs, Hans sent a raffle of charges around the room.

Zel didn't wait for T-ROLLs vision to clear and start shooting at anything that moved. She darted after the android that had bolted out of the room. It had the latest augments installed by Lisbeth's minions, but Zel was fast. She had a clear view of it, got on a knee, and took a deep breath. The android looked back at her and smirked. *Smirked.*

Pulling the trigger, Zel didn't stop until the rifle overheated, but the android had shattered the plexiglass of the elevator with a single blast and flew up the tower even before the first charge left the barrel.

"Zel, stop and listen to me," a voice in her ear spoke.

She didn't care to hear the rest. Tearing the earpiece away, it crunched under her boot as she dashed toward the stairs.

By the time she got to the lobby, her muscles burned, sweat beaded her skin, but Zel pushed forward.

She cursed Lisbeth's love for tall buildings as she ran higher up the tower. Her implants were non responsive, Hans and G were fighting with T-ROLLs, but Zel didn't care. She had to get to the android before it escaped.

Gasping for breath, Zel emerged onto one of the last unfinished floors of the tower. Wind and rain were so strong here, Zel had to press herself against the walls to avoid being swept into the darkness of the city.

A silent click-click of mechanisms told Zel the android was still here. Hiding in the shadows, waiting for the moment to kill her and be free.

Taking one last breath and gripping the rifle hard in her hands, Zel turned a corner.

Sleeping Beauty stood in the middle of the room, not caring for the wind and rain. It waited for Zel; she knew it, but for a moment she forgot all about it. A step ahead of it stood its master.

Lisbeth was a beautiful woman. Too young for someone to have so much power at her fingertips. She had been born into money and blessed with a bright mind. Her heritage paid for the first ROLL's facility. By the time she was twenty-five, every soul in the city had implants manufactured in her factories. Few knew she tested them on orphans in her care first. Not many of them survived the trial phase, but even those who did, Lisbeth would discard as easily as a broken toy. Those who knew about her projects didn't dare to oppose her. After all, there was no competition. Once you cut your ties with ROLL, there was no coming back. No maintenance for the bionics meant that you either joined Raiders or got killed for parts. Scientists and politicians who voiced doubts died in the most unusual consequences. The news of their deaths swept under the rug by the media companies Lisbeth owned.

Anger made Zel clutch the rifle so hard it dug painfully into her hands. She hated this woman. She hated everything she had done to the city.

A smile Zel knew all too well grew on that face of sharp angles and high cheekbones. "Rapunzel. So good of you to join us."

"You've crossed a line, Lisbeth."

Lisbeth's laughter was a soft tinkle. Yet another thing perfect in a body that had not a single implant. She, more than anyone, knew they couldn't be trusted.

The android didn't even budge as Lisbeth walked toward Zel with her hands in the pockets of her high-waisted white suit trousers. Lisbeth still didn't see a threat in Zel.

"There are no lines for people like me. No one to stop me."

"You're wrong," Zel said and pointed the muzzle of her rifle straight at Lisbeth's chest.

The android took a step toward them, but one glance from Lisbeth had it backing away.

Wind threw Lisbeth's white locks into her eyes, and she brushed it with more annoyance than she had showed Zel.

"You're still holding onto that grudge?"

"It killed my parents. It decided that it was the only solution, and it shot them." Zel was shouting, but she didn't care. It's not like anyone besides the android would hear them. Zel planned to have it in a recycling center before the clock stroke midnight.

"It?" Lisbeth asked. "I taught you better than that. Call it by the name I gave it."

"I would rather be thrown off this tower."

"You might yet get your wish, Rapunzel," Lisbeth said, and leaned closer. The muzzle dug deeper into her skin. Her white jacket was flapping in the storm that raged around them. "Snow White did only what she was ordered."

Zel stumbled back, memories from that night flooding her vision.

She was looking down a barrel of a gun hot enough to make her flinch. An android stood in front of her, and three lifeless bodies lay around them. Ma, Da, and Aunt Kira. The thing had killed them before waking up Zel and dragging her into the living room, where everyone lay dead. Zel knew what would happen next. She saw it each time she closed her eyes. She had screamed and cried, begged for it to spare her, but the android stood unmoving until its chest exploded into pieces. It fell down into the black ichor that fueled its mechanisms.

"The room is secure," said the first T-ROLL that had entered the room. She would later discover his name was Otto, and she would learn to hate him with her every breath.

He lowered his rifle and let Lisbeth pass. The woman walked closer to Zel and picked her chin, forcing her to look her in the eyes.

"My dear child," Lisbeth said in a soothing voice. "What do you say I make you strong enough so this will never happen again?"

Zel didn't fully understand what it meant. Still, she nodded. She would never feel that weak again.

Lisbeth climbed to her feet and motioned to the other T-ROLLs. "Bring her in for the Project Rapunzel."

Zel blinked, the tears clogging her throat. She had lived through countless surgeries, survived trainings she should have not. She was the only girl who had accepted the implants among the group of twenty. But this was never about her.

"Snow White," Zel said. She shook her head as if she could dislodge the memories. "With the name like that, it was yours."

Zel had lived fueled by hate and anger. She had survived

everything with the only goal in mind. Not to let anyone develop another AI like the one that killed her parents.

Among everything else, Lisbeth knew how to read people. She knew how to stroke that side of Zel. To make her do anything Lisbeth wanted, and she knew nothing would ever change that.

The rifle was still set on kill, but before Zel could pull the trigger, Lisbeth pushed the weapon away and ducked under. Bullets flew across the floor.

Sleeping Beauty rolled away before any charge could damage it. One of the basic rules Lisbeth must have programmed into it. Protect itself before anything else. Zel hated it even more then. *Would it even defend its creator?*

Zel didn't have time to dwell on that thought. Lisbeth had kicked her in her gut, sending her flying back. No need for implants when she had trained in Krav Maga.

Fighting for a breath, Zel climbed to her feet. It was too late. Lisbeth threw a punch. Zel's face flew to a side with a crunch of something in her jaw.

Zel had trained to fight with her implants, to be attuned with them every moment until it became unconscious. With the neurotoxin still pumping through her blood, she felt crippled, missing a part of herself that she hated as much as she loved.

Hans and G were still nowhere to be seen, and Hunter would have no angle on this side of the building. Zel was utterly alone and when Lisbeth drew her knee into Zel's stomach, she didn't even try to stop it.

Better to die than to see the city crippled even more by this woman.

Another gust of wind made them stumble, and Zel saw an opportunity she didn't think she would have again.

She rammed into Lisbeth and took her by surprise. By the time Lisbeth realized what she was doing, Zel had carried her to the edge. She could see the android running toward them, trying to save its creator, but it would not make it here in time.

"We'll meet on the other side," Zel said and jumped into the night.

***

Zel was still screaming, but it took her a moment to realize she was no longer falling. She stopped and closed her mouth. She looked around, but still could not make any sense of it.

The world was upside down, and somewhere sixty floors below, Lisbeth's body lay sprawled in a puddle, her white suit stark against the mud.

A powerful set of arms hauled Zel back to the roof and away from the edge.

"Are you all right?" Hans was patting her legs and arms, searching for an injury he would not find.

Zel barely heard him, her gaze fixed on the deformed android. Its legs had stretched to circle the closest columns. The sensitive mechanics in its arms had broken when it caught up Zel, but it still looked at the group with a tilted head.

"Why?" Zel muttered under her breath. "Why did you save me?"

The android twitched its head the other way before the light went out of its eyes. G was at its side, running diagnostics and reattaching cables, but Zel was too stunned to see anything.

She didn't say a word as they walked back to Hans's van. Nor as they loaded the android with G still working on it into the back.

She just climbed behind the wheel and drove away. Someone might steal her bike, but she couldn't find a reason to care. Everything she knew and believed in had been crushed that day, and she killed the woman who had held all the answers.

They arrived at their hideout just as Hunter jumped down from his jeep. "Is it still alive?"

That question shook Zel out from her haze.

"Why would you care?" she said.

Hans and G lifted their heads from the back of the van, where G had her hands full of ichor as she dug through the neural connections. Zel thought them beyond repair, but G would not let go. She was like that. An idealist. Even after surviving what Lisbeth had done to her.

Hunter blinked. His bionic eyes had trouble finding focus for a moment.

"It was Lisbeth's latest project," he said. "It could be of so much help."

"It's an AI."

"So?"

Zel stumbled away as if physically struck by that one word.

"It saved you," Hunter said, stepping closer, not missing a beat. "Lisbeth had connected it to the network and let it browse it for a year with no supervision or restriction. It had absorbed all the knowledge and tracked every step of everyone in this city. It discovered your file and contacted me. Even if it owed its creator its life, it saved you."

"AIs are outlawed."

"Your implants are outlawed," Hunter spat back.

Zel was reaching, she knew that, but she still threw her last argument, her voice barely above a whisper. "It's an android. There is not a single part of it that's human."

"Look at me, Zel. Really look at me. I come from the same project as Snow White."

Zel didn't have to look. She knew his features by heart. While T-ROLLs had constructed Snow White from nothing and made her look like a human, they've picked Hunter from a group of disabled orphans. Starting with a mechanical spine, they put augments in his arms and legs. They had replaced his lungs and his heart. Violet implants for eyes. They hadn't left a single part of his body untouched. Even the face was half gone. Everything below the bridge of his nose was just a metallic skull with no artificial skin covering it.

"The only difference between me and Snow White is that I have a human brain," Hunter said, his metallic voice as low as it would go. "Yet you fight by my side as you do with Hans and G. The modifications Lisbeth made you go through are far less than what she did to me, but can you tell me you're still completely human?"

Zel turned back to the van. She hated to hear those words. And most of all, she hated that he was right.

"What? What, G?" Hans cried out. "I can't understand you when you blur the words."

Even if Hans had grown up with G, she lost him when she was signing fast. It wasn't too fast for Zel. She had spent too much time with G in that van, while they stormed Raider's hideouts and raided T-ROLLs' outposts even if Hunter forbade them. Zel would always understand her half-signs and splintered sentences, even when her implants weren't there to help her.

Despite herself, she marched across the room and picked the ER. They've snatched one of the Emergency Regenerators from a T-ROLLs' outpost on their last outing in case Hunter might need one someday to restart his augmented heart.

G caught the ER. A click and turn, and the android's chest lifted as if the thing had just taken a breath.

"Connect power supply to the main frame motor, please," it said.

G did as Sleeping Beauty said, and with a whiz, the android sat up.

"That's much better," it said, and Zel swore she saw the thing smile. The android turned until its implants focused on Zel. "What about GRIMMS?"

No one moved.

"Did your circuits got fried or something?" Hans finally asked. "Ghost Reconnaissance and Infiltration Mechanically-enhanced Militia Squad, or GRIMMS." The android motioned at the room with a whir of her finger. "You might actually get people who'll join you once you pick up the name for this squad."

Lisbeth had been the last actual human in this city with no augments or implants, and yet the android who didn't even have a brain and was making stupid jokes had more humanity than her.

Zel snorted and shook her head.

"Welcome to GRIMMS, Sleeping Beauty."

Be it in writing or reading, **Iren Adams** has a passion for fantasy and sci-fi. She's usually writing about mystical creatures, magic, and dystopian futures. You can find her short stories in Write of Passion Literary Journal, Dragon Soul Press Anthologies, or join her community of book-lovers on Instagram (@irenadams.writes).

Wilds of the Mind

by Bethany A. Perry

It began as a cure for Alzheimer's.

"Never lose another memory!" the purple billboards screamed. "Visit our website today: StoreU.com. Unlimited cloud storage!"

They gave me these stickers I could put up all over the house. "StoreU.com—find your precious memories now!" My dad could look at them anytime, close his eyes, and hook up to his memories through an implant. It was like having a brain outside his brain, one whose memory cells were as easy to access as a wish.

In the end, even the wishes dried up.

I sat there on the toilet the morning of his funeral, staring at those happy purple stickers, my life as I'd known it—feeding him, dressing him, telling him who I was when I could muster the strength to do it—over.

I didn't pull up my pants before I leaned off the toilet and picked at the corner of the sticker. It came up enough to get a nail under.

The nail ripped off instead of the sticker, and I wore a Band-Aid to the service.

Afterward, the funeral director handed me the urn and a small box that fit in the palm of my hand.

"What's this?" I opened the box. Inside rested a smaller plastic box and inside that, a metal chip so small I'd need a magnifying glass to see it.

"His StoreU implant. We can return it if you like and they will refund your deposit. Or you may keep it."

I closed the box and turned it over, its cool surface slick. It caught on the sticky bandage where it'd started to curl up. "Why would I want to keep it?"

The thin man shrugged, his drawn face a shade darker than the rich, russet-brown urn I cradled in my elbow. "Some keep them for sentimental value."

My fingers closed around the box. "What will StoreU do with it?"

He shrugged again, his fitted suit jacket shifting up and down with a whisper of the silk that lined it. "Destroy it, I suppose."

I left, urn cradled in my arm, metal box clutched in my hand.

***

It sat on a closet shelf next to the urn. I didn't know what to do with until it gathered so much dust, the surface of the box was a dull grey instead of shiny black. The rest of the StoreU stickers came off the walls, except that one in the bathroom. Every time I sat there on the toilet, I stared at the half of the sticker that absolutely would not come unstuck. Now it read, "U.com—now!" and I wondered if Dad even remembered how to read before the wishes stopped coming, or if the purple was enough to trigger something in him. Not that any of that made a difference, but the distinction seemed important.

"Get your deposit back," my sister sighed over the phone. "The chip isn't of any use to you now. That deposit will pay your rent until you find a new job."

A new job. Something to do besides look after Dad.

"Yeah. I guess that's a good idea."

When I searched how to return it, the sponsored results came back with two things. I always scroll past those, but the second result caught my eye.

"*Retrieve the memories StoreU stole from your loved ones—contact* RestoreU *today for your free estimate.*"

Stole? Hm.

The receptionist at the front desk didn't look up. He handed me a clipboard without speaking. I took the implication to mean I should fill out the attached form with the attached pen, and sat between two people who'd already finished theirs.

The woman on my left, a chipper blonde-headed white woman, didn't disguise the way she wanted to peek at my form. Her eyes glanced down and away each time I looked up. And the man to my right, a long-faced Indian man in a tuque against the cold winter day, crossed one knee over the other and gave me a warm smile before going back to his phone.

I filled out the form in my chicken scratch and signed the documents piled behind it. All the fluff they include, like the terms and conditions on a credit card.

Mr. Brown Hair Blue Eyes receptionist made a copy of my license while I waited to be called. I must have registered surprise when I was called before the people on either side of me even though they'd been waiting longer, because the pale woman in a smart business suit with the clipboard shrugged and said, "Your case worker was available before theirs."

More surprise, but this time I controlled my expression. I had a case worker already? I came in for a simple estimate.

When I met the caseworker, a man who clearly thought he was Dick Tracy with his fedora, three-piece suit, and watch phone, I understood why an estimate wasn't as simple as the ad had led me to believe. Surprise, surprise. This is why I always kept scrolling.

With a ball-point pen he clicked and unclicked after every sentence, he led me around a brochure about their services. But first he began with a warning.

"StoreU isn't just a benevolent memory storage company. They're thieves who take your memories and use them for their own gain."

Even since I'd read RestoreU's ad, clicked on the website and scheduled an appointment, that hadn't made sense to me. I leaned forward and asked why. "Why would they want my memories?"

"Not just yours," Dick Tracy said. He scanned my application with quick, jerking eye movements that put me off in a non-specific way. "Your father's too. Anyone they can get their greedy little mitts on." He curled his nose while he said this, frowning with such ferocity I couldn't help but frown a little with him.

"But why?" I asked again.

"Listen," he said, going back to his computer. "Let me get you that estimate, and we can get down to business."

***

I hadn't been home more than ten minutes before I decided Dick Tracy, the blue-eyed receptionist, and the smartly dressed assistant were all part of a company who existed to do nothing but swindle scared, angry, sad people, most of whom had probably just lost a loved one. Why else would their ad only pop up when I searched how to return the chip, but not when I searched for StoreU's contact info as Dad slid further down the hole of no retrieval?

I crumpled up the estimate—sixteen thousand dollars—along with Dick Tracy's card, and threw them in the trash. Curious or no, I'd be damned if I was going to pay twice what I paid for the implant itself just to find out why StoreU might want to steal memories. Luckily the estimate had been free, and as I sat on the toilet and stared at that ripped purple sticker, I thanked my lucky stars grief hadn't talked me into giving those swindlers my credit card.

***

The coffee shop buzzed, something I hoped to replicate in my insides when I ordered a large latte with extra espresso. Since I hadn't decided whether or not to return the implant to StoreU, much to my sister's consternation, I needed a job. I had to get back out into the world, and explain that gap in my resume.

As I waited for my order, I used the free Wi-Fi to put in applications. I'd had skills once but it'd been so many years since I used them, I didn't bother looking for a job in my field. Instead, I started with an application for this very coffee house. It wasn't far from home, so I wouldn't have to crawl out of my depression sleep too early to get here. And it seemed a bit like witchcraft, making brewed concoctions that helped people get through their day. That attracted me to it. I could use a little magic in my life after all the wishes had dried up and left both Dad and I without a spark.

She sat down at my table without so much as a "hi" and lowered the screen of my laptop until she could peer over it into my widening eyes. "Busy?"

I couldn't find any words to communicate my surprise, so I just sat there with my mouth open, catching flies as Dad would have said, nodding.

I should have told her to get lost. I would have been better for it.

Probably.

Thin but very red lips formed a smile and she leaned closer, her arms crossed and resting on the table. "Giving away more of your data as we speak? Who are we giving it to this time?"

Before I could get my brain into gear, she spun my laptop to face her. She barked a laugh. "This place?" She rammed a pointer finger into the table. "A coffee shop? You're giving all your data to this place? On public Wi-Fi?"

Finally my brain caught up, even as I tried to count the freckles on her pale, upturned nose. "Who are you?" I spun the laptop back around and closed it harder than I should, the snap of the screen hitting the keyboard loud enough to make the people at the tables closest to us turn around.

She waved them off and they went back to their coffees. Throwing her long brown hair the same shade as her deep eyes over her shoulder, she leaned closer to me. "There's better questions to answer than that one, and you know what they are."

I still couldn't get over how she'd just sat down like she'd been invited, and how her coming hit my psyche like a breath of fresh air that smelled like the earthy perfume she wore. She may have caught me off guard but as I stared at her, trying to think of the "better questions" she alluded to, the synapses in my brain lit up like firecrackers, shooting neurons across their paths in a way Dad hadn't been able to do for years before he died. Her visit somehow wasn't just welcome, part of me had been expecting it. Waiting for it. Longing for it.

They called my name at the front counter.

In the time it took me to glance up at my steaming hot coffee and back to her, she was gone.

***

Days passed before I opened my laptop again to continue the job application frenzy. When I did, a piece of paper fluttered out of it and landed face down on the table Dad inherited from his mom, which I guess was mine now. I stared at the paper, knowing exactly where it came from, and my synapses started firing again. I didn't move my hand to pick it up, not intentionally. No, the synapses did that for me. My hand twitched on its own and tweezed the paper between my fingers.

I turned it over.

Sure enough, a phone number. No name, just a number. But it was from her. It still smelled like her earthy perfume.

I carried that thin piece of paper around the house for an hour, just walking from spot to spot where I would stop for several seconds, look at the paper, and pace some more. My socks dragged across the carpet, creating a charge that shocked me on the finger when I went into the bathroom and shut the door. Why I still closed the door is beyond me.

It was sitting on the toilet, staring at the ripped purple sticker, "U.com—now!", when it hit me why I hadn't dialed the number as soon as I picked up the paper. I didn't know the question. But that sticker, that sticker gave it to me.

"Why do they steal the memories?" It was the first thing I said.

She laughed into the receiver, her breath a crackle on the other end. "There you go, now you're getting somewhere. I don't want to talk over the phone. Your number has been sold a hundred times over by now. Meet me where we first met." She hung up without waiting for an answer, or giving me a time to meet.

I dressed as fast as my limbs would work to pull on clothes.

The coffee shop sat dark. Seems like coffee shop owners think no one wants coffee late at night. But she leaned on the bricks next to the front window, her arms crossed, a thick jacket covering the curves I'd hardly gotten a chance to ogle earlier. That wasn't important now, not if she could answer my questions.

Without a word, she led me into the alley behind the coffee shop, an alley that stretched another block behind other shops and diners. Once we were safely in the shadows of the buildings and away from the orange of the street lights, she held out her hand. "Give me your phone."

I hesitated. I didn't even know her name.

She stopped walking and glanced over my shoulder at the street. "Give me your phone, now, or you'll never see me again."

Even without much light, the hardness of her expression—her pinched lips, her narrowed eyes—shone through. She meant it.

I handed it over.

She slid an earring off and poked the arm into the SIM card slot. The slot popped open and she pulled the card out. Holding it between two fingers, she snapped the slot closed, handed me my phone back, and slid the earring back on. "Either get a new one, or buy a burner."

With that, she pulled a phone from her pocket, the screen reflecting what light hit the alley. She walked a few more steps into the dark, almost disappearing in the shadows, and chucked the card and phone into a dumpster. The phone clunked.

A car with its brights on crawled down the road.

From the shadows, her arm snaked out and grabbed my collar. She jerked me into the shadows with her and the dumpster. The dumpster reeked, and I covered my nose to keep from dry-heaving. I could almost hear the maggots crawling around in the trash. Her hand clenched my shirt long enough for me to feel the heat of her creeping into my own cold skin. She'd caught a bit of my chest when she grabbed me, and while I wanted her to ease up, the pinch of her nails, the tearing, burning sensation it caused, was more than I'd felt in months. Maybe longer. Life had been a dream I floated through, disconnected from the world, myself, my own skin, and it was the pain of that pinch that finally woke me from it.

More synapses lit up. I never wanted her to let go.

She stood, dragging me with her, and peeked over the dumpster. And she released me.

I sighed.

"Let's go." She took off down the alley at almost a jog, and I followed behind in silence.

We walked for half an hour, down more alleys, around buildings, between cars and discarded boxes. The only creatures who saw us were the rats.

Occasionally I would spot a purple sticker and even without being able to make out the words, I knew what it said. I'd memorized it.

When I was good and lost, she stopped. We stood in a space between four buildings that was just large enough for a confluence of electrical boxes and plumbing pipes. Water dripped on my shoulder. Each drop was like the tapping of a finger, insisting I listen, insisting I stay awake. But her first sentence caught me so off guard, I may as well have still been sleeping.

"Have you ever baked a cake?"

Struggling to figure out her point, I sputtered out a yes.

"Each ingredient alone doesn't do anything. Flour doesn't rise on its own. Dry cocoa doesn't do much without sugar. Put all the ingredients together and you get cake."

I pinched myself where she'd pinched me, where the skin was still tender. It thrust my brain into gear. "My dad's memories alone don't do anything."

"Right. But when you combine them with farmer John's knowledge of fertilizer, Betty Crocker's knowledge of buttercream..."

Her point clicked home. "You get cake. Or a bomb."

She nodded, her deep brown eyes all pupil. "What's the next question, then?"

I waited for it to come to me. I didn't know if she'd get tired of waiting, if she expected me to know immediately. The walls closing us into this strange corner oozed cold and I wanted to curl up and go to sleep. Forget I'd ever seen RestoreU's ad. Forget I had a dad.

"Let me ask you a question, since you can't think of one." She did nothing to mask the exasperation in her voice.

"OK."

"How much did you tell them at RestoreU?"

My next question required no thought. "How did you know I went there?"

She grinned, her teeth reflecting what little light made it to us, the strange shadows elongating them, making them look like wolf teeth. "I could find out what you ate for breakfast this morning, if I wanted to."

My mouth hung open. Again. "How?"

"It's called a digital footprint, and most people's are so thick it's more like a digital forest. But the right algorithms can break it into useful pieces, and those useful pieces can get sold to StoreU or any corporation with enough buying power. Or stolen, by someone like me."

Heat raced up my neck into my face, tightening my forehead and making my ears ring. "You stole my…my…"

"Your data." She smirked. "I…" She trailed off before finishing, her head cocked to the side, eyes glazed with a far-off look.

I drew in breath to speak, but she crushed a finger across my lips, mashing them into my teeth.

I took the hint and said nothing. Just let her continue listening.

A full minute passed before she said more. When she did, it was in a whisper so soft that to hear her, I had to lean close enough for her breath to tickle my lip. "Do you hear that?" she asked.

I started to lean back so I could listen too. She clutched my hand and I stopped, my mouth just a few inches from hers, and I listened.

In the deep night, a sound broke the dripping of water, the whine of electrical lines and boxes. A high-pitched drone, something like a fly but much too consistent, too mechanical.

She dropped my hand and turned away, her muscles tense like she was preparing to fly. But I didn't have her number anymore, and if I never saw her again, I'd never know why that ripped purple sticker haunted me. Day in, day out. I had to ask her the question she wanted me to ask. And at the last moment before she ran away forever, the water dripping on my shoulder electrified my brain and the questions came to me.

"Wait." It was me who clutched her. "How do they know whose memories they want? How do they get the right people's memories? Or is it chance?"

She kissed me.

Full on the lips she kissed me, her mouth warm but tight, the sharp intake of breath through her nose the only sound.

For the first time since before Dad's diagnosis, every nerve ending sang *I am alive.*

I am alive.

She ended the kiss before I had the chance to wrap her in my arms. If I'd had that chance, I don't think the embrace would have ever ended. But it did, and thinking about it later brought tears to the back of my throat. Thick and hot, making it hard to breathe.

Gripping the back of my neck, her nails digging into my skin again, she stayed next to my lips. "I knew you'd figure out the questions."

And she was gone.

The drone flew through the alleyway and over my head before I found my way out of the back streets, but I tucked my ears into my coat, shoved my hands in my pockets, and tried to make sure it didn't get a look at my face. It followed me for a block, until I was back onto regular streets, and then its high-pitched whine disappeared.

***

I thought about that kiss for longer than I rightly should have.

I am alive.

The thought came to me throughout random hours of the day, knocking me over with its ferocity, its fiery will. I didn't know where to find her, but I couldn't dismiss the building hope I'd see her again. Soon.

Even with several better offers, some within my skill set—what there still was of it after all those years as a caregiver—I took the job at that coffee house, just hoping to see her again.

She never came in.

But I kept thinking about what she said. About the data, about the memories, about the cake. Or the bomb.

I set up a fake social account and followed all the people I could find who had friends or loved ones that'd signed up for StoreU. And I gathered as much chatter as I could find about RestoreU while I was at it. Two birds, one stone, as they say.

I tracked the jobs of the people who said they had StoreU implants. When I did this work, everything she'd said to me, including the drone that was clearly there to spy on us, crowded my mind. So I hid in the only room without a window, the bathroom. And I stared at that ripped purple sticker as I compiled list after list.

I won't lie. Some part of me hoped to find her in the lists.

But for the most part, I gathered information. And over time, the pattern became clear.

This Nobel winner with the graying temples didn't get the implant. But her wife did.

This supercollider physicist didn't get the implant. But his adult daughter had early-onset, and there she was, on the steps of the London branch of StoreU, standing in the middle of a photo-op, telling people the implant was perfectly safe and it let her live a normal life.

And here, the link between them. A professor from North Dakota who'd retired in the nineties, who'd written a book long, long ago, about as-yet-identified but since-discovered elements that could change the trajectory of war as we knew it. Nothing but conjecture, and his work was never taken very seriously because he meant it as more of a warning than scientific theory, but if you put these three minds together, you could create something not just dangerous, but powerful.

If there's one thing people could sell, it's always been power.

***

She appeared again when I least expected her to, which I've found is always the way things happen. Maybe that's because all we expect is: go to work, go home, sleep, repeat. Something like her, a flame to light the insides of my mind and smolder in my belly, is never expected.

I was getting gas for a trip I wanted to take out of town. I'd decided to bury Dad's implant in the forest, a kind of funeral for who he was. Symbolic more than anything, since the memories were in the cloud and I didn't know how to retrieve them. But I needed to move forward, to let him go so I could get on with my life, and this was the only way I knew how.

When I got back from grabbing a soda for my road trip, she was there. Sitting in my car.

It took all my strength not to kiss her from the moment I saw her. Her thin, red lips cracked a smile as if she could read my thoughts. She pulled the seat belt across her breasts and leaned into me, one arm stretched out.

"Just drive." She keyed the ignition.

I don't remember the drive out of town. I don't remember deciding to drive to the mountains. I just remember pulling off the road at an overlook and turning off the car. It ticked while we sat in silence, our breath mingling as the car heated up in the afternoon sun.

"Did you figure it out?" Her question quivered in the space between us.

I nodded, suddenly nervous like she was a teacher with the test key and I was just a high-schooler with a crush who hadn't studied. My palms began to sweat and I wiped them on my pants. "I know why they choose who they do."

"I knew you could get it." She licked her lips and I all wanted was for her to kiss me for being smart. The fire smoldering in my belly leapt into my throat as I waited. But instead, she repeated my own question back to me. One I'd asked months ago. "How do they get the right people's memories?"

I deflated, the fire in my throat turning sour and tasting of stomach acid instead of hormones. I swallowed and tried to meet her eyes, but failed. "I don't know. I spent too much time studying the people they choose to understand how."

She rested her elbow on the center console of my little car and nestled her chin in her palm. Her brown eyes widened and a grin creased one side of her face, highlighting a dimple in her cheek. Just the sight of her made me want to do better. To be better.

I pinched the spot where she'd pinched me on that first night, trying to clear the fog that'd settled in my mind. Sometimes I feared that fog, that it was the beginning of what had happened to Dad. But I had years left until it'd happened to him and I knew where this fog came from. Certainly not my head, much further south than that.

"Data?"

She whooped and clapped, a wide smile stretched across her face that rivaled the sun falling through the windshield.

And thank whatever gods might be out there, she kissed me again. This time her lips weren't tight but instead open and inviting, and I took no time at all remembering to kiss her back. The synapses in my brain that'd responded to her when we first met exploded again, lit up like a pinball machine, happy chemicals firing around my brain like they were bouncing off the bumpers. I sank my hand into her hair and pulled her close, fully intending to never let her go.

But Dad had a saying about all good things.

She pulled back enough to break the seal of our lips and smiled against my mouth. "I told you you could do it. I've been waiting so long for someone to get it." A laugh escaped her mouth, breathy and light, and I'm pretty sure I fell in love with her right then and there.

But now I had new questions and she surely had the answers.

More synapses fired, corralling the questions and forming them into words, one at a time. I didn't let go of her, but I did back up enough to see her eyes. "How does that work? The data?"

She opened her door and stepped out.

I joined her, the thin mountain air cool in the back of my throat. Spring had come and sprinkled the mountain with pollen and fresh breezes, and the sneeze that came along with that first intake of breath felt almost as good as the kiss.

Hands gesturing, she spent the next half hour pacing and explaining. I tried desperately to give her input from time to time, to sound smart so she'd kiss me again.

"Data is precious. We've known this for a long time. And yet we give it out every day. To our bank, to our employer, to our digital TVs. They know what we eat, what we watch, what we read, what we see, what we feel. And every time you sign a release like the one you signed at RestoreU—"

All the paperwork I signed like a good little drone. Data releases.

"—you give it away. For nothing."

"And they break it into manageable pieces and sell it."

Her eyes lit up. "Yes! They sell it. To advertisers mostly. But also to companies like—"

"StoreU."

She pointed finger guns at me. "Now you're getting it."

I didn't want to ask what a company like StoreU did with the data, didn't want to sound like I couldn't figure it out on my own, so I tried to talk my way into the point. "They sell a service so they have ads. They target the ads?"

"Not just their own ads. Here's where it gets sinister. They target you with all kinds of ads. Food, drink, games, medications, anything that's been shown to decrease memory. Anything that's been shown to correlate to an Alzheimer's diagnosis."

I leaned against the car. It was the only thing holding me up. "They make you sick?"

She took several small, slow, careful steps toward me until we stood face to face again. "They make you sick, and they take your memories. They feed them to the cloud and what they don't use for information or profit, they use to turn around and start the process over again." She gripped my shirt, pulling me closer, and buried her face in my shoulder. "They've already started it with you."

I hugged her to me, but all I wanted to do was run away. "They've started it with me? What do you—"

"StoreU sold you to RestoreU, and you gave them everything. You gave it all to them."

It was a really large stack of papers to sign.

I conjured Dick Tracy's face just so I could imagine punching it.

It helped, a little.

I kissed her neck. She didn't pull away, so I did it again, and I whispered against her skin. "How do I get out of this?"

The tendons in her neck stiffened. "You don't. But someone else might be able to."

I slid my hand down to hers and squeezed. "We run?"

"We run."

***

Becoming someone else is easier than you think it is when the only people who're really left to care about you are a sister who's tired of your depression and a stranger that needs someone to lean on. The one and only thing I still had was the thing I didn't bury after all, Dad's implant. I left my identity, my sadness, my loneliness, all of it. Gave it to her, and the firecrackers she lit in my brain blew it away like smoke.

We got a little place in a nothing town in a nowhere state and she taught me to mine data for our new identities. She taught me how to read the data, how to manipulate it, how to save people caught in the trap of targeted lives.

The freedom she showed me turned the world right-side up, when it'd been upside down all my life. Without targeted ads at every turn, I could finally rely on my own mind to make decisions, to choose things for myself without relying on someone else to choose them for me. No purple billboards had my name on them.

It was exhilarating.

And exhausting.

But we lived together in sheer bliss, she and I. I learned all the secrets about her that not even the Internet knew, and she learned all of mine, such as they were. We loved, and laughed, and laid in not just on Saturdays but on any day we wanted to, having coffee in bed and telling each other stories.

The news piece about my sister penetrated the pink glow of sex and happiness. It might have been the only thing that could. She'd been found guilty of stealing—our father's implant. The DA, someone I was unsurprised to recognize, stood on the cold marble stairs of the courthouse and spoke to the press.

"It's certainly not the only case of implant stealing we've found, but this one became high-profile because of the circumstances." Dick Tracy smiled, his teeth a perfect and straight white, his brown suit creased and pressed within an inch of its life. He didn't list the circumstances. He didn't enumerate the reasons my sister had been treated to such a demanding trial, why she'd been prosecuted to the fullest extent of the law. But he stared straight into the camera when he said, "If someone comes forward with the implant, the DA's office is prepared to vacate the conviction before sentencing."

I snapped the antenna TV off and we sat, our silence thick.

"They're trying to flush you out. With everything you know, you're a liability now."

I turned to her, my mouth open again. Nothing came out, if anything could. I wouldn't let my sister rot in jail, not when I could so easily fix it.

I zipped up my jacket and pulled the hood over my head. Large sunglasses obscured my eyes, and a purple medical mask hid the rest of my face. "I'll be back soon."

She sat on the bed where I'd left her, having detangled my limbs from hers and left her in a sprawl of sheets, blankets and pillows. Her knees crooked in front of her, she lay her palms flat on her cheeks and shook her head, her hair falling over her face. "No you won't."

I crawled onto the bed with her and took the mask down. Easing some of the hair out of her face with one hand, I cupped her chin with the other. "We'll always be together in my heart."

She kissed me with tears running down her face. They mingled between our mouths and when I leaned back and licked my lips, I tasted salt.

***

A woman comes to visit me sometimes. She's got long brown hair and sad brown eyes and thin red lips, and she always looks like she's been crying. I don't know her, but she brings me food and we chat. She's very nice. Her being there makes my constant headaches feel better. When she leaves, I almost never want to let her go.

On the nights that she visits, I cry in the bathroom after she's gone. There's a spot on the wall in front of the toilet where something has been painted over, and when I run my hand over its raised edges, all I can remember is this:

It began as a cure for Alzheimer's.

Bethany A. Perry (she/her) is a sci-fi/horror/fantasy writer who builds miniatures in her spare time. She has published five novels and several short stories and poems. You can catch her writing the sequel to her latest book from Cloaked Press, "Lexa Dean and the Wellspring" on Facebook and Twitter. Find all the deets at bperrywrites.com.

Thank you...

Thank you for taking the time to read our collection. We enjoyed all the stories contained within and hope you found at least a few to enjoy yourself. If you did, we'd be honored if you would leave a review on Amazon, Goodreads, and anywhere else reviews are posted.

You can also subscribe to our email list via our website,
Https://www.cloakedpress.com

Follow us on Facebook
http://www.facebook.com/Cloakedpress

Tweet to us https://twitter.com/CloakedPress

We are also on Instagram
http://www.instagram.com/Cloakedpress

Join us on TikTok @Cloakedpressllc

If you'd like to check out our other publications, you can find them on our website above. Click the "Our Books" button on the homepage for more great collections and novels from the Cloaked Press Family.

Printed in Great Britain
by Amazon